THE ALICE CURSE

MEGAN VAN DYKE

THE ALICE CURSE

MEGAN VAN DYKE

CITY OWL
PRESS

THE ALICE CURSE
Reimagined Fairy Tales, Book 3

CITY OWL PRESS
www.cityowlpress.com

Cover Design by MiblArt. All stock photos licensed appropriately.

Edited by Heather McCorkle.

For information on subsidiary rights, please contact the publisher at info@cityowlpress.com.

Hardback Edition ISBN: 978-1-64898-353-5
Paperback Edition ISBN: 978-1-64898-352-8
Digital Edition ISBN: 978-1-64898-354-2

Printed in the United States of America

PRAISE FOR MEGAN VAN DYKE

"Van Dyke puts an imaginative spin on "Cinderella" in her second Reimagined Fairy Tales romance, The Ugly Stepsister, which takes place after the traditional tale's happy ever after. Van Dyke keeps readers guessing with a clever, twisty plot that proves stories are always filtered through the point of view of their tellers. The hero and heroine make a swoon-worthy pair, and supporting characters add color, especially rebel Mina and her brothers. This adult fairy tale will captivate fans of fantasy romance." — *Publisher's Weekly*

"A fun, sexy, swashbuckling read. Hook is a swoony, caring, protective surprise of a hero, and he meets his match in the dauntless and sassy Tink, who'll go toe-to-toe with a pirate any day. Magical creatures, seafaring adventures, plot twists and turns, steamy kisses (and more!) await in this exciting, reimagined version of the story of Captain Hook and Tinker Bell." — *Amanda Bouchet, USA Today Bestselling author of The Kingmaker Chronicles*

"A seductive reimagined Neverland fairytale dusted with magic, passion, and adventure that will hook readers from page one!" — *InD'Tale Magazine*

"Such a wonderful retelling. Fast paced, well plotted, full of glorious pirate action and a great enemies to lovers romance at the heart of it." – *The SFFRomCast Podcast*

"Van Dyke's action-packed debut puts a sexy, adult spin on Tinker Bell and Captain Hook. On this daring adventure, mermaids become the least of their problems, as Hook and Tink come under threat from their mutual enemy, Blackbeard. As they spend time together, they learn the complicated truth behind each others' storied pasts—Van Dyke does a good job making Hook and his crew sympathetic—and a fiery passion grows. The steamy scenes, explosive battles, and adventurous treasure hunt make for a gripping tale." — *Publisher's Weekly*

"Packed with steamy romance, adventure, and an unforgettable cast of characters, Megan Van Dyke's clever reimagining of Peter Pan, centering Tinker Bell and Captain Hook, is an absolute treasure. The writing is effortless and draws you in immediately, leaving you fully immersed in a fantastical world that feels both familiar and fresh." — *Paulette Kennedy, International Best-selling Author of Parting The Veil*

"Keep your hands and feet inside the ride at all times. Ladies and Gentlemen we are going to Neverland. But not the Neverland you remember from your childhood. Hook and Tink are amazing in this new twist on a classic." — *Melody Caraballo, author of Unhinged Witch*

"Megan Van Dyke's story resets the balance of Neverland, turning an imaginary playland into a world that lives and breathes through every scene. Highly recommend!" — *K.J. Harrowick, author of Bloodflower*

"A delightful, sexy romp set in a fresh, yet familiar fantasy world. Perfect for anyone who has shipped Tinker Bell and Captain Hook!" — *Jeffe Kennedy, award-winning author of Dark Wizard and The Forgotten Empires*

"A fun read that hooks you from chapter one with vivid characters and a smooth, fluid writing style." — *Desirée Niccoli, author of Called to the Deep*

"Megan Van Dyke just became a one-click author for me." — *Ashley King, Author of Painting the Lines and Forever After*

"A fun and sassy retelling that's impossible to put down." — *Kat Turner, author of Hex, Love, & Rock and Roll*

To everyone who needs a short and pleasant escape from life. May this book be that for you.

1

*I*t's funny how time affects some things but seems to flow around others like a boulder in a river, leaving them untouched and ever the same. To Eliza, Folly Hall was one of those places. Or at least she thought so as the carriage rocked to a stop along the gravel drive, leaving the front of the manor framed by her little window. She scooted along the cushioned seat and pressed her palm against the glass pane.

The bright sun overhead gleamed off the copper accents on the roof, all shined up like age could never turn them green. The greyish-blue walls might have received a new coat of paint, too, for they looked fresh as they did when she used to stay there with her Grandmama as a girl. She sighed and pushed open the door, eager to be away from the confining transport. Eliza gave one last look at the velvet interior and clicked her tongue. Her parents probably paid a small fortune to have their daughter delivered in style. Too bad they hadn't considered her comfort—nor had the carriage maker. She'd felt every jarring bump on the drive there, and the velvet did little to comfort the hard seats beneath.

But then, her parents never did care much about her feelings. Life was all a show to them, every act a plot to garner political favor. In truth, that was probably the only reason they bothered to attend the reading of grandmother's will, or opted to hold a gathering or remembrance.

Well, there was the money of course, the inheritance Papa was sure to reap from Grandmama's death. Who could forget that?

Gravel crunched as the driver hopped down. "Oh, miss!" He practically tripped over himself as he stumbled to dip a bow. "Ya should a' let me do that."

Open the door? Eliza fought the urge to roll her eyes. She wasn't some high-born incapable of lifting a finger to help herself. Her parents weren't either, though they might act like it and think it their due now with the favor her father had earned from the royals of their country, Gamor. She'd heard more than one passing whisper on her journey here about his likelihood of being named the new governor.

"It's no bother," she said instead. Eliza reached into her coin purse and procured a generous tip.

The man's wide-eyed gaze locked on the coin. Perhaps her parents hadn't been so generous after all.

"T-thank you, miss." He clutched the coin like it might vanish. "I'll bring your trunks."

With a polite smile and nod, Eliza turned her back on the man and studied the manor once more. Even the gardens remained immaculate, stretching out around the house. In particular, the hedge maze was well trimmed and just as intimidating as it had been in her childhood where it stretched far above her average height.

She'd spent so many lazy afternoons among the hedges, often listening to her Grandmama tell wild stories about a strange world and its odd inhabitants. She'd loved to hear about magic and the things those people could do. Her made-up stories were so different than the real world. Humans with magic were non-existent in their country of Gamor. Some foreign lands could boast a few, but even those were a rarity. The merfolk and pixies had their abilities, but both races were somewhat reclusive, and Eliza couldn't claim to have met either one, though she'd studied them plenty in her work at the library.

A sudden heaviness rooted her feet to the ground. Her parents would be inside. Eliza's lips drew thin. Even now that Grandmama had passed and could no longer influence Eliza with her peculiar ways and nonsense tales as they referred to them, they wouldn't let her be alone with Grandmama, or her spirit, or whatever remained in Folly Hall.

"I'm sorry, Grandmama," Eliza whispered, closing her eyes against the sting of tears at their corners. "I should have come sooner."

But she hadn't. Her letters never said she was ill.

Still, that was no excuse. Eliza shook her head and squared her shoulders. She might have been a horrible granddaughter, staying away so long, but the past was unchangeable, and no amount of wallowing in it on the drive would help matters.

The knot in her throat grew thicker with every step, but Eliza forced herself across the short length of the drive and up the half dozen steps to the front porch. She reached a hand toward the door when a servant pushed it open wide, sending her stumbling back a step.

Servants. She gave her head a little shake. Eliza had forgotten what that was like. Years of boarding school followed by study at university, and finally her life as a scholar at the great library in the Gamorean capital afforded little waiting on and much hard work. But she preferred it that way. It was much better than life under constant scrutiny, clawing after every morsel of praise and acclaim one could add to their name. Some of her colleagues couldn't quite understand why she didn't want an *easy* life following in her parent's footsteps and being a darling of society. But only someone who'd never suffered it would call it easy.

"Miss Eliza." The butler inclined his head where he held open the door. "How you have grown."

She forced a smile for his benefit. "Thank you..." *Blast it.* She couldn't remember his name, though his features were vaguely familiar. The staff had always been kind to her when she stayed here with Grandmama, but it had been so long.

"Albert."

"Albert," she repeated. "My apologies. It has been a long journey."

He ushered her inside. "And quite a long time."

She couldn't miss the note of condemnation there. Eliza barely stifled a wince. A long time indeed. And while her parents deserved her cold shoulder, Grandmama hadn't, not even if she'd been a bit strange and absent-minded.

"They're waiting for you in the parlor." Albert led her through the wood-paneled walls of the hallway. Portraits of former mistresses of Folly Hall hung on the wall, their varied gazes staring at anyone who ventured down the crimson carpeted walk. Eliza hated the hall as a child, and that sentiment certainly hadn't changed.

Other servants passed by carrying vases of flowers. One held a long cloth with gold stitching. No doubt they were setting up for the gathering of remembrance to be held the next day, though the decorations were a bit bright for such a somber affair.

Albert knocked once on the parlor door before opening it. Eliza's breath hitched as she took in the small gathering inside. Her parents, she expected, though it'd be a lie to say she was ever quite prepared enough to see them. However, an unfamiliar spectacled man sat on the sofa, his face creased with consternation.

"Ah, there she is!" Mama set aside her tea and nearly leaped to her feet as if she were actually thrilled to see her daughter. A crimson dress hugged her form, entirely out of place for the reason they were there. So were the styled, brown ringlets in her hair and the make-up on her face. Papa and the stranger both could have stepped out of a business meeting given their tailored coats and styled accents. Only Eliza dressed appropriately in a dress of navy blue, a grey shawl around her shoulders to fight off the chill.

Eliza barely managed a stiff "Mama," before the woman gathered her in a loose hug and placed a kiss upon her cheek.

"It's been so long, my dear." She held tight to Eliza's upper arms, looking her over, probably searching for a hair out of place or an unseemly wrinkle marring her clothes. She wouldn't find much. Her mother's incessant preening over her appearance was one of the few things from her childhood that stuck. Though, the fact that the boarding school mistresses insisted on perfection too probably hadn't hurt. They weren't known for grooming and training the daughters of the Gamorean elite for nothing. However, Eliza was likely a dark mark on their record for choosing to become a scholar and librarian rather than a pretty thing on the arm of some noble.

If she was being honest with herself, that was one reason she'd chosen that path. It was one thing that couldn't aid her parents. Being a well-heeled woman of society, or even the subject of endless scandal, certainly could. After all, there was nothing quite so powerful as a name on someone's lips—in praise or admonishment.

But a scholar stuffed in a dusty library? They were easily ignored and forgotten. Just the way she preferred.

"Right on time. Didn't I tell you she would be?" Her father said to the stranger. A little more silver colored his hair than she remembered, but it only added to his air of superiority.

"What is this about?" Eliza asked. She focused her gaze on Mama, the most likely to give her a straight answer.

Surprisingly, it was Papa who answered. "Mother's lawyer has come to read her will."

That, she expected. As Grandmama's only child, Papa stood to inherit quite a fortune, not to mention the manor itself. But some bit of information still seemed to be missing. Why wait for her?

Mama finally released Eliza from her scrutiny and led her by the arm to the sitting area where the men waited.

The lawyer rose to his feet and gave a polite bow. "Miss Eliza Carroll. It's a pleasure to meet you."

"And you." She nodded in return.

"He insisted that you be present before he'd begin," Papa said, only letting the slightest bit of his irritation show through. Eliza could see it, though, the twitch in his nose that told when something annoyed him.

Her mother slid her arm through Eliza's and drew her to sit beside her on the settee. "She must have left you something. Isn't that marvelous?"

A knot welled up in her throat before Eliza forced it back down. Marvelous, yes...and so unmerited. She didn't deserve anything for the few letters she'd sent of late and even fewer visits.

A sudden sweat broke out on the back of her neck. Whatever Grandmama had left wouldn't be pleasant. How could it be when it'd remind Eliza of all her failings? Even if it were just a small sum, how could she spend it without considering how little she deserved it?

"Shall we get on with it now?" Papa asked. He crossed his legs and leaned back in the wide armchair. An unlit cigar already hovered in one hand, the other fumbling with a match like he was used to a servant lighting in for him. Eliza nearly rolled her eyes. He probably was.

"Yes, well." The lawyer shifted on the opposite sofa as if it were hard as a board, though the plush furnishings Grandmama favored were anything but. He took his time gathering papers from his leather bag and holding them up to read. The older gentleman adjusted his glasses and set the papers down, not even bothering to read from them. "I'll get straight to the point then."

Her mother's arm tightened against hers before she leaned forward, anticipation evident in her glittering eyes. Eliza's shoulders dropped. No doubt her mother already imagined the changes she would make to the manor and how they might use it as a summer home or showpiece of sorts. It was smaller than their sprawling city estate, but it had a history to it, one they might weave and show off at parties. Politicians and royals alike loved a good yarn.

"The late Mrs. Carroll was very direct in her wishes and desired to keep her estate and finances together."

Her father, having lit his cigar, blew out a hearty puff of smoke and nodded along. A grin already twisted up his features, giving them the cruel edge that made her stomach turn over.

The lawyer adjusted his glasses once more and shifted his gaze to Eliza. "She willed the full sum of her property and holdings to the sole inheritance of Miss Eliza Carroll."

Mama shrieked—a sound caught between shock and outrage. Papa choked on his smoke.

Eliza could do no more than blink. Someone may well have sinched her corset tighter, for air grew thin, and a sheen of sweat broke out on the back of her neck.

The estate, the settee on which she sat, the roof over her head, and even the very ground beneath her feet belonged to her.

"Nonsense!" Papa shouted at the older gentleman, who simply handed over the papers. Mama jumped away from her like she was a monster crawled up from the sea. Heeled shoes thumped across the carpets as she started pacing, hand on her brow, near hysterics.

Spots danced in Eliza's vision, and it took all she had not to let the darkness creeping in at the edges steal her away. What should have been theirs was now hers, and they surely would make her suffer for it.

The papers shook in Papa's grip before he practically threw them back at the lawyer.

The familiar pulse of an oncoming migraine started to beat behind her eyes.

Oh, Grandmama. If you wanted to punish me, there was no better way than this.

2

inn emerged from a hole in the ground as rabbits often do, with a twitch of his ears and shimmy of his backside. The hint of a chill crept up his paws, so different from the perpetually pleasant ground in Wonderland. In fact, nearly everything about the Other Land was unsettling, from the twinkling lights in the dark sky to the way the plant life was far too many shades of green and brown rather than the colorful array he was used to.

Worst of all, though, was the tug around his middle, like a thick rope that could never be seen or severed. It urged him back through the hole, back to Wonderland, for none of its residents were ever to leave its borders.

Except, of course, for Alice.

And that was precisely the reason he ventured here this evening.

The previous Alice passed a number of days before, a death that was felt by every soul living. Wonderland must have an Alice, and the time between one and the next was fraught and treacherous at best. Or so others said. He'd been too young to remember the last time between Alices. His ears twitched as he adjusted to the sounds of the world—the crickets and their off-kilter notes, and the frogs whose croak might kill a man for its poor symphony.

The rulers of the Red Court charged Finn with bringing the new Alice to court.

He rubbed his twitching nose with a furry, white paw.

So ridiculous. As if he needed one more reason to earn the king and queen's ire. Finn couldn't fail, couldn't be late, or it'd be off with his head.

It wasn't enough that half of Wonderland wanted him dead. The previous Alice seemed determined to set the rest of it against him, too. Not that he'd done anything to earn her scorn. Rather, he'd quite liked the old Alice and her tales of the Other Land. She'd been kind to him where few were, and yet, this was how she repaid him? Forcing him into an agreement to be the one to retrieve the new Alice—her granddaughter— probably some spoiled child if the stories of her kin held any truth.

He reached for the pocket watch inlaid with decorative stone from the shrine of the original Alice, only belatedly realizing he lingered in his alternate form. Magic shivered across his fur, and a moment later, Finn's body tingled and stung as it shifted into its true shape.

With a shiver and shake, he stepped forward. An odd habit, some said. He didn't need to truly step out of his other skin, but it always felt right to move from the spot his rabbit form once occupied and onto fresh soil.

"Much better."

At his proper height, Finn could see the upper floors of the human house rising above the nearby hedges—which disconcertingly were similar to the ones the Red Queen favored in her gardens. The structure was just as the former Alice had described with all its Other Land boring symmetry. She'd even painted him a portrait, just to be sure, not that he needed it. He adjusted his human clothes—always a touch wrinkled after such a shift—and sought out an object in his pocket. His hand closed over the watch. Its pull alone was enough.

The new Alice resided within, in a room along the right wing of the house, if he wasn't mistaken. Finn released the watch, leaving it to thrum along his leg through the fabric of his trousers.

Such an object could have fetched a hefty sum. *Be the one to wield the enchanted pocket watch of Alice and bring her to Wonderland! A hero for the coming age!*

Except, if he were to sell it, or to fail... *Off with my head.* He shivered.

He much preferred to keep it atop his neck and to keep living, however troublesome a life it was sometimes. He wouldn't even be a hero for bringing this Alice back. It'd simply be a task done, one to maintain favor with the monarchs. They'd be the heroes if all went according to plan, assuring Alice granted the Red Court her favor.

For all his magic and the titles people of the court bestowed on him—queen's favorite, king's ward—the monarchs often saw him as no better than a clever pet. Or a delivery boy in this case.

Hmm... Not a boy, a man. At least they gave him that much respect, however much he loathed that facet of the queen's regard.

Finn made his way through the labyrinth of hedges toward the house. The path spilled out into an open space with a gurgling fountain and far too many of the blasted frogs that set his teeth on edge. Someone opened a door to the house, just visible beyond the vast rose garden and little pools that occupied the space between them. Laughter and conversation spilled out with the light from within.

Alice wasn't alone.

The dirt trail gave way to a path of small rocks that crunched far too loudly under his boots. He winced, waiting for the inevitable complication of Other Land humans coming to investigate.

Though, if he were truly honest, which he was—sometimes, he might enjoy that. Other than the former Alice and her stories, he knew little of the Other Land. It'd be tempting to stay a while, to linger, if not for the damnable magic pulling him back toward the portal like a swift current. It had less patience than the queen, and hers was next to none.

Still, it would be best not to cause a ruckus and complicate his purpose. Eventually, the White Court would find their way to the portal and come for Alice themselves, and he couldn't have that. At least, not until he had her well in hand on the way to the Red Court.

Finn picked his way through the shadows toward the house. Whatever the people were doing, they seemed to prefer to stay indoors. A stream of carriages arrived, causing such a commotion he could have skipped blindly through the rest of the garden and never been heard. People exited the carriages dressed in blues and blacks and greys—such a depressing sight—and entered the house. The liveliness inside was far from their somber clothes. Finn smoothed a hand down his coat, his lips curling as he considered the various shades of red, gold, and green stitching. Perhaps these humans lacked taste. *That must be it.*

He frowned. Or worse, they were as hard and stoic as the White Court.

Laughter burst from within as another couple was let inside. He shook his head. Of course not, the White Court didn't favor such shows of emotion, not like these Other Landers.

The pull of the watch took him around to the back of the sprawling home, and annoyingly, tugged him upward. He tucked loose strands of his long hair behind one ear as he gazed at the windows high above. *Alas, Alice must be on the second floor.*

His lips quirked up in the corner. Luckily fate saw fit to provide him with a sort of ladder. A sprawling trellis clung to the side of the building, barely visible beyond the vines crawling up it. The bit of wildness, at odds with much of the orderliness of the house's exterior, sparked an ember of mirth dancing in his heart, not to mention its convenience. He'd always loved to climb. The act got him in trouble as a boy on numerous occasions.

Finn found a foothold and began his ascent, only to have the trellis snap under his weight and send him tumbling to the ground. Air whooshed from his lungs as his back slammed against the ground. He sat up, rubbing the back of his head.

Fate was a tricky bitch.

The easy way was always a trap. Didn't he know that already?

But, if Alice was up there, he needed a way up too. He'd stick out like a sore thumb among these drab people with his colorful attire. Or nude. A laugh caught in his chest. Now that would be entertaining.

With a soft groan, Finn pushed to his feet and examined the wall. The trellis might be poor support at best, but the brick façade underneath showed promise. The vines had done their damage, burrowing out holes and grooves in the mortar. Not much to work with, but enough.

Moments later, he clung to the wall outside a second-story window. Muffled sounds from the gathering rose from below, seeping out every nook and cranny to tease his ears, but nothing came from the room beyond. He thought it empty—the watch having led him astray—until he looked within. A young woman sat in front of a vanity, pushing at her brown locks like they wouldn't quite stay in place how she wanted.

Alice?

He'd expected a little girl, like the one the previous Alice showed him a painting of in one of her last visits. And though he could only see the back of her head and a hint of the profile of her face through the blurry glass, it was enough to know she was a girl no longer. Too bad. Children were easier to enchant and beguile.

A woman then. He tilted his head, taking her in. Highborn and haughty, or more reserved and demure? The previous Alice wasn't entirely sure. Apparently, it'd been some time since she'd actually seen her granddaughter. But this woman wasn't bursting with laughter like the people downstairs. A black dress hugged shoulders that hunched in slightly. She shook her head, slammed her hands upon the table, and stood.

Anger? His lips quirked. *What an interesting Alice.*

She bent to pick up something off the floor. As she held it up near her table lamp, turning it this way and that, the truth of it struck him so hard he nearly fell again.

The magic mirror. Or a shard of it.

Retrieving the new Alice used to be simple. She'd be called to the manor by the power of Wonderland, and someone would simply step through the mirror and bring her back with them.

Easy. Done before the tea turned cold.

But the previous Alice shattered the mirror. An accident, she'd said, but he couldn't help but wonder. Between that and her insistence that he travel the old, hidden—*and don't forget, long*—way to retrieve the new Alice, he suspected some game at play.

But that Alice was dead, so who moved the pieces?

Either way, nothing good would come from that mirror now if anyone in the White Court saw Alice through it. At least it was too small for most to pass through.

Finn pressed in closer to the window glass. "Don't look, Alice. Throw it away."

She jolted, then froze. Finn sucked in a breath. Just as she started to twist toward the window, he ducked.

Too close. Far too close. It wouldn't do for her to see him yet, not until he reasoned out a way to bring this Alice back through the rabbit hole with him.

A voice spoke within—high, lilting, and sharpened with sugared bitterness that set his teeth on edge. He dared to peek through the window once more. Another woman had entered the room. She appeared a little older, wearing a violet dress that brought out the blonde notes in her brown hair. Her mother? The late Alice only had one son. Without any daughters for the title to pass to, it fell to her next closest relative, her granddaughter. This must be the woman her son married. His nose wrinkled. *Hopefully Alice has better taste than her father.*

Alice replied, her words inaudible, but it was enough to taste the warmth in her tone, to roll the notes around on his tongue and determine them palatable.

Her mother poked at her hair where Alice had pinned it back behind her ears and shoved a stray strand back in place. *Too bad.* That wayward bit was his favorite, the one that refused to submit to pinning and prodding.

Finn sighed as Alice's mother led her from the room.

At least he'd found her. Now, he needed to get her to Wonderland.

3

*E*liza had yet to descend the stairs to the gathering, and it was already unbearable. Her corset, which fit moments ago, dug at her ribs, her hair wouldn't stay in its pins, and every burst of laughter made her see red.

This is a gathering of remembrance, for goodness sake! Did these people have no shame? She'd yet to set eyes on the crowd, but Eliza doubted if any of them truly knew her grandmother other than by reputation. Her parents had organized this and sent the invitations.

Eliza's hands balled into fists at her side, ones she slipped behind the skirts of her dress lest her mother notice. The house belonged to Eliza now. She could order them all out this very moment. She should.

Poor Mr. whatever-his-name-was practically fled the house, red-faced and flustered, in the wake of Papa's outrage the day before. Eliza had run after him, much to Mama's dismay, and gave apologies on behalf of her *shocked and bereaved* parents. That had calmed him some, at least enough to admit he understood why Grandmama left the estate to Eliza instead of her son.

The lawyer might have understood, but Eliza still didn't. She was no better than her parents really, living her own life, however quiet and aloof it might be, and leaving her grandmother to weather life alone save the occasional letter. A poor service after all the times they spent together when Eliza was a girl, before her parents became convinced Grandmama was a bad influence and sent her off to boarding school. They didn't like Grandmama's stories of strange lands and magic that had filled her childhood afternoons. A head full of nonsense wasn't fitting for a future lady of society. Plus, they couldn't be bothered to raise their own daughter after all, having *more important* matters to see to.

"There are quite a few important guests downstairs," Mama whispered. She didn't spare a glance to her daughter as she led her toward the top of the grand, sweeping staircase. All her focus lay straight ahead on the guests—likely nobles or others of political importance—that she planned to impress. "We should have cinched your corset tighter," she mumbled. "You've let yourself go. No wonder you wear such shapeless dresses."

Eliza winced. Fashion mattered little in the library, nor did her waist size. Whether it was because of their important guests or Eliza's inheritance that Mama chose to scold her about her weight, she couldn't say. She wasn't overly plump exactly, but she'd never have the thin, willowy form of her mother no matter how tight her corset. Plus, she quite preferred dresses she could move in with ease.

The few names Mama rattled off during their short walk were meaningless to Eliza, who did her best to stay far away from the politics of the realm.

"I think they'll be excited to see you," Mama said.

Eliza fought back a sigh. She was probably right. Not because any of them cared a wit about her, but because it would elevate them in the eyes of their peers, having conversed with her parents' elusive daughter.

The rush of sound rolling up the stairs was enough to send the start of another headache building behind her eyes. So many lately. The one yesterday had lasted much of the afternoon. The migraines were always troublesome when they came on, seemingly out of the blue, but at least they'd been infrequent most of her life. The last few months or so, however, they'd been bad as ever, leaving her bedridden with pain and nausea on a number of occasions.

Figures came into view below, dressed in their best austere colors of mourning, though from the smiles on their faces and occasional laughter, none of them appeared the least bit remorse at Grandmama's passing. They crammed the space, buzzing around like flies near a corpse. That thought hit a little too close to home, making her tear up, but she hastily blinked the tears away. They wouldn't do in front of guests, and she'd shed plenty already when she received the news of Grandmama's passing. Several heads turned her way, and she began her descent of the stairs beside Mama. A demure grin stretched her features, snapping into place as easily as donning a mask at a ball.

Strangers swarmed them the moment Eliza left the bottom step. It took everything she had not to turn and flee or push away offending hands as they drew her near for a hug, patted her cheek, or a number of things that made her skin crawl. Perfumes warred for dominance and increased the steady throbbing in her head.

Mama did most of the talking, which was just as well. Eliza couldn't muster more than polite one-word replies and nods. One of the house staff wandered by with a tray of saucers filled with bubbling, pale-amber liquid. How lovely it would be to down one in a single sip. Maybe two.

Well, lovely for blurring her senses enough for the night to be less awful. Not so lovely for her building headache. But then, that pain might be a worthy price to pay to escape the people around her.

Eliza limited herself to taking a single cup. The cool crystal against her palm gave a strange sort of comfort. The bubbling liquid dancing on her tongue was even better.

She needed every bit of it as her father yelled through the crowd and beckoned her over. With her mother, at least she could be a pretty flower in the shadow of her splendor. Not so with her father.

Eliza picked her way through the crowd toward his summons. Her father stood with a few other men, mostly older than him. One managed to snag Eliza's attention where most of the others had not. He was younger, maybe no more than a few years her elder, if that. His dark blonde hair was trimmed short to fall at his ears in artful waves, and he wore a tailored coat of navy blue with gold thread that complimented his tanned complexion well. His wide shoulders and strong features caused a fluttering in her stomach that had little to do with the drink in her hand. This stranger was truly the handsome sort, even if his mere presence here spoke ill of him. Most likely some son of one of her father's political allies.

"Ah, there she is," Papa said.

Eliza forced her smile just a bit brighter.

"The lovely Miss Carroll." An older man with a bushy mustache held out his hand to her.

She took it, instantly hating how his sweaty palm dampened her skin. The revulsion only grew as he drew her hand to his lips and placed a scratchy kiss on its back.

"Your father has been telling us all about you," he continued once he released her hand.

So many vague details, I'm sure. Eliza took a sip to avoid responding. Her father knew little about her life.

"This is my son, Fredrick." He gestured to the attractive young man at his side.

At least the son was a far cry more attractive than his father. Taking after his mother, perhaps? Not that she had any idea who that was.

He dipped his head. "A pleasure."

"Indeed." She returned the gesture.

"Surely you recognize Commodore Harrington?" Her father said by way of filling in the gaps for her. "The pride of the Gamorean navy, and his son, intends to follow in his father's footsteps, isn't that right?"

Ah, that explains it. Such a man would be a valuable ally in Father's pocket for his run at the governorship of the province. That alone might ensure Papa's success.

"An honor." Eliza dipped a curtsy, careful of the drink in her hand. It was best to play the dutiful daughter. Any minute now, Papa would dismiss her, and she could find a dark corner to hide in. "Though do the pirates not make your endeavors quite fraught these days?" Perhaps that would get him wishing her away.

"Not since Captain Blackbeard disappeared," Fredrick replied with a broad grin. "Some say he's finally dead. It certainly makes our work easier."

The men laughed, clearly pleased with themselves and not at all put off by her comments.

"Speaking of work, your father says you are employed?" The commodore raised a brow. "At the national library?"

The insult was near unmissable. Eliza forced her grin brighter. "I am indeed."

"Such dreary work for such a lovely lady, don't you think, Fredrick?"

Fredrick's gaze raked her form, so much more prying than his courteous greeting a moment ago. The other men nearby murmured their agreement.

Eliza stood a little straighter. "Well, I—"

"It is indeed," her father answered. "But our dear Eliza thought it to her best advantage to learn as much as she could about our glorious country, especially if she were to play a prominent role in society one day."

The nearby conversations swallowed up her airy snort. *Hardly.*

"There have been many offers for her hand, but none seemed quite worthwhile to draw her from her learning," he continued.

Had there been? If so, they weren't made to her. She'd had some requests of the more passionate and less marriage-minded sort. A few that interested her enough to agree to, at least for a time, but her father wouldn't know that, surely.

The older man gave a knowing chuckle. "I am pleased that my Fredrick is the exception."

Eliza swayed on her feet and nearly dropped her glass. "Papa?" she asked, her voice rising precariously high.

He ignored her and rambled on about Fredrick's many accomplishments and virtues, but they were no more than a dull buzz in her ears. The words were for her, but he barely paid her any mind. None of them did.

A silent scream built in the back of her mind, waring against the rising pound of a headache.

"Papa," she demanded, finally snaring his attention. "What is this about?"

It couldn't be what he implied. It couldn't.

"Your mother didn't tell you?" He seemed genuinely surprised, but then his nose twitched, giving him away. "You're to be engaged to Fredrick. Isn't that wonderful, darling?"

She looked from one man to the next. They all knew. Even Fredrick had a certain smugness glittering in his eyes that turned all his fair looks foul.

"B-but we just met," she stammered.

"Then it's fortunate he is here tonight for you to become acquainted with one another," her father said. "Yours will be the pre-eminent wedding of the season—no, the year! Why, I can't remember the last time two great families came together in such a strong match."

And there it was. He planned to use her, his own daughter, to solidify his political alliance. She was the bargaining chip, his ticket to further success.

She stared at him, uncaring of the way her mouth gaped open in shocked horror.

A hard glint lay in his eyes—a bit too much drink, and something worse, the spark of vengeance. This was her penance for inheriting Grandmama's estate, to be sold off in marriage like the property he'd hoped to acquire.

But no one owned her.

"Excuse me." She spun on her heel.

Voices erupted behind her, but she ignored them all. The crystal saucer slipped from her grip to shatter upon the floor. Eliza ignored that too. Blood rushed in her ears as she gathered her skirts in her fists and shoved through the crowd.

Apologies were the last thing on her mind as she bolted toward the stairs. But there was her mother standing at their base, waving to her, trying to grab her attention.

A half-strangled scream slipped through Eliza's lips as she turned abruptly in the opposite direction. People leaped out of her way, a few too slowly, earning a nudge or two in the process. A drink spilled down her arm as one man jolted back. It didn't matter. She needed away. *Out. Air.*

Finally, she burst out a side door and stumbled down the stairs into the gardens. The chill of night cloaked her, sharpening her senses with each gasped inhale.

She'd made a scene, the very thing she always tried not to do. People would talk about her abrupt exit for months. It might garner even more attention than her engagement, which she'd quite literally run away from.

An engagement. A sob caught in her throat.

Did her father think she'd actually go through with such nonsense? He must to have arranged it. All her years of trying to escape the shadow of her parents, to forge a life that was her own, and he had to go and do something as horrible as this.

Shadows danced along the gravel path, hinting at a pursuit.

She couldn't face whoever it was. Mama or Papa? Her would-be fiancé? A brittle laugh slipped from her lips. She couldn't go back in there.

Eliza raced through the rose garden, around the little pools with their golden fishes, and into the hedge maze. No one would follow her there, not on this chilly night. She hugged her arms around herself. A shawl would have helped, but she'd had no time to grab one or the wherewithal to think to do it.

"Marriage. To a complete stranger." She shook her head and wandered further into the maze. "They must be joking."

Except this was no joke. The tight vice around her chest, worse than any tightly strung corset, was proof of that.

She wiped at the tears attempting to escape and run down her face. "I'll simply refuse. I have my job, my inheritance. They can't possibly force such a thing on a grown woman."

Or could they? Eliza swallowed the knot in her throat. Her father was notorious for getting what he wanted. He hadn't risen from a nobody of reasonable means to the likely next governor of the eastern mainland for nothing. Besides, she was a woman. In this society, her rights were limited.

The path ahead spilled out into a small, open area. A large tree, a willow perhaps, draped its branches over a stone bench. An opening in the hedge loomed to either side of the space, offering the wanderer a choice of directions. Eliza chose neither and, instead, huddled down on the cold stone. The clear sky gave off a show of stars and let the moon cast its light over the space, providing plenty of illumination to see by.

The top floor of the house gleamed like a beacon beyond the hedges. She'd walked farther than she'd realized, but the stillness of the night, punctuated by the croak of frogs and chitter of bugs, was a comfort compared to the riotous party inside the manor. This far away, she couldn't hear it at all. *Thank the Mother and all her saints for that.*

Eliza looked to the stars. "Grandmama, what should I do?" Silently she added, *I'm sorry they corrupted this night that should have been in remembrance of you.*

"Alice."

Eliza sucked in a breath and jolted to her feet. "Who's there?"

She glanced around, but the space remained empty.

Alice. The name caught like a loose thread and wouldn't let go. It was common enough, but it was more than that. Something Grandmama said long ago. A memory just out of reach.

"Grandmama?" The start of a bitter huff of laughter followed her question. That was wishful thinking, and such thoughts never bred anything but cruel hope.

A rustling sound nearby had her almost leaping out of her skin. Eliza twisted around, prepared to greet a monstrous demon, when a white rabbit hopped from the hedges near the bench.

"Oh." She sagged with relief. "You frightened me."

Scared of a little rabbit. She really was a mess this evening.

It seemed to give a little shiver and folded its ears down over its head.

"Poor thing." Eliza crouched. "It's cold out tonight, isn't it?"

It rubbed a paw at its nose.

The act had Eliza grinning, perhaps the first true one of the night. "I won't hurt you," she promised.

The rabbit hopped forward as if it understood what she said. But that was more nonsense, of course it couldn't understand her, no matter how much she wanted it to.

Eliza slowly stretched out her hand toward the rabbit and waited.

It inched forward, ears twitching.

So close. Almost. Eliza stretched her fingers, rocking forward on her toes.

She nearly brushed one fluffy ear when it stilled, turned, and leaped in the opposite direction.

She sighed, content to let the wild creature hop away, when it did the most peculiar thing. It stopped and turned its head back toward her. Eliza couldn't shake the thought that it beckoned her to follow, however ridiculous that might be.

Happy for the distraction and with nothing but sorrows to occupy her time otherwise, she spoke to the rabbit. "You want me to follow you?"

The fluffy thing took another hop and looked back again.

Eliza bunched her dress to keep from stumbling and waddled along after it until it neared the base of the willow. Its branches hung low, dripping like long, spindly fingers ready to grab her by the hair and drag her away. A shiver raced across her skin, and she dropped her skirts to rub at her arms.

The rabbit hopped again, this time landing near a large opening at the base of the tree, which she'd swear hadn't been there a moment ago. "Your home?" she asked it.

It seemed to nod in return and took another hop. Her brows drew together.

She inched closer until she could brace one palm on the trunk of the tree. "I can't possibly follow you in there, but thank you for your offer."

Carrying on a conversation with a rabbit. How ridiculous.

"Eliza?" someone called in the distance.

The fine hairs along the back of her neck rose.

The voice wasn't close, but still loud enough for her to know it wasn't either of her parents. Her fiancé? Eliza shivered.

"I don't want him to find me yet," she said to the rabbit, never turning from the direction of the manor.

"He won't." A human hand latched onto her arm and tugged.

A scream raced up her throat as she tumbled backwards, but the sound never escaped before another hand clamped over her lips. And then she was falling, tumbling into darkness.

4

*S*o this is Alice.

Finn brushed a stray strand of hair away from her face and adjusted her unconscious form in his arms. She was lovely, this Alice, if a little too pale, almost like she avoided the sun on purpose. Some of her dark brown hair had fallen free from its pins and hung toward the ground in little waves. Her painted red lips were slightly parted and just plump enough to make them tempting. Not too skinny, with the perfect softness in her curves. A tender heart toward animals too. He grinned. Or rabbits, at least.

He'd planned to wait until she returned to her room and steal her away then. That would have been easiest—well, except the getting down from the second story with an unconscious woman in his arms part. But, a small sprinkle of sleeping powder would have kept her from running away. Fate, for once, dealt him a favorable card and sent her running out into the night instead. She never even heard him following behind her through the hedges.

"Fleeing an unwanted marriage?" he asked her sleeping form, not that she could answer.

The man must be hideous. Finn gave a little shrug as he trotted along the path. It was the Other Landers' loss. Alice had more important things to do than wed some random man.

Though, if things went smoothly, she could be back in time to do that too.

The thought had his jaw stiffening. She'd been in tears. She didn't want that.

He shook his head. Alice's affairs in the Other Land didn't matter. The important thing was getting her safely back to the Red Court.

At least he wouldn't be carrying her all the way back. Now *that* would be a trial. "But where is that damned horse?" he mused, scanning the nearby woods.

He should have tied it up. But time between Wonderland and the Other Land flowed strangely, especially where Alice was concerned, and it wouldn't do any good for him—or the poor horse—if he came back to find it starved to death.

With a sigh, he knelt near the base of a large tree and laid Alice's sleeping form on a stretch of moss. His fingers moved of their own accord, brushing a lock of hair back from her face again, maybe that same one that caught his attention in her rooms. It was an enticing bit of hair, wild and unruly. A clue to the woman herself? Though she looked orderly and proper in her appearance. Well, she had until he pulled her through the rabbit hole. Shifting worlds was always a bit unsettling, probably why she fainted.

Finn reached into his pouch, one enchanted to hold things many times its small size, and pulled out a soft blanket. *Poor Alice.* He touched her cool cheek. Her world was colder than Wonderland, and she still held its chill. He tucked the blanket around her. With its dark coloring, it would help disguise her presence. Not that he planned to be gone long, only until he could track down that damn horse.

With Alice secured, Finn reached out with his senses. Even in human form, they were much stronger than most. He filtered through the myriad scents, searching for the one he wanted. His nose twitched as he caught it and turned in the horse's direction. "There you are."

Finn sprinted into the woods, only slowing as he neared his quarry. He gave a sharp whistle, and the horse raised its head from where it nibbled on a tuft of bluish grass.

"Thought you'd run off," he scolded before rubbing a hand down the mare's neck. He checked the saddle and was about to leap onto it when another scent demanded his attention.

He stilled. "Bandersnatch."

The horse gave a pitiful whinny. Finn stoked its neck again. "Terrifying indeed," he concurred.

They weren't common in these woods, but little went as it should when there was no Alice to decide who reigned over Wonderland. It wasn't a fresh scent, but not old enough for his liking either. Such a beasty could have made a tasty snack of his horse with its swift speed and razor-sharp teeth.

Or Alice.

He leaped into the saddle. *Shit.* He should never have left her.

If anything happened to her, it'd be his head that would roll. Not to mention whatever havoc it would wreak on the land to lose another Alice so soon. Had it ever happened?

He couldn't think, couldn't sort through the many lessons he'd learned of their history as he raced through the woods on horseback, pulse beating wildly in his throat.

Moments stretched like years until he leaped a fallen log and drew the horse up just short of the tree where he'd left her. The blanket sat crumpled in a shadowed heap on the moss.

"Shit." He jumped from the saddle, boots slamming onto the ground. "Alice?"

Where could she have gone? The moon was bright overhead, but there were still far too many shadows. He strode away from the horse and sniffed at the air, searching. No Bandersnatch—*thank the ancient kings*. But where—

Movement in the corner of his eye caught his attention. Finn raised his hand just in time to catch the thick branch whistling through the air toward his face. It slammed against his palm. He closed his fingers around it, holding it still as Alice tried to jerk it away.

The hint of a grin twitched on his lips. "There you are."

"Stay away from me you, you—" She jerked on the stick, but he held firm. Alice threw her weight backward, nearly spilling to the ground in her feeble attempts. To be fair, she didn't know he'd trained in combat for years, and she didn't have a chance at beating him. Though he immensely enjoyed watching her try.

In one quick move, Finn twisted the stick, pulled it from her grasp, and sent it sailing off behind him. "Finneas, at your service, Alice." He bowed.

He snapped his head back up to see her standing there wide-eyed and fuming, fists bunched at her sides. Something swelled in his chest. She was even more lovely when she was furious.

And possibly a good actress. She recognized him. Apparently, she hadn't been as unconscious as he'd thought. His grin widened. *Most interesting.*

Her gaze coasted down him before snapping back to his face as if she just now got a good look at him, or the best she could at night. "Take me back this instant."

The sharpness in her tone brokered no argument. Only someone used to getting their way could be so forceful.

He relaxed his stance. At least she was smart enough not to attack again. "I thought you didn't want *him* to find you yet?"

Her lips parted, and she stood a little taller.

"That's no excuse to steal me." She notched her chin higher. "Do you even know who I am?"

"Of course. You're Alice."

She huffed and shoved at her hair. "I'm Eliza Carroll. If you know what's good for you, you'll take me back before my parents grow worried." She crossed her arms. "Or my fiancé. His father is the Admiral of the Gamorean navy."

She could almost be convincing if he hadn't overheard her laments.

Finn tilted his head to the side. "Oh yes, you seemed so pleased with that arrangement."

Alice stumbled back a step.

"So *eager* to go back to him," he prodded.

"I—" Her arms fell to her sides, hands in tight fists once more.

"I'm afraid you're needed here, Alice." Slowly, he drew near. Finn expected her to retreat. An entirely un-rabbit-like part of him yearned to give chase. Instead, she held firm, staring up at him as he neared.

Brave woman. An excellent quality. She'd need all of her bravery for what was to come.

"I am not Alice. You have the wrong person."

"But you are." She was so close now. He could reach out and touch her, but he held back. "Your grandmother never told you?"

"Grandmama…" Her hard expression shattered. She swayed on her feet, and her gaze dripped toward the ground.

He felt terrible for bringing up the previous Alice. Well, almost. The sooner she realized who she was, the better for both of them.

"She was the previous Alice, and you are the next," Finn continued.

Alice shook her head. "Her name was Eloise. Eloise Carroll."

"In the Other Land." He touched her arm, and Alice gasped. "Here, she was Alice, as are you."

"You're ridiculous." She jerked away. Her lips pinched together, and that hard shield slipped back over her features. "I'll find my own way home."

Finn sighed. *So difficult.* Maybe he should have used that sleeping potion after all, though it'd be so much easier to have her cooperation.

She stalked into the trees. He let her go. Alice wouldn't get far in these woods at night, and there was no way he'd lose her scent—lavender with a hint of clove. *Intoxicating.* A bit of it clung to his clothes, every whiff sending a subtle wave of warmth coursing through him.

A roar rumbled through the night. His hair stood on end. Alice stopped abruptly and then jumped behind a tree.

He shook his head. Little protection that would be from a Bandersnatch. The roar was some distance away, but with their swiftness, that distance could shrink in minutes.

Finn crept up on Alice. "Frightened?"

She screamed and whirled toward him, her back plastered against the tree trunk.

"Y-you!" She swatted his arm. "How dare you!"

He smirked. *Because it's so delightful to see you furious.* But to her, he said, "Come now. We don't want that terrible beastie discovering us."

"T-that… That roar. Nothing like that exists near Folly Hall."

"No." He tapped a finger on his lips. "I'd wager it doesn't."

"These trees…" She ran her hand along a branch. "You…" Her gaze picked its way down his form once more and back up. The shadows that cloaked her form weren't enough to dull the spark of understanding burning in her eyes. "This isn't part of Gamor, is it?"

He merely shook his head. "This is Wonderland."

She pinched her eyes closed.

"What are you doing?" His brows drew together as he took in the odd reaction.

"This is a dream. You're a terrible, bad dream."

He snorted. Him? A bad dream? *Hardly.* Now an emissary of the Court of White finding her? That could be a nightmare, as it would be if the Bandersnatch found them.

"Dear Alice. This is anything but a dream."

Her eyes snapped open. "I am not Alice." She pursed her lips, and he had the strangest urge to run his thumb over them.

"Ah, but you are, whether you believe it or not. And your grandmother ordered me to find you and bring you to court." He leaned in, drawing close even as she tried to mold herself against the tree. "Believe me," he whispered in her ear. "You'd rather go with me than be left alone out here. There are much more terrible things in these woods than me."

"Grandmama." Her throat bobbed.

"If I am a bad dream." He fumbled over the word. *How could a dream of me ever be bad?* "Then you'll wake up eventually. But if I'm not, do you really want to be alone here?" He stepped back and held out his hand. If Alice had any sense, she'd take it.

As if to punctuate his point, the Bandersnatch roared again—louder this time and much too loud for his liking. Finn fought against the urge to race for his horse and simply raised his brows.

The woman visibly shivered, and it certainly wasn't from the cold, not here in Wonderland where it was almost always perfectly pleasant.

Hesitantly, she placed her hand in his. *So soft and warm. A perfect fit.* His brows drew together, and he pushed away that thought.

"Fine." She swallowed again and stepped closer to him. "But if you try anything, I swear you'll regret it."

He fought down a laugh and led her to the horse. "I quite look forward to that."

5

A *dream—it must all be some terrible nightmare.* That was the only explanation for the roar that sounded like nothing Eliza had ever heard, the azure colored bark of a tree that should not exist, or the numerous plants that she had no name for. Eliza loved plants. She'd studied the ones in Gamor, and further reaches of Neverland, to a great extent both in books and in person, but the trees the horse trotted by... they were not of her world.

The sky made no sense either, green-tinted moonlight filtering down from a sky without stars. Slight variations in the dark carpet of the night hinted at something up there, but the bright white pin-pricks of light and the constellations they formed were gone, almost like someone had thrown a sheet over the sky and only a teasing hint of them slipped through.

The whole place was wrong—odd, to say nothing of the man at her back.

He was quite unlike anyone she'd ever met. Finn, that's what he'd called himself anyway, had hair so pale it looked white in the moonlight. *Truly, it might be white.* But he wasn't old, far from it. His strong, balanced features lacked any wrinkles. He'd lifted her onto the horse as if she weighed nothing, and all that lean muscle coursing his body was unmissable where he sat behind her in the saddle.

She'd tried not to lean into him, to sit perfectly stiff and still in the saddle, but that lasted all of a minute. Finn had simply laughed, tucked her back against his chest, and that was where she'd stayed. Damn him for the way the intimate touch made her head spin. She'd love to say it was the corset's fault, but that would be a lie. Sitting astride the horse and against his solid form, that no amount of clothing or the blanket wrapped around her could disguise, stirred up way too many feelings that were entirely inappropriate for a strange man she'd just met.

He hadn't been at the gathering of remembrance. He'd have stood out like a blossom against the winter snows with the bright crimson and gold of his coat, to say nothing of his hair where it hung loose past his shoulders with its strange color.

Nothing about the night made any sense, not from her father's pronouncement to that very moment. Maybe she'd fallen while descending the stairs and hit her head. She was prone to clumsiness.

But when the fog cleared from Finn wrapping his arms around her and tucking her against his chest, an old memory surfaced. At least, she thought it was a memory.

Eliza sat with Grandmama on the bench near the willow tree, listening to one of her stories about a strange land. The stories were common in their time together, but in that particular one, she'd given the land a name.

Wonderland.

"Is it truly wonderful then?" Eliza had asked with all her youthful eagerness.

At that, her grandmother's expression had changed. All thought of homes made of cake and fountains of cream vanished at her shadowed look. "It could be," she'd said.

Grandmama had tucked her close into her side. Years later, Eliza could still smell the scent of her favorite peppermint candies that often clung to her, just as she had then. "I hope you never have to go there," she'd said.

Little Eliza was so confused. Why wouldn't Grandmama want her to go to a world of wonders, one she told her about all the time? She knew the stories were just that, and no one could go to a land of imagination, but she'd wanted to all those years ago.

Finn slowed the horse as he navigated over an old wooden bridge.

"Where exactly are you taking me?" Eliza asked, the first words she'd spoken to him since their hasty flight from the terrifying roar they'd heard.

The first town or building she saw, she'd make a run for it. That was the plan. She'd offer whomever she encountered a hefty reward to get her away from Finn and back home. Who would turn down a small fortune? Her parents would pay it, she was sure, and if not, she had her own inheritance now.

If this wasn't a bad dream, and she certainly hoped it was, she needed to get away from this stranger, however oddly handsome he might be. If it was a dream? Well, she'd wake up anyway, and whatever fortune she promised wouldn't matter.

"The Red Court," he answered.

Not a place that existed.

"And we're almost there?" she prodded.

He huffed. "Hardly. It's a few days' ride, at least."

Days. She gaped. Eliza pushed at her dress and the corset underneath. Dream or not, she wanted to be comfortable and was far from it at the moment. Not to mention that her legs had begun to chafe. "You cannot expect me to ride all that way in this."

"Hm." He leaned in, his breath warm on her cheek. Eliza gasped as his arm wrapped tight around her middle. "Indeed. We'll get you something more appropriate when we visit the Duchess."

Finn released her, but it took another moment to gather her wits and respond. "Which Duchess?" Perhaps that would give a clue to where they were.

He shrugged. "She's simply called the Duchess."

A cry of frustration caught in her throat. No one she knew went by a title alone. He couldn't have taken her that far away in the brief time she'd fainted. It was more evidence to this being a dream conjured from her childhood memories, but shouldn't she have woken up by now? Her arm throbbed from the number of times she'd pinched it.

Finn slowed the horse further and eased it off the path into the nearby woods.

"What are you doing?" she asked.

"Stopping for the night," he replied matter-of-factly.

"Out here. In the woods?" *Oh no, no way.* She'd never slept outdoors in her life.

His hair tickled her cheek as he leaned in close. "Afraid of a few bugs?"

She rolled her shoulder to shove him away, earning a small chuckle. The man had no sense of personal space.

"What about the Duchess? That roar we heard?" *Damn it all, how have we not come upon anyone else?*

Finn leaped down from the horse and took the reins in hand, leading them further into the woods. "The Duchess is still some hours away. You may want to rest before then." He glanced up at her. "I certainly do. You can never be too prepared with that one," he said, almost to himself. "And the terrible beasty?" He shrugged. "We've ventured outside its territory. I don't scent it here."

Scent? She blinked at him. As if he were some tracking dog? But he ignored her once more and found his way through the trees with enviable skill given the darkness. She could make out little enough of their surroundings, and what she did see—blue tree trunks and bright-colored flowers—made no sense given the approaching winter. Such things baffled the mind and asked her to accept what she couldn't. Though, oddly, her earlier headache had completely vanished.

More evidence that this place couldn't be real. Her headaches never went away so quickly.

"Not afraid I'll run off in the night?" She couldn't help herself. Something about the quiet night and the very strange bug sounds—almost symphonic in their harmony—made her deeply uncomfortable. Awkward conversation with Finn was a much better option.

He stopped and looked back over one shoulder. "I guess I'll have to sleep with my arms around you."

She stiffened. "You wouldn't."

Finn grinned before turning back to the woods and resuming his careful trek. "Oh, I certainly would."

The indignation of such a suggestion! She pulled the blanket tighter around herself. If he tried something like that, he might just get an unfortunate kick between the legs sometime during the night.

"This looks like a good spot for a rest." Finn tied the reins to a branch.

Eliza eyed the small glen, which looked about like all the rest save for the little clearing void of trees. "Here?"

"Of course. It's dry. Off the main road. There's plenty of moss to sleep on."

Moss...as a bed.

He held a hand up to her. "Shall I help you down, Alice?" He always drew out the last two letters in a hiss that set her teeth on edge.

"It's Eliza," she said. Still, she took his hand. Better that than slip in her heels and break something. Her body slid against his as he helped to lower her to the ground. The skirts of her dress bunched between them. A strong arm around her back held her firm, even once she no longer needed his assistance.

"Eliza." Each syllable stretched between them as if he took the time to taste each one as it rolled across his tongue.

The sound of her name on his lips sent a flush burning up her neck and the air growing thin, especially as he held her gaze with his startling amber eyes.

Eliza all but pulled herself from his embrace and smoothed out her skirts. Damn her traitorous body and the effect he had on it.

Finn reached into the pouch tied to his waist and pulled forth a large flask—one that shouldn't have fit in such a small space, and she certainly hadn't heard jingling about in their trek. He offered it to her. "Thirsty?"

She licked her lips without thinking. He grinned. *Damn it.* She snatched the flask.

Water never tasted so good, and no matter how much she drank, the flask always weighed the same. *How delightfully odd...*

Stranger still was Finn's little pouch. She had to be stuck in a dream because he pulled out something almost as long as her, shook it, and it sprang into the form of a tent before planting itself on the moss.

Eliza blinked as Finn procured other items: a bed roll, another blanket, bread. Her mouth watered. She'd been too upset and nervous to eat dinner, and that had been hours ago, at least.

Her brows scrunched together. Why would she be hungry in a dream? Eliza shook the thought away and crossed the space between them. "How are you doing that?"

He tucked the long loaf of bread under one arm. "Doing what?" he asked as if he truly wasn't sure what she asked about.

Infuriating man. "The bag." She gestured to it. "It can't possibly fit so many things." The flask alone would have taken up the entire thing.

"Ah." His grin returned. "No wise person would go on a quest to fetch Alice without an enchanted pouch to keep all their things safe and dry."

An enchanted pouch. If such a thing existed, she'd have read about it somewhere, but she hadn't. "That doesn't exist."

"The Other Land really is a dreadful place, isn't it?" Finn's expression dropped into a pout. "Would you like to touch it?"

Tempting as it was, it was still attached to his hip, and putting her hands there was out of the question. "No thank you." *Nope. Not happening.*

He shrugged and passed her the loaf, nearly whacking her in the stomach with it. "You should eat something."

"Bread was the only thing that fit in your pouch?" She examined it in the moonlight. It looked ordinary enough, golden brown and crisp, with a few splits in the crust across the top. Strangely, it even felt a bit warm, as if it had been in the oven not long ago, but that made no sense. Though, little in this place did.

"I didn't know what you'd like, and everyone likes bread."

Likes, might be a strong word. Tolerates would be better, but she didn't argue with him further. Instead, she broke a chunk off the end and took a bite.

Eliza groaned in pleasure.

This was not bread. It was cake. And chocolate. And spice. And yet savory too. Everything she could have wanted from a meal.

Finn's chuckle caused her face to heat. "See," he said. "I told you everyone likes bread."

Bastard. She yearned to throw it at him, but it'd be a shame to waste something so delicious.

After a few mouthfuls, Eliza ventured a question that kept racing around in her mind. "So, you're taking me to the Red Court. Why exactly?"

He smoothed out the blanket he'd laid in the tent and glanced back at her. "Because the previous Alice ordered it."

Right... She tapped her foot, waiting for more.

A sigh slipped from his lips. Finn crossed his legs and made himself comfortable near the edge of the tent. "You can come and sit." When she didn't move, he shrugged and continued. "You're to meet with the king and queen and stay there for a time until you're anointed the new Alice and declare the Red Court in charge of Wonderland."

The bread suddenly lost its flavor on her tongue. She had a good feeling he didn't mean the monarchs she'd once glimpsed at the university when they came to deliver a speech. Nor did his words really make any logical sense.

"If I am this Alice, and the king and queen want me to reside with them, why didn't they come for me themselves? Or send a whole host of people to deliver me there? Why send you?" She thrust an accusing finger at him.

Finn leaned back on his arms, a cocky swagger to his actions. "You don't think I'm enough."

This time she did throw the bread at him. He plucked it from the air before it could touch the ground and took a sizeable bite straight from the loaf.

Eliza crossed her arms and scowled at him, waiting for a better answer. He took his time chewing the bread, holding her stare all the while. It was disturbing the way she couldn't tear her gaze away from his lips or his strong jaw as he chewed. Watching someone eat shouldn't be so mesmerizing.

Eventually, he swallowed. "It should be easier to bring Alice to court. Step through the magic mirror into your world and bring you back through. But the previous Alice, your grandmother, shattered the mirror on her side."

Her brows drew together. Early that night, she'd found a broken piece of mirror that had slipped under the vanity. She rubbed her fingers together at the memory of its eerie coldness. *But why shatter it?* Her arms fell loose at her side.

"Who can say why?" he said like he had plucked the question from her mind. "Perhaps she feared the White Court might reach the mirror first and claim you?"

"The White Court?"

He nodded. "Wonderland has two courts, White and Red. It's Alice who decides which one reigns."

A dull headache began to build behind her eyes, but it felt nothing like the usual ones. This one was born of pure confusion and frustration. "Then shouldn't you take me to both courts? What if I prefer White instead of Red?"

The normally jovial expression Finn wore turned hard and sharp in an instant. "You would not like the White Court. They're hard and cruel."

Her lips thinned. "Shouldn't that be for me to decide?" This was all too much like her parents and their political games, trying to move her as a piece to be played for their gain. Didn't anyone understand that she just wanted to live her own life?

"If you trust me on anything, trust me in that. I'm from there. Your grandmother didn't want you there. Neither do I. Besides." He set the bread aside. "They'd probably kill me on sight if I went back."

She sucked in a breath. The casual way he spoke of death chilled her to the bone. That, and what it said about him. "You're an outlaw?" She took a step back.

"Only in certain places." His grin returned.

Great. Just great. What were you thinking, Grandmama? Unless... "How do I know it's really my grandmother who sent you? Maybe you made it up."

Nothing else about this world or him made sense, so why should that?

He fished around in his pack and drew something out. Eliza didn't get a good look at it until he rose and came to stand a foot away from her. Always a bit too close.

The object he held out made her eyes widen in surprise. Even in the dim moonlight, she could make out the little painting, one her grandmother had commissioned during one of the last times she'd stayed with her when she'd been a girl. Eliza trailed her fingers across the small, tarnished frame. She'd loved that blue dress and its lacey hem.

She jerked her hand away. "You could have stolen that from the manor."

"I didn't, though."

His golden eyes were unflinching, too full of something she couldn't name, which stirred up too many emotions, so she looked away.

"Ask me something. What's something only someone who knew her would know?" He stepped forward.

Eliza stood a little straighter. He was so close, not enough that they touched, but almost.

It was impossible to see him where he loomed behind her, but his nearness threatened to overwhelm her. Eliza shut her eyes, remembering the day the portrait was painted. She'd been playing in the garden that morning and listening to Grandmama's strange stories of other lands and creatures. *Of here?*

"What did she smell like?" Eliza asked at last. If he truly had such a great sense of smell, he would know the scent from her memories, the one that always clung to her grandmother.

Silence reigned for a moment. Long enough that she nearly opened her eyes to see if Finn still stood behind her, though she hadn't heard him move.

"Peppermint."

Eliza whirled around so fast that she nearly fell. Her gaze landed on his face, utterly devoid of humor. A half-sob crawled up out of nowhere and tore from her lips. He knew. He truly had known her. Worse, he probably knew her far better than Eliza did.

She didn't fight it as his arms encircled her. The opposite, she buried her face against his chest to hide the tears trying to slip free. She sniffled, inhaling his scent, all cedar and spice, the very opposite of peppermint.

Every moment that passed lessened her conviction that it was all a dream. She was sore. She hungered. She desired. And she had regrets. So many regrets.

"Shh, dear Ali— Eliza." His long fingers slid through her hair and caressed her scalp. "It will be better in the morning. There's little that rest and a hot cup of tea can't fix."

A huff of laughter shook her chest. What an odd thing to say. But something about his gentle caress and the warmth of his body against hers stilled the momentary panic and sorrow that had overtaken her.

Her grandmother may have truly sent this man to find her, to bring her here, and for that reason, if no other, she decided to trust him. At least for the night.

6

*E*liza had been quiet that morning as they continued their trek on horseback. In fact, she'd said little at all since their conversation about her grandmother the night before. She believed him, in that at least, which made everything so much easier. The headstrong woman even trusted him enough to ask for his assistance loosening the strings of her corset before she snuggled down under the blankets.

She was peaceful in sleep, serene in a way she hadn't been earlier. Though traveling to another world was probably quite the shock. He'd spent too much of the night watching the steady rise and fall of her chest and the way her eyelashes fluttered.

The previous Alice first showed him a portrait of Eliza years ago, the same one he carried with him now. He wasn't sure why she'd shared it with him then or even why she'd ordered him to be the one to retrieve Eliza from the other land and bring her to Wonderland…the slow way.

It still made no sense. Almost as if Alice wanted her granddaughter to have to traverse Wonderland, to see and experience it before the Red Court took her into their keeping until anointment day. Even her death fell exactly on the day after the full moon, in Wonderland anyway, ensuring that Alice would have to spend time here before her anointment, even if Eliza were retrieved the moment Alice took her last breath.

But why?

Why force her granddaughter to endure the danger-filled forest or the threat of the White Court? If he could go back in time and change one thing, he would ask her that. Well, no, that wasn't entirely true, he'd have changed events long before then, but still, he wished he could understand her reasoning.

Eliza twisted to glance behind them, accidentally rubbing against him in the saddle. The action stole all his thoughts, drew everything down to the feel of her against him.

What a terrible distraction.

He'd often wondered what the new Alice might be like, but his imaginings always drew her as young, like the portrait, never so...*so troublesome*.

A few times in their journey, she'd looked like she was about to speak but then held her tongue. Silence was far more frustrating than anything she could say. Too many thoughts were bred there, and too often since he met this Alice they grew in directions they shouldn't.

"See something curious?" he asked if only to distract himself from the feel of her where she nestled between his legs in the saddle.

Eliza turned forward again. "Your trees are just so odd. Blue, violet, crimson. Their leaves too. But none of them seem to be falling like they would in autumn. It's too warm for that. And the flowers..." She shook her head. "That one was the size of this horse! Why, I could have slept in it."

Laughter rumbled in his chest. "You wouldn't want to rest in one of those. It might close up and never let you out."

She shivered. "It's so different from home."

So true. Maybe that was the reason for her silence, drinking in the scenery. It was much more varied than the Other Land, or the little of it he'd seen.

"Finn?" She twisted to glance at him out of the corner of her eye.

The use of his name drew him in until her hair tickled his cheek. "Yes, Eliza?"

A small shudder ran through her form, and he mused it had little to do with man-eating flowers. This Alice was so demure, so proper. The Red Court would be quite the shock.

She swallowed and looked away again. "What will happen to me once we reach the Red Court?"

"Ah." At least she'd stopped insisting this was some dream. Things would go better for them both if she faced what was to come with open eyes. "You'll stay there until the full moon, at which time you'll visit the shrine and be anointed as the new Alice."

Her lips pressed thin. "And after?"

What then indeed? "Alice decides who rules in Wonderland. She could stay, or she could go home for a time."

Heavy silence lingered between them as she digested his words. "Only for a time?"

The remorse in her words hit him harder than it should. Yes, she was Alice, precious to all, but it was something more than that. She was just a young woman, her whole life ahead of her, but trapped by choices that were not her own and forced into a life that wasn't of her choosing.

Just like him.

"Wonderland needs Alice. Without her, things become strange. Dangerous." She had no idea what the lack of an Alice could do. He hadn't experienced it for himself, but there were plenty of stories and records.

Compulsion drove the courts to war, to battle for dominance if Alice were not to choose. Terrible beasties like the Bandersnatch left the deep woods and raided towns and villages. The sky refused to darken into night.

Only Alice could restore balance and order.

"Why not just declare me this Alice here and now and turn the horse around?"

He sighed. "If it were so easy, I would."

She looked at him then, a hard glare through narrowed eyes. "Would you?"

"I would do as Alice commands."

Eliza twisted around, seeming to shrink in on herself. "Then, once this is over, will you take me back, Finn?" Her voice was thin, barely a whisper.

He almost thought he made it up when she spoke again, "Will you make sure I get home again?"

His reply leaped out before he could think about it. "Yes."

Alice could request the favor of anyone, but he... His brows drew together. He wanted to. Not just because she was Alice, but he wanted her to have whatever taste of freedom she could take.

A cloud cast its shadow over them and pulled her attention. "Even your sky is odd."

He laughed at that. He quite liked the green tint that clung near the horizon, fading into the blue as it drew higher. "Or perhaps it's yours that's odd?"

When she didn't rise to the question, he asked another. "I thought you weren't eager to return to your fiancé?"

"I will not be marrying him." All her softness of moments ago faded. She even sat a little straighter.

"No?"

"Certainly not."

"Hmm," he mused. "Poor fellow. Is he not handsome then? Not everyone can be charming as me."

She smacked him on the leg. The horse whinnied at the disturbance. "Irritating man," she scolded, though her words lacked bite.

Finn bit his lip, holding in a laugh. She'd smack him again for that, and the horse might not forgive them a second time.

"He...he's handsome enough," she said. "In his looks. But he'd never said one word to me before agreeing to the marriage. I'm sure he just sees me as a tool for him to use to his advantage, just like my father." She all but spit the last word.

There was no love lost there. Perhaps this Alice was not free in the Other Land either. "Then what do you wish to go back for?"

The tension fled her shoulders in a sigh as she nestled back against him. Finn fought the urge to nuzzle her closer and instead focused on leading the horse.

"My work."

"Oh?" Rooftops edged beyond the trees ahead. She hadn't seen them yet, once she did, he'd lose her to curiosity, but he still had so much he wished to ask her, to learn. Every word was a little gift, a drop of water in the empty well of his years of musing on what she'd be like.

"I'm a scholar, a librarian, at the great library in the capital." Her voice rang with pride, and it warmed something deep within him. "It's quite a competitive position, I'll have you know. I was one of the youngest admitted to my position, and I won't lose it getting lost in this—" She waved her hand around.

"Wonderland," he supplied for her.

"Exactly. This Wonderland."

Should I tell her? It might ease her worries. That decided it. If it made the journey easier for her, it was worth sharing. "Time flows differently for Alice than most."

"What?" She twisted to look at him again.

"When Alice is in Wonderland, time all but stops in the Other Land. Mere hours or minutes will have passed when you return." Once Alice left Wonderland and went back to her home, the flow of time would become more consistent between the two worlds, according to former Alices. Though the time between Alices wasn't always as certain, leaving even the steady crawl of time uneven.

She blinked, her brows pinching together. "That's absurd! Time cannot just stop."

Finn shrugged. "That's Wonderland."

"Nonsense," she muttered, facing forward once more. Eliza stiffened before perking up and leaning forward in the saddle. "Is that—"

He bound an arm around her middle. "Careful now."

He wouldn't lose her to a fall from the horse. What a terrible way to go.

Eliza huffed and sat back against him in the saddle. "That's where we're going?"

The hope in those words was unmissable. *Poor thing.*

"Yes, the Duchess owns the largest manor in town. She should have some clothes you can wear. Fresh food. Maybe even a warm bath." The thought of Eliza sinking into the steaming water brought a smile to his lips.

He jolted in the seat as Eliza reached back and patted his satchel, coming precariously close to patting something else entirely.

"You couldn't fit a change of clothes for me in there?" she teased. Of course he could have, which she well knew after she'd watched him pack away their tent this morning.

His arm remained around her waist after her earlier wiggling, and now he took the time to splay his palm wide over her middle. Eliza drew in a breath as if he touched her skin rather than the layers of fabric between them. She was in for quite the awakening once they reached the Red Court if such a simple touch stole her breath and drew a flush to her cheeks. Finn leaned in, savoring her awkwardness and the way his touch seemed to set her on edge. Only when his lips ghosted over her ear did he reply. "I didn't know what size you'd be. What clothing you'd prefer to wear." He slid his palm along her stomach and over one hip. "Or not wear."

She smacked his leg again—hard.

The horse gave a plaintive cry and nearly bucked. Only Finn's quick use of magic, words whispered for the ears of the animal alone, calmed her.

"Easy girl," he said, switching back to the human tongue. He reached around and patted the mare's neck as the woman in his arms panted. From the near tumble or him? He bit his lip, holding in another laugh as he let his long hair fall forward to hide his expression.

"Anyhow," he continued when they were back on their way, "we can't stay long."

Eliza huffed in irritation. "Why not, if we have until the full moon?"

So innocent to the world. He could almost envy her for that. "The White Court will be after you. Sooner or later, they'll learn about the hidden path to the Other Land and come for you. They may be hunting for you already. I cannot let you fall into their hands."

She hugged her arms around herself. "They're that terrible?"

The question gave him pause. In theory, they were not bad. Law and order ruled. It kept peace and harmony among the people, a life without the worry of lawlessness or danger. If one followed the rules... However, the punishment for breaking them could be harsh, severe, and without mercy. He of all people knew that. If not for the Red Court taking him in, he'd have died years ago, hunted down by the White King's guards.

"Yes," he said at length, unwilling to elaborate on the memories that still haunted him.

Though the lack of mercy was one thing the courts shared. He'd been ordered to bring Alice to the Red Court, and if he failed, it would cost him his head.

7

The town was simple and extraordinary all at once. Some things were much as Eliza expected—cobbled streets, a little river running along the edge of town, a water wheel hard at work, a gurgling fountain, and children playing in the streets. Some of the houses and shops were entirely ordinary—simple one or two-story constructions of wood, stone, and brick like she'd seen all her life.

But others...

She blinked for the millionth time, always expecting her eyes to have been playing tricks on her, but they weren't. Or if they were, it was quite a long ruse.

One house balanced on its cornerstone, the only part of it that touched the ground, with the rest slanted precariously into the air. Another had no outer walls at all, leaving the occupants in full view of everyone who passed by—even the man reclining in a copper tub. A few had no doors or windows that she could see, and one was so impossibly skinny she had no idea how someone could live there with any level of comfort. A table and chair couldn't sit next to one another in such a narrow space.

Her lips pursed as she considered the oddities. Perhaps they were like Finn's strange bag, different within than without, but this wasn't the time to inspect them. Finn hustled their horse through the streets at a gallop, leaving a wake of turned glances and exclamations behind them.

"Shouldn't you slow down?" she asked, gripping the saddle for dear life.

He had leaned forward once they entered the town, all but hiding her between the sides of his open coat where it fell around them both. His white hair whipped behind them like a pennant, and he didn't seem to mind that hers probably lashed him half the ride.

It was the wrong question to ask because he simply wrapped one arm around her and pulled her against his hard body. Heat crept up her neck, and she fought the urge to wiggle. It wouldn't do her any good, and he only seemed to enjoy it. Did he not realize that she could feel almost all of him in this position? The man had no sense of propriety at all.

"I won't let you fall, dear Eliza," he said against her ear.

Dear Eliza.

She nearly groaned. The way he said her name, drawing out the syllables and letting them roll across his tongue, was absolutely maddening. He packed so much intimacy into her little name, one might think they were lovers. However, she hardly knew him better than her would-be fiancé. Finn was polite enough, other than his lack of personal space, but he was still the thing she loathed most, another man seeking to use her for his gain.

Perhaps Grandmama had put him up to it, as he'd said, but it changed little.

Finn didn't slow until they drew near a massive estate near the edge of town. It reminded Eliza a bit of Folly Hall with its double-door entry and grand staircase sweeping up toward it. But unlike Folly Hall, this place was walled. Vines crept over the high stone structure like creatures trying to escape. Other trees and shrubs grew beyond the stonework, hinting at gardens surrounding the sides, and possibly the back, of the estate.

It went without saying that this must be the Duchess's residence. The suspicion was confirmed as Finn stopped the horse at the base of the stairs and leaped from its back with enviable grace and ease.

A liveried man—perhaps the Duchess's butler—with a pink rose pinned to his lapel burst from the double doors and hustled down the stairs.

"Sir Finneas." He removed his top hat and gave a sweeping bow. "To what do we owe this honor?"

Her brows drew up at that. If it was an honor for Finn to visit the Duchess, he must rank quite highly in the court. *How very interesting.*

Finn merely nodded in acknowledgment. "Is the Duchess at home? I thought to ask for some respite for my companion and myself if she were so inclined for our company."

"Indeed, she would be most honored!" The man fumbled while replacing his hat, nearly sending it tumbling to the ground. The moment it settled, his gaze drifted to Eliza. "Oh, my lady." He gave an awkward bow.

By the time the butler looked up, Finn was halfway back to her, his arm outstretched to help her down. No sooner had she taken it than his other settled around her waist, and he hoisted her to the ground as if she weighed almost nothing. At least this time she didn't slide halfway down his body. They'd had quite enough closeness on the ride there.

Finn looped her arm through his like a proper gentleman and led her to the stairs. The butler gazed at a passing cloud, completely lost in thought, until they stood directly before him, and Finn cleared his throat. "Do you have a man to see to my horse?"

"Oh." The butler startled as if he'd forgotten they were there at all and blinked rapidly. "Oh, of course," he said before bellowing some name she didn't quite catch.

The piercing yell made Eliza stiffen and wish to the Mother and all her saints she'd known to cover her ears. A moment later, a younger man shoved through a squeaking metal gate and ran to the foot of the steps. His mussed red hair had a few leaves sticking out of it like he'd just woken from a nap beneath a tree.

"See to their horse," the butler ordered.

"At once." The younger man bowed.

"Give her a good rub down," Finn called. "And plenty of food. We leave this afternoon."

"So soon?" Eliza asked as they turned to follow the butler inside.

Finn patted her arm. "We mustn't be late."

"But we have—"

He gave her arm a little jerk and leaned in quickly. "We'll talk later, darling." He pulled out the last word as he often did her name, letting it linger in the air.

She sucked in a breath, indignation rising into words, and then swallowed it down at his pointed look. He didn't want the butler to know who she was. *Interesting.*

And fair, if they were truly in danger. She'd play along for now, as long as he didn't call her darling again.

The butler led them up the stairs, carpeted in a garish pink that contrasted sharply with the teal wallpaper bearing golden birds. *This* was where he planned to find clothes for her? If the Duchess's fashion taste matched her decorating, Eliza would rather stick with her stuffy dress and the corset; however, uncomfortable.

At the end of a long hall, the butler rapped on the door before cracking it open. "Guests, Duchess. Sir Finneas, and..." He glanced back at her, perhaps only now realizing he didn't have her name. Nor did she give it. "And his companion."

"Well, don't leave them in the hall. Show them in," commanded a voice so soft and sweet it belied the order in the words.

The butler swung the door wide and ushered them in with a hurried wave of his hand. Finn, however, took his time, somehow making his long-legged stride slow and purposeful as he led Eliza into the room.

The teal and gold walls weren't as alarming thanks to the cream flooring and floor-to-ceiling windows draped with flowing, sheer curtains. Furniture dotted much of the space, all polished, dark wood and cushions the same color as the marble floors. The room might have been pleasant, if a bit eccentric, had it not been spotted everywhere with pink—pink rugs, pink pillows, pink flowers in vases on all of the tables. Each spot of bold color stood out like a sore thumb among the rest.

The Duchess reclined on a settee, wearing a long, poofy dress in a similar shade as the walls. With a few golden accents, she could have blended right in with the furnishings. And like the rest of the room, she sported that jarring bit of pink in a rose pinned to her dress and a few other blossoms woven through the silver hair piled upon her head.

Eliza forced her gaze to the woman's face. She remained sitting as Finn brought them near. While her voice was soft and gentle, her features were anything but with her sharp cheekbones, hard jaw, and pointed chin. The amethyst eyes in her pale face might have been gemstones for their hardness.

"Duchess," Finn bowed. Eliza curtsyed as best she was able with her arm still looped through Finn's.

"To what do I owe the pleasure?" she asked.

Finn stood a little straighter, his head high. In that moment, he looked regal, like a royal himself. How had she not noticed that side of him before?

"I hope you might loan my companion some clothes." He gestured to Eliza. "Perhaps you might even indulge us with a hot bath and a warm meal before we continue on our journey."

The Duchess pursed her lips. Eliza fought the urge to squirm as the woman inspected her with her careful gaze. "Poor dear. She looks dressed for a funeral. And that dirt on her hem..." She clucked her tongue. "Did you drag the poor woman through the forest, Finneas?"

Before either had time to answer, something jolted in the fabric of the Duchess's wide poofy sleeves. Eliza leaped back with a gasp as a small bundle lifted its pale pink head.

The piglet gave a little whine and squirmed in the Duchess's arms. "Shh now, Baby," she crooned. "Settle."

It still squirmed, but at least Eliza's racing heart calmed. A piglet. She hadn't even seen it, buried as it was in the woman's dress. Finn simply patted Eliza's arm, unfazed by the animal's sudden appearance. Had he known it was there all along?

She reigned in a sigh. *Probably.*

The Duchess petted the piglet, soothing it back into rest. Finn took the moment to press his case. "The Red Court would look most favorably on your assistance."

"Hm... But it hasn't been decided who shall rule yet, and such a favor might disadvantage me with the White Court if they ever found out." Her fingers brushed over the pink rose. "We're careful to show our neutrality in these turbulent times."

A missing piece clicked into place so hard that Eliza nearly gasped. All the garish pink suddenly made a certain sense. With courts of Red and White, what better way to show indifference than unmissable splashes of pink?

The Duchess waved a hand through the air in Finn's direction. Her long, gold painted nails shimmered in the light streaming through the windows. "You know I care for you, dear Finneas, but to pick a side before Alice makes her choice can be quite...trying."

Finn shifted on his feet, his arm through hers tightening. "The White Court doesn't need to know of your involvement."

Her sharp gaze shifted back to Eliza. The Duchess pursued her silent inspection again, all the while stroking her pet. At length, she said. "I can't let this poor woman go around like that." She gestured up and down Eliza's form. "Of course, I'll lend her some clothes."

Eliza let out a sigh. Perhaps this would work out after all.

"A bath too, I think, and plenty of food." She smiled, but it only sharpened her features more. "I could never let a fellow woman go hungry. However..." Eliza held her breath as the Duchess shifted her attention back to Finn. "I'm having a small tea party out in the gardens this afternoon, and you simply must attend. I insist."

"We cannot be late—" he began.

The Duchess cut him off with another wave of her manicured hand. "Nonsense. You have plenty of time. Besides, it would do Alice well to experience life outside the courts, don't you agree?"

Finn went utterly still.

Eliza swayed on her feet and clutched him tighter. "I'm not—" Her voice cracked. "My name is Eliza."

The Duchess's expression softened for the briefest moment. "Of course you are the new Alice, dear." Her attention shifted back to Finn. "Why else would the Red Queen let her favorite white rabbit off his leash?"

A barely muffled snarl slipped from the man at her side, but all Eliza could think of was the Duchess's words. *White rabbit.*

Eliza jerked her arm from his and stepped away. "You were there. In the gardens."

It hadn't been some random animal. It was him. He drew her to the hole in the tree and pulled her in. Distantly, she'd known—maybe—but she hadn't fully accepted it until that moment.

His hard jaw shifted. "Yes."

The Duchess rose in one smooth movement, all but tossing her pet onto the cushions of the settee and striding to Eliza. The older woman was shorter than she'd expected, near her height, and far less intimating standing than sitting. "Now, now." She wrapped an arm around Eliza and turned her away from Finn. "Don't fret, dearie. Let's get you a bath and some clean clothes. My maids will see to all your needs."

Eliza glanced over one shoulder at Finn, numerous emotions swirling within her. He was safe...ish. Familiar—or as familiar as anything here. But the Duchess's comments wove their insecurities around Eliza. The Red Queen's leash?

Finn stepped toward her, concern erasing the frustration that had stiffened his jaw and narrowed his bright amber eyes. "I would stay with her."

In the bath? The unspoken question taunted all the confusing emotions she couldn't begin to process and drew a blush to her cheeks.

"No harm will come to Alice under my roof. I promise that." The Duchess squeezed her shoulders.

Unable to form a reasonable protest, Eliza let herself be led away.

8

*H*e should never have brought Alice here. It was a mistake to trust the Duchess.

They'd always been on friendly terms, but the old woman saw too much. He should have thought about that and been prepared for their secret to be discovered. Requiring them to attend a tea party? He snorted air through his nose while he paced the hallway. To expose Alice to even more people, anyone of whom could share her identity and their location with the White Court, was a mistake.

A wiser man would have turned and left right then, Alice in tow.

But the Duchess was right on one score. Alice's clothes were dirty and not fit for travel at all. The poor woman had to be in discomfort, yet she'd not once complained about it. He'd packed extra clothes for himself but hadn't bothered to change this morning. It felt wrong wearing fresh clothing when she could not. Not to mention a bath would do her spirit well. She'd had more than one shock since coming to Wonderland…and before.

The thought of her being forced into marriage with some man she'd barely met and didn't like set his teeth on edge. She deserved better than that. He rubbed the back of his neck as he made another crossing of the nauseatingly pink carpets. She deserved better than being taken to the

Red Queen and King too. They'd lock her in a gilded cage until it was time for her to be anointed Alice.

But what choice did he have?

He'd promised the previous Alice to bring her there, and the Red Queen commanded it. One slip up, one failure, and the Red Queen would see that he lost his head, however much others thought she favored him. The king might not be able to save him from that, just like he hadn't saved him from his wife's attentions.

Once, he thought the man his savior—he *was* his savior—plucking him away from the White knights ordered to pursue and end him. He'd taken pity on the poor boy who'd just lost his mother minutes before he arrived. King Jasper gave him a home, a place of safety in a world that wanted to end him simply for defending his mother's crime. A harsh punishment, even by White Court standards, and he'd only been a boy.

Finn and the king had been close for quite a time, especially when the king trained him up to become one of his own trusted knights. But that was years ago. Lately, King Jasper saw more in the bottom of a wine glass than in the people around him, an opportunity his wife pounced on. Queen Victoria got what she wanted, and no one else got a say.

His *leash* was tight enough to choke him.

Finn pulled at his coat collar and stared at the door at the end of the hall. Alice—*no, Eliza*—had been out of his sights for over an hour.

Too long. Far too long.

His feet stilled on the rug. If something happened...

He shook his head. He'd know, surely. And the headstrong woman wouldn't thank him for barging in on her in the bath, tempting though it might be.

His hand balled into a fist at his side. Such thoughts were dangerous. She was Alice. He'd deliver her to the Red Court and then get far away from those brown eyes and her bewitching scent. To do anything else would tempt the queen's ire. Sharing was a skill she refused to practice.

Finally, the door cracked open.

Breath caught in his throat as Eliza appeared at the threshold. A green dress hugged her form, trailing to the ground. Only two thin straps held it on her shoulders, plunging down in a vee that exposed a tantalizing amount of flesh between her rounded breasts. A thick swash of gold was bound around her middle just below those breasts. Between that and the cut, it was impossible not to stare at the one place he shouldn't. A few blinks later, and he still couldn't form a coherent thought.

Holy ancient kings. He scrubbed a hand down his face before forcing his gaze up to hers. She didn't quite look at him, her gaze carefully trained on the wall as she steadily drew near. The previous dress she'd worn did little to favor her appearance, but this one did almost too much. It wasn't better for traveling in either, but he guessed that wasn't the point. Hopefully, the Duchess had something else in mind for their departure. If it was for Alice's benefit, he wouldn't put it past the Duchess to grant Eliza an entire wardrobe. She was always trying to curry favor with whoever was in power, and who held more sway over that than the future Alice?

"They tried to dress me in pink," she mumbled, coming to a stop in front of him.

He barely choked down a laugh. "You don't like pink?"

She sighed and slipped her arm through his offered one. "Some shades. But not..." She dropped her gaze to the ground for emphasis. *Indeed.* The variation the Duchess picked to demonstrate her neutrality was rather horrid. The significance of the choice wasn't lost on him. The Duchess wanted Alice to appear neutral, her decision still in play. If she dressed Alice in Red or White and her ultimate choice went the other way, it would be a stain on the older woman's reputation.

Green and gold was a fair compromise, showing favor to neither court. Plus, it was stunning on Eliza. "I'm glad you argued for something else. You look lovely."

The column of her throat bobbed, but she didn't say anything, not until Finn led her through the mansion and out to the back gardens where the butler informed him earlier that the tea would be held.

The moment they stepped out into the bright, early afternoon light, Eliza drew them to a halt. "What am I to say to them?" She flicked her gaze up to him, the first time she'd really looked at him since their audience with the Duchess earlier.

The sight alone stirred something in his chest. "Anything you want."

She raised her brows. "Just not my would-be title, I suppose?"

"Except that." His jaw stiffened. Unless the Duchess had already spoiled her identity to whomever she'd invited. A distinct possibility, unfortunately.

"Fine." All the fire and stubbornness rose to the surface. "I have plenty of experience dancing around the truth and entertaining people I don't know a wit about."

"Do you now?"

A wry grin twisted her lips. "My father is a politician, and I attended a boarding school for *proper young ladies of society.*" The disdain dripping from her words fueled an odd sort of pleasure burning in his chest. "You could say I was trained for this."

The spark of amusement died. Perhaps she was, without even realizing it. The Red Court might not be as overwhelming for her as he feared. "Well then," he continued, attempting to push that dark thought away. "Shall we go to tea?"

Her nose twitched, and she looked up at him again, adjusting her grip on his arm. Her gaze coasted down his form, and he couldn't help standing a little straighter. "We match a bit."

Now that she mentioned it, their outfits did go together in a way, sharing similar golden accents. *Good, let anyone who attends this tea know whose side you belong at.* The thought shocked him, but he did his best not to let it show.

"A coincidence." That much he was sure of. He hadn't known what she'd wear when he selected his clothes, and surely the Duchess hadn't planned such a thing. "Does that bother you?"

She looked him over again before raising her chin and leading them deeper into the garden. "No. It doesn't."

Something fluttered in his chest, causing the start of a grin to pull at the corner of his mouth. Perhaps tea wouldn't be too terrible.

9

*E*liza wasn't lying to Finn. She had practically trained for this sort of thing her entire life. What she wasn't prepared for, however, was the strangeness of Wonderland. Within the manor, she could almost forget she wasn't back in her world and visiting some member of society with an unusual taste in décor. Out in the gardens, however, it was impossible to miss all the things that existed but shouldn't. Oddly colored plants and trees were just the start. The flowers as big as her were back again, and she made sure to give them an extra-wide berth, even earning a chuckle from Finn.

Eaten by a flower? *No thank you.*

A nearby tree dripped shimmering balls of something blue. Another had leaves that stuck straight up. One bush looked more like an animal creeping across the ground, its roots rising into the air. Eliza sighed with relief when the path ended in an open grassy space set with a long table. That was almost normal, even if the grass was violet.

The Duchess sat at the head of the table, her voluminous dress trying to squeeze itself out beneath the armrests. Her pig, Baby, lay on the grass beside her chair. Two others already sat at the table with her, one to each side.

"Ah, there you are!" The Duchess called. She clapped, and her butler jolted out of his stupor and rushed to see them to their seats.

Eliza was shown to a seat next to a man of upper middle age in an exceptionally tall hat. He bounced with glee in his seat and set her teeth on edge. Finn ignored the butler as he pulled out Eliza's chair and then plopped himself ungracefully into the seat on her other side.

Tiered trays of pastel foods covered the table along with multiple kettles spouting steam, though she could see no flames or anything else to keep them warm. Fine porcelain dishes were set at each place, their cream surfaces painted in pink roses. By the looks of things, they were only missing one more guest.

"Oh, where are my manners?" the Duchess exclaimed.

Eliza wiggled into the cushioned seat and forced a polite smile.

"Dear friends." She drew out the words. "You may remember Finneas, he has come to tea with us before."

Oh? Eliza raised a brow at that and shot him a look from the corner of her eyes.

"Maddoc and Harry." Finn looked first at the man in the hat and then the one across from him before picking up a white napkin and spreading it across his lap, the picture of a refined nobleman. "It's nice to see you once more."

The two strangers nodded, but all their focus was riveted on her, their too-wide eyes seeming to pry her very clothes off to get a look at her soul.

"And this, friends,"—Eliza held her breath—"is Eliza. A visitor to my estate."

The breath slipped from her lips, some of the tension within her uncoiling. "It's nice to meet you both."

Maddoc took her hand in his and lifted it to his lips, placing a kiss on its back before she had the chance to pull away. "It's so nice to have such lovely company for tea." He froze, dropping her hand, and twisted toward the Duchess. "Not as lovely as you, of course, my sweet."

The Duchess laughed and swatted playfully at her companion.

Eliza retrieved her hand and scrubbed the back of it against her skirts under the table. Quite the eccentric this man, the opposite of his companion who'd yet to utter a word. The buttons on Harry's vest pulled tight across the girth of his chest, looking as though they could pop off at any moment. His too-small green hat sat askew on his bald head, and the only hair she could actually see on him was his bushy grey mustache.

"Should I recite a poem for you, my dear? Perhaps a song?" Maddoc looked to the others expectantly.

"A song! A song!" Harry raised the teacup in his wrinkled hand, splattering liquid over the rim and onto the table.

The two older men leaned over the table, debating the merits of songs to serenade their guests with.

None would have been Eliza's preference, unless their singing voices were significantly better than their normal ones, and likely not even then. Eliza's smile grew stiff as she fought against the urge to excuse herself from the madness. A gasp slipped from her lips as Finn laid his hand upon her thigh and gave a little squeeze. She shot her gaze to him and received a tight smile.

"Are the tea parties here always so...lively?" she whispered. This was not at all what she was expecting.

A hint of mirth twinkled in his eyes. "Often livelier."

Oh, Mother above. This mistress at her old boarding school would faint to witness such a display. And such theatrics at the library? Never. Worse was Finn's hand still resting on her thigh. She couldn't think straight with him touching her like that. But she couldn't bring herself to ask him to move it either. It was an odd sort of comfort.

Maddoc half climbed onto the table, jostling the dishes and sending a few of the little green cakes tumbling onto the teal tablecloth.

"Oh, stop it, you two," the Duchess ordered. The two men stilled like scolded little boys and plopped back into their seats with muttered apologies. "Eliza hasn't even had a cup of tea, and you start such nonsense. What would she think of you?"

She opened her mouth to respond, unsure what to say, but the Duchess saved her by rambling on. "Eat, dear. You must be famished."

"Are we not waiting on one more?" Eliza nodded toward the open place setting. Her old lessons crept to the front, as they always did in formal settings, reminding her it would be rude to eat until everyone was seated. But then, so was singing and banging on the table, and this was Wonderland after all.

The Duchess waved her hand in the air. "She'll be along. Now eat, I insist."

Eliza cut a glance to Finn and mouthed "she?" But he only shrugged and finally, *finally*, removed his hand from her thigh. Relief and loss warred in its wake, and she couldn't determine a winner.

She supposed it didn't matter if someone else was coming since she wouldn't know them anyway and took her time examining the vast array of delicacies. In front of the tiered trays stood little signs that said "Eat me" and nothing else. Harry began pointing them out one by one, giving them various names that she'd never heard and that didn't seem to fit the delicate designs. Like so much else, Wonderland made no sense.

Pleasant acknowledgment was the best she could muster before reaching for what appeared to be a little cake with violet frosting.

"Here." Finn plucked the azure one next to it from the tray and placed it on her plate. "You'll like this one better," his voice dropped to a whisper as he added, "trust me."

She held his gaze a moment longer, searching for information and finding it, for once, easy to read. Whatever the other cake contained, she wouldn't like it. *Fair enough.* He'd been trustworthy so far.

Before she could take a bite, another person sauntered into the clearing, their presence demanding the attention of the table and bringing it to silence for the first time.

"Chesa." Finn managed to pack so much into her name, just as he often did hers, but she couldn't pick out all the varied threads. Surprise, but not. A touch of anger. A dash of resignation? But mostly, a fullness that suggested history between the two.

As much as she was curious about Finn's reaction, she was even more interested in this woman who painted a very opposite portrait of the Duchess. Purple trousers hung tight about her waist, flaring out into air clouds around her long legs. Her shirt was tight too, baring a strip of her dark-skinned mid-drift, and though it crept all the way up to the base of her neck, the garment left her arms completely bare. An enviable outfit in its apparent comfort and airiness, though something her mother might have fainted at.

Chesa's black hair was pulled behind her head to trail down her back and bore a wide streak of pink. Not the wilted-petal pink the Duchess displayed, but a bright and vibrate shade Eliza quite liked.

Though her outfit and streak of color in her hair would be enough to demand attention on their own, it was her eyes that Eliza had trouble tugging her attention from. The bright greenish-blue was mesmerizing, and Chesa seemed to know it as she met Eliza's gaze and gave a tooth-filled grin.

One moment she was there, and the next, she vanished as if she'd never been.

"Where—" Eliza began.

A voice spoke just behind her. "Now, here's a new face."

Eliza screamed, jolting in her chair and nearly falling into the pastries. Only Finn's quick hand on her arm steadied her as she twisted toward the unexpected voice.

Chesa loomed behind her chair, her head tilting to the side as she took in Eliza with those strange, bright eyes. Eliza fought the urge to lean farther away. Finn moved his hand to the small of her back, a steady presence giving her strength—and keeping her from falling into the pastries.

"Now, now," the Duchess scolded. "Are you all trying to scare dear Eliza away and spoil my tea?"

"She just—" Eliza stammered.

"Yes," Finn drawled. "Chesa can do that."

Chesa ignored them. "Eliza," she said, drawing her name out and rolling the letters across her tongue as Finn often did. Her attention dropped to Finn's hand at her back—his side nearly pressed against her own. "With the rabbit."

He stiffened, and Eliza's lips thinned in indignation. Though she'd regained her steadiness, she leaned into Finn as a show of support and raised her chin at the newcomer.

Chesa's grin only widened.

"We have a place set for you just there." The Duchess motioned to the seat opposite Finn.

Finally, Chesa blinked and stepped away from her, shifting her gaze to the rest of the assembled. "Next to mad ole' Harry?" She stalked around the table.

Harry grumbled as Chesa rounded the table. "You didn't say she was coming."

"Or were you the mad one, Maddoc?" She asked, seeming genuinely confused.

"Well, I—" he began, drawing himself up.

"Both, perhaps?"

The men shot Chesa angry glances, but she ignored them.

Eliza slid back down into her seat, never taking her gaze off the newcomer, and Finn did the same. His hand came to rest on her leg again. It took effort to ignore the touch. Support or something else?

Chesa leaned on the back of her assigned chair but didn't sit. "I'm not quite hungry yet, but don't wait on my account. A quick stroll through the gardens might be just the thing for my appetite." Her feline-like gaze coasted down the table to land on Eliza. She fought the urge to squirm, not wanting to go anywhere with this strange new woman.

The odd gentlemen and even the Duchess were preferable. For all their eccentricities, she at least had an idea of what to expect from them. This woman, Eliza had a feeling she could spend years with her and never know her at all. And that was a dangerous thing over a game of polite conversation, especially when her identity was best kept a secret, or so Finn insisted.

At the last moment, Chesa's attention shifted. "Well, Finn. I think you have much to tell me."

He leaned back in his chair, the picture of collected calm, though the hand on her leg squeezed almost painfully tight. "Oh, do I now?"

Chesa's grin widened.

Bitterness teased Eliza's tongue and her lips pursed of their own accord. Finn released her leg, giving it a little pat under the tablecloth and out of sight before he rose.

"I'll just be a moment," he said to Eliza. Finn looked to the Duchess and gave a short nod. "Duchess."

"Fine. Off with you two." She shooed them away and settled back into her cushioned seat. "But just a moment. Then you owe us a tale over tea."

The twitching smile he gave didn't meet his eyes. "Of course."

Eliza watched them leave. Chesa sidled up to Finn, who didn't aim even one passing glance in her direction before they rounded a hedge and were out of sight.

Only once they'd vanished did she realize she clutched her skirts in a death grip. She smoothed her hands across her lap, pasted a smile on her face, and looked at the rest of the table occupants. Harry poured more tea from a little pot emblazoned with the words "Drink me," and offered her a cup, which she gratefully accepted. The Duchess had half leaned out of her chair, feeding cakes to her piglet.

All the tension and worry of moments ago smoothed out like the napkin in her lap. She didn't need Finn at her side. This wasn't her first meal with strangers. Far from it. She was a Carroll for goodness sake. Navigating such an affair was in her blood, and for all that she didn't care for her family, that trait served her well both personally and professionally.

In a way, it was freeing to be without Finn. She was simply Eliza here, even if the Duchess knew differently. And with Chesa gone, the remaining company felt suddenly...comfortable. At least these people didn't vanish only to reappear directly behind her. A little shiver raced over her arms. Another oddity she'd have to ask Finn about sometime.

Harry passed her the delicate cup, all the while explaining its many qualities and taste notes like a master of his craft. Perhaps he was.

One advantage of being stuck in this strange world was the knowledge she could gain. No records of such a land existed, not that she'd ever found in the great library, and she would know. It was the duty of new scholars to reshelve borrowed books, and she'd handled thousands of them. If she couldn't go home, she might as well make the best of her time here and get to know these people. *Think of all the books I could write about the wonders of Wonderland.* It might be enough to get her promoted. A genuine grin spread across her features. And wouldn't that just annoy her father to no end?

Eliza took a bite of the cake—plum and vanilla rushing over her tongue—before she leaned toward the odd man at her side. "So Maddoc," she began. "Do tell me about yourself. I'd like to know everything."

The Duchess caught her eye and gave her a pleasant smile, which Eliza returned. Perhaps this afternoon tea wouldn't be so terrible after all.

10

*I*t took everything Finn had to keep his calm demeanor in check as he left the table and wandered into the gardens with Chesa. Of all the potential guests, he never expected her, but he should have. She had a habit of showing up at the most inconvenient times. And given who he was with and what he'd been sent to do, Chesa was bound to show up at some point.

"So, what is this catching up we must do?" he asked innocently. There was only one reason Chesa bothered with him. Alice.

"Your companion didn't expect to see me," she said matter-of-factly.

Because I didn't either. Finn expected her to be waiting back at the Red Court, but he should have known that Chesa never did what was expected. She was a law unto herself, beholden to no one, something that no one else in Wonderland could honestly claim.

"You didn't tell her about me?"

Finn gave a casual shrug that belied the tightness between his shoulders. "Why would I?"

Chesa skidded to a halt. "I'm Alice's guardian." Her unnerving gaze narrowed. "You thought to keep her a secret? As if such a thing could exist in a world where I do."

He fought down a sigh. Chesa was the last person who would ever harm Alice, but confuse and unsettle her? She already had. Not to mention that chaos followed behind Chesa like a cloak.

"We haven't gotten to that yet." He'd avoided just about everything that might give her concern. The task of bringing Alice to court was risky enough as it was. Why complicate it further? "And *I* was charged with bringing her to the Red Court."

A poor decision on the previous Alice's part. She was usually such an intelligent woman, but assigning him this task was a terrible mistake. It should have been Chesa. Alice was her responsibility. Though Eliza wasn't officially Alice yet, he still couldn't understand why she asked him, of all people, to deliver her granddaughter to the Red Court.

"Curiouser and curiouser. You just happened to stop for tea?" Chesa prodded.

Finn's lips thinned. She probably looked for some fault to report back to the monarchs. "We stopped for food and clothes. The tea was a requirement to get those. A party that you just happened to be invited to." He gave her a side-long look. "I'm sure that's no coincidence."

"Isn't it?" she asked before wandering off down the path, seemingly lost in thought. Sometimes Chesa lived in a world of her own, lucid one moment and then off in a daydream the next. Probably some side-effect of her long life. In all the years he'd known her, she never aged. Supposedly, she'd been the same for generations—a unique trait even among the many varied magics and powers that people or creatures possessed.

Finn fought the urge to roll his eyes and followed after her until he was in step at her side once more. "I don't know how you discovered us so quickly."

Chesa grinned in that way that set his teeth on edge. "So quickly? You assume I just discovered you? I have my ways, or have you forgotten that?"

How could he? She'd gotten him into trouble more than once at the Red Court. With her ability to come and go, and sometimes even linger unseen, Chesa gathered more knowledge than any one person should have the right to. Nor did she have any problem doling it out—when it benefitted her, of course.

"Does she know who she is?" Chesa asked.

"Yes."

"Hmm," she mused, not bothering to look at him.

"Why exactly are you here, Chesa, if you already know who she is?"

"I can't just enjoy an afternoon tea?" She shrugged. With a sigh, she continued, "It's my job to make sure Alice is safe."

The implied insult, that he might let Eliza come to harm, dug under his skin. Finn fought the urge to let his annoyance show and cocked one brow instead. "Scaring her at tea accomplishes that?"

"I wanted to get a measure of her." Chesa halted on the path once more. "And you." Her lips twitched. Chesa raised one finger in the air just in time for a purple butterfly the size of her hand to land on it. "Seems you're taking your responsibilities seriously for once."

"Don't I always?" His heel ground into the pathway.

"No. You don't." The butterfly took to the air once more.

A grin twitched at the corner of his lips. She had him there. The important things, though, ones that kept his head on his shoulders, he took seriously.

"She's not Alice yet. Not officially." He resumed their walk, eager to put those old memories behind him.

"Close enough. And too naïve for her own good. That won't do her any favors, in either court."

Finn let out a throaty grumble. "I'm taking her to the Red Court."

"Indeed," she said, unaffected by his threat. "But knights of White are already on the ride."

Shit. He kicked a stone on the path and sent it tumbling. *Already?* He thought they'd have more time. "And you're here to help us evade them?" he pressed. It was worth a shot.

Chesa's expression dropped, seeming weighed down by the world. "I cannot interfere in Alice's choice. You know that."

The sorrow in her voice touched something in him. He almost felt sorry for her, for this mysterious woman trapped in time, forced to watch after one Alice after the next in a seeming eternity. How many lifetimes had she lived, all in the name of protecting Alice?

"But you are supposed to keep her safe. Eliza is bright. Stronger than you know. She had more backbone than I expected." He rubbed at his chin. "She tried to smash my head in with a branch the night I brought her here."

Chesa snorted. "Seriously?"

"Seriously. She wasn't raised to be Alice, not really, and I think that might help her. But if the White Court gets her, if her headstrong resolve comes against their hardness, it could break her."

She crossed her arms and stared up at him, the hint of a genuine smile erasing her sorrow from moments ago. "One might think you like this Alice, this…Eliza."

Her name on Chesa's lips twisted something tight in his gut that he tried and failed to ignore. "She'll make a good Alice, I think."

"Hmm…" Chesa drummed her fingers on her arms as she leaned in close, near enough that he could see the little flecks of iridescence in her eyes. "I think I might understand why the previous Alice gave you this task."

His brows arched. "Do you?" Because he sure didn't.

Chesa ignored the question and sauntered down the path. Finn hurried to catch up again.

"Time reveals all things in the end, but do try to keep dear Eliza safe for me."

He shook his head. *Always speaking in riddles.* Maybe too much knowledge was to blame, or too many years of life. Even if it never affected her appearance, it had to do something to her mind. He'd be madder than Maddoc if he'd lived as long as her.

"You could help us, you know," he pushed. "Protect us from White. Keeping Alice safe isn't making her choice for her."

"Well, we should return," she replied, completely ignoring his words. "You always do hear the most interesting stories over tea, especially when the guests indulge in Dormaus tea."

His pulse skipped a beat. "What did you say?"

"Dormaus tea. You didn't smell it? Harry is known to favor the stuff."

Shit. He sprinted back toward the clearing. Dormaus tea could turn even the most stalwart person into a bumbling idiot with just a few sips. He'd been so focused on the company at the tea party he hadn't paid enough attention to the tea. If Eliza drank that, it could ruin everything.

11

*H*orror rooted Finn's feet to the ground at the edge of the clearing, nearly sending him tumbling end over end. Eliza stood on her chair, spinning in circles as she rambled on about something —the panic churning through him turned her words into a buzzing hum. Harry did the same, opposite her, much to the amusement of the Duchess and Maddoc, who laughed and cheered. Eliza held her hand down to Maddoc, who took it, and, wobbling, climbed onto his own chair. Only the butler retained any sense of normalcy, but he just stared up at the passing clouds, seeming to miss everything going on around him.

"Well," Chesa sighed. "So much for keeping her safe."

Finn saw red and whirled on the woman at his side. "This is your fault." He thrust an accusing finger at her. "You knew what kind of tea that was, and you still led me away to discuss nonsense you already knew."

She poked him in the chest—hard. "Nothing is nonsense. There is sense in every little thing if you have the wisdom to see it." She dropped her hand and cut her gaze to the table. "And they do seem to be having a merry time."

A joyful giggle erupted from the table, from Eliza. The tea's fault, he knew, but it still twisted something in his chest. He'd never heard that sound from her. Not that he'd known her long, but a wicked tea had caused something he'd yet to manage.

Finn stalked across the grass.

"Oh, dear Finneas!" The Duchess wiped tears of laughter from her eyes. "Join us! Join us!"

His jaw stiffened. *What a mess.*

"Finn!" Eliza twirled toward him. His steps faltered. The bright smile on her face nearly undid him. Her cheeks flushed a rosy pink. Her lips were bright red with stains from the tea. The look she gave him would slay anyone, and he was no exception.

"Isn't this tea party marvelous?" Eliza flung out her arms, the motion sending her wobbling and the chair beneath her doing the same.

Shit! Finn sprinted the last few feet and lunged just in time to catch Eliza as she tumbled in his direction, arms flailing. Something caught between a screech and giggle slipped from her lips before she crashed into Finn, and they both tumbled to the ground.

He took the brunt of the fall, Eliza slamming into his chest and knocking the breath from his lungs. Finn's head smacked on the grass— the stuff not near as cushioning as it ought to be.

"Oh." Eliza wiggled atop him as she tried to sit, her backside grinding against his cock. *Ancient kings help me.* The woman had no idea how that affected him or the forbidden desires it stirred. She was Alice. He had to deliver her to the Red Court. Nothing more.

She shoved at wayward strands of hair that had fallen free from where they were pinned behind her head, smearing violet frosting across her cheek in the process.

Without thinking, he brushed his thumb across her skin, wiping away the sweet blemish.

Eliza caught his gaze and sucked in a deep breath. And then she glanced up and said, "How did we get down here?"

He sighed. *How indeed?*

Finn eased Eliza off his lap and helped her to her feet. The others still carried on as if they hadn't just fallen. Chesa had taken her seat—finally— and selected a few of the unspoiled sweets from the varying trays as if nothing were amiss and half the table wasn't covered in smushed cake and spilled tea, its occupants in varying states of madness.

He'd hoped to leave as soon as this dreadful tea was over. No, actually, he'd hoped to leave shortly after they arrived, but nothing went the way he planned—not this afternoon or being assigned this task to begin with.

"You simply must try the little green ones." Eliza lunged between the chairs and across half of the table, nearly poking one as she pointed it out to Chesa.

The other woman smirked and took the cake. "What do you think of a Wonderland tea party" —Chesa's gaze flicked to him then back— "Eliza?"

A strangled breath slipped from his lips. *If she called her Alice...* His jaw stiffened. Not that any of them would likely remember a thing once the tea wore off.

"It is..." She made to tap a finger on her lips and missed. "Wonderous." Eliza giggled at her joke. She grabbed the arm of her chair and squeezed toward the table to retake her seat.

Oh no, not happening. Finn slung an arm around her chest and pulled her back, ignoring Eliza's protests.

"Duchess, we'll be needing a room," he said.

The piglet sat in her lap, his front feet on the table as he ate straight from her plate. She dabbed at her eyes and reigned in her laughter. "Of course, of course. Duckworth!"

The butler jolted from his stupor, taking in the table and its occupants with rapidly blinking eyes.

"A room for our guests," she ordered.

Finn's teeth ground together. The Duchess still had her wits about her, and yet she'd let this happen to Alice? He'd have to have a word with her later. Likely several.

"B-but the tea!" Eliza protested as he led her back toward the house.

He sighed. "You can have more later."

Some regular tea. At least the promise got her to follow along without trying to drag him back outside. He planned to keep her far away from the wicked stuff, at least until she was safely at the Red Court. His fingers flexed on the bare skin of her wrist, finding her hammering pulse. Maybe even then, too. There were far too many people who would try to take advantage of Alice if they found her in such a state.

The butler threw open the doors to a lavish bedroom bedecked in crimson and gold—quite to Finn's taste, honestly.

"Do you need anything?" the butler asked.

"No." Finn snapped. And then he looked at Alice, at her bleary eyes and stained dress. He turned back to Duckworth. "Apologies. Some water and food. *Simple* foods. And fresh clothing for the lady." He cut his gaze to Eliza for emphasis. The right side of her bodice was damp, likely with tea, and food was smeared across her skirts.

"It will be done," the butler replied. His gaze flitted past Finn, and the man froze before coughing in his fist.

"What—" Finn's question vanished the moment he turned and spied Eliza pulling at the ties binding her dress. The wide golden sash around her middle had already slipped to the floor, and she tugged at the laces at her back. With her flushed face, the scene painted an entirely different image than the truth.

The sound of the door closing knocked him from his stupor, and Finn bolted across the room to her. "What are you doing?"

"Help me, Finn." The desperation in her voice and pout on her face chipped away at his resolve. He helped with the laces of her corset, but he'd barely loosened the thing before stepping away to give her privacy. The way she pulled her bottom lip between her teeth sent an entirely different message.

"Please." She jerked at the laces again, only making them draw tighter. "The vines are crushing me. I can't get out."

Vines? Shit. Hallucinations. He should have known. *Damnable tea.* At least she hadn't tumbled off her high and into the pit of sorrow. Hopefully, she'd be asleep before that misery descended and not wake until long after that and the rest of this nonsense passed.

"Hold still." He swept her hair over one shoulder, exposing the back of the dress that already hung a bit loose in places thanks to the removal of the silken belt. In moments, he had the bow undone and loosened her laces enough to earn a grateful sigh.

"Much better." Eliza shoved at the thin sleeves, and before he realized what was happening, the dress fell to puddle around her feet.

"Eliza…" He scrubbed a hand down his face. Ancient kings damn him, but she was a sight standing there in just a thin slip of creamy material that did little to hide her form. It ended halfway down her thighs, baring legs he couldn't help but gaze at as she stepped out of her heels. His throat dried as she turned toward him. Her long hair tumbled over her shoulder, spilling around one breast and hiding it from view, but the other pressed against the fabric, dusky nipple teasing below.

His cock went hard in an instant. He couldn't help it. She was a dream, with curves in all the right places and a body that begged to be kissed, caressed, and pleasured.

Finn twisted around and pinched his eyes shut. She wasn't some random woman he could desire, she was Alice. Worse, she probably had only half a clue what she did.

"Finn." She drew his name out, hooked him with it like a fish with a lure, and begged him to turn. It was one of the hardest things he'd ever done not to.

"Am I ugly?" She sniffled. "Is that it?"

Damn tea. Finn's fist tightened at his side, nails digging into his palm. This was not the time for it to take her into the well of sorrows.

"No, Eliza." The words were so rough and coarse it shocked him.

He refused to peek, wouldn't indulge his desire when the Dormaus tea influenced her behavior. But still, he could feel her as she drew near and circled to stand in front of him, as if she poured out magic into the air. But then, she was Alice, and who wielded more power here than her?

"Th-then why won't you look at me?"

The pain in her words cut him like a blade. If only she knew. If she was fully herself and came to him like that it'd be impossible to turn her away —Alice or not. "You're not yourself, Eliza."

"I'm not?" He could picture her brows scrunching together, her red lips drawing into a pout. "Then who am I?"

Who indeed? "Tell you what. If you get in bed and pull the covers up, I'll look at you plenty in the morning if that's what you want."

"You promise?"

"Absolutely." She wouldn't want him to look at her then. He was certain of that. All the better, he shouldn't—couldn't—want to see her.

His pulse hammered in his throat as he listened to the sounds of her sliding into the sheets, hopefully still wearing that slip if nothing else. The butler hadn't returned with new clothes yet, and Finn wouldn't insist she put the dress back on, soiled as it was.

There was one thing he'd insist on, though. Finn reached into the magical pouch at his waist and searched by touch until he found the item he sought. In a weird twist of fate, it was lucky he hadn't used the sleeping potion on Alice that first night.

"Are you in bed?" he asked.

"Mm-hm," came her answer. "Will you be joining me?"

The question shot a bolt of yearning straight between his legs. If only he could. Finn adjusted himself, trying to hide the proof of his desire before he turned and cracked open his eyes.

The sight of Eliza nestled in the bed, the crimson coverings pulled up just below her breasts, nearly brought him to his knees. No one had had that effect on him in a very long time, not since he was free to choose his lovers.

Of course fate would see fit to tease him with Alice. Fate always was a wicked bitch.

He settled on the edge of the bed, a respectful distance from her, and passed her the little vial. "You should drink this. It'll…help morning arrive sooner."

Her pinched brows smoothed out, and a grin stretched her face. "Oh, well then." She grabbed it from him and tipped it back.

Too trusting, Alice. Far too trusting.

Another reason he'd never let her near that tea again. Eliza would never do something so foolish as to drink something like that if she knew what it caused.

She passed the vial back to him. "So sweet."

Sugar always went down easier than something foul.

Finn started to slide off the bed when Eliza grabbed his coat. A glassy sheen shone in her eyes, and he nearly cursed under his breath.

"I'm a terrible person," she said.

He shook his head. "I've known many terrible people." Some would say he was one himself. "But you're not one of them."

"I am." She sniffed.

"Rest, Eliza. Everything will look better in the morning."

She only clutched her fist tighter on his clothes. "My grandmother…"

Alice?

"I wasn't good to her. Not in the end. Not for a long time. I was a terrible granddaughter. I don't deserve her inheritance. I shouldn't be Alice."

He didn't stop to think before he brushed that wayward strand of hair away from her face. "It's just the tea making you think that."

"No!" She jerked him closer. "It's not." Tears welled and fell. "I barely wrote to her. I hadn't visited her in years. She practically raised me as a child, was the best family I ever had, and yet I…I…"

Unmistakable truth rang through the haze of the tea. Her confession mirrored some of the things the previous Alice had told him—bits of stories here and there locked in his memories.

Finn eased further onto the bed with his legs stretched out near hers. "Your grandmother loved you."

Breath caught in her throat. "She can't have."

Her hand fell from his coat, but he didn't leave. "She did. She talked very fondly of you."

Her eyes blinked rapidly, the sleeping potion trying to take hold. "But I was far away. I only focused on myself, my life."

Finn brushed the back of his hand along her face, smoothing her hair behind her ears. Eliza leaned into the touch, her eyes falling closed and not reopening.

"That's what she wanted, Eliza. She wanted you to live. To be free." *Until Wonderland would come to claim you.* A heaviness settled in his chest. Until he came to claim her, to bind her as Alice and steal her freedom.

Her breathing evened. Finn carefully inched himself away. Soft fingers grazed his where he still had one hand propped near her face. "Don't leave me, Finn."

He sat back on the bed, tangling his fingers with hers and savoring her contented sigh. "I won't."

12

"Wake up, Eliza."

Someone shook her gently, drawing her from a dream of drinking tea with rabbits while perched on spotted toadstools. The scene dripped away like water splashed across a wet portrait, replaced with a familiar face just visible in the dim, flickering light of the room.

"Finn?" His name came out as a hoarse whisper, her throat full of cotton.

"Shh." He placed a finger over her lips. "We have to go. Now."

Eliza could only blink, trying to regain her bearings, as Finn slipped from the edge of the bed and crept to a curtained window.

How had she gotten here? Where was here? She rubbed her eyes and glanced around, trying to pick out what she could of the surroundings with only the low-burning candle on the nearby table to provide light. It was the room she'd changed in at the Duchess's manor, but why was she inside? In bed?

Last she remembered, she was sipping tea in the gardens and listening to Maddoc's tales of misadventures in the Red Court. Her brows scrunched together. *No, there was more than that.* The memories hung like ribbons before her, blowing in the breeze, almost visible but just out of reach. There was a tea so sweet it stuck her teeth together like pure honey.

Maybe some dancing? She sat and her gaze dipped to her chest. A ball of warmth caught there and spread outward. *By the Mother in her high heavens, I'm nearly naked!*

Finn rushed back to the bed. "Come on." He extended his hand. "We have to go."

Apprehension prickled along the back of her neck. "But I'm—" She gestured to herself. "What happened? I can't go like this."

"I'll explain later." His hand dropped to something strapped to his side that hadn't been there earlier—a sword.

An icy chill gripped her, and she leaped from the bed, no longer caring about her state of undress.

Finn averted his gaze. "There are clothes on the settee," he said in a rapid whisper. "Be quick."

Eliza raced to them, scanning them over with a hurried glance. The horrid pink dress they'd tried to have her wear before stood out immediately. Another in pale blue lay next to it. But the third outfit, with dark trousers and an airy-looking blue shirt, similar to the one Chesa wore, showed promise.

She grabbed it without a second thought, shucked her slip, and started to pull on the pants. "What's going on?" she asked as she dressed.

A choked sound slipped into the silence behind her, followed by shuffling. She nearly turned to look when Finn answered.

"The White knights are here."

Her stomach turned over, and she nearly fell getting her legs into the pants. Gooseflesh crept up her arms as she hastily pulled on the shirt and shoved her feet into the low boots she'd worn here.

When she turned, Finn stood near the window, peeking around the edge of one heavy drape. Moonlight spilled in through the crack, painting his face in pale shades.

"Here as in…" Her voice was suddenly too loud, too damning.

He turned to her. "In town. Right outside the manor."

She couldn't help it. She had to see, had to know. Eliza rushed across the room, blew out the candle, and slid up beside Finn at the window.

She'd seen the Gamorean military a number of times. They were common in the cities, especially near the coast where pirate raids were all too common. But most of their uniforms were simple—matching shirts and pants bearing military insignias, swords strapped to their back or sides. It was said they wore armor into battle, but thankfully she'd never witnessed that, and the pictures she'd seen illustrated in books were so much simpler than these White knights. Moonlight glimmered off bits of pale metal. Spikes seem to extend from their arms, elbows, and shoulders. Elaborate helmets she couldn't quite make out hid their faces.

One knight trotted slowly by on their horse, a string of townspeople with their hands bound trailed behind him.

Eliza sucked in a breath. "What are they doing?"

Finn wrapped an arm around her, pulling her close. Her heart skipped a beat, and she thought to draw away but leaned into his warmth instead.

"I don't know," he admitted. He drew her away from the window, sliding his arm from around her shoulders and taking her hand. "But we have to go."

She swallowed the tightness in her throat and nodded.

"Don't let go. Don't make a sound," Finn said, leading them to the door. He cracked it open, the hinges giving a slight squeak, before poking his head outside.

Eliza held her breath, waiting to hear the voice of the butler or someone else, but no one answered.

Without a word, Finn pulled her into the hall and shut the door behind him. The manor was eerily quiet. Only the rare gas lamps burned low in their sconces along the wall, leaving most of the space cloaked in shadow.

They'd just made it down the grand staircase to the lower floor when the familiar clop of hooves slipped like a whisper through an open window. Finn's hand tightened on hers. She dared a glance at him, taking in the hard set of his jaw. His hearing was better than hers, and even she'd heard that. What more did he pick up?

Halfway down the hall toward the back gardens, a hard pounding echoed from the main door. Eliza jumped and bit back a screech. Finn adjusted his grip on her hand, and only then did she realize her nails dug into his skin. She loosened her hold and suppressed an apology as he picked up their pace, moving at a near jog through the manor until they reached the back door. Only then did Finn finally halt.

"I need to get the horse," he whispered, so quiet she could barely make out the words.

Eliza nodded in return.

Once again, he opened the door painfully slowly before looking out. Every second that ticked away set her nerves further on edge. Someone would answer the pounding at the door. Would they look for them in the manor? Had they come for her?

Finn's ears twitched, likely hearing something she could not over the wild fluttering of her pulse. He looked at her once, his gaze unreadable, before leading her out into the gardens.

Together, they crept around the edge of the manor, Finn with enviable grace and silence. Muffled sounds teased her ears from the front. Conversation? She couldn't pick out the words.

Suddenly, Finn drew them to a halt. He leaned down, so close his long hair swept over her shoulder. "There are knights near the stables."

Shit.

He pulled her closer, his lips barely a hair's width from her ears. The warmth of his breath stirred up a mess of emotions that almost drowned out his next words. "Hide over there." He pointed. "I'll come for you."

A chill swept over her as he pulled away, seeming to fade into the shadows.

Hide there? She gazed toward the garden path. *With the flowers that might eat me alive?*

The White knights had to be preferable to that. Still, she nodded, biting her lip and watching Finn creep toward the stable building beyond the nearby hedges.

A loud sound from the front of the manor urged her into action. She raced across the grass, quiet as she could, and disappeared into the nearly overgrown pathway choked with strange trees and bushes that might literally consume her.

Eliza hugged her arms about herself, inwardly wishing for Finn. She dropped her arms with a small huff. She relied on him too much. She wasn't some child. Still, it'd be a lie to say his presence in this strange place wasn't a comfort. But relying on a man, on anyone, wasn't like her. All her life, she'd strived to be the very opposite of her mother, of the woman her parents groomed her to be—just some pretty, polished lady on the arm of a powerful man. Instead, she strived to stand alone, to be her own woman, even if that woman preferred a dusty library of ancient books to a society ballroom.

Sounds ahead drew her attention, and Eliza stilled, prepared to turn and run. But then she noticed the wall, its height reaching far above her head. The sound came from the other side of it. Unless the knights, or whomever it was, were prepared to scale the thing, she should be safe. She glared at the nearby plant life. *Safe-ish.*

Light flickered from the wall. Eliza drew a shaky breath. *Impossible.* It came again, but this time, she spied its source. A hole.

Quietly as she could, Eliza crept near, the sounds beyond becoming clearer.

"I-I swear," someone stammered.

Eliza crouched and squinted through the opening. A person knelt in a grassy space a little distance from the wall. Their hands were clasped in front of them as they begged the closest White knight. There were two of them surrounding the poor soul, and in the dim threads of moonlight, their attire was even more intimating, casting dark, pointy shadows across the villager on their knees.

"This one knows nothing," said one knight, his voice like boots crunching on gravel. "Away with you."

The villager nearly stumbled rising to their feet. Was that blood on their face? Dirt? She squeezed closer to the wall. Before she could figure it out, they turned and ran for their lives in the opposite direction.

"They check the manor?" the other asked.

Her breath caught. They had to mean this one.

"Checking now. Nearly had to break down the door."

"Good." The man let out an eerie laugh. "If our squadron finds Alice, we'll get a promotion for sure."

Eliza shivered. "They're looking for me," she whispered.

"Of course they are."

A scream crawled up her throat. Eliza whipped around toward the unexpected voice, only to have Chesa slam her hand over her mouth as the first note of the screech slipped free. Her head throbbed where it smacked against the stone, and though there was nowhere to go, Eliza attempted to scramble backward, away from the strange woman.

"Shh, don't scream," Chesa whispered. "Promise?"

The wall scrapped her back through her shirt, and Eliza stilled. Chesa tried to quiet her. She hadn't called for the knights. *An ally?* At length, she nodded.

Chesa dropped her hand, and Eliza took a moment to rub at the ache at the base of her skull. The other woman noticed and winced. "Sorry about that." A slight grin pulled at her lips. "I see you've recovered from the tea."

Eliza scowled. Was that how she'd lost the whole day? "You terrified me sneaking up on me like that."

Chesa ignored her and squeezed in to glance through the hole. "They're gone," she whispered.

Finally, some good news.

Chesa leaned back and sat on the ground next to Eliza. Her head cocked to the side. "You were worried about the villager."

"Of course." *Who wouldn't be?*

"That one got off easy, just a little nick above the brow."

Her brows drew together. Had she seen that?

Chesa rocked back, her palms on the ground as support. "Others have fared worse this night. Broken doors. A few buildings burned." Her oddly colored eyes slid to Eliza. "Broken bones."

She gasped. *My fault.* They searched for Alice, for her, because someone must have seen them arrive and reasoned out who she was. "If I turn myself in, they'll stop. They'll leave these people alone."

"Is that the path you wish to take? I won't stop you." She tapped a finger on her lips, her nails oddly long. "Though it might end poorly for Finn."

Eliza had pushed to her feet before the last of what she'd said sank in. Something tight and terrible gripped her chest, and her gaze snapped to Chesa's. "What do you mean?"

"He didn't tell you?" She looked up at her, blinking innocently. And then, with a quiet snort, "Gallant fool."

She shook her head before rising to her feet. Every second that passed was pure agony.

"If he fails to deliver you safely to the Red Court, he may very well lose his head." She drew a finger across her throat. "The Red Queen has little tolerance for failure, even among her favorites."

Her knees nearly gave out. Eliza grasped a nearby tree limb for support. If Finn failed to deliver her, if the White knights got her instead, or anyone else for that matter, he could be executed. And this was the court, the monarchs, he planned to take her to, that *her grandmother* insisted she be taken to. What little she'd eaten the day before tried to crawl back up her throat.

"Why?" Eliza forced out.

Chesa raised one shoulder in a half-shrug. "It's my duty to guide and protect Alice."

Protect me? All she'd done was nearly scare her out of her skin—more than once.

"Losing Finn in such a way would not be best for you or Wonderland. Alice should not be anointed in tears. Though…" Her gaze was suddenly worlds away. "That is how it began."

"How what began?" Eliza asked.

Chesa ignored her questions again. "You might be the Alice we need. The pieces move in strange ways."

She fought the urge to shake the other woman. None of it made any sense.

Suddenly, Chesa looked down the garden path, seeming to return to the present. "He comes for you."

"Finn?" Eliza twisted around, searching for any sign of him.

When she looked back, Chesa was gone.

13

"Where..." Eliza turned in a circle, peering into the shadows of the night-drenched garden. However, Chesa was nowhere to be seen. She'd simply vanished like she had at the table, but this time, she did not reappear.

Distant shouts sent her heart leaping into her throat. Eliza froze, her head twisting toward the sound. Wood crashed. Horses shrieked their displeasure, as did a number of men. The fine hairs on the back of her neck rose. A tiny voice within yelled at her to turn and run, to flee into the gardens. But this wasn't the maze outside her grandmother's manor—not the safe, comfortable place she often retreated to as a child.

This was Wonderland. This garden could eat her alive.

The thunder of hoofbeats carried through the night, growing louder. Finally, Eliza snapped into motion, turning and sprinting down the overgrown path. She'd be damned if the White knights would catch her if it meant forfeiting Finn's life.

The path grew narrower as she fled. Sudden turns and walls had her slipping on mossy stones, her breaths coming fast and hard. A branch seemed to lower of its own accord and swipe its sharp fingers across her cheek. Pain bloomed in their wake, but she pressed on. The hoofbeats drew closer.

Something wrapped around her leg and pulled, sending Eliza tumbling to the ground. The air fled from her lungs. Color danced in front of her eyes. It jerked again, tugging her to the side—off the path. *No, not happening!*

Eliza scrambled to twist around, catching sight of a vine thicker than her arm. It retreated into the underbrush. A brightly colored flower, big as her, seemed to vibrate in anticipation where it loomed beyond some benign shrubs.

"No. No!" Eliza kicked and flailed. "Get off!"

Her heel smashed into the vine, and it loosened. Another shake and she was almost free. And then a dark shape rounded the corner. The ground vibrated from the thump of the horse's hooves. Terror locked her in its grip. The moment was all the vine needed to regain its hold and drag her across the mossy path.

Eliza screeched, bucking on the ground. A stream of moonlight illuminated a fall of white hair.

"Finn?" His name was somewhere between a prayer and a sob.

"Hold still."

Another sob escaped as Eliza dug her fingers into the ground. His voice was the best sound in the world.

Finn drew the horse to a halt, its front legs kicking in the air. It hadn't returned to the ground when he leaped from its back and pulled the sword sheathed at his side. The blade whizzed through the air, glimmering in thin strands of moonlight, as Finn brought it down on the vine, severing it in one go.

An inhuman screech rattled through the underbrush. Eliza stared in horror as the flower shook, sending all the plants around it swaying like they were caught in a storm.

"Eliza." Finn's urgent tone dragged her focus to him. The sword was sheathed once more, his hand outstretched. She took it, and he hauled her to her feet. The last of the vine slipped from her leg. Eliza made to kick it away, but Finn wrapped her in a crushing hug.

"You're safe." His palm smoothed down her arms, along her back. *Checking for wounds?*

She ached, but already his embrace soothed the pain away. All too soon, he pulled back. His gaze caught hers, filled with so many things she couldn't pick them out.

"We have to go," he whispered. Distant sounds teased her ears and raised the fine hairs along the back of her neck. They wouldn't be alone for long.

Before she had the chance to nod, Finn lifted her into the saddle. He leaped on behind her and had the horse in motion a moment later.

"How do we get out?" she asked.

"A gate. At the back." Finn turned the horse, the same mare as before, down another path before making a sharp turn around a tree.

Eliza held on for dear life, praying the horse's footing was better than hers. Finn leaned his chest against her back, a literal shield against the world. He was at risk because of her, and she hadn't known. They had so much more to fear than just the White Court and the monsters creeping about in the dark.

And it was her grandmother who set him on this mission, who forced him to risk his life for her. If only she could talk to her one more time. Ask why—why any of this?

The garden path spilled out into a grassy area, larger than the one they'd had tea in. The stone wall loomed, a large metal gate teased the world beyond the garden's borders

"Finn..." Eliza leaned further into him as they galloped toward it. Masses of vines wound through the bars of the gate and clung to the surrounding wall. The blasted thing looked like it hadn't been opened in years.

The horse reared just in front of the gate, and Finn leaped from its back. *Poor girl.* Eliza patted the animal, whispering reassurances.

Sounds of riders giving chase rose behind them. Eliza wove her fingers into the horse's mane. They had minutes. Seconds.

Finn turned and spoke to the horse in a language she couldn't place. The horse seemed to nod in agreement and began to walk backward.

"Finn!" Eliza twisted uneasily in the saddle, looking back toward the overgrown gardens, waiting for the inevitable shapes of their doom to burst free from the plant life.

"Keep her steady." He'd already turned back to the gate.

Eliza gasped as a pale light formed between his hands, glowing like the moon. "Mother above..."

Steadily, it grew. Finn's face creased in concentration. His lips curled back in a snarl, a groan ripping free from his lungs. And then, he shoved the light at the gate. It flew from his hands, barreling into vine and metal and bursting it wide with a screeching groan.

The light zipped off across the fields beyond before fading into nothingness.

Eliza shivered.

Magic.

She'd read about it plenty, but seeing it, such raw force drawn from nowhere, was something else entirely. And this...this was more than humans should wield, more than they could from her understanding. In the north of Neverland, some claimed to be blessed by a Goddess— *perhaps another name for the Mother?*—and given strength beyond normal humans. To the east, across the Cerulean Seas and the far mountains, some could work spells and enchantments. The merfolk had their curses. The pixies, their dust.

But this? A summoning of light and Chesa's ability to vanish were new —unrecorded.

Finn returned to the horse and leaped up into the saddle, breathing hard.

She twisted to catch a glimpse of his face, the flush on his cheeks, the determination in his eyes.

So much power, so much grace, in this strange man.

His gaze dipped to hers, a question lingering there she couldn't make out. Finn pulled her closer, and her breath hitched.

And then they were off. All thoughts of the question vanished as they slipped through the twisted metal and cut vines that used to be the gate and galloped across the field in the moonlight toward a looming forest.

It was hours later when Finn, barely awake, deemed them safe enough to stop for the night. The sky had begun to lighten, hinting at dawn not far away. Several times over the last hour, his head had dropped, coming to lay on Eliza's shoulder. If she wasn't worried about him falling off, she'd have let him sleep. His strong form laid over hers was oddly comforting, if not exactly comfortable. He must have used so much energy forming his magic, and who knew if he'd slept at all. Probably not, alert as he'd been when he woke her. He'd slept little the night before too.

"Let me." Eliza gestured toward his satchel.

Finn only blinked, half-awake, as he dropped the horse's reins so she could drink her fill from the nearby stream.

"I'll set up the tent." She held out her hand, waiting.

"But you're—"

"Quite capable," she interrupted. "You got us away from there. Now, let me help."

With a weary yawn, he untied the magical bag and passed it off to her. Finn said not a word as she went about setting up their little camp. The bag was especially helpful, letting her hand find exactly what she needed each time she reached inside. When the tent was set up—perfectly to her discerning eye—she pulled Finn from the stump where he'd nearly fallen asleep with his head propped on his fist.

"Rest now," she said, tucking him in like a child.

"If they find us—" His gaze searched hers.

"I'll keep watch." She was tired as well, but she'd do it. Finn had already done so much.

He swallowed, then nodded, seeming to trust her words.

"There's just... Chesa came to me in the garden."

His eyes widened. "Chesa." He tried to sit, but Eliza forced him back down.

"It's fine. Nothing happened. But..." The words tried to stick to her tongue, but she forced them out. "She said it would be your head if you failed to get me to the Red Court, if the White knights got me."

"Yes."

The single word turned her stomach over.

"It's what the Red Queen threatened." A bitter smile twisted his lips. "And she's not known to be forgiving."

And this was the woman, the court, her grandmother wanted her to go to. Eliza pushed down her worries, locking them away until she could wrestle with them later. "I won't let that happen," she promised. "I won't let you die."

He rubbed his thumb against the back of her palm, the barest trace of connection. "So brave, my Eliza."

Butterflies erupted in her stomach at the way he said her name.

"I should let you rest." She made to crawl from the tent, but Finn grabbed her wrist, and she twisted back to him.

"Stay with me, Eliza." The vulnerability in his gaze reached straight into her heart. This strong brave man, letting a sliver of weakness through, was a wonder in himself.

A memory flashed before her eyes, hazy and blurred, but there all the same. Before she'd fallen asleep, she'd asked the same thing. *Stay with me.*

And he had.

The tension fled her body. "Of course I'll stay with you, Finn."

14

*E*very step drew them closer to the Red Court, to the promise of safety from the White knights and the beasts of the wild. Each second, Alice's anointment neared.

And Finn dreaded it. All of it.

Only days ago, that had been his goal. If the magic mirror had not been shattered, he'd have delivered Alice there immediately, dusted off his hands, and been done with her—task complete.

But that was before—before she tried to attack him in self-defense, their flight from the Bandersnatch, and their time riding together. Before sharing a tent. Before the tea party and the flight through the gardens.

Eliza held his hand that night as he gave into exhaustion from a lack of sleep and the use of strong magic.

That alone would have been enough, but during the last day and a half, she looked at all the world with wonder and asked myriad questions about everything from the chittering, furry animals that ran across the path in front of them to the river tinted red from the sap of nearby trees.

Her inquisitiveness made him smile—truly smile. Her sharp wit spurred interesting conversation. But mostly, she was kind.

And it had been a long time since anyone was truly kind to him.

Eliza craned her neck, looking toward the gilly underside of the giant mushroom cap looming many feet above. Her hair tickled his cheek, but he didn't mind. Rather, he savored the casual way she was with him now —comfortable and trusting. His arm tightened around her.

"That may be the largest one yet," she said.

Finn chuckled. "That's nothing compared to some of the others deeper in the forest." He'd longed to see her expression if she caught sight of one of the tall violet shrooms that tried to touch the clouds.

"Really?" She twisted in the seat, and he took the opportunity to trail his fingers along her side. "Can we go there? We have time, right?"

When she asked like that, her voice full of passionate curiosity, he was so tempted to say yes. But he shook his head with a sigh. "Too risky."

Her shoulders drooped. "Because of the White knights?"

"Just so." They hadn't seen them since fleeing the Duchess's gardens, but they were out there. They wouldn't stop hunting for Alice, not until her anointment on the night of the full moon—still many days away.

He'd be a fool, the worst possible protector, to deviate from their course and take her anywhere but straight back to the Red Court. But then, he'd never been the wisest of rabbits, prone to wandering, day dreams, and getting up to no good.

In fact, he was the very last person the previous Alice should have picked for the job.

Though he did have considerable skill with magic and a blade. Finn had few equals there. Perhaps that was why she'd chosen him. He vowed never to let the White knights touch her and had the talent to live up to that promise.

Still, only a fool courted danger, and more than the knights prowled the woods. He hadn't told Alice about the claw marks he saw gouged on the side of one shroomy stalk or the undeniable scent of Bandersnatch in the air.

Wonderland was restless without an anointed Alice. All the terrible, wild beasties came out to play.

"Perhaps we can stop for a rest?" She beamed at him over one shoulder. "And maybe you could sketch that one for me?" She pointed at the red-capped mushroom towering overhead.

He arched a brow. "It'd be hard to forget the look of that one."

"A present subject is always best for sketching, didn't you say so yourself?"

Ah, that I did. She'd found his sketchbook tucked away in his bag the night they'd left the Duchess. He'd been frustrated, finding it out and open in their tent the next morning. *Didn't remember packing the darn thing.* But Eliza's praise for his work quickly washed that away. As had her curiosity, her desire to know about all the drawings he'd sketched on its pages.

Every time they stopped for a short rest, she asked for new ones, eager to learn about all the things her world lacked. How could he deny her?

But in this instance, he might have to. "We're close to the Red Court now."

So close they'd see it soon. The moment they passed the edge of the mushroom forest, the towers would come into view where they stretched up from the city near the shore, the gleaming waters behind them. A stunning sight, if only the people inside were half so lovely.

"Oh, well, if it's close, maybe we can come back here?"

He stiffened and put some space between them—or as much as he could astride the same horse. The monarchs would never let her leave until her anointment. And after...

Finn drew the horse to a stop.

She had no idea what they were riding into. It was the one topic he avoided, too afraid to give her cause to run again, to send her fleeing to the White Court, which was even worse, or making some foolish attempt to get back to her world.

"Finn?" Her fingers trailed down his arm, stirring up too many feelings —guilt most of all.

But what if they went to neither court? She could still be anointed. He'd see to that. But until then, they could run. See all the wilds of Wonderland. With his senses, they could avoid most troubles. And if danger found them, his magic could keep her safe.

He dropped the reins and cupped the cheek she turned his way. She gave a short intake of breath at the touch, color rising to her face.

"Eliza, if I said I'd take you anywhere in Wonderland you wanted to go. If we didn't go to—"

The breeze carried a familiar scent, one he should have expected but didn't. His ears twitched as he tuned into his senses, hearing the sounds of approach he should have heard minutes ago, might have, had he not been so distracted by the woman in his arms and what lay ahead.

"What is it?" She leaned closer to him. "What's wrong?"

"The Red knights," he whispered.

The sand in the hourglass ran out. The clock stopped ticking. He was out of time. His journey with Eliza, their easy company, was at its end. His stomach hollowed out, and his chest constricted, making it hard to breathe.

Of course the knights would come for them. It was a wonder they hadn't found them sooner. The Red King and Queen would not risk losing Alice. If not for the previous Alice's wish, they'd have sent their whole army to claim her, protection of the court be damned.

Finn's eyes fell shut. He wrapped his arms around Eliza, all focus given to her form against his, her scent in his nose, and her quavering whisper as she said his name again.

He loosened his hold and pried his eyes open, quickly spying the source of her concern in shadows moving through the distant mushrooms.

"Don't worry," he said, as much for her as for himself. "You're safe. They represent the Red King and Queen."

Finn dismounted, doing his best to shake away his worries and regrets and to be the confident, proud man they expected. He gave a loud whistle that made Eliza startle and clamp her hands over her ears.

Should have warned her.

Answering calls trilled from the forest—confirmation of their allegiance. The knights gave up all pretense of stealth and rushed toward their position. Finn whispered magical words of comfort to the horse and rubbed down her neck. Anything to keep her calm.

Eliza had become a statue atop the mare, shoulders back, head high, eyes wide. She could command a battalion with that look alone. And she'd need all of that courageous pride now.

"Finneas." Lizardo pulled free his helm with its plume of crimson feathers.

Finn's lips twitched at the sight. White knights loomed about, and yet these fools stalked through the forest in elaborate red armor more appropriate for a ceremony than war. They may not know about their enemy searching for Alice, but they should have expected it. Without Alice, the magic of Wonderland would put a fire in the heart of its warriors and urge them into conflict to see which court would dominate. Only Alice kept the peace, her decision choosing who would reign and preventing all-out war and destruction. They were fools to ignore the White Court's lust for possession of Alice and her choice.

"Lizardo," he replied, not bothering with a nod or bow of acknowledgment for the man's rank as captain. He hadn't earned it, not through skill or seniority anyway. But the Red Queen enjoyed him in her bed and liked to reward her favorites...so long as they pleased her.

The man's eyes hardened, but Finn ignored him, instead gesturing to Eliza. "May I present, Alice."

She cut him a hard look at the use of her title, but said nothing. The knights dropped to their knees, even Lizardo. When she glanced at Finn again, it was with a raised brow and question in her eyes. She didn't flush nor back down from the show of respect. His lips curled up in one corner. Rather, she embraced it like a queen.

"Alice," the captain said, a note of awe in his voice. "We're to escort you to the Red Court."

Finn's smile vanished into a hard press of his lips. That bastard tried to claim the honor of delivering Alice. He wouldn't be slighted or risk the queen thinking he'd failed. Not now.

"Thank you," Eliza replied before he could. "But I already have an escort." She looked at him, her sharp grin lowering into a gentle smile.

"B-but, Alice..."

"You heard her." Finn climbed back into the saddle. Lizardo's gaze dropped to his arm as it reached around Eliza to grab at the reins. A scowl cut across the man's features before dropping away under Eliza's steady look.

"You may follow after us," Eliza commanded.

Pride swelled in his chest. *Yes, she has a chance after all.* She could handle what was to come.

"Finn?" She arched a brow at him and then quietly, just for his ears, "Let's leave them in the dust."

He inclined his head, lips quirking up in one corner. "As my Alice commands."

Finn snapped the reins, and they took off at a gallop along the worn dirt pathway. Red knights jumped out of the way to avoid the horse. Muffled curses echoed in their wake. Lizardo would hate him even more, but it was worth it to see the way he cowered before Eliza.

Wind caught in his hair. Eliza squealed and leaned into the horse. It was freedom. Joy.

But as they broke through the edge of the shroom forest and he caught sight of the towers of the castle stretching toward the sky in the distance, his heart plummeted.

This moment was but a fleeting taste of what he longed for and could never have.

15

*E*liza's breath caught in her throat as the first glimpse of the Red Court came into view. Spires topped with twisting red roofs shone like rubies in the sunlight, glimmering against the strange green-tinted sky. She stretched up in the saddle, hoping for a better view, a hint of what lay at the base of the impossibly tall towers.

The mare hopped a rise, sending Eliza wobbling in her perch. She'd never been an exemplary rider, not like some of her boarding school classmates who made riding a graceful art. But it didn't matter, not with Finn there to steady her before fear could take root and grow. Whatever moment of uncertainty had come over him vanished with the appearance of the knights. *Our escort.* Her nose wrinkled at the thought. Ones they'd left in the dust.

It was so like something her parents would do, sending an unnecessary swarm of people to create a grand entrance. The very notion of it grated against all the rebellious desire she'd tended over the majority of her life.

As they crested the last rise, the view opened up before her. The heady rush of their flight swirled with the awe of the city, leaving her flushed and lightheaded. The ruby spires she'd seen were just the barest hint of the Red Court—a pennant waving above a stall of goods in the market. A sprawling structure of pale stone rose around the base of the three towers.

More ruby roofs dotted the various levels, creating an almost checked pattern from their place atop the hill where Finn had drawn their mare to a halt.

The size of the main manor—at least twice that of the Gamorean royal house—would stun anyone into silence, but rolling out from it like a blanket across the landscape around the rise on which it rested was a bustling city. More structures of pale stone, but color too—a riot of shades warring for attention like a quilt sewn of far too many thread colors.

Beyond that… Eliza sucked in a shuddering breath as her gaze caught the glimmer of sunlight on water. It was hard to see from here, past the city and all its exuberance, but she'd swear it was the sea, stretching out toward the horizon in an unchecked stretch of blue that ended in a line of bright green where it met the sky.

"It's quite the view from here," Finn said.

"It is." She shook her head, words failing to form on her parted lips. Wonderland was wondrous indeed. How could her world not know of this place? Surely something like this would have been recorded somewhere in the great library.

The sight alone made her ache for the knowledge the city offered. So much to see, explore, and learn. For the first time, being Alice didn't seem so bad at all, not if she could spend time in this place. It would be a worthy holiday away from her routine life. A chance to visit a strange new city that even her precious books couldn't take her to.

"It's incredible," she said at last. "I was nervous, but now…" She shook her head, her body feeling as light as it had in years. "I can't wait to see the city. Is it as lovely as it looks from here? What's your favorite part?"

Eliza leaned forward in the saddle hoping the extra inches might help her discover something new. One beat passed, then another. Finn moved in the saddle, the only sign he hadn't vanished into the heavy silence spilling from him.

"Finn?" She twisted toward him, all the lightness from moments before constricting into a tight band that tugged her ribs toward her spine.

The hard set of his jaw and distant gaze were so at odds from a moment ago, as if they viewed a city of ruins rather than the colorful wonder before them.

He gave a slight nod, like he answered some unspoken question, and turned the horse away from the city.

A tingle of apprehension slid down her spine. "Finn?"

His attention snapped toward the shroom forest a moment before riders burst from the path heading in their direction. The Red knights. They must have had horses nearby, at least the handful that approached at a steady gallop.

"We're waiting for them?" Eliza ventured. But no, even as she spoke the words, she knew that wasn't right.

Still, Finn remained silent, gaze averted.

Each second he didn't respond increased her desire to flee. Something was wrong, very wrong.

These were the knights. He said they were safe. She glanced back toward the city. Was it not so lovely to him?

"Forget the maze was closed?" Lizardo asked as he drew up beside them.

The maze? Eliza looked back once more, this time focusing on the gently sloping land between them and the Red Court. Now that he pointed it out, it was unmissable. Hedges higher than her head rose up from the ground like the garden maze outside her grandmother's manor. But unlike the manor, whose maze took only minutes to traverse, this monstrosity stretched as far to the sides as she could see, as if it might ring in the entire city beyond.

"Of course not," Finn replied, all the hardness of moments ago absent from his voice. "Just eager to show our Alice the view."

Right. Eliza nearly snorted. She'd believe that as much as she would believe her father telling her that he was proud of her. But the easy look on Finn's face said she wouldn't be getting any answers. Not while they had close company. She met Lizardo's questioning gaze and notched her chin higher. Nor would she cower before this stranger, especially given his obvious dislike of her companion.

The man quickly looked away and urged his mount down the hillside toward the maze. Finn followed, settling into an uneasy silence once more.

A gate of black iron stood at the entrance to the hedges, its high points topped with crimson designs that appeared to be in the shape of hearts. A strange decoration for such a place.

Multiple carriages and people stood outside the barred gate, seemingly waiting for entry.

"Why such a hedge maze?" Eliza asked as they neared.

"Protection," Finn's reply came swiftly, hanging in the air like there might be more.

"Not worried about fire?" she prodded. Unless these hedges couldn't burn. No such plants existed in her world, that she knew of, but this was Wonderland, so who knew?

Finn snorted air through his nose, and Eliza savored the hint of humor it contained, the first bit since his odd turn upon seeing the city. "It's happened a time or two, or so the records say." She felt his shrug. "Though such a blaze would make it hard for an enemy to approach with the Red Court unaware. The maze as well. Unwary travelers have been known to get lost in its pathways and never be seen again."

Eliza scoffed. He must be joking. Who would want their citizens or travelers to suffer such a fate?

Finn leaned in. His breath ghosted across her cheek. A jostle of the horse had his lips coasting across her ear and Eliza's middle clenching tight. "Never go into the maze, Eliza," he whispered.

The warning drenched all the melting feelings his fleeting touch elicited.

And yet, here they were, at the gates of it. "But we're..." She gestured ahead.

"The Red Court sends escorts to see travelers through, and some of the knights know the safe paths. We'll be safe today."

"And you know those paths, Finn?" she asked.

He tucked her closer to him and dropped his voice to a whisper. "I do. I'll keep you safe, Eliza."

"Finally!" A woman barked near the gates. A navy dress cloaked her curvaceous form, trailing all the way to the ground aside from the slit that ran dangerously high, revealing one pale legged that tapped on the ground with impatience. Blonde hair was piled on top of her head, and one upturned hand held a long, thin pipe of some sort that trailed a tendril of smoke into the air.

"We've been waiting here for ages," she continued. "How long does it take someone to open this thing up anyhow?"

The woman's look of disdain rolled across the cluster of riders, snagging on Eliza, or rather, the man at her back.

"Ah, Finneas," the woman crooned. All at once, her pinched lips and upturned nose smoothed out into something more pleasing, more knowing.

The sharp pang of jealousy hit Eliza's gut like acid. Only as the woman's gaze shifted ever so slightly to her did she remember to smooth out her own pinched lips and furrowed brow.

"Pilla," Finn replied in a congenial tone that twisted Eliza into knots and had her shifting against him.

Stupid, worrying about some random woman. It wasn't like Finn was hers. He was her escort. And though his touch teased more, all he promised was to deliver her to the Red Court. His task was complete— almost. She didn't know him that well, had never asked about any lovers, and certainly couldn't expect more from him, but her heart was known to wander far from what those around her expected. He was strange, Finn, and not just his long white hair that would have him standing out in any crowd back home. He often stood too close and wielded power she struggled to comprehend. *He turns into a rabbit, for goodness sake!* But he also loved to draw and tell tales about the world around them.

He seemed to enjoy making her laugh, something she often forgot she could still do.

Years at a strict boarding school or surrounded by the false laughter of her parents and their so-called friends could do that to a person. Not to mention her life in the library—a quiet, comfortable place, but one where laughter wasn't often welcome.

"Surely you can help out an old friend?" The woman—Pilla—sauntered their way. "I simply can't understand this delay."

"Things are always strange in these...uncertain times," he replied.

Lizardo edged his horse between them. "I'd ask you to keep your distance."

Pilla gave a dramatic eye roll and a sigh. "As if he or his cute companion have anything to fear from me."

Cute? A touch of heat rose to Eliza's cheeks. The guards might know who she was, but this woman certainly didn't. All the better, really. The last thing she wanted was another hold-up or awkward display.

"The wild beasts are much more of a threat," Pilla continued berating the man and swishing her long cigarette at him. "Why, we passed Bandersnatch scratchings on the road here, and I do believe her majesty would be quite displeased if her friend were set upon by such a creature."

Bandersnatch? Eliza gasped and cut her gaze to Finn out of the corner of her eye.

He gave the briefest nod. His palm landed on her thigh in what was likely a show of support, but to Eliza, it made the whole world blur. She barely heard Pilla continue to ramble her frustrations.

"Come now, Lizardo," Finn said. "Surely you can let them through with us. What could it hurt?"

The captain narrowed his eyes. "I will not risk—"

"You'd delay our arrival further?" Finn cut in. He led the horse into a trot, circling around the man to near the gate. "Send a rider ahead. Her majesty will want to greet her guests. You don't want to upset her, do you?"

Eliza could almost taste the smile in Finn's words and she certainly could see the impact of it in the red hue rising to Lizardo's cheeks. "Of course not," he ground out.

Pilla had fallen silent during the exchange, her gaze firmly fixed on Eliza in a way that was impossible to ignore. She drew her cigarette to her lips before letting out a long stream of smoke from between her red lips, which closed to a knowing smirk.

Blast it all.

The captain approached the gates with a large golden key. No sooner did they groan open than a pair of riders appeared around a bend in the hedge. Both drew up short. "Captain," one exclaimed. "You're back. Then..."

The man's gaze fell on Eliza and the base of her neck burned. Was it going to be like this with everyone they met?

Once again, Finn stepped in. "On the way to the Red Court. Precisely. So glad you've returned to show these travelers through the maze."

The two new arrivals looked from Finn to the captain, who added, "Well, what are you waiting for? See to your duties."

Finally, the two new riders trotted by, never looking away from Eliza as if she was some two-headed monster rather than a woman. As they did, the captain gave orders to his men. One he assigned to ride ahead with urgency to inform Their Majesties of their *guests*, the other to see that the travelers awaiting entry followed, but at a distance.

It all seemed like too much until a distant roar rumbled through the quiet, sending Eliza's hair standing on end. But it hadn't come from the mushroom forest behind, it was off to the right. *Within the maze?*

Only Finn's thumb rubbing circles on her thigh kept her from leaping out of her skin or demanding they turn back. "I told you, Eliza," he whispered. "Never go into the maze."

16

The journey through the maze was, blessedly, unremarkable. The path seemed simple, but if Eliza had to make the reverse trip on her own, she was dubious about the chances of success. The tall hedges often blocked the view, and sometimes even when the ruby spires were visible, it seemed they traveled the wrong way. Eventually, the path opened wide before them. The towering hedges dropped to waist height. Great fields spread out to the sides, ringed in by distant hedges. One contained many rows of wooden seats, perhaps indicating a space for events or games. Pennants were staked along the sides of the pathway, flapping in a gentle breeze and showing off a golden crown ringing a red heart.

At the far end of the path loomed another gate with a procession of people filling through it toward them. At its front rode two people on horseback, crowns of gold and ruby glimmering on their heads. Eliza swallowed the lump in her throat and sat a little straighter. She pushed at her hair, trying to smooth the rogue strands into something presentable. On the ride there, she hadn't minded her appearance—the bit of dirt on her clothes or her tangled hair. Now, every hair out of place stirred up a mess of worries. She'd seen the Gamorean royal family a few times, but Eliza was below notice despite her parent's furtive social climbing.

However, these royals, for she had no doubt that's who headed their way, were here for her—to greet their Alice.

"Don't be nervous," Finn whispered at her back. "Head high. You're stronger than they know."

And he must believe her far stronger than she was, especially as her hands trembled and spots swam in the edges of her vision.

The procession halted as they advanced in a slow trot. Eliza should divert her gaze, look at the ground, the other people, or the maze, anything but stare the monarchs in the face. But somehow, she couldn't quite manage that. Both were regal and in their prime, likely not much older than her parents. The king's rich brown hair was liberally streaked with silver, adding an air of seasoned confidence to his strong features and square jaw. As he leaped from his horse, his height and strength were displayed to great effect, showing a man still powerful in both body and spirit.

Even so, it was the queen who drew her focus. Attendants situated a short set of stairs and helped their queen down from her horse. She maintained her perfect posture with every step, not an auburn hair out of place. She'd have been the apple in the eye of Eliza's boarding school mistress. Well, except for her attire. A fitted ruby bodice flared out into wide skirts, and though the material appeared voluminous, it was quite sheer, teasing her legs from ankle to the apex of her thighs. Black hearts speckled the fabric of her skirts. A large one dominated the bodice of her dress, barely covering her voluptuous breasts and leaving much of her cleavage in full show.

Finn drew the horse to a halt, slid down, and gave a dramatic bow, his arms flaring wide in a show of subservience. For some reason, the act set Eliza's teeth on edge.

No sooner did he rise than he reached up to help her off. But the action was formal, distant, and so unlike the rest of their journey. He'd always pulled her off into his arms, their bodies touching probably more than was necessary—Finn was always a little closer than was truly proper. At first, it rankled her sense of propriety, but now, she missed it. The change was as cold and sudden as his shift in demeanor earlier.

What's wrong? She tried to ask via a glance, but his attention wasn't on her at all. His focus was where hers really should have been, on the monarchs waiting near their retinue.

The answer to it all came suddenly as a blink of her eyes. Formality reigned. Slipping back into a lifetime of lessons and expectations was as easy as donning her shoes. Eliza smoothed out her features and dipped into a flawless, deep curtsy that even her exacting mother would have praised.

When she lifted to her full height once more, tall and straight as the queen, she slipped her hand through Finn's offered one, a respectful distance between them. She was used to this. She could do this. However much she hated this part of her life, it was a part of her, and she wouldn't cower, though she yearned to sink into Finn's side or flee from sight.

"Your Majesties," Finn announced when they were mere feet away.

Eliza dipped into another perfect curtsy.

"May I present, Alice."

Her breath caught. She wobbled just the slightest bit on her feet. The title should have been expected. But still, hearing it from Finn, so formal and detached, shook her.

"Alice, welcome to the Red Court," the king said, his voice rich and booming.

"She is quite darling, isn't she? And so well-mannered." The queen sauntered closer, waving a lace fan in one hand.

"Quite pretty too," the king added.

"Indeed she is." A grin pulled at the queen's red lips set in a flawless face.

Eliza's cheeks heated, especially as both monarchs eyed her with obvious interest. If either was bothered by the other's compliment or its implications, they didn't show it.

Finn dropped Eliza's arm and stepped away, leaving her to the queen's exacting inspection as she looked her over head to toe like a merchant inspecting new wares. Eliza's gaze caught on the ruby pendant hanging from the chain around the queen's neck. It was somehow safer than looking her in the eye or daring a glance at the king.

Of all the times for Finn to leave her alone.

The queen tipped Eliza's chin up with the edge of her fan and smiled brightly. "We're pleased you're here at last, Alice."

The hint of a smile twitched at Eliza's lips but didn't quite stay. Something sparkled in the queen's golden-brown eyes that she couldn't decipher. The intrusive look may well have stripped her nude there in the gardens.

Everything in her urged her to look away, lest the other woman reach down into her soul, so she did, glancing at Finn as if he could somehow save her from that moment.

His stiff expression broke for a fleeting moment. "She prefers to be called Eliza."

As always, he filled her name with such richness that it twisted her up inside. And the queen, this woman who saw too much, noticed. Her grin twitched. She snapped the fan closed, the edge sweeping across the soft skin of Eliza's chin in a stinging line that caused her to startle.

"Does she?" That intrusive look slid to Finn, and finally, Eliza could breathe again.

"I suppose she's not the anointed Alice quite yet, just our dear Alice in waiting." The queen crossed to Finn, her gaze stiff but easy at the same time, almost like a predator taking carefully concealed steps toward their prey, having not decided whether to pounce or let it run away.

"I thought you might like to know, Your Majesty," Finn replied. All the playful easiness she'd come to appreciate about him had vanished.

The queen stopped in front of Finn and glanced back over her shoulder toward Eliza. Her eyes narrowed as her smile grew. "Well, Finneas, dear." The queen caressed his cheek, the act familiar and intimate in a way that made Eliza's chest ache. "I'm sure you have much you can tell me about her later. I am *so* glad you're back."

And then, without the slightest hesitation for their audience, the queen rose on her toes and dragged Finn's face down to hers, locking him in a deep, passionate kiss.

Eliza blinked. Once. Twice.

In one moment, all the time she'd spent in Wonderland suddenly seemed a dream. Upside down, twisted, and never once real.

She was a foolish child alone in a world of strangers, just like she'd always been, and there was only one way to survive in such a place.

17

*F*inn yearned to scream, pull away, and shove Queen Victoria back.

It didn't matter how many times she threw herself at him, it never got easier. Life would have been simpler if he could pull together a drop of desire for her, but there was nothing there but loathing—at least on his part. Not that it mattered to her. The queen took a lover of whomever she liked, and if they dissented? Well, off with their head.

The king was free with his attentions as well, but at least he was more discreet in his conquests, and Finn hadn't heard of him punishing any who refused his advances. The king and queen might be married, but their alliance was political, not romantic. Other people shared their beds far more than each other.

It wasn't a secret that he was one of Victoria's favorites. Even the Duchess had called him the queen's pet, and she wasn't wrong, but he'd never expected her attention so soon on his return.

There should have been time to find a way to ward her off, to shift more of her attention elsewhere, to warn Eliza.

His nails dug into his palm, nearly drawing blood.

The queen finally pulled away, grinning in smug satisfaction. Finn forced himself to look at her, to shutter away all the emotions raging through him. "It is a pleasure to be back, my queen." The evenness of the words shocked even him. Though, he had a great deal of practice in the matter.

When the queen finally turned away, he dared a glance at Eliza. He expected shock and confusion. He dared to hope for sadness or jealousy, anything to hint she might desire him even half so much as he did her. However, Eliza didn't even look at him.

The stalwart woman stared at the king and the rest of the procession with her head held high, back straight, and the hint of a pleasant smile playing about her lips.

A blade to the stomach would have gutted him less.

She didn't care, not at all.

He'd been a pleasant companion, a protector, a source of information about the world around her—nothing more. There'd been nothing in the stray touches or lingering looks.

Finn blew out a huff of air through his nose. He'd been everything he was ordered to be, all he should ever be to Alice. He'd been a fool to hope for anything more.

It'd been years since he'd cared for anyone or could even hope to care for someone with the queen's attention on him. There was an excellent reason he avoided romantic liaisons—he quite liked his head on his shoulders. The queen wouldn't kill Eliza, but she could make her life miserable in other ways. It'd been a mistake pointing out her name, showing that he might have more than respectable feelings for her. Eliza was the smart one. It was better for both of them that she didn't care. Still, his traitorous heart ached at her indifference.

"Dearest Alice." The queen looped her arm through Eliza's as if they were the best of friends. "I can't wait to show you our lovely court."

"I'd like that," Eliza replied, the portrait of regal congeniality. "It took my breath away when I first saw the spires. They glimmer like rubies. So apt for such a lovely queen as yourself."

Victoria gave a hearty laugh, and he barely restrained his grimace.

The woman he cared for, complimenting the one who made his life miserable? Eliza hadn't seen beyond the queen's fair façade yet. Once she did, well, she better be a good actor.

His teeth ground together as he watched them walk arm-in-arm over to the king—another person who presently tempted him to violence. He liked the man, typically. He'd offered shelter years ago when he'd desperately needed it and seen that he was educated and trained. But if he made a play for Eliza, Finn might have to do...something.

Finn swallowed the tightness in his throat and looked away.

You'll do what? His small, inner voice of reason taunted.

He pinched his eyes closed. *Nothing.*

Eliza was a grown woman. She could make her choices, and the king wouldn't risk offending her by aggressive pursuit. He had more sense than his wife with her flair for the dramatic.

"She fits right in."

Finn jumped at the unexpected voice. His eyes snapped open to find Chesa standing at his side. "Of course, she's Alice," he said after regaining his composure.

"One might think she was groomed for this role all her life, but she wasn't, was she?"

"No." She hadn't known a thing about Wonderland or her role, which bothered him as much as anything. The previous Alice had been wise, balanced. Not telling her beloved granddaughter about this world and then sending him—alone—on a ridiculous mission to bring her here didn't fit the woman he'd known.

"Perhaps..." Chesa mused, a finger tapping on her lips.

Finn arched a brow. "Perhaps?" He'd take anything to distract him from watching her walk away with the monarchs.

"Some Alices have known and been prepared. Some have not. All have failed."

That drew his attention. "Failed at what?"

Chesa still stared, her nose twitching, at where Eliza had disappeared with the monarchs into the retreating crowd. "I don't think she can do it alone."

"Do what?" It took effort not to shake the woman. Half the things she said never made any sense, but it hadn't bothered him in the past. But that was before she talked about Eliza.

Finally, she turned her head toward him, but Chesa's gaze was far away. "You'll help her. She needs you."

His fists balled at his side. *She clearly doesn't want me, you fool.* "Alice doesn't—"

"Finneas, you rogue!"

Pilla's throaty exclamation had him grinding his teeth. Everyone had to choose this moment to bother him when all he wanted was to drown his sorrows in wine.

With effort, he turned away from the still aloof Chesa toward the approaching woman. She'd lit a new cigarette, its smoke swirling into the air where she waved it about on its longer holder. "Pilla."

Her carriage stopped at the head of a line, presumably waiting for the crowd to clear. He fought the urge to pinch the bridge of his nose. Couldn't the knights have held them back a little longer? *What a mess.*

When he turned back to Chesa, the woman had vanished.

Ancient kings be damned! How dare she leave him with her vague comments and no answers?

"Ignoring me, now?" Pilla asked.

Finn forced a smile. "Of course not. Only Chesa was just here—"

Pilla waved a hand in dismissal. "You know her."

He barely suppressed a sigh. That he did—though no one could claim to truly know the mysterious woman, much less when she might choose to reappear or where.

"But you!" She shoved him playfully. "Riding into the court with our new Alice in tow."

His eyes widened.

"Please. You think I wouldn't notice?" She took another drag on her cigarette and blew it out. "But you don't seem pleased. Did Victoria not promise to reward you properly?" She raised her brows, the implication clear.

He coughed and looked away. "Your friend, the queen, was most generous." If she thought to *reward* him further, he'd endure. His life depended on it.

"Mmm, Alice's Champion," she mused. "Might be a fitting title." Pilla looked him up and down, her interest obvious enough to make his insides recoil.

One advantage to being a favorite of the queen—she didn't share, which Pilla should know since she was a favorite as well. Finn forced a twisted smile, one he often donned at court, that painted him a far more dangerous animal than the rabbit he could become. "Anything for my queen."

The other woman's grin dropped, and she gave a little huff.

"You'll be wanting to say hello to her too, I believe," he added.

She wrinkled her nose and turned away. "Indeed."

A sigh slipped from his lips. Now, if only he could become something useful like a hawk and fly away—far, far away.

18

*E*liza flopped onto the bed, exhaustion pulling her into the cushioned mattress. All motivation to do anything other than curl up into a ball and sleep vanished. She couldn't even find the will to shed her clothes or wash away the makeup painted on her face, especially as the first pulses of an oncoming headache built behind her eyes.

Each of the handful of days she'd had since she arrived at the Red Court had been the same. First, there'd been sitting awkwardly in the throne room between the king and queen while citizens came to gawk at their new Alice as if she was some type of prize or work of art to be displayed. *What nonsense!* She'd been excited for the tour of the city, but with the wall of knights keeping the crowds at bay and the queen's too-tight grip on her arm, she'd seen little and enjoyed even less of it.

It was like being stuck at one of the society parties her parents loved, only she was the center of everyone's focus, unable to slip away to a quiet corner. The attention made her skin crawl. The faked smiles and too-bright laughter chaffed her nerves, especially the queen's. She could pretend to be the kind and bubbly monarch all she wanted, but Eliza had a lifetime of experience seeing past the masks people wore. Beneath, she was just as bad as many of the society women back home, and the marks on Eliza's arm where the queen's nails had dug in when she'd lingered too long in parts of the city proved it. There was no genuine kindness there, whatever glittering show she put on.

The king's not-so-subtle interest didn't help matters. The queen didn't care, but Eliza did. Fair he may be, but she was not one for sharing lovers, as these monarchs so obviously were. Worse, he was otherwise aloof and seemed to turn a blind eye to whatever his wife did, whether kicking a servant when her tea was too cold or threatening another with beheading when they dared drop the smallest bit of food on her sleeve at dinner.

Not an idle threat, especially from what Chesa had told her in the gardens. Eliza hadn't seen the strange woman no matter how often she'd looked, though there was another face she searched for even more often.

Finn was never far from her thoughts, no matter how much her voice of reason told her she shouldn't search for him. But she hadn't seen him. Not once. A few times, she thought she may have glimpsed him, only to turn and discover it a trick of her mind or wishful thinking.

Searching for him herself? Out of the question. Guards were assigned to watch her at all times, for her protection, they insisted. *Right...* Most often it was the Tweeds, or that's what everyone called the identical twins who shared everything, even a name—*who named both their children the same thing?* They were nice enough, if not the sharpest of men, but the constant supervision when she stepped outside her rooms rankled.

Though she hadn't seen Finn, she'd heard about him plenty. A skilled warrior, good-natured, and well-liked. One of the queen's favorites. Her stomach twisted into knots, what little food she'd managed to eat over dinner sloshing precariously.

That kiss haunted her every thought.

How could he desire such a horrible woman? Did he? Or maybe he didn't have a choice, but why hadn't Finn told her that?

Eliza grabbed a pillow, pulled it over her face, and screamed her frustration into the quiet room.

She was just a job to him. Finn delivered her safely here, and now his work was done. Why press through the crowds to meet Alice when he already had?

Did he know she'd asked about him? That she longed to see him? A humorless laugh slipped free as the pillow slid away.

When she'd asked after him, the queen had merely laughed, a dark, bitter sound. The king said he was busy. Lizardo huffed and turned away.

It shouldn't matter. If Finn cared at all, he'd have at least shown his face instead of leaving her alone with these strangers who made her skin crawl.

Eliza summoned the last bit of her energy and sat on the mattress, clutching the pillow to her chest.

"What were you thinking, Grandmama?" she whispered. She could have prepared her, told her something, anything.

Did her grandmother think she was like her parents? That she might like this ridiculous attention and all the vanity and vagary that went with it?

This room had been her grandmother's while she was here, or so the queen said. And it was grand—expansive, well furnished, the perfect gilded cage for their Alice. But nothing about the room reminded her of the grandmother she knew.

But what Eliza knew was old, worn away by time, and blurry at the edges until she wasn't sure if the memories from her childhood were real or dreams.

"I should have visited. Written more often." Maybe then she'd have understood more, been prepared. Though, that still didn't explain Finn.

Eliza squeezed her eyes shut as his face flashed to mind. Her nails dug into the silk-covered pillow. With an exasperated sigh, she flung the pillow. It crashed onto the writing desk, knocking over a wide candle and splattering wax everywhere.

"Saints!" Eliza leaped to her feet and rushed to the mess.

She hadn't had occasion to use the sheets of paper or fancy pens—who would she write to anyway?—but ruining any kind of page with such a stupid display of emotion was criminal in her mind. And the books. A small, pained whimper slipped from her lips as she noticed the splattering of wax along their spines. She'd been so excited to read them whenever she had a moment's peace, and now she'd abused them so.

At least the spill had gutted the flame instead of letting it catch.

Eliza grabbed the most offended book from the neat row and wiped at the wax along its spine, uncaring of the warmth against her skin. "Not too bad. You'll be okay," she promised it.

If anyone heard her, they might think their new Alice was a little daft, but Eliza didn't much care what they thought. Books had a spirit all their own, and she often spoke to them in whispers while she worked—it was better than complete silence.

She gave the spine one more wipe and frowned. It would need more attention once the wax dried. Eliza went to set it aside when something slipped from between the pages and fell to the floor.

Her brows pinched as she stared at the folded paper. Following her curiosity, she set the book aside and picked it up. Eliza often found little notes stuck in books. Sometimes they were notations about the work itself. Others were leftover scribblings someone forgot to remove before returning it. She expected more of the same, so when she flipped open the page and saw her name scrawled across the top, her legs nearly gave out.

No one in Wonderland called her Eliza—no one except for Finn. But she'd seen his balanced, slanted writing in his notebook. This was different, with far more loops and flourishes. And it started the same way as so many other letters she'd received over the years.

Tears stung the corners of her eyes. *Grandmama.*

On unsteady feet, she wandered back to the bed and sat before reading the letter.

Dearest Eliza,

> *I so wish I could be there with you right now. To see you again and hold you in my arms. Better yet, I wish I could have prepared you for all that you must endure. It must seem strange to you, this world. I told you some about it as a child, but it was years ago, before your father put a stop to your staying with me. How I loathed that. But there is no time for regrets anymore. You're here. You're the next closest woman of my blood, the next Alice. And maybe you can be the last if you're able to break the curse.*

Curse! What curse? Eliza jolted, nearly dropping the page before reading on.

Many in Wonderland don't see it that way. Alice brings peace. Alice brings stability. But not for Alice herself. We're bound here, far from home, forced to choose or let the people and the land war until only death reigns.

I tried that. I tried not to choose, and the horrors it wrought were unspeakable. You must choose, my dear, unless you can break it. No curse is absolute. All magic has a weakness, a loose thread, as it were. And if you pull just right, the entire thing will unravel.

Do what I could not. Find the thread, Eliza. You deserve to be free, to live your life as you would. I hope you've done that, my dear girl. I hoped that without the knowledge of what awaited you, what life until now was yours and yours alone.

But be aware, the courts may not want the curse removed. They would stop you if they knew what you attempt, because to remove it brings change. Red has its faults, but they are kinder than White in their way. Chesa will help you.

Eliza nearly snorted. She hadn't seen the strange woman in days, and little she'd said made any sense.

I've commanded Finneas to see you into Wonderland. He's not like most of the others, but that may be best. I have a feeling—

Eliza turned the page, but the other side was blank. There had to be more. She rushed back to the book, flipped open the cover, fingered through the pages, then shook the thing—much to her shame. Still, no more hidden notes appeared.

She grabbed at the next book and the next until a pile of books lay on the ground, all devoid of her grandmother's words.

"Damn." She scrubbed her hands down her face as she sank into the desk chair. The rest of it must have gotten lost, probably sometime in between when her grandmother left and she arrived. The room had been spotless when she arrived, and the careful attention of maids any time she left the room kept it that way. Could they have found it?

She chewed at her bottom lip and glared at the darkness outside the window. Any inquiries would have to wait for dawn. Deep inside, she knew this was something she couldn't ask the monarchs about. The warning on the page was a clear enough indication of that.

Eliza ran a tentative hand along the edge of the note. A curse, one the royals wouldn't want broken. If they'd known of this letter, they never would have let her get her hands on it, that she was sure of.

Eliza read over the letter again.

What did you want to tell me about Finn, Gran?

Is he my ally? She sighed. Once, she'd have agreed, but that was before he dropped her on the city doorstep to kiss his queen without telling Eliza anything about what she was walking into or his personal relationship. Her cheeks heated. Not that it was her business.

Eliza refolded the letter and clutched it like a precious talisman in her palm. If only she had the rest.

She pinched the bridge of her nose. "Chesa and Finn, huh?" she whispered.

But first, she had to find them again.

19

*F*inn should have stayed in his burrow. That was the only thought racing over and over through his head as he reclined in his chair, boots on the table, and listened to Lizardo fret over the activity of the White knights in the Red Court's territory.

It was pleasant in his little rabbit hole. Quiet, warm, and smelling of rich soil. Too bad he'd never bothered to make it human-sized and could only hold his alternative shape for so long before the drain of the magic became too much.

He didn't often retreat to that secret space under the courtyard of the royal manor. Only when he desperately needed a break from everything or to evade the queen when she was in one of her moods—lusty or furious. But ever since his return, it was the only place he wanted to be. Far from the royals. Far from talk of the new Alice. And somewhere he couldn't accidentally catch a glimpse of her that would have him drowning his sorrows in his favorite red wine.

He'd had a few—glimpses of her and bottles of wine—over the past few days. She still looked at the world with wonder...sometimes. Others, she just seemed distant or bored, rather like he was while waiting for the king to arrive.

Perhaps he'd been a coward, hiding away after promising to keep her safe and eventually return her home. He hadn't lied…exactly. She was safe and returning her home now would be disastrous for all of Wonderland. It was better that way. Easier. He'd never focused on much other than his own wants and desires, why should a new Alice change all that?

The plan had been to slip out, grab more wine from the kitchens, and retreat again, but no, Lizardo just had to find him in the hallway and insist Finn join their little meeting with other high-ranking knights. The others didn't much like him, but his magical skills were too strong for the king to ignore. Servitude in the royal army, protecting the Red Court, was a condition of offering him sanctuary and letting him lead an otherwise errant life of drinking wine, sketching, and trying to stay atop the shifting sands of court politics and royal favor.

Better than losing his head to one set of monarchs or the other.

Finally, King Jasper entered the room, his current lover by his side. Finn quickly slipped his boots from the table and righted himself in the chair. Others in the room drew quiet and bowed their heads in acknowledgment.

The king dropped into his usual chair at the head of the table and waved a ring-decked hand through the air. "Well, what is it?"

Sometimes the king showed more enthusiasm over dinner than he did threats to the court. Though, such threats were rare when Alice decided who ruled. The last Alice had reigned long, with both she and the one before choosing the Red Court for the duration of their reign. Red ruled Finn's entire life, and the king's life for that matter. White had not ruled in living memory, likely why they marshaled their troops now. The White Court didn't just want Alice, they needed her.

Finn's nails dug into his palm. They would never get their hands on her. The White Court, and that bastard, King Alvar, would destroy her. Maybe not in body, but in soul. Finn fought the urge to rub at the ache in his chest. Alvar had much practice in cruelty. For all that the Red Court was eccentric, White was cold and callous.

"It's the White knights, Your Highness." Lizardo bowed before taking his seat. "They've been more aggressive in their pursuit of Alice than we anticipated."

Eliza. Finn corrected silently. She was more than Alice, more than some piece on a game board to be shown off and then hidden away. Though wasn't that what he'd done? Tuck her away in the Red Court for safe keeping? True, he'd thought to do otherwise for a moment there, but in the end he'd been a coward, handing her over and then hiding himself away.

"Yes, and we sent scouts to the northern wood to get a measure of their movement." The king waved his hand in the air, his disinterested gaze panning the room. He hadn't always been so aloof. When Finn first met him, he was the opposite—a younger man at his peak, full of life, and brimming with excitement. Somehow, the years had snuffed that spark out of him.

Lizardo swallowed and shifted in his seat. Finn sat a little straighter in his, the wine in his too-empty stomach suddenly foul. "They have not returned."

The king stilled. All the air in the room seemed to be sucked from it in an instant.

"Only…" The captain looked to the man at his side. "Well, show him."

The younger man visibly paled as he rose, clutching the box in his hands as if his life relied on not dropping it. The polished wood, so pale it resembled bleached bone, told Finn everything.

A warning from White. A threat.

The young man set the box on the table and removed the lid. The king rose in one sharp movement, his chair tipping over and clattering to the floor behind him.

A bloody heart lay within—a human heart by its size. Stabbed through its center was a small silver sword. One of the guards gave a choked sound and fled—hand over his mouth. Others cursed. Even Finn couldn't contain the expletives that spewed forth. But his worry wasn't only for the Red Court, and the obvious threat to their rule—their symbol, or the organ on which it was based—presented so violently. His worry was for Eliza and the role she unwittingly played in the assault.

Only King Jasper remained stone-faced and silent, glaring down at the offending gift. A closer look showed a small piece of paper secured on a little tuft of white. Well, it was white, until blood from the punctured heart soaked into its base leaving a grizzly stain.

The foul gift contained a message.

Short. Simple. To the point.

So very White Court that Finn could guess the words before the king snatched the tiny scroll from the box and read it aloud.

"Deliver Alice before her ascension or suffer the fate of your scouts."

inn propped his elbows on the railing as he looked out over the training yard and the squadrons of warriors amassing together, each led by a high-ranking knight.

Not him, though. His lips pursed as he watched them forming into ranks, each person barely the size of a bug from his perch on the balcony high up in the manor's towers. The king wanted him close. Finn wasn't foolish enough to think it some gesture of affection, even if the man had taken him in and named him his ward all those years ago. Finn turned his palm up and willed the magic flowing through him to coalesce and dance in the air, a shimmering ball of raw power. *That* was why he was ordered to stay close. A last defense if the worst should happen.

King Jasper might be disinterested in war these days, but he was no fool about it. Why waste your best weapons in the field when you could have them guarding your side and your most precious treasure?

Eliza.

Finn snapped his palm into a fist, disbursing the magical show. He should be thankful for the command to stay close. It meant he'd be closer to *her*. But it also kept him sitting on his hands, idle, as he so often was. Waiting for what? Time ticked on, and by the time the king let him fight, it might already be too late. The desire to rush into battle had anticipation spiking through him. He could do something—anything, even just release some pent-up frustration. Perhaps that would compensate for his cowardice in delivering Eliza as ordered. Not to mention he'd be farther from the queen…

But no, life was never so kind to him.

"Enjoying the view?"

He whirled toward the voice at his back, spying a grinning Chesa. The racing of his heart slowed in recognition. Not a threat. Though he never could decide whether to consider her a friend. She dressed in Red Court fashion with a long gown of yellow that accented her dark skin and vibrant hair—it held more streaks of pink than last he'd seen it. The woman changed her hair almost as often as she changed clothes, though rumor said she never aged and looked exactly the same as she had decades ago.

"Haven't seen you around much," he replied, ignoring her question.

"You haven't been around to see me." Her head tilted to the side. "Or anyone else."

Finn's nose twitched. The woman knew way too much. He turned away from her, back to the sight below. However, she didn't leave as he'd hoped. Instead, she took the space next to him, gazing with her curious eyes at everything and nothing.

"You want to be with them." Chesa glanced meaningfully at the warriors training in the yard.

"The king ordered me to stay here." *How do you know that?* Was what he really wanted to ask, but he knew better than to expect her to answer anything about her mysterious ways.

"You make him happy," Chesa said.

Finn snorted. The woman really was crazy if she thought that. "Wine makes him happy. And his lovers."

Chesa's head tilted to the side. "Acts to fill an endless hole. His true love is dead."

True love? "Who?" Not the queen, that he knew. Their marriage was purely political. The queen descended from the royal line, but lacked any real magic. Hence why she took a husband with powerful magic from one of the noble families. It may also have been the reason King Jasper ignored his wife's atrocities. His position might still be precarious after all these years.

"Loss leaves its scars," Chesa said, ignoring his question. "But sometimes they take years to show."

Chesa gestured toward the soldiers. "You want to be there, but you're needed here."

He rolled his eyes. "To fix the king's broken heart?" Not a chance. The man was the closest thing he had to a father, and thankfully the king had never shown the slightest interest in him that way either.

"No," Chesa replied. "Alice needs you here."

His breath hitched. Finn snapped around toward the manor at his back as if he could somehow find her through the walls. "She's in danger?"

"Not presently." With her nonchalant tone, Chesa could have been discussing the weather rather than the fate of Wonderland.

"But she will be," he said, offering a carrot for her to grasp. The warmth of the sun was nothing against the sudden chill from within.

"The ink is not dry. The future unset."

Finn's teeth ground together. "Tell me what you know. Tell me how to keep her safe." He'd promised it. He would do it. A failure at most else he might be, but in this, he would not let Eliza down, not if she really needed him.

Chesa merely blinked at him and smiled. "You see, that's why she needs you."

"She doesn't want me." The confession tasted bitter on his tongue. She hadn't sought him out, hadn't asked after him. *Damn it all.* He'd scraped together the last of his pride in front of the king and dared to ask about her less than an hour ago. All he'd been given was the stinging knowledge that Eliza hadn't asked a thing about him.

"You're a fool, rabbit." Chesa's eyes were clear as he'd ever seen them, her gaze so sharp and intense she may well have peeled him open and looked at his soul.

"You were there the day we arrived." He drew himself up higher. "She turned her back on me the first moment she could."

Chesa smirked.

She's fucking grinning at me.

"After you kissed the queen," she said.

He bared his teeth, something much more feral than a rabbit lurking under his skin. "I didn't want to."

Chesa raised one brow, her smile never dimming. "And does she know that? Does *Eliza*,"—she drew out the name, almost like a caress—"know that? Does she know why you've hidden yourself away in your burrow?"

"She…" *Fuck.* He'd told her little about the queen. He'd been too afraid, too…ashamed. His shoulders drooped. But for her to be bothered by that or offended somehow, he must mean something to her. His stomach knotted in on itself.

Chesa shoved him—hard. Finn stumbled back into the railing. "What the—"

"Eliza needs you if she's to break the curse."

If her previous revelation was shocking, this one shot a bolt of lightning straight through him. "Curse? What curse?"

The woman's vision clouded, and she looked past him, far out to the distant horizon. "Do you think there was always an Alice?"

His brows pinched. Truly, he'd never given it much thought, but now that she mentioned it, the ascension always took place at the shrine of the first Alice.

The first.

"If there's a first. There's a last." The wind snatched up Chesa's voice, drawing it out like an echoing whisper. "She could be free. *You* could be free."

Dark laughter caught in his throat. What a nonsense thing to say. Exiled and wanted dead by one court, honor-bound to serve the other in gratitude for his life. Ward of the king. Favored of the queen. There was no freedom for him, only life in invisible chains or on the run in the wilds.

But it was there, the hope of something more, a terrible spark that never could die out no matter how dark his life got.

And Chesa had just dropped another cloud over him. A curse. Eliza in danger? It was almost enough to kill that spark until she dropped a branch of kindling to that treacherous bit of hope. If it burned brighter, it might consume him, and he'd die in its flames. But maybe he could help Eliza first.

"How can I free her?"

Chesa took her time meeting his demanding gaze. Her eyes blinked rapidly before clearing again. All her sharp features softened as she said. "Maybe she was right, choosing you. I think. Maybe."

His fist tightened in impatience. "Who?"

The horizon drew her focus again. "Alice."

"The former or the current?" Damn confusing woman.

Chesa leaned on the railing. The breeze caught at the ends of the short hair falling to her neck. "She searches in the library. A lover of books, that one. She's had many interesting conversations with them."

Finn fought the urge to tap his foot, all but ready to shake Chesa to get a clear answer from her when she said, "But what she needs isn't there right now." She glanced over one shoulder at him and grinned before vanishing from sight.

She needs you. A voice whispered in his head. Chesa, his own thoughts, someone else? He had no idea, but it no longer mattered. He had to get to the library.

20

The queen's goons waited outside the doors to the library. Eliza was in there all right. He'd heard the Tweeds were ordered to stay by her side at all times, and the brief glimpse he'd had of her the other day confirmed that.

It should be me.

The Tweeds might have more brawn than the average guard, especially put together, but they were always a bit lacking in the brains department. Unfortunately, they weren't dumb enough to let him in without an argument. He pursed his lips and slipped back behind the bend in the hall. At best, they'd alert Eliza of his presence, and though he yearned to see her, he still couldn't fully believe she felt the same about him. She might send him away without ever speaking to him, and then where would he be?

If she was in danger, or might be soon, as Chesa alluded, he had to regain her trust. That started with talking to her.

A distraction might work. Something small. Not enough that they'd rush Eliza away to safety, but something to tug their attention from the doors long enough for him to slip through unseen.

If anyone else lingered on the other side, he'd have to deal with that when the time came.

Finn glanced around the corner once more. It was a good thing most of the court was too obsessed with planning and preparations for the upcoming ball to honor Alice to spend much time in this wing. At the other end of the hall loomed a stately marble bust of a former queen whose beauty was only rivaled by her love of books—pity this one would have to go. At least there were other tributes to the former monarch.

A small sparkle of magic collected in his hand. It wouldn't take much. One well-placed marble of energy was all he'd need.

One of the Tweeds' heads bobbed forward before jolting upright. *Falling asleep on the job, huh? This should wake him up.*

Finn sent the tiny orb zipping down the hall. It struck the side of the bust. The marble sculpture tilted, wobbled. Then it fell, shattering across the stone floor and spraying debris in myriad directions. The Tweeds startled and rushed toward the disaster, just as he expected.

No sooner had they left their post than Finn shifted into his alternate form and darted toward the library door with his unnatural speed. Being a rabbit was terribly convenient sometimes. He slid just before the door, letting his backside careen into the wood and knock it slightly ajar. A second later, he was through. A solid kick closed it behind him.

His ears twitched as he raised on his hind legs to better see the room. The cluster of chairs and settees near the door was blessedly absent of life, as were the nearby shelves.

Another twitch of his ears, and then he heard the sound he sought— the slight scrape of one book against another as something was pulled from a shelf, followed by the softest, gentlest sigh.

"You're not in the right place either," Eliza said, somewhere out of sight.

Just the sound of her voice made his little heart race like it might burst. Between the scent of books and the lingering cocktail of perfumes clinging to the seats from their long-past occupants, he could just make out her scent. He homed in on it with his rabbit senses, let it consume him and carry him off in a way that even the strongest wine couldn't. Finn's head swam, and he almost forgot why he was there, almost let himself drift off into a pleasant trance.

The gentle tap of Eliza descending a ladder slipped through the air, followed by a soft thump. Curiosity drew him closer. Either she hadn't heard the sculpture shatter or was too absorbed in whatever she did to mind.

Finn crept along the floor past the first few rows of shelves until he caught sight of her through an empty space where a book or two may once have rested on the lowest shelf. He wedged himself into the hole for a better look. The baby blue skirts of Eliza's dress swished around her ankles as she ascended the ladder once more to reach the highest shelves. Small stacks of books occupied the space around the ladder's base.

"Ridiculous," she said, scowling at the shelves and adding a book to the nearly bare top shelf. Eliza tucked a wayward piece of hair behind her ears, the motion so natural but so enticing that Finn couldn't draw his focus away, even as the strand tried its best to slip out of place again. What he wouldn't give to touch it.

Eliza lifted another book, flipped open the cover, and thumbed through the pages. With another sigh, she shook her head. "How is anyone supposed to find you if you're in the wrong place?" she asked the book.

Ah. His nose twitched. *Organizing the library?* Though Chesa had said she searched for something. Perhaps she'd been lurking among the shelves, too, watching Eliza work her way through one book and then the next. Yes, she searched, but more than that, she was calm, at peace. She...fit.

Watching Eliza stretch on her toes upon the ladder rung to select a worn leather-bound book off the shelf was as natural as the green-tinted horizon. In their days of travel, he'd never seen her so relaxed, so at ease. She certainly hadn't been that way when they arrived, nor when he caught a glimpse of her during her tour of the Red Court.

This was a dance of sorts, a quest for perfection that the Red Court library could never satisfy. No one had told Eliza that the books liked to rearrange themselves at night. No one really knew why or how they might choose to align themselves. Each day was a surprise. It was why none of the shelves were labeled. If anyone bothered, it would all be wrong the next day anyway.

All Eliza's careful work would vanish with the rising of the sun tomorrow.

He should tell her, save her the time and trouble. But watching her was the most pleasure he'd had in days.

"You!"

Finn jumped, his ears smashing against the top of the shelf. But Eliza wasn't looking at him. She scowled at the book in her hand. "I swear I shelved you yesterday." She pinched the bridge of her nose, her careful balance on the ladder the only thing keeping her from tumbling off. Finn made to move to steady her, only belatedly realizing he was still a rabbit and scurrying back into his hiding spot.

"A duplicate?" she asked the book before flipping open the cover. "No, bloody hell, you have a stamp like the other one." She stopped her foot, sending Finn's nerves fraying. "If someone moved all my hard work..." Eliza shook her head, tucked the book under her arm, and turned back to examine the others on the shelf.

Experienced in such precarious situations or not, he couldn't leave her in an unsteady perch. Even if she didn't want to speak to him, he could hold the books for her.

Finn hopped out from the shelf and transformed back into his human self. Sometimes the change was uncomfortable, a stretching and pulling of the body and soul. But with his gaze glued to the woman in front of him, none of that mattered. He expected his racing heart to slow and her scent to stop addling his senses like the strongest drug. But somehow, her nearness in this form only made it worse.

"Eliza," he said, just the barest whisper to get her attention.

A mistake. Finn expected Eliza to pause, hand on the spine of a book, and glance over her shoulder at him. He should have known better. This woman never did what he anticipated.

Eliza shrieked, spinning around so fast that a book flew out of her hands. It whizzed straight past his head to slam into the shelf behind him. The ladder tipped precariously on one leg. The other book she'd tucked close dropped to the floor as her arms flew out to balance herself.

Too little, too late.

Finn lunged forward and grabbed Eliza as her heel slipped from the rung. She fell into his arms, her chest slamming against his. The momentum sent them tumbling backward, and it took every bit of Finn's concentration to shelter her in the cradle of his arms and brace for the impact of the fall. His shoulder slammed the shelf, adding a groan to Eliza's lingering shriek. A book fell loose and whacked him on the head just as they tumbled onto one of her piles of misplaced books stacked on the floor.

21

*K**ings of old, what a horrible idea.* Finn's head throbbed and spun, but he held something precious in his arms—a woman he feared might be lost to him.

"Finn?" she squeaked.

Eliza's face loomed inches from his. She straddled his body, warm and solid atop him. Though his perch was far from ideal, with a book digging into his back and bruises already making themselves known, it had been days since he'd been so comfortable.

More of her brown hair had fallen free from where she'd pulled it back, and it hung over her shoulders, brushing his cheek. He wanted nothing more than to tuck it behind her ear and tug her closer against his chest. Or better yet, maybe discover what those perfect strawberry lips tasted like. But he didn't dare breathe, much less move, for fear of shattering the moment.

Her brows drew together. Her lips parted as if she planned to speak but lost the words. Whatever she might have said vanished as the doors to the library burst open.

Finn groaned, and his head fell back to thump against the floor. *The Tweeds. Of course.*

"Alice!" One of them called.

Thundering footsteps headed their way. There wasn't time to right themselves before the twins barreled to their row.

"Are you all right?" they asked at the same time. "What happened?" one added.

Eliza all but leaped to her feet, pushing at her hair and brushing at her skirts as if the situation were far more scandalous than the truth. "I'm fine."

Thank goodness for that.

"Wobbly ladder. That's all," Eliza said. She bent to pick up one of the fallen books, completely ignoring him on the ground.

Finn couldn't summon the urge to move. One brief moment, one word. That's all he got before she ignored him again. And now her faithful guards were here to drag him away.

"You," one of them scowled.

Finn raised his head just enough to see the two large men staring at him in confusion.

"The library was empty. How did you get here?"

As if he'd tell them about his little destruction of property in the hall. Finn tucked his hands behind his head and summoned an easy smile to his lips. "Been here for hours."

Finally, Eliza turned his way, an unreadable expression on her face.

One of the twins snorted. "Out. No one disturbs Alice."

"I caught Alice. Or would you rather she tumbled into the shelves?" He drew up one knee and braced the other ankle over it, a far more casual posture than he felt, especially with that damn book under his back still poking at his spine.

Eliza's eyes narrowed as if to say, *"You're the reason I fell."* But she held her tongue.

One of the twins merely grunted. "Come on, rabbit."

The insult struck him like a hot poker. He snapped up into a sitting position, teeth slightly bared. It was one thing coming from Chesa, but these two? *How dare they...*

"He can stay."

Finn's mouth dropped open. The fury of moments ago died in an instant.

"But Alice—"

Eliza snapped her impassive gaze from him to the twins. "He was helping me before I fell."

The lie rolled so smoothly off her tongue that even he almost believed it.

"Besides," she continued. "Who found me, protected me, and brought me to court? If Finneas intended me harm, don't you think he'd have done so already?"

Finn's brows arched toward the ceiling. What an unexpected turn of events. However, the use of his full name fluttered between them like an awkward bird with a broken wing.

The twins looked at one another. One rubbed the back of his neck.

"Well?" Alice asked. Her foot tapped a steady rhythm on the floor.

When they still didn't answer, she waved them off. "You're disturbing my work. Now go."

The burly men retreated like scolded hounds with their tails between their legs, uttering no more than a whispered grumble in unison, "Yes, Alice."

Neither he nor Eliza moved until the library door clicked closed once more. Even then, Finn couldn't bring himself to break the weighty silence, especially since Eliza still stared toward the doors. He could read little of her expression in the slight profile of her face visible to him.

"What are you doing here, Finn?" Eliza's whispered words were delicate and thin, like glass about to shatter.

He dared not move for fear of cracking the fragile thing between them. "I'm here to help you. As you said."

"Sneaking up behind me and scaring me half to death is helping?" Finally, she turned toward him, the barest hint of a smile on her face.

He shoved to his feet. "I didn't mean to. I...I saw things going differently."

A sigh left her, and she shrunk in, clutching her arms around herself. Her gaze cut away. "So did I."

The sorrow etched between her pinched brows said her words had little do with a fall from the ladder. The tension hovering between them was almost tangible. The pressure of its weight sat on Finn's chest, heavier than a whole stack of books. "I wanted to check on you and ensure you were okay."

Eliza snorted air through her nose. "Why wouldn't I be?" She looked at him again. "I'm Alice. Protected and guarded at all times before being stuck back in her room like a bird in a cage. How could I be anything but okay?" She spat the last of the words. Eliza's arms fell to her sides, one hand squeezed into a fist.

Now it was his turn to wither. She was a prisoner. A precious and well-kept one, but even a gilded cage has bars. And he brought her here— led her to the door and tossed her in. No wonder she was cold toward him.

"I'm sorry, Eliza. I did what I had to, but I might be able to help you get free."

"Oh yes, what you had to. That's what you call passing me off as soon as you could? Giving over your burden to others so you could go kiss your queen?"

The accusation stung like a slap to the face. "I didn't want to." A shiver of magic rolled under his skin, a beast in its own cage yearning to be unleashed.

Eliza rolled her eyes and looked away. Suddenly, the distance between them was too much. The mere feet filled with words left unsaid. Finn moved in a blink to stand in front of her. Eliza gasped, stepping back, and he let her retreat. But she didn't go far, just a step, and one sharp breath before she stared up at him with wide eyes.

"I didn't want to kiss her, Eliza. I don't want her. I never have. But I have no choice." It was treason to speak the words, damnation if anyone were to hear him. But she needed to know. She *had* to know. "If I displease her, it'll be my head that rolls, do you understand? I know what it's like to be trapped here. Safe, alive, pampered, but a prisoner all the same."

It had been his life for years. A ward of the king, one of his esteemed knights, and the queen's favorite. It afforded him all the luxuries he could want: the finest rooms, expertly tailored clothes, and all the vintage wine he could drink. But one offense, one step out of line, and he could become the next victim of the queen's temper.

Eliza's lip wobbled as her expression shattered. "Finn..." She reached for him before letting her hand drop and pinching her eyes shut. "I didn't know." Unshed tears glimmered in her eyes when she opened them.

Those salty bits of water snapped something in him. Before he could think, he crossed the short space between them and pulled Eliza into his arms, cradling her head against his chest. *This is where she belongs*, his traitorous heart whispered. But that little voice was wrong. She didn't belong with him. She didn't belong in Wonderland at all.

"There may be a way to free you. To get you out of here."

Eliza stiffened in his arms.

"Chesa said it's a curse that brings Alice to Wonderland," he rushed on before he could think better of it. "There was a first, and there can be a last. You could be the last."

She squirmed against him, just enough to look up at him while staying in the cradle of his arms. "My grandmother left a letter. It said the same thing."

"Alice left you a letter?" Now that was a surprise. To risk putting something like that in words wasn't like Alice, but then, the more he learned, the more he was certain he knew nothing about Alice and what she was forced to endure.

Eliza nodded. "She said Chesa would help me, but I've hardly seen her. And you..." She trailed off, swallowing visibly.

What about me? But when she didn't continue, he said, "Chesa sent me here. She said I could help you. What are you searching for?" *Figures the flighty woman would ignore her charge as Alice's protector.* Though, as Chesa had said herself, Eliza wasn't anointed as Alice, not yet anyway.

With a look to the shelves, Eliza drifted from his arms, leaving an ache in the space she vacated. She ran her fingers lovingly across the spines of the books. "Anything to help me understand the curse or the previous Alices. It's part of history. There must be something."

One would think. But so many things where Alice was concerned made little sense. Chesa said what Eliza sought wasn't in the library but where else—

The doors to the library groaned open. Finn whirled toward the sound, stepping in front of Eliza.

One of the Tweed's voices flooded in. "You can't disturb—"

"Nonsense."

Pilla. Finn's jaw stiffened. Nothing good followed the sound of her voice.

"Lady Pilla—" One of the twins stumbled after her into the room.

"As I told you, the queen sent me."

Every muscle in his body drew taut. He'd managed to avoid the queen since his return. Did Pilla come for him?

"Alice, dear?" Pilla called, her voice unnaturally pleasant.

The relief he expected didn't come. The thought of Eliza stuck with these vultures of women set his teeth on edge. Eliza merely sighed, shaking her head as she stepped to his side and gave him a tight smile.

Finn grabbed her hand, the act so sudden he forgot what he planned to say, to do. A spark of something slid up his arm from where they touched, tingling under his skin. The slight gape of her lips and widening of her eyes mirrored his own.

Don't go. He mouthed.

It was stupid. She had to go to the queen.

Her fingers tightened on his, brief and comforting, and then they were gone. The sharp rap of footsteps he'd somehow missed drew closer, louder, deafening, as Pilla rounded the shelves.

A wave of her hand showed off her lit cigarette on its long holder before she burst into sight with her billowing skirts that bore a jarring combination of red and lime green.

"Smoking in a library?" Eliza scolded in a low whisper.

Finn's lips quirked up in one corner. Leave it to Eliza to worry about the books.

"There you are, dear." Fleeting disdain washed across Pilla's features as she took in Eliza.

"Lady Pilla," Eliza gave a respectful nod in the woman's direction.

"The queen sent me to fetch you for your final dress fitting. Wouldn't want to keep her waiting."

Finn barely held back a snort. *No, best not to do that.*

Pilla slid her gaze to him. "You've been strangely absent." She took a drag on her cigarette and blew a puff of smoke toward some unsuspecting tomes.

A small squeak slipped from Eliza, almost a strangled sound, as she stared down the offending cloud.

"I'm sure our queen would like a word with you as well, Finneas," Pilla continued.

His heart dropped into his stomach.

"Surely not at a dress fitting," Eliza said smoothly, batting away the smoke. "It wouldn't be proper for Finneas to see me like that anyway, don't you agree?" She slipped her arm through Pilla's, smiling up at the woman before cutting her gaze to him.

"Yes, well—" Pilla stammered, suddenly straight and stiff.

"We shouldn't keep her majesty waiting. Besides, I'm eager to see how the dress she commissioned came together."

The tight pinch of her cheeks said she was anything but excited about the dress. Eliza did this for him. A reprieve, if only a temporary one.

"I'll look for that book you wanted." Finn dipped a bow toward Eliza, his focus never leaving her face. *I'll help you. Find me here.* All the things he couldn't say, he threw into that look.

The softest touch of color raced to her cheeks. "Th-thank you, Finneas. That would be lovely."

The slight crack in her voice nearly undid him. There was hope.

She blinked rapidly before turning to Pilla once more. "Shall we?"

Without a backward glance, Eliza left, her guards trailing behind.

22

*E*liza barely heard two words Pilla said as they walked the halls of the manor to the queen's quarters, the Tweeds trailing just a few steps behind.

Finn hadn't abandoned her as she'd feared. He wasn't in love with the queen.

Dizzying hope turned all her surroundings into a colorful blur. She'd tried to deny how much she'd missed him, to push it away and focus on more important things—when someone wasn't dragging her around the Red Court, and a headache didn't threaten to split her head in two. Not that people here let her do much, even if she was supposed to be their precious Alice. She'd been close to begging just to get time in the library. In so many ways, these people were just like her parents and their friends. They wanted a smiling woman of good manners to sit on her cushioned seat and look pleasant. Nothing more.

There may be a way to free you.

Finn wanted to help her, or so he said, but an undeniable truth shone in his eyes when he spoke to her. An honesty she rarely saw. That offer was as much a wondrous revelation as the one about him not being in love with the horrible queen.

The bars of her cage suddenly didn't stifle her quite so much, though she still longed to be free of it. Maybe there was a chance. Maybe—

A riot of sound startled her from her daydream as Pilla led her through a set of grand double-doors. A gaggle of women stood in an expansive, lavish sitting room dotted with gaudy crimson furnishings her mother would love. The queen stood at their center, a commanding presence, though she was shorter than many of the colorfully dressed courtiers around her. The wide skirts of her crimson gown fanned out to her sides. She had a certain intensity that could make even the most stalwart person feel like a mouse about to be preyed upon by a cat at play.

It took an effort to keep her face neutral and her steps even—not that Pilla would have let her falter or turn and run. The other woman would drag her into the room with an iron grip if it pleased her queen.

Queen Victoria fanned herself with a black lace fan, her grin growing sharp as Eliza entered the room. "There's our dear, Alice."

Eliza's hands tightened into fists. This woman kept Finn as her play thing. Eliza's flickering smile fell. Instantly, the queen's eyes narrowed. *Blast it.* Thankfully, Pilla took that moment to drop into a curtsy, dragging Eliza with her. A shuddering exhale slipped from Eliza's lips as she dipped her attention to the floor. She should know better than to let her hate show. Hadn't she had years of disguising that very thing at the endless stream of social events and lessons she attended while at boarding school?

Eliza forced a pleasant smile as she rose, adding a little brightness to her eyes as she gazed at the queen as if she were pleased to be in her presence. She could muster this, just like old times. After all, her fury would serve no one, least of all Finn.

He wanted to free her, yet, he was more trapped than she. Bitter emotion stung at the corner of her eyes, trying to form an errant tear, but Eliza blinked it away.

"Alice is so eager to see her gown for the ball," Pilla said, releasing Eliza's arm.

The queen's momentary irritation fled. Her head tilted to the side. "Is she?"

"Oh yes, Majesty." She snuffed the end of her cigarette in a dish of sand. "She said so herself, didn't you, dear?"

Eliza dipped the tiniest curtsy once more. "Yes, Majesty. I look forward to it."

"Well then." The queen drew two fingers to her mouth and let out a sharp whistle.

Another group of women lingering near the far wall jumped to attention, rushing forward with arms full of fabric. The queen's courtiers flooded forward like a human tide. None too carefully, they led Eliza to a stool placed amid large mirrors, all the while crooning and cooing over her like hens.

Eliza loathed the false interest, the hands touching her that nearly made her skin crawl, but she could weather this storm. After all, it was nothing new, not really.

"Take off your dress, dear." The queen ordered from just outside the swarm.

"My—my dress?" Eliza stuttered, cheeks suddenly aflame. She gasped as someone pulled at the ties at her back.

"So modest," the queen laughed. Other women echoed her, still pawing at her clothes. "Of course, how else would we see your gown?"

She'd changed in front of her classmates many times in the school dorms. She'd lain with lovers. Even the maids here helped her dress at times. It wasn't like no one had seen her nude, but somehow this was different, invasive, where the rest had been natural.

There'd be no escape. The queen always got her way. Even Alice was no better than a puppet ripe for her ministrations, or so the woman clearly believed.

Such a tyrant wouldn't be conquered by force. Eliza cut her gaze to Pilla, who lit another cigarette. But some could claim her confidence, it seemed. She had no interest in becoming the queen's lover, but a feigned friendship, perhaps? If anyone were to know the history of Alice, it should be the queen.

Eliza pulled her hair in front of her, fully baring her back. "Help me, ladies?" she asked, but all the while, she kept her focus on Victoria. The woman's eyes widened ever so slightly before her grin grew.

She grinned in return, shutting down her panic as the women worked to loosen her dress. The ironic thing Eliza had learned those years ago: she may hate the game, but she was terribly good at playing it.

A few minutes later, the head seamstress had helped her into the gown...if one could really call it that. It didn't lack for fabric. The whole thing weighed enough in the back that Eliza had to stand a little straighter to support the massive crimson bow at the base of her spine and its ribbons, which trailed down to her feet. It'd be a miracle if she could sit comfortably in such a thing, though perhaps she wasn't meant to.

The front was cut much shorter, exposing her legs up to mid-thigh before tapering down into the long length at the back. That alone might have created a scandal back home, but she could tolerate it. It was the top that had her chest burning in an unending flush.

The gauzy material covered her arms, shoulder to wrist, and rose up to her collarbone. But it was far too thin—teasing every curve and shadow of her breasts and doing nothing to hide the soft bud of her nipples. There'd be no underthings, no corset, not with the deep v in the fabric that plunged to her navel, exposing her cleavage and threatening to spill her breasts for all to see.

"It's just like one of my favorites," the queen said as she paced a circle around Eliza. The other women had moved back, giving the monarch space to inspect her creation.

Eliza gasped as Queen Victoria trailed fingers around her middle, her grip tightening before she came to a standstill just behind Eliza, one open palm planted firmly on either side of her chest. With the fine material layered so thinly, she could feel everything, as if the woman touched her bare skin. Eliza didn't dare pull her focus from the mirrors, especially not as the queen looked into them as well, her gaze hooding as her lips quirked up in one corner.

"A perfect dress for our Alice, don't you think?"

The women murmured their agreement.

A sigh caught in Eliza's throat as the queen released her and moved to circle her again. "You'll be radiant on the dais with me. But... Hmm..." She tapped a manicured finger to her lips. "You need some jewelry, something grand. Ladies!" She clapped, sending the women hurrying to the side of the room to gather things the queen had no doubt already selected.

"What do you think, dear?" The queen asked, drawing close.

Eliza trained her attention on the woman's face. From this angle, the slightest glance downward would give her an eyeful of the woman's breasts where they all but spilled out the top of her dress. A conservative choice compared to others she'd seen in the past few days.

"It's quite unlike anything I've ever worn," Eliza answered honestly.

The queen nodded slowly, appeased.

"Are all Alices given such hospitable treatment?"

The queen stopped her pacing, contemplative. If she noticed the bare hint of sarcasm Eliza laced into the words, the woman showed no sign of it. Instead, she said, "I only knew the last. But yes, I think she quite enjoyed it here."

A scoff lodged in her throat. The grandmother she knew? *Hardly.* But then, how well had she really known her? Tightness grew in her chest, and Eliza fought the urge to rub at it. *Not well enough at all.* And she should have, could have. If only she'd written more or visited. She'd stayed away to avoid her parents, been a coward. Her grandmother had deserved better, even if it meant Eliza had to face her parents if they dropped by for a visit—which they would have done if they'd learned of her presence.

The queen grabbed a necklace from a silken pillow and held it up in front of Eliza. "No. Not it." She threw it toward a random woman who scrambled to catch it as another stepped forward bearing her offering.

"Do you know what the previous Alices were like?" Eliza asked. If she was to be the queen's plaything, at least she could make use of the time.

"The previous Alices? Why, they were Alice, of course."

As if that answers anything.

The queen scowled at another necklace and waved it away. Eliza feared the woman wouldn't continue until she said, "They were each wise, that I know for sure, for Alice has sided in favor of the Red Court for generations."

"Is White so horrid?"

The women gasped. One wobbled like she might faint. The queen stilled where she grasped another necklace, ready to lift it from its pillow.

"The White Court?" The queen accented each word.

It was the wrong question to ask. The queen grinned, but she didn't look at Eliza until she lifted the necklace and held the thing by its ends. The short, wide length, dotted with rubies, reminded Eliza of the fancy collars worn by the hounds of one of her father's friends.

"I-I'm sorry, I'm so new here," Eliza said. "I only wished to know more about Wonderland."

"Step down, dear." The queen ordered, ignoring her comment.

Eliza complied, a slight tremor to her step.

The queen advanced until their feet nearly brushed, gazes leveled with one another. Everything in Eliza begged her to look away or flee, but she held steady. This close, she could make out the fine age lines that the queen attempted to hide with her make-up. Victoria huffed a small bit of air through her nose before circling Eliza and fitting the collar-like necklace on her. Eliza swallowed as the weight settled on her skin. The queen trailed her fingers down the front of Eliza's neck as if smoothing the piece into place, but halted, palm still pressed against her skin.

"The White Court," she accentuated the words again, "is the opposite of all we are. Cold. Callous. Plain. Devoid of fun." The queen met Eliza's eyes in the mirror. "You would find no joy there, Alice."

"But here"—she pulled away her hand, and Eliza remembered how to breathe—"You will have all you could ever want and need. Clothes. Jewelry. The finest foods. Lovers, perhaps?" She quirked a brow. "Whatever you desire, we can provide it to you."

Freedom? For me? For Finn?

One look in the queen's eyes was enough to know the answer. She may promise all the worldly goods in her palace, but she would never give her what really mattered. A comfortable cage was still just that.

"All we ask is your loyalty to the Red Court. For you, dear Alice, to let us continue to bring all that our court has to offer to the people of Wonderland."

The surrounding women nodded, down to the last courtier and seamstress.

Eliza swallowed the tightness in her throat. It seemed like so little to ask when she put it that way.

The queen cupped her cheek, drawing close as if they were intimate friends. "You wouldn't want to deprive the people of all this, would you?

You've seen our Court and how we care for them. You don't want them to suffer at the hands of White." The queen shook her head. "You surely can't want that, right?"

"No, of course not," Eliza responded, near breathless.

"I thought not." Victoria patted her cheek before stepping away.

"Your Majesty," Eliza forced the honorific. "What would happen if you hadn't found me?" Not that she had, but the woman seemed to want all the praise no matter who did the work.

The temperature in the room seemed to drop, the lingering quiet full and heavy.

"Disaster." For once, the queen looked almost somber. "If there is no Alice, she cannot choose. If Alice does not choose, we are compelled to fight for control of Wonderland. You, my dear, stop all of that with a single choice." The dark look vanished into a carefully crafted smile. "Don't worry. We won't let it come to that."

The comment was meant to reassure, but it did nothing of the sort. If she fled, if she did not become Alice and choose, the penalty would be bloodshed. And it wouldn't be the sharp queen who bled, not at first anyway. Eliza needed to break the curse, to somehow undo the madness that moved the pieces of this world like players across a game board.

"That'll do for the necklace," the queen said, her tone so light the previous conversation might never have happened. "We need bracelets, rings." The women hurried away again.

"What happened before there was an Alice?"

"Before?" The queen's brows drew together.

"Chesa mentioned there was a first," Eliza continued.

Pilla snorted. Of all the courtiers present, she was the only one not fetching jewelry. Instead, she had stationed herself near the mirrors as if she were one herself. "Half of what she says is nonsense," she said.

Perhaps more. Chesa confused her almost every time she saw her, which was rare enough in itself, but that didn't mean what she said wasn't true, only that they didn't understand it.

"She's Alice's protector, is she not?" Eliza pushed.

"More of a companion." The queen waved her hand as if the

conversation was beneath her. "Though the years have made her mind fragile at best."

"How old is she?"

"Old enough that no one knows. If only we all could be so lucky in our looks," Pilla said, a touch of disdain in her voice. "But if Chesa can't tell you all you wish to know, you surely won't find it searching through that dusty old library with Finneas."

"That's not—" Eliza began to protest. It was exactly what she'd been doing.

"Finneas was in the library? With you?" the queen asked, incredulous.

Oh... Oh no.

The queen's gaze narrowed. "You were alone with him?"

Eliza stepped back, pulse hammering. "I—He wouldn't harm me. He brought me to you, after all, on Alice's orders."

The queen's lips thinned further. The absolute stillness of her form was more horrifying than words. "Out! All of you!"

The force of the order made Eliza flinch back. A few women gasped.

"But, your majesty—" Pilla started.

The queen silenced her with a look. "You too. I wish to be alone. I will select the jewelry myself."

Eliza took another step back, her bare foot landing on a stretch of gauzy material from the obscene bow at her back. "The dress…"

Victoria's turned-up nose wrinkled. "Ladies, take Alice's things to her room and help her change." She clapped her hands together. "Now!"

Everyone hustled to obey, rushing to the door in a wave of women and clothes, even a wide-eyed Pilla. Eliza was just about to the threshold when another order stopped her cold.

"Alice, dear." She drew out the endearment, too sweet to be anything but its own sickly poison.

Eliza's spine stiffened. Her heart tried to climb up her throat as she turned back toward the queen. Her smile was blinding, a sharp contrast to her fury.

"If you see dear Finneas again, please remind him that he's overdue to pay me a visit."

A visit…

The queen's eyes hooded with obvious meaning.

Bile burned the back of Eliza's throat.

"Of course, Your Majesty. I'll tell him." *I'll tell him to run. To flee. To never look back.* If Finn had a way for Alice to escape, perhaps he could take it for himself.

23

*F*inn scowled at another book and forced himself to replace it on the shelf rather than tossing it to the floor. There was no need for order when the library would rearrange itself in the night, but he did it for her, for Eliza. The first book he'd looked at, he'd tossed to the ground, and instant regret had churned through him. Her scolding voice had echoed in the back of his mind, her frown and pinched brows lingered in the corner of his vision. If only she was actually there to reprimand him. He'd scooped the book up with uncharacteristic tenderness, checked it for damage—something he never did, and returned it to its place on the shelf.

Hopefully, she'd come. If she did, a poor, abused book might ruin her mood. He couldn't allow that.

Finn glanced toward the curtained window, the sun's rays slanting in and showing the aging of the day. Perhaps he should have spent his days reading instead of idling away his time sipping wine or sketching the passing clouds. Time had been endless then—infinite, with no urgency. But everything changed when the previous Alice gave him a mission—her last command as Alice—to retrieve her granddaughter. There was never enough time anymore. It pounded like a ticking clock in the back of his mind. *Hurry. Don't be late.*

The day was almost done. The ball would begin in mere hours, and Eliza had yet to appear.

He'd shown up at her door mid-morning, eager to see her, to assure himself of her safety if nothing else. But the Tweeds would not bid him entry.

Alice has a headache, they'd said.

She had so many of them. It was the only reason he accepted their refusal to grant him entry. He'd returned an hour later with a pouch of herbs and a steaming kettle. Long ago, his mother had suffered a similar malady, and the blend had always helped her.

Strangely, he could remember little of his mother anymore, just the basic shape of her face and her hair pale as his. But some things were startling clear all these years later—the warmth of her hug, the way she held him like a precious treasure, the sing-song quality of her voice, and even the blend of herbs he used to gather for her when her headaches struck. His chest tightened at the old memories, the longing that never ceased. She was the only one who'd loved him, and she'd given her life to save his when they'd fled from the White knights and into the wilds.

He should have died there too. He would have if King Jasper hadn't found him and offered shelter.

Finn shook away the memories. None of that would help Eliza. Perhaps the herbs hadn't either since she'd yet to appear, but it was worth a try. Would they make her attend the ball even if she was ill? His fingertips slid from the spine of a book. Sharp nails dug into his palm, nearly drawing blood.

They would. *Damn them.*

Noise from the hall, too muffled to make out, caught his attention. Magic shivered across his skin, his body groaning in pain as he shifted into his rabbit form. The sudden change in height and shape made his head spin.

Find a hiding spot. Get in it.

He bolted for an open nook on a low shelf. Finn couldn't afford to have someone report his presence to the queen. She'd seek him out, of that he had no doubt, and denying her was impossible. The thought of kissing her again, or more, made him ill. It had been one thing when it was only he who suffered. He could handle it. But something about Eliza seeing them together or knowing what transpired made everything worse, even if she now knew it wasn't his choice.

The door cracked open, and his heart kicked up a notch.

"Really, I'll only be a little bit," Eliza said. Her voice was a magic of its own. It made his head swim more than the strongest wine.

"We must ensure your protection, Alice," one of the Tweeds said.

The tap, tap, tap of her foot carried through the space. "Be on with it then."

Finn wedged himself further into the space as the Tweeds made a quick and sloppy pass through the library, ensuring it was empty. His nose twitched. He'd have to have a word with the king about it. Shifters were rare in the Red Court but much more common in White. It'd be too easy for someone—like him—to hide just out of sight. With the White Court's recent threat, Eliza needed better protection. She needed *him*.

Keeping her safe if White grew bold would be worth the queen's attention or ire.

"We'll be right outside, Alice." The Tweeds departed with a click of the door behind them.

"Of course you will," Eliza mumbled, barely a whisper to his acute hearing. A deep sigh followed, then the tread of her shoes across the floor as she ventured further into the library.

"Finn?" The hopeful note in her whisper nearly undid him.

She came for him.

He yearned to leap from the shadows, transform back into himself, and pull her into his arms.

Don't scare her again. A small, rational voice whispered.

Slowly, he hopped out from his nook on the shelf. A sharp intake of breath was the only tell that he'd been spotted. He craned his head upward, gazing at Eliza high above him with one delicate hand over her parted mouth.

A shiver of magic sent his body twisting and popping back to his human form. He didn't mind the twinge of pain or the strange sensation that made his stomach turn in knots. It was an easy price to pay for the woman standing in front of him.

"Finn," she gasped before shaking her head. "I'm not sure I'll ever get used to that."

"Is it so odd?"

She glanced up at him from under her lashes. "Animals don't become humans. Or the other way around. Not where I'm from anyway."

What a boring place the Other Land must be. "It's an uncommon trait, even here, but some of us can."

"Not just you?"

"No, there are others." His half-brother, for one. Finn's throat dried, and he shut out the thought. "How is your headache?" he asked quickly, switching the topic.

Her eyes widened in surprise. "Much better. One of the maids prepared a tea—something pungent and oddly sweet."

"The sweetness comes from the Toadal plant. I'm glad to see that it worked."

Eliza's head tilted to the side. "How did you know I was ill?"

"I came by your room this morning," he admitted, a sudden warmth spreading through his chest at the admission.

"Oh." A slight flush touched her cheek before her gaze cut away.

When she didn't speak again, he continued, "My mother used to suffer as you do. The tea helped her."

Eliza's gaze snapped back to his. "You brought the tea?"

"Yes."

The soft sigh that slipped from her lips nearly undid him. She reached out, fingers grazing his, the touch pricking and sparkling up his arm like magic. "Thank you, Finn. Really." Then her hand was gone, pulled back to her side as if she hadn't meant to touch him, but oh, how he wished she hadn't retreated. "Sometimes, when they come on like that, I'm in bed all day." She dropped her voice low. "Though missing the ball might not have been a terrible thing."

"You don't want to go?" he asked.

She shook her head. "Balls are not to my liking, and the dress..." She pursed her lips. "It's not one I would pick."

A hint of amusement pulled at his lips. "Perhaps I can offer a distraction until then?"

Her gaze swept across him. A pink tongue slipped out to moisten her lips. All thoughts of books vanished in the wake of the look in her eyes. She couldn't possibly want—

Eliza gave her head a little shake. "Yes, we should look while we have time."

Right. For information about Alice. If only she were anyone else in the court, but no, he had to desire Alice, the one woman he shouldn't want. And if they could break the curse, if he could get her away from here and back to her world, she'd be gone—possibly forever.

But she deserved that. He *owed* her that for bringing her here, the former Alice's orders or not.

"I've been searching for books that might be helpful, as I promised," he said quickly to distract his spiraling thoughts. "But I'm afraid I haven't found much that's useful." They were the opposite of useful. In fact, many of the histories and records he'd uncovered were carefully devoid of details about Alice. They included her title, her choice of court, and little else. Some didn't even mention Alice's real name.

Despite their lack of success so far, Finn and Eliza searched through one shelf after another. Eliza removed books, thumbed through them with practiced ease, and replaced them with gentle precision. Finn did the same, though less quickly. Eliza was a master at work among her books.

"You!" She all but shrieked.

Finn jumped to attention, nearly dropping the book in his grasp.

Eliza drew up straight, scowling at the tome she held as if it had personally offended her. A tangle of hair had slipped over one ear, and she pushed it back.

"I swear I came upon this exact book yesterday and the day before." She held the cover open toward him, displaying handwriting written in messy crawl on the inner cover. "It's the same handwriting and everything. Why would someone put the same odd note in the same book three times? I just—Ugh!" She huffed in annoyance.

He didn't mean to smile, but he couldn't help it.

Eliza's scowl deepened and she snapped the book closed. "What *are* you grinning at?"

He bit his lip, trying to get himself under control before he said, "It's almost certainly the same book."

Her head snapped toward the shelves she'd been working at yesterday, three rows over. "But I..." She looked back at him. "It's that popular then? But why would someone move it?"

Oh, Eliza... The grin returned, and this time Finn didn't try to stop it. Rather, he relished the hint of offense and disapproval that crept back over her features. "Eliza..." He plopped the book he held onto a shelf without looking and strode to her.

"Don't *Eliza* me." She drew herself up, her chin notching higher. This was the Eliza he first met, proud and headstrong, not the meek Alice the Red Court tried to shape her into.

He stopped a few feet away and leaned on the edge of a shelf, careful not to trust it to his full weight. "The library of the Red Court rearranges itself each night."

She merely blinked, her mouth dropping open.

"Didn't you wonder why it was so disorganized?"

Various emotions flickered in broad display across her face. Her lips closed, then parted again. "Bloody hells!" She stomped her foot. "So all that work I did the other day was for nothing?"

He nodded. "Gone with the setting of the sun."

Eliza shoved the book onto the shelf with a huff. "What nonsense! How can a library be useful if no one can find what they're looking for?"

"Perhaps fate decides?" he offered.

She glared at him.

Finn's grin stretched wider.

"You knew and didn't tell me."

He shrugged.

"How am I supposed to find anything of use?" She asked herself, her voice rising higher. Eliza broke into motion, pacing back and forth between the shelves. "If I don't know where I've looked, it'll take ages. What if I sleep in here?" She glanced at him, but he couldn't say whether the question was for him or not. "Would the books move then? Or what if I took some of them out and moved them elsewhere?"

There were thousands. Even if that worked, it would be an

undertaking in itself, and someone would be bound to ask questions they wouldn't have a good answer for.

"Eliza," he said, but she continued to pace.

"What if I marked them?" She turned on her heel, her pace increasing. "No, no, I can't do that."

"Eliza," he said again, trying to draw her attention, but she was lost in her dilemma, panic rising in her voice.

"Maybe if I—"

Finn stepped into her path, and she stumbled right into him. She gasped, stilling, her gaze finding his. Without thinking, he reached up and pushed a lock of hair behind her ear, that same one that always liked to escape.

"Eliza." He dared to cup her cheek, to feel the slight shiver of her skin against his. This time, she didn't pull away. If anything, she leaned the slightest bit closer. "What if the answer isn't in the library?"

Chesa had said as much the day before. That what she sought wasn't here.

"Then where?" she whispered.

"I don't know." The honest truth. But if it wasn't here, spending days dismantling the library wouldn't help. He'd gone along with Eliza's request because she wanted it, and he wasn't about to push her away again. But there had to be another way to get the answers they needed.

"I've tried to ask about Alice, but no one will tell me much of anything, and the queen—"

He flinched and dropped his hand.

Eliza stepped back. "I'm sorry."

"You have nothing to be sorry for." He closed the space between them again. It wasn't her fault that just mentioning that woman made his skin crawl. Avoiding her forever wouldn't be possible. A reckoning was coming.

"But she—"

He stopped her with a finger to the lips. "Her actions are not your fault."

Soft lashes dropped to hide her eyes before she looked at him again. "Why are you helping me, Finn? It can't be earning you any favors."

"Can't I just want to?" One brow arched. When she didn't respond, he continued, "I didn't know your grandmother well, but still, she was kind to me." So few ever were. "She didn't expect anything in return and didn't want anything from me." Another rarity. "The only thing she ever asked of me was her final command—to be the one to bring you here."

Oh, how I wish I knew why. He was strong enough—capable. But a solo recovery of Alice through a strange doorway, an act forced by the previous Alice after she shattered the magic mirror, made no sense. It risked too much.

Eliza dropped her gaze, nodding absently as if all that made sense. "I..." She visibly swallowed before staring back up at him—the sincerity in her gaze nearly stealing his breath. "I want to help you too, Finn."

"Me?" The shock of it drew his shoulders back.

She nodded. "Alice must stay. If we cannot solve this curse, I must choose. I can't let Wonderland fall to ruin."

"We don't deserve you."

Her smile nearly broke him. "You do. I can't leave yet, but you don't have to stay."

Something inside him cracked, spreading warmth through his chest. "Eliza."

She closed the last of the distance between them, her body pressing against his as she cupped his cheek. "Get away from here, Finn. Away from her."

His arms wound around her, pulling her close and eliciting the softest gasp. Her hand slid to his chest, but she didn't break their held gaze. "And go where?" He'd be a wanted man by both courts. He would risk it—for her. Alone? *No.* He wouldn't leave her.

Absently, she licked her lips, the smallest hint of her pink tongue slipping out. "Go back through the doorway to my world. The estate is mine now. You can live there."

How many times could the woman leave him speechless? Apparently, a few more. If only what she proposed were possible, but no one could leave Wonderland, not for long.

"Once I'm Alice, I'll return home," she continued. "They can't keep me then, right? I'll set it all to rights. I'll— What *are* you smirking at?" Her brows pinched in annoyance.

Truly, he couldn't help it. "Once your mind is set on something, there's no swaying it, is there?"

Her lips thinned in answer.

"But, Eliza, you forgot one important detail," he said, his smirk growing.

"And what would that be?" She raised her chin higher, her face so close her breath ghosted across his skin.

Finn leaned in until their noses nearly touched, finding the gold flecks in her eyes sparkling like sand on the shore. "I have no intention of leaving you behind."

Eliza's eyes grew wide. There was an audible hitch to her breath as Finn touched his lips to hers. A tingling rush roared through his veins at the feather-light contact. He dared not move. He may have started this, stolen the first touch, but Eliza would have to take the leap with him. The graze of his lips was a question, a hope, and only she could answer it.

24

*B*reath caught in her throat at the soft touch of Finn's lips to hers—barely there at all. The simple act sent a lightning bolt straight down her spine, making the fine hairs on her arms stand on end.

Eliza stood frozen as a blazing fire burned her up from within, threatening to melt her into a puddle at his feet. But he didn't move, didn't press the kiss or claim her lips as she suddenly so desperately needed him to. His eyes had fallen shut, given nothing away, or was that hers? She couldn't think, couldn't reason beyond that fleeting whisper of intimacy.

I have no intention of leaving you behind.

Stupid. Didn't Finn understand that she wanted to save him too?

No, not just wanted—needed. She needed him.

Her guide. Her knight.

Eliza leaned into the kiss, unable to wait, to hold back. Her lips met his, and something about the action shattered the frozen moment that had locked them in stillness. Finn's arms drew tight around her, molding her body to his. He met her kiss with reverent passion as if he had only waited for her to catch up before carrying them along together.

He kissed her. He wanted her.

And, oh, how she wanted him. Such a simple, natural thing, the only thing that made sense in this world of strange nonsense. The realization came almost too late. How ridiculous that she'd had to all but lose him to realize how much she wanted him.

"Ahem."

Eliza's heart nearly burst out of her ribs as someone cleared their throat nearby. Finn broke their kiss and shoved her behind him so quickly that her head spun. She might have wobbled right into the bookshelves if instinct hadn't forced her to grab ahold of his shirt to steady herself.

"Chesa," Finn growled.

Eliza peeked around him. Chesa leaned against the opposite row of shelves, a book open in one hand as if she'd been casually standing there reading for much longer than the duration of their kiss. Worry knotted itself in Eliza's throat. How much had the other woman seen? Or worse, heard?

The book snapped shut, causing Eliza to startle.

The odd woman's gaze was as alert as she'd ever seen, flickering between her and Finn with interest. "The queen comes," Chesa said.

Bloody hells.

Finn tensed, back stiffening under her touch.

"Here?" Eliza squeaked.

"Presently," Chesa said.

Finn twisted his head toward her.

"You have to run. Hide," Eliza implored.

The queen had simmered with fury at the mention of Finn helping her in the library. She couldn't let her find him here.

Finn took her hand in his. There was no time to savor the touch before he hauled her toward the one door out of the library. Shelves passed in a blur. Just before they reached the entrance, realization stuck her feet to the ground.

"The Tweeds," Eliza said in a harsh whisper.

He whirled toward her, eyes wide. "Damn." His attention snapped across the room.

The window? "We can't. We're too high up."

Finn gripped her hand tighter. "We have to—"

"Almost out of time," Chesa erupted, her voice melodic as a song. She appeared from nowhere on the long sofa in the sitting area, her legs stretched out on the cushions and a book open in her lap.

"How did—" Eliza shook her head. It didn't matter. Finn had to get away. An idea spilled out before she fully had time to process it. "Become a rabbit."

"Okay." He gave one sharp nod before releasing her hand. A shudder rolled through his body before he vanished into a cloud of sparkling mist that disbursed almost as quickly as it appeared. A white rabbit sat at her feet, nose twitching.

The sight nearly broke her. He trusted her completely, without question, when she had only the barest hint of a plan.

Now to hide him. Eliza bounced on the balls of her feet, scanning the room. The rabbit tried to hop away, but Eliza scooped him up.

"Almost here," Chesa said.

Panic held her in its thrall. Muffled voices slipped through the door.

So Eliza did the first thing that popped into her mind. She threw herself down on the couch next to Chesa's feet, spread out the skirts of her dress, and shoved rabbit Finn beneath the fabric. "Be still," she whispered.

No sooner had she fluffed her skirts to hide his form than the doors burst open. Pilla sauntered in, the billowing skirts of her crimson gown nearly trapping her in the doorway until she pushed through with a huff. For once, her cigarette was absent. "There you are, Alice."

Eliza cut a stern glance at Chesa. *I thought you said it was the queen,* she tried to say with a scowl.

Chesa shrugged one tan shoulder before glancing down at her book. "No matter which eyes see it, the knowledge is the same."

Nails dug into her palm. *Not the same at all!*

Eliza turned back to Pilla, forcing a smile.

"You should be getting ready," Pilla scolded. "The queen is almost dressed and wishes to see you before ball."

"Oh?" When Finn twitched ever so slightly against her stocking leg, Eliza sat a little straighter. "What does she want?"

"Who knows," Pill huffed, bracing a gloved hand on her hip. She sighed and straightened herself up. "My apologies, Alice."

Eliza's brows crept skyward.

"But she's in one of her moods, you know?" Pilla waved a hand through the air. "Anyhow, it won't do to be late and upset her further." She cut a glance at Chesa. "You too. I believe Alice's guardian is to join the royal procession?"

Chesa tore her eyes from the book. "Oh, we'll be there right on time. I just need a moment more with our Alice, and then I'll see that she's dressed."

Pilla notched her chin higher. "Her majesty ordered me to see to it."

Of course. Always wanting to pander to the queen. Finn's little heart pounded so rapidly she could feel its thump against her skin. It was nearly as distracting as the soft touch of his fur.

Chesa swung her feet around and planted them on the ground. "Her Majesty will not mind me seeing to it. I am Alice's guardian after all," she said, her voice suddenly full of authority rather than the wispy musical tone it often held. "Besides, don't you want the maids to see to your own hair and makeup? This is a very important ball, after all. One must look their best."

Eliza bit the inside of her lip, holding back a traitorous grin. The dress alone said Pilla was already dressed for the evening ball, and yet... The woman's lips parted. Her hand reached for her upswept hair. "Yes, of course." She rocked on her heels, blinking rapidly. "Well, as long as you're not late."

Chesa gave a toothy grin. "I'll make sure Alice is right where she needs to be."

"Fine." Pilla turned on her heel, then swung back around and dipped a curtsy. "Alice."

Eliza gave no more than a nod as the woman turned and all but fled. If she couldn't manage to call her by her correct name or knock, for goodness sake, then that was all she would get.

"Ridiculous woman," Chesa remarked to the closed door.

The furry companion under her skirts picked that moment to wiggle, sliding higher up her thigh and brushing the hem of her underthings. A flush stole up her chest, flooding through her neck to her face. She jerked back her dress, revealing the white rabbit plastered to her leg, his little nose daring to rub against the silken fabric she wore to cover her most intimate areas.

"Out of there, you!" Eliza shooed Finn from his hiding place.

Sparkling dust erupted, and Eliza lurched back with a squeak. The cushion dipped. And then Finneas sat on the armrest of the sofa, his booted feet planted on the cushion next to Eliza. She placed a palm over her racing heart. "You could have warned me."

He grinned, leaning down with his elbows on his thighs. "You seemed quite adamant that I move."

"Ridiculous." Eliza rolled her eyes and tore her gaze from his smirking face. Looking at his lips brought to mind too many memories from minutes before, and she wasn't ready to repeat that show with an audience present.

Speaking of... Eliza turned toward Chesa, giving Finn her back, but he spoke first. "How long have you been here?"

All the delicious warmth from moments ago dropped into a hard ball in Eliza's center.

That toothy smile returned. "Long enough."

The weight of it pulled Eliza down into the cushion. One look into her alert, clear gaze, so uncommon from her few encounters, and Eliza knew. It wasn't just the kiss Chesa had seen and heard.

A deep growl rumbled behind her, a sound unlike man or rabbit. "If you tell—"

Chesa held up a hand, somehow silencing Finn. "I protect and guide Alice, remember? How would speaking a word of your secrets serve her?"

"But the queen?" Eliza stammered.

"Doesn't need to know." Chesa accentuated each word.

Finn leaped from the arm of the sofa and began to pace across the carpets, one hand massaging his forehead.

"You'll keep this a secret?"

She inclined her head. "Some things are as certain as the rise and fall of the sun."

"You knew she was coming," Finn mumbled, almost to himself. "Why not tell us sooner?"

Chesa leaned back, crossing one leg over the other. "And ruin the fun?"

Fun? Eliza swallowed. *Oh.* That flush returned, hot as ever.

"Besides," she continued. "I wanted to see what you two would do. Quite amusing."

Finn gave a very un-rabbit-like growl. Eliza shared the sympathies, but arguing with Chesa would get them nowhere. Rather, she was grateful to finally have the woman show up for once.

"If you're to be my guide and guardian, why not help us find what we're looking for?" Eliza asked.

"Books that talk about Alice?" Chesa gave a knowing grin. She really had been there far longer than they realized. "And why would you need those?"

Finn shot her a warning glare, but she ignored it. It was time for a leap of faith, to trust that the grandmother she'd known as a girl was the same woman who left her the letter saying to trust Chesa. "I want to break the curse."

Every second was punishingly long as Eliza awaited a reply.

Finally, Chesa said, "Good," the comment devoid of any surprise. Finn let out an audible sigh.

"This one may have held what you sought… Once." She opened the front cover, revealing tattered scraps where dozens of pages were torn out of the beginning of the book. "But no more. What you seek is no longer in the library, but you're on the right path."

Eliza's brows drew together. "Someone borrowed the book?"

Chesa gave a wry smile. "What you must find to break the curse isn't in any book, Eliza."

"Then tell me." Eliza slid across the cushions until her leg brushed the other woman's. She wanted to grab her and shake her. *Bloody hell.* She would beg if it would help.

"I can't." She shrugged. "If I spoke it, it could no longer be. Only time will tell you."

"Only time…" Eliza gaped. A scream crawled up her throat, aching to be set free as her nails dug into the cushions.

"That's ridiculous!" Finn snapped, a mirror of her barely leashed fury.

Chesa gave a meaningful look toward the doors.

Damn. Eliza tensed. *The Tweeds.* Collective silence reigned for a beat, then another, but the doors didn't open.

Satisfied, Finn marched the short steps to the couch. "If you know, tell her," he begged. "Help her. Free her. Aren't you supposed to do what's best for Alice?"

Chesa rose to her feet in one fluid motion, advancing on Finn until their feet nearly touched and their faces were inches apart. "I. Am."

Finn stepped back, but the hardness of his features didn't break. "The White Court is after Eliza. They sent a threat promising violence if she's not handed over."

"What?" That had Eliza bolting upright. He'd never said a word about it.

"I didn't want to alarm you."

Eliza joined the tense circle. "Well, you have. And you kept it from me." She wasn't sure which was worse, the threat or the lie.

He ran a hand through his hair. "I thought if I could get you out of here, keep you safe, it wouldn't matter."

The admission grated like coarse sand. "Well, it does." A sudden thought strangled her with its horror. "The ball tonight…"

Finn looked at her. "We know. All guards are on duty, in the manor, on the grounds, and throughout the city." He took her hand in his. "I will protect you, Eliza. I promise."

"She is safe here as long as you are at her side," Chesa said with a calm certainty that Eliza believed. Chesa might not make sense most of the time, but the things that did had been right thus far.

Finn would protect her. Somehow, she was sure of that too. But by watching out for her, he'd put himself in danger. "If you go to the ball, others will see you. *She* might…" Her throat tightened, refusing to let the horrible thoughts free.

His fingers gripped hers. "I can still protect you even if I'm out of sight."

He'd be there. He'd risk it for her. Somehow, the thought of not seeing him, of wondering about him, made the tumultuous feelings twisting within her worse, but she couldn't ask him for more. Already he risked too much.

Instead, she simply nodded. "Just tell me next time there's a threat against me."

Finn cocked his head to the side. "Technically, it was against the Red Court."

Eliza rolled her eyes. *Not making it any better, Finn.*

"I will be at your side, Eliza," Chesa promised. Somehow, that was reassuring, too, even if they were barely acquaintances. "But now, we should get you ready. I promised after all."

"Right." She slipped her hand from Finn's. "I'll see you...later." *Not at the ball.*

"Soon," he promised with a small bow.

"Soon," Eliza echoed. Something more than words passed in the silence—a promise.

Chesa twined her arm through Eliza's and pulled her toward the door. Her heart lurched as she twisted to look at Finn where he stood stoic in the middle of the room. If only they could have had a few more moments alone.

"Leave a few minutes after us," Chesa tossed over her shoulder to Finn. The strange woman pulled Eliza closer, demanding her attention, and said, "How about I tell you about your grandmother while we walk?"

Suddenly, walking away was a little bit easier.

25

To think Finn once looked forward to these balls. Before the queen set her eyes to him, each one excited him with its free and festive nature—so different from the White Court of his youth with its rules and formality. Plus, there were wine and partners aplenty. What more could he want? Now, he wished for nothing more than to hide in his burrow. He frowned at the mass of people filing into the expansive ballroom and tugged at the stiff collar of his uniform. The king's commanders dressed in their finery, expected to attend the ball but also stay alert for trouble. Many of the Red knights bemoaned missing the celebration, being forced to patrol the outskirts of the court for any sign of trouble. He'd have given much to trade places with them.

The queen would be here. Eliza would be here. And though he longed to see her again, the thought of sticking to the shadows and seeing her dance with various partners was enough to make his teeth grind together. Red Court balls were often far from chaste, some couples and groups choosing to indulge their desires on the chaises spotted around the floor or even against a wall. Once the drinks started flowing, laced with preventatives to ensure the festivities didn't result in a rash of children months later, any number of things were bound to happen.

Would anyone dare try for more with their new Alice? That was a sight he'd never be able to suffer.

A servant passed by carrying a tray laden with saucers of wine. Finn snatched one and tipped it back, letting the sweet liquid bubble and slide across his tongue.

"Drinking on the job?" Lizardo edged into Finn's periphery.

Finn shot him a side-eyed look and took another sip. "One drink can't hurt." *Ancient kings, I need it to get through this night.*

"Hrmp." The captain crossed his arms and stared toward the arriving guests. "So long as it's only one. If there's trouble…"

Yeah, yeah. He, of all people, knew what was at stake. "Have they been warned of the danger?" he whispered. Finn tipped his head toward the gaggle of people in their finery.

"Of course not," Lizardo snapped. "And disrupt Alice's ball?"

Alice's ball… She seemed to loathe the idea of it as much as him. But then, he wasn't surprised the king had ordered the threat to be kept quiet. Why cause a stir until it was necessary? Everyone knew that Alice's arrival was a fraught time. Forcing all the guards to their posts this night wouldn't be that unusual. It was probably why the king ordered them to don their dress uniforms rather than anything useful for battle. A clever illusion of happiness and security for all the people.

"Still," Lizardo continued, "best to keep an eye out." He slid his attention to Finn. "Interesting that you would request to be posted out here rather than at Her Majesty's side."

"I'm sure you'll take up that post well enough." The man did just about everything he could to look good in front of the queen. His looks were average at best, his form a little too burley for her taste. Without his constant pandering, he'd have never earned her affections, but he was grateful the man tried. Finn had even slipped him a few pointers, tipped him off to the queen's more…private interests. Any person she took to her bed helped dissuade the woman's interest in him.

"Indeed." Lizardo stood a little taller. "Speaking of, they should be arriving soon."

Without so much as a farewell, the captain strode for the main doors into the ballroom. He squeezed his way into the mass of bodies before disappearing into the bright light and sounds of laughter seeping from the doors.

It was better in the manor's halls—no queen to spot him, yet still far from potential trouble at the edges of the court or the hedge maze. In fact, the worst thing he'd have to endure would be the drunkards later in the night who couldn't find their way back to their beds.

It was a lovely plan. It worked for all of a few minutes until the noise in the ballroom drew quiet, and the herald's voice tickled his ears. He announced the monarchs. A cheer rose from the crowd. Then another hush descended as if the air was sucked from the room. From his vantage, Finn caught sight of the crowd in the ballroom pressing forward, some rising on their toes for a better view.

"And now, lovelies, the reason our glorious King Jasper and Queen Victoria have hosted this ball tonight. And isn't it a grand one?" Murmurs of acknowledgment rose to fill the intentional pause. "Their Majesties are pleased to introduce the next Alice. May her reign be long, and her blessings always favor our esteemed Red Court."

Finn wasn't sure when it happened or how. One minute he was out in the shadows of the hall, content to linger there. But by the time the herald had finished the introduction, he'd slipped into the ballroom and stood next to one of the crimson draperies hanging from the wall just inside the ornate golden doors. Breath caught in his throat as Eliza entered the far side of the room on Chesa's arm. Her hair was swept back, as it often was, but ruby pins adorned the rich, dark waves. Equally large stones hung like drops of blood from her ears, matching the necklace flush against the skin of the column of her neck. The jewels alone were a wonder, as fine as the queen's and likely from her own collection, but it was the gown that left his throat suddenly dry. The dress left little to the imagination, plunging to her belly button and revealing creamy skin among the swaths of crimson. A cloud of red surrounded her waist and legs, but the fabric was nearly as insubstantial as the mist that liked to cling over the hedge maze in the morning. Every step she took onto the dais with Chesa displayed her legs—shadows in the cloud, visible but not quite.

The outfit alone boiled his blood, but worse was the look on her face—impassive, vacant, and cold. A stark contrast to the crowd's rising cheers, swooning sighs, and unfiltered joy.

As she came to the side of the king and queen, she forced a smile, earning more love from those gathered. But the act sliced him up inside. A pretty bird in a cage, singing for the crowd when all she wanted was to fly free, to fly home. Guilt wracked him. He'd brought her here. He'd done this to her.

Finn skirted the wall, nearly knocking into a table laden with sweet delicacies while aiming for a better look.

Eliza's gaze panned the crowd almost lazily, never settling.

Music rose amid the chatter, the musicians striking up a song and warring to be heard.

The king took Eliza's hand, pulling her away from Chesa, down the short steps, and onto the dance floor. The man had saved him, given him a life here, but at that moment, Finn loathed the way his hand settled onto the small of Eliza's back, just above a ginormous bow. He hated the genuine smile on his savior's face as he gazed at the woman Finn loved.

He—

Finn halted abruptly, an island in the crowd surging to join their monarch on the dancefloor. Someone bumped him. Another cursed. Something wet splashed onto his hand. He hardly noticed any of it.

He gave himself a shake and stumbled back toward the safety of the wall—when had he left it? *It can't be. I hardly know her.* But then, when had anyone seen him as more than the king's ward? A Red knight? The white rabbit? The queen's favored?

Titles one and all, but not him—not the man lurking beyond all that.

Life had been the same charade for years.

And then the former Alice had to go and send him on his quest, turning his life inside out and upside down. His only worry had been performing his duty successfully. Find the girl and bring her back to the Red Court lest he lose his head in penance for failure.

He'd returned, but not the same.

Finn shoved through the crowd, back out the doors of the ballroom, and into the hall. His actions were not his own as he fled into the night, seeking quiet and solitude.

I love her.

Losing his head might have been the preferable choice, quick and all but painless. Loving Alice? There was no happy ending in that story.

26

*E*liza nearly cried in relief as the last notes of the song warbled in the air, and her partner released her with a gallant bow. The move was just as stiff as the man's dancing, which earned her sore toes and a rip in the long train of her dress.

For the millionth time, she scanned the crowd, searching every face for the one she sought. In some ways, she was glad of his absence. The queen was never far, and if Eliza spotted Finn, that horrible woman might as well. After all, there were worse dangers than sore feet and unsavory dance partners.

But her heart rarely listened to reason in its wanting.

"Care for refreshment?"

Eliza spun to find Chesa at her side, a saucer of pale liquid extended in one hand. She could not have been more relieved if the Holy Mother stood before her.

"Please." Eliza took the glass, barely restraining herself from chugging the sweet liquid. In mere hours, the strange woman had transformed from an acquaintance with a fancy title to a possible ally. At least she gave her moments of respite during the horrible evening. Eliza could have used a friend like Chesa during her youth. Perhaps then, the various gatherings her parents forced her to attend would have been more bearable.

"Lady Alice—" someone began before she lowered her glass. Eliza's spine stiffened, a sharp dismissal souring the wine on her tongue.

"Our dear Alice is dancing with me next," Chesa replied without missing a beat. "Off with you. Shoo, shoo."

"My savior," Eliza said as the man hurried away.

Chesa shrugged one tanned shoulder, the airy sleeve of her dress moving with her. "It's my duty to watch after Alice." She plucked the empty glass from her hand and handed it off to a nearby waiter without even turning in their direction.

Eliza nearly snorted. "I thought you weren't my protector until I was anointed?"

"I don't have to be Alice's protector to save you from another horrible dance partner." She took Eliza's hand in hers. "Come."

It was the best and easiest thing anyone had asked of her all night. Eliza didn't even mind that Chesa practically dragged her across the dance floor toward the dais. Dancers tripped over themselves to part for them. It might have been the first thing Eliza grinned about in hours.

Without the dancing to distract her, she couldn't help her gaze from wandering the room. Faces aplenty stared back, unabashedly inspecting Alice and her guardian, who, Eliza gathered, rarely attended such public events. Thankfully, one sharp look from Chesa warded off anyone else who dared approach.

Beyond the dancers, other moving forms came into view. Some entwined together on the various furniture near the edges of the room. A trio—no, quad—on the floor. Creamy flesh met dark skin in a dance that had nothing to do with music. A sudden warmth settled low in her belly.

"Are they...?" Eliza tilted her head in the group's direction.

"Having sex?" Chesa replied as if they discussed the weather.

Eliza swallowed. "Yes. That."

"Haven't you been paying much attention to the Red Court?" She raised one brow, dyed a bright pink to match her hair.

"But here?" In the ballroom of all places.

Chesa merely shrugged. "The Red Court is the court of pleasures, Eliza. Do you not think they're enjoying themselves?"

Truthfully, she tried not to look too closely. Sex could be quite pleasurable with the right company. She'd had a few casual affairs that were...not terrible. But in a ballroom? No one in Gamor would ever consider it. The scandal it would create could never be lived down. Her mother might have died of shock if she'd witnessed such a thing at a society ball.

The dance floor became more appealing by the moment. At least then, Eliza could focus on counting her steps and avoiding an ill-placed boot rather than being rooted to the ground, unable to look away from the illicit show.

Eliza turned to the woman at her side, desperate for distraction. "You're quite present today." Terrible wording, but the best her racing mind could conjure.

"It's an important day," she replied.

"Because of the ball?"

Chesa turned to her, a slight cloudiness across her eyes that wasn't there a moment ago. "Tonight could shift the future of the courts."

All the warmth of moments ago fled. A terrible, creeping sensation crawled down Eliza's spine. She searched the sea of crimson for anything amiss, any sign of the White Court trying to make good on their threats.

Eliza bounced on her toes, unable to stand still any longer. "You think they'll—"

"Dearest Alice." The familiar deep voice silenced everything she planned to say. King Jasper stood at her side, his hand outstretched. "May I have the next dance?"

He'd had two already, more than anyone else. No one dared ask for more than one when there was a room full of people eager for the next. Eliza paused, waiting to see if Chesa would intervene on her behalf as the king's heavy-lidded gaze swept her from head to toe, then back again.

Please. She begged The Mother or whatever deity would listen.

He wasn't a bad man, not like some she'd encountered over the years, but he'd had enough drink this night that his desires were no longer hidden behind carefully guarded features. He wanted more than a dance—more than she wanted to offer.

But who could say no to a king?

Eliza forced a smile and placed her hand in his. "Of course."

As he pulled her to the dancefloor, she looked back once for her companion, but Chesa had vanished.

Figures she'd disappear when I need her.

The newest melody kept a quick tempo, leaving little time for conversation, thank goodness. But it didn't stop the king from pulling her close at every opportunity. His warmth swarmed her senses and the sweet scent of the wine on his breath swept over her skin in a way that made her want to wretch.

If only the queen were around to claim her husband. However, fidelity seemed far less important in the Red Court than in Gamorean society. The monarchs had shared little more than a forced smile, and everyone seemed to know who their favorites were.

As the song drew to its final notes, the king guided them toward the edge of the dance floor.

Almost there. Just another moment. Eliza scoured the room for Chesa without luck. She even tried to catch the eyes of the dancers nearby, desperate to partner with someone else—anyone else.

"Alice, dearest." Eliza gasped as the king cupped her cheek, drawing her face entirely too close to his. "Perhaps you'd like to take the air with me?"

Air. A hysterical laugh caught in her throat. As if that was what he truly wanted.

Was this how Finn felt with the queen? Trapped. Caged. Fearful that rejection would only lead to something even worse?

Spots swam in her vision. Her breath became short.

"Y-your Majesty…"

The world spun, taking her words with it.

Then a palm touched her back, the briefest connection that steadied her and gave refuge amid the storm.

"Apologies, Your Majesty, but Alice promised me a dance as favor for her safe journey here."

Eliza nearly sobbed in relief at the sight of Finn. Dressed in the crimson and gold of the royal guard, he blended right in with the crowd. Had he been here this whole time? Watching? Waiting? Keeping an eye on her as he'd said?

"Ah, Finneas." The king dropped his hand from her cheek, and Eliza could breathe again. "Alice and I were—"

"Your Majesty." Another man drew close, bowing before the monarch. Young and fit, he cut a stunning image in his crimson long coat. The man's slicked-back blond waves almost glimmered in the light.

"Gryph," The king replied, surprise and pleasure mingling in the wake of the name.

"I hoped we might share a moment." Gryph's brows rose in suggestion. "There is something I've been eager to show you."

The king released her, his attention given over to the newcomer. "Indeed."

Something fluttered awkwardly in Eliza's stomach at the unsaid words passing between them.

"Well," the king said and blinked away his drink-induced haze. "By all means." He took the man's hand and quickly looked back at Finn. "Do keep an eye on our Alice, will you?"

"As my king commands."

Eliza stood frozen in wonder as Finn bowed to the retreating monarch and his companion. She's prayed for a miracle, and the Mother delivered in the form of Finn.

"Well, Eliza?" Finn held a hand out to her and gestured to the dance floor.

For the first time all night, she accepted with joy.

27

Eliza is safe. She's here. He repeated the reminder over and over, trying to calm his racing heart as he led her onto the dance floor. She wasn't with the king or lured away into some ill encounter.

Something had urged him to return—tugged at him like a loose thread until he broke free from the shock of his earlier revelation and ventured back to the ballroom.

Her palm fit perfectly against his as they began the dance. His other hand found purchase on her hip, his thumb smoothing up and down the fabric as a reminder that she was real.

The slow, easy melody gave him time to look her over and ensure she was none the worse for wear, at least physically. He loved her. She was in his arms, safe. The beginning of a grin pulled at his lips.

"How did you manage that?" Eliza asked.

That grin vanished as surely as it came. Seeing Eliza in the arms of the king, that look on his face, was enough for Finn to see red. It was only dumb luck that Gryph was standing nearby, sipping a drink and looking entirely too bored for such an event. A minute later, and he'd have been too late.

He couldn't be late. He couldn't let his emotions distract him again, not with Eliza's safety on the line.

"Gryph owed me a favor. I called it in," he replied as evenly as possible given the torrent of emotions spiraling through him.

"I'm glad." She dipped her focus before locking eyes with him once more. "You saved me, Finn."

His hand tightened on hers. "I'll always save you, Eliza."

The melody shifted, and Finn took the opportunity to pull her close, their bodies nearly brushing one another as they glided amid the sea of people. The crowd could have been a herd of Bandersnatch for all he saw of them. Only one woman mattered—the one in his arms.

"Is it safe for you to be here? Dancing?"

Finn twirled her around before bringing Eliza back, drawing her chest against his and savoring the slight parting of her lips at the contact.

"The night is quiet so far. Not a peep from White." *Thank all the ancient kings for that.* The bastards would probably wait until they were all exhausted and hung over.

"Oh." She blinked rapidly. "Well, that's good."

And unexpected. The longer they went without trouble, the more horrible it would likely be when it arrived. White wouldn't give up, not with King Alvis in charge.

"What I actually meant," Eliza said, "was is it safe for you to be out here?" She held his gaze. "In the open. Where *anyone* might spot you."

He skipped a step in the dance, tripping over his own feet. *Damn.* All his worry about the queen had fled at the sight of Eliza in the king's arms. In another beat, he swept Eliza back into the flow of the dance and forced a smile. "It doesn't matter."

"It does." She scowled. "At least, maybe dance near the edge?"

A fair and wise idea. He couldn't bring himself to leave her, not now.

A few more stanzas of the song had them moving through the crowd, dancers parting for them as if their careful flight was part of the natural rhythm of the music. Some openly stopped to gape as Eliza moved through their midst. She was a beautiful dancer, following his lead with trusting ease.

The dancers thinned near the tables and furniture dotted near the walls. The song's tempo slowed to a near standstill, begging the couples to linger in stillness like the rocks jutting up from the sea near the edge of the shore.

"Better?" he asked.

She merely nodded, never breaking eye contact with him. He could drown in her brown irises, so warm and inviting. The intelligence sparkling there only fueled his interest, making it too easy to lose track of time and place.

A loud moan tore through the peaceful melody. Every muscle in his body tensed, seeking danger. Eliza gasped as his gaze landed on a trio nearby engaged in their own horizontal dance on a chaise, barely a scrap of clothing left on any of them. One man, quite pleased, retreated to the side as another took his place with the woman.

Eliza snapped her attention back to him, a deep flush painting her cheeks. "They're..." She shook her head.

"Such pleasures are uncommon in your world?" he asked, genuinely bemused. It wasn't so out of place for revelers to let their pleasure spill out in various ways in public, at least not in the Red Court.

"Not in the ballroom," she responded, her form suddenly as stiff as her words.

Finn turned them until Eliza's back was to the scene, saving her from the view. Though it gave him quite the show as the man raised the woman's ankles to his shoulders, her dress bunched around her middle. Still, she wore more than the man whose pants hung around his ankles, revealing a less than pleasing backside—an unfortunate consequence of lingering near the edge of the dance floor.

"The Red Court is a court of pleasures," he said. "If they all consent, then who is to complain?"

Eliza stared determinedly at his chest, refusing to meet his eyes. "Don't they worry about potential consequences?" she asked in a sharp whisper.

"Such as?"

She squirmed a little in his arms, and damn if her modesty didn't bring a grin to his face.

"Such as children." Finally, she looked at him again. "How would she even know who the father was?"

Now that did give him pause. Apparently neither Chesa nor the monarchs had told Eliza about the finer details of Red Court balls. For what purpose? His hand flexed on her side before he answered. "Have you tried the wine tonight?"

Her brows pinched. "Yes, but don't change the subject on me." She swatted lightly at his chest.

"I'm not." He watched her carefully. "Was it not a bit sweet? All the drinks are laced with a contraceptive. No children will come from tonight's pleasures—assuming the participants partook in the drinks."

Eliza drew still, her lips parted. "Well… That's certainly practical."

Leave it to Eliza to find reason in the ways of the Red Court. The noise behind her grew as the couple reached another climax.

"Perhaps the edge of the dance floor was a terrible idea after all." She all but dragged Finn away, not that he minded.

She'd given up the dance completely and charged back toward the heart of the ballroom as the musicians changed to a livelier selection.

"Lady Alice," a man said, stepping in front of her.

Eliza leaped back, her body finding rest against his chest, but even as the shock faded from her, she did nothing to increase the space between them.

"May I request a dance?" the man, whose name he couldn't place, held out his hand.

Finn sighed. One dance. That's all he'd get before they stole her away, but at least he'd gotten that much. It was more than he'd hoped. His fingers were still entwined with Eliza's, and he made to let her go, but she held tight.

"I am dancing with Finn."

The statement all but knocked the breath from his lungs.

"Excuse us," Eliza said. Finn was helpless but to trail after her, a heady ball of desire knotting deep within him.

Abruptly she stopped, turned to him, and positioned her hand on his shoulder. "Well, shall we?"

Laughter burst from his chest. "So determined to avoid a poor dance partner?" His hand found that spot on her hip again, but she didn't leave space between them like before. Instead, she leaned in until her breasts nearly grazed his chest. All thought narrowed to that brief touch. Any more contact and the desire twitching in his cock would be plain for anyone to see.

"Perhaps I only want to dance with you," she said.

He blinked, unsure what to say. The words were a dream he'd never dared believe possible. "Not worried the people will consider your rejection rude?" he managed at last.

Eliza's nose twitched. "I'm not sure I care what they think. If I have to attend this horrible ball, the least they can let me do is dance with whom I choose. And I choose you, Finn."

Breath was suddenly hard to come by. He was the safe choice—familiar. That was all, or so he tried to convince himself. But as he stared into her eyes, their bodies moving in time to the dance, all he could think of was the moment they had alone in the library and the softness of her lips against his. Eliza's tongue ran across her lips. The simple act struck a bolt of desire straight through him.

"Eliza." He leaned in closer, his forehead nearly touching hers. This close, he could make out the flecks of gold in her eyes.

Her fingertips grazed his neck, sending a shiver rolling across his skin. "Yes, Finn."

He'd have to be a damned fool to kiss Alice in front of everyone, but when she blinked at him and pressed her chest against his, no one else mattered. "I want to—"

"Finneas!"

That horrid voice all but ripped him away from Eliza, sending him stumbling back and bumping into a nearby woman who yelped in offense.

The happy dream of moments ago shattered, its remnants slicing worse than broken glass. Finn forced himself to turn toward the woman approaching from behind. The other dancers moved away, leaving them stranded in the open, prey to the queen's advance.

Tonight, she wore a dress much like Eliza's, an intentional decision, no doubt—dressing the new Alice in her style. A sign for all the court that required no explanation. But unlike Eliza, she couldn't carry it off. Eliza's soft curves and dark hair were shown to advantage in the gaudy gown. The queen appeared all the more a tyrant, a woman more likely to slay someone on the dance floor than offer them her hand.

"Your Majesty." It took all he had to keep his voice even, force the barest smile, and bend at the waist in a courteous bow.

"I was hoping to see you tonight." Her gaze clawed down his form, then back up again. "Before tonight, actually."

Pilla stood behind the queen with a cluster of other women, something almost like pity on her face when she glanced at Eliza—she hadn't moved, almost as if the queen had turned her to stone with a single thought. She didn't have that kind of magic, though. The queen, for all her rank and reputation, had little at all.

"And dancing with our Alice." Victoria drew near, circling like a predator.

"I requested the dance, Your Majesty," Eliza said. She held her head high, did not bow, did not shy away.

Bright, beautiful woman.

"With my Finneas?"

If the queen noticed how Eliza stiffened or how the knuckles of her fist turned white, she didn't comment on it. But he saw it. The pain that raced across her face was unmissable, fleeting as it was.

"Well." The queen turned his way, sauntering up to him until the cloying scent of her perfume nearly made him gag. "Enjoy your dance with our dear Alice, but I hope to see you later. I'll be retiring to my rooms soon. I do fear my feet are worn out. The rest of me, though, is quite energetic yet." She giggled, a sound like scratches against glass. Her ring-decked fingers trailed down his cheek. It took the last of his control not to flinch away. "I have missed you in my bed, Finneas."

Eliza's eyes went wide. She stumbled back, swaying on her feet. Finn's nails cut into his palm as he fought the urge to reach for her, to do anything but stand perfectly still under the queen's inspection.

"Let's remedy that. Shall we?" She trailed her fingers down his chest, digging in her crimson-painted nails over his heart.

Finn swallowed the tightness in his throat. "Of course, my queen."

There was nothing else he could say.

A sharp smile broke across the queen's face. "Good." She turned to Eliza, her grin growing. "Have a lovely night, dear Alice."

With a swish of her skirts, the queen turned and melded into the crowd with her ladies.

28

*I*t took everything she had to remain upright. Never in her life had she wanted to cause such a scene—scream at the queen, hurl a glass of wine at her, or simply collapse into a tearful heap on the marble.

But Eliza Carroll didn't make a scene. No woman of breeding would dare. Only the years of careful practice kept her emotions in check as she watched the queen retreat without even a backward glance, having no idea the destruction she left in her wake.

No, that wasn't true. The horrible woman likely knew exactly what she'd done.

How could she think Eliza would choose Red after this? How could White possibly be worse?

Tears stung the corners of her eyes. Perhaps the White Court *should* attack this night. Maybe she should go to the gates and open them wide herself. That would show the bitch that Alice had her own claws.

Guilt gnawed at her, a little voice of reason piercing through the madness. Death to the innocent wasn't a fair. They didn't deserve punishment for their queen's behavior. But there had to be another way, a better choice than granting her favor to the Red Court and granting the illusion that she condoned such behavior.

"Eliza." Finn filled her vision, his hand closing over her tight fist.

Something caught between a sob and laugh burst from her as she took in his expression. How could he be so calm?

"It'll be all right, Eliza."

She blinked, and his serene appearance was gone, or perhaps she missed the truth behind the sheen of tears trying to blur her vision. His hand trembled. His chest rose and fell in quick succession. He might school his features—far better than she could—but he wasn't okay, far from it.

"I'm so sorry," she whispered, conscious of the onlookers. "I shouldn't have asked you to dance." She should have sent him away the moment she was free of the king, but no, she had to be selfish and dance with him.

Now the queen had her claws in him. He couldn't turn down such a direct command, not without consequence.

"It's not your—"

Eliza shook her head and brushed past him, refusing to hear anymore. It *was* her fault.

Finn caught up with her in a handful of steps. "I can't stay here," Eliza said before he could pick up where he left off. "I have to get out of here."

"Breathe." Finn slipped his arm through hers and urged her to slow her pace. "I'll take you to your room, but don't run. Don't panic."

If anyone but Finn had asked, she would have screamed. Don't panic? How could she not panic? They hadn't even left the ballroom before the Tweeds stepped into her path. Of course they were there. Weren't they always?

"I have a terrible headache." She placed the back of her hand against her forehead. It wasn't entirely a lie. The queen's little speech made every part of her ache. "I'll be retiring early."

The twins looked at each other, mirror images in their looks and formal, crimson attire, much like Finn's. Though they were similar and always together, she'd begun to note the small differences between them—the way one liked to rest his hand on his sword pommel or how the other usually spoke first. He didn't disappoint this time either.

"We'll escort you to your room."

"That won't be necessary," Finn said. "Alice is safe with me." He patted her arm.

The twins looked to one another again. This time, the second one spoke. "The queen charged us with guarding her."

Eliza's teeth ground together. If she had to say goodbye to Finn here, she might fall apart.

"And the queen charged me to bring her to court and keep her safe," Finn replied. "Besides. The queen asked me to join her this evening. Alice's rooms are on the way."

How could he say it so calmly? As if a horrible fate didn't await? When the Tweeds looked to one another again, Eliza summoned the last of her calm and spoke up. "I'd feel terrible if you missed such a ball. Relax. Enjoy it. I will be safe with Finn. That's an order from your future Alice."

Another look passed between them, and she nearly lost her temper, but then the one on the right nodded and said, "As Alice requests."

Thank the Mother. At least someone in this bloody place respects my wishes.

Sliding between the Tweeds and out of the ballroom was like stepping through another rabbit hole and into a new world entirely. Noise faded. Warm, dim light replaced the blinding glare from the ornate chandeliers. A fresh breeze ghosted down the hall, stripping away the overwhelming cloud of perfume and sweat she'd lingered in for far too long.

The slight chill of night crept across her skin, each prickle reminding her of the horrors that awaited. Finn was stiff at her side, his attention both straight ahead and far away.

What could she say? *I'm sorry?* He knew that. It didn't fix anything. *Don't go? Brace yourself for whatever horrors that woman will dole out? Flee to the wilds?*

He should go—save himself.

Eliza's thoughts spiraled, chasing each other through her mind like hounds after a hare. There was no good outcome. Nothing that wouldn't leave scars—internal ones, if not external.

All too soon, they stood in front of the doors to her quarters.

"I could have the guards call for your maids." Finn was stiff as he removed his arm from hers. In short minutes, he'd become as formal as the twins he'd replaced as her escort.

"No, thank you," she said, the words so quiet she wasn't sure he'd heard them, but it was the best she could do. Her voice had left her, strangled by the same piercing tightness that dug into her chest tighter than any corset.

Finn opened the door, revealing the dimly lit room beyond. The maids had already been there to check on things, light some candles, and turn down her sheets. The room should be inviting, but Eliza couldn't make herself enter. She whirled toward Finn, a thousand words poised on the tip of her tongue, but the only ones that slipped out were, "Don't go."

His eyes widened a fraction, the only reaction he let slip through the cold, hard mask he'd worn since leaving the ballroom. When he took her hand in his, she gasped at the contact, the little sparks that ignited in her blood at the simple touch. Finn raised her hand and placed a chaste kiss on its back. "I must."

No. Please. She begged silently, her fingers suddenly tight around his, refusing to let go.

A set of guards paced down the far hall. They stopped, staring in their direction.

Finn pulled his hand away. "Good night, Alice."

Alice. Not Eliza.

He gave a stiff, formal bow and turned on his heel.

Eliza lurched into the room and threw herself against the door, slamming it with a satisfying bang.

Tears stung the corner of her eyes. Breath drew thin and harsh. Eliza collapsed to the floor, the wispy fabric of the dress gathering like a cloud around her.

The thought of Finn going to the queen turned her stomach. How was she supposed to be okay with that? The horrible woman all but threw the command in her face. Somehow, she knew Eliza cared for Finn. Knew and didn't care. Worse, she worked to destroy the beautiful, fragile thing that grew between them.

"Did you bring me here to suffer, Grandmama?" she whispered into the gloom while brushing an errant tear from her cheek. "Is this my punishment for failing to write and visit as much as I should have?"

Oh, how she regretted that now. Grandmama had been a certainty. Eliza could write later, visit later, or so she'd told herself. Grandmama would always welcome her back. She'd been so certain of that. But death had other plans.

"I was brought here to be Alice, to decide the fate of Wonderland, but I've never had less authority in my life."

A whisper of sound teased her ears from somewhere in the room. Eliza held her breath, listening. It came again, barely audible. "Take it, Alice."

Her hair stood on end. "Who's there?"

Eliza turned this way and that, searching the shadows.

"Take your power." The voice said again, a hint of familiarity in its whispered tone.

"Chesa?" Eliza's brows drew together. She hadn't seen her since the king requested another dance. "Are you there?"

She paced the room as silently as possible, searching, listening, but the voice did not come again.

"My power?" Eliza echoed, staring at her hands in the flickering candlelight.

Can I order the queen to stop? Demand she leave Finn alone?

The Tweeds listened when she gave a command. Pilla had listened to her command. Would the queen? She drew herself higher, swallowing her apprehension. If Alice truly determined the fate of Wonderland, could she not order the queen to stay away from Finn?

She had to try, had to do *something*.

And if the nasty woman still dug in her claws? Well, there was always the White Court.

A fire ignited in her soul. Its light burned away the dark despair that threatened to swallow her. Eliza wiped her eyes, straightened her spine, and marched toward the door.

Her palm closed over the cold metal of the handle. She could do this. She would.

When Eliza pulled the door open, her heart threatened to leap from her chest.

"Finn."

He stood wide-eyed across the threshold, his hand raised as if he had been about to knock.

All her bravery from moments ago shattered, the pieces sticking themselves together into something else entirely.

"Eliza." He swallowed and finally lowered his hand. The way he said her name, like the sweetest prayer, made her knees go weak.

He's here. He's here. He's here.

No other thought could take hold but that one.

She stepped back. Finn entered, closing the door quietly behind him before leaning against it.

"I thought you were going to the queen," she said, then hated herself for uttering that title.

His gaze caught hers, held. "I was."

The admission hit her like a fist to the ribs, but she forced herself to be still, to wait. "But?"

"I couldn't do it."

"No?"

He shook his head. "What I want is right here."

A flush of warmth crept up her neck.

Finn pushed off the door and took her hand in his. The simple connection was enough to steal her breath. The expansive room was suddenly small and stifling.

"Eliza." He knelt on one knee. "I could never be with anyone else in a world where you exist."

She wasn't sure when she knelt or how her palms ended up pressed against his cheeks. But suddenly, his face was just in front of hers, sharing the same breath, the same warmth, and uttering the only truth there was to share. "Me either. I meant what I said on the dance floor. I only want to be with you."

Finn's eyes widened just a fraction, the last sight she had before his lips crashed against her. It wasn't the tentative kiss from the library—the barest whisper of touch that made her question whether it had truly happened at all. This kiss was all-consuming, the truest confirmation of his words that anyone could offer.

He lifted her as if she weighed nothing, never breaking their kiss. Her arms encircled his neck, her legs his torso, but she didn't need to hold on. He'd never drop her, never let her fall.

The tip of his tongue flicked against her lips. Eliza parted for him, eager to deepen their connection, lost in the feel of Finneas against her.

Something solid pressed against her back. The wall? The ridiculous bow dug into the base of her spine—cushion and obtrusion at once. But that didn't matter, not with his taste in her mouth, his scent filling her nose, and his strong body cocooning her. He was the sweetest cage, the only one she ever desired to be trapped in.

Moisture grew between her legs as she rubbed herself against him, desperate for more, for all of him. The kiss alone was a wonder, sparking fire in her veins, but it wasn't enough. Not nearly enough.

29

*I*f he died at that moment, Finn would die a happy man. Whatever punishment awaited in his future was worth it. Even if he lost the safety of the Red Court, his easy life, *she* was worth it. The taste of Eliza's lips was better than he could have dreamed, sweet and intoxicating. They were the richest wine and blurred his thoughts more with one taste than an entire bottle of Wonderland's finest.

Eliza's ridiculous dress bunched up between them, a barrier blocking the feel of her that he so desperately craved. She kissed him. She wanted him. Even his dreams hadn't been so generous.

Then she pulled away, tugging his heart right out of his chest.

"Finneas."

Ancient kings. The sound of his full name on her lips nearly brought him to his knees. It might have had he not held her pressed against the wall.

"I want you," she said in a hoarse whisper. Her lips found his again, a teasing press followed by a sharp nip of teeth at his bottom lip.

Little minx. A grin twitched at the corner of his mouth as she pulled back, their heated breaths mingling. "What exactly do you want from me, Eliza?"

"I want… I want…" She licked her lips.

"Say it. Tell me."

She ground her hips against him, driving him mad. "Must I?"

"Yes," he nearly growled. He'd take nothing less.

"I want you to fuck me, Finneas."

The words alone nearly made him come. His cock was hard as a rock, desperate, eager. But he wouldn't rush things. He adjusted his grip until their fingers were twined, only the press of his hips against Eliza and the wall at her back keeping them upright. Finn positioned their bound hands on either side of Eliza's head, and she let him, completely open to his attentions.

"Please," she whimpered.

He groaned. That little whimper tried to undo him, but he wouldn't be dissuaded. Finn dipped his head, trailing kisses along the column of her neck, her collarbone. He pushed down the sleeve of her dress, baring one shoulder and lavishing it as well.

"Finn…" Eliza wiggled against him, and he bucked back lest she have him coming in his breeches. She slid a bit down the wall, the damn dress getting in his way. That wouldn't do at all.

Eliza squealed as Finn took her in his arms once more and carried her to the bed. He laid her upon the coverings like a precious work of art, all stretched out in her brilliance, her legs dangling off the side. Candlelight illuminated the profile of her face and the flush of her cheeks. It sculpted out the curve of her breasts with teasing shadows. She reached for him, but there was so much more he desired to sample first.

Finn captured one of her legs, tracing his fingertips across her skin and the gooseflesh pebbling it. As he lifted it, the dress slid up, bearing her underthings—a horrible shade of crimson to match the dress. Those would have to go. He slid his fingers under the hem, savoring Eliza's gasp and how her body tensed in anticipation.

"Are you sure you want me?" he asked.

Eliza grumbled. "Must I beg?"

"You should beg for nothing." He tugged the material. Eliza raised her hips, allowing her undergarments to slip down her legs and reveal her to him.

That sight did bring him to his knees. He pulled the last of her underthings free and tossed them away. *Ancient kings.* She was wet. He could see the slight glisten of her desire on her curls. A knot of pure lust pulled tight and taut deep within him. Only a woman worthy of being Alice could undo him with just the sight of her.

Eliza leaned up on her forearms, barely visible over the mass of her dress. "Are you still there?"

"Always." He grinned. "But this—" He gathered a fistful of her dress. "Needs to go."

"I couldn't agree more." Eliza slipped to her feet, their bodies pressing together in the most delicious way as she occupied the narrow space between him and the bed. She turned, giving him access to the ties at the back. He tugged at them, earning a gasp as he accidentally tightened them instead.

"Damnable thing," he grumbled. It floated around Eliza like a crimson cloud, but getting it off? A nightmare.

"Just rip it."

He tugged at the back once more, but it held firm.

"Here." She twisted toward him once more, her hand at her chest over the deep vee plunging almost to her navel, only little threads of beads holding it together.

He sought her eyes and held her gaze as he slipped his fingers into either side of the gaping vee, the flat of his nails sliding against the soft skin below.

Without another moment's hesitation, he jerked the dress apart. Fabric ripped. Beads tinkled to the floor. Eliza shrugged out of the gown, and he finally allowed his gaze to trail downward. Her breasts were perfect—full globes and dusky nipples he couldn't wait to taste. And the rest of her? He scrubbed a hand down his face as he took in her graceful curves, the thatch of curls between her legs, and back up to her parted lips and the unshielded look of desire burning in her eyes.

What had he ever done to be blessed with such a sight?

"Do I get to see you?" Eliza stepped out of the dress and kicked it away. She trailed her fingers along the collar of his coat and down his chest, stopping at his heart, her palm settling over it. Did she feel how it raced for her?

"As my lady wishes." He took that hand, raised it to his lips, and kissed it once more before stepping back.

Eliza settled on the bed, watching as he shed one piece of clothing and then the next. Her fingers drifted between her breasts and down her stomach, venturing lower. Finn groaned, nearly ripping his own clothes off in his eagerness to get to her.

When he finally shed the last piece, he had to restrain himself from leaping on her like the animal lurking under his skin. A woman like her deserved so much more than that.

Finn trailed his fingers down her cheek, grazing the side of her face. "No second thoughts?"

The look in her eyes answered the question before she ever spoke. "Never."

He captured her lips with his, gently urging her back onto the covers. She was a soft, gentle warmth to the cold harshness of his life. Perfect. A breathy whimper escaped her as he left her mouth, traveling down to her chin, her neck, her breast, leaving little kisses with each step. Eliza gasped, her back arching up to him as his mouth closed over the lovely bud of one nipple. So delightful, and a perfect fit for his palm as he took the other in hand. He savored its fullness.

Reluctantly, he released his prize, continuing down her stomach until he reached the juncture of her thighs. Eliza parted for him, baring her most intimate self. *Glorious.* His cock throbbed and twitched, aching with its eagerness to be inside her.

"You're stunning, Eliza. Inside and out."

Her lips parted, but he didn't wait for her to speak before he sought that place between her legs.

She gasped at the first contact. At least, he thought she did. Everything blurred at his first taste of her, already so wet and sweet. She wanted him —of all men in Wonderland, how did he get so lucky as to have Eliza crave him? Maybe it was damnation, a curse all its own. No good could come from loving Alice. She'd told him from the start that she wanted to go home, back to her world. Once she was anointed, she could, but he could never follow, at least not for long. Mere minutes in her world and the tug of Wonderland tried to pull him back across the ground and down the rabbit hole. And then there was the fact the queen would be more than furious if she learned of his true feelings.

Still, for all the risk and heartache it was sure to bring, he couldn't make himself regret a moment, especially not as Eliza moaned his name and rolled her hips toward him as he lavished her.

This night was a gift. No matter what the future held, he wouldn't let it touch this moment.

"Finneas." Eliza's fingers slid through his hair, caressing his scalp and tugging him closer.

He smoothed his thumbs along her inner thighs, urging her legs wider. The precious nub between her legs taunted him, and he didn't hesitate to tease it back. The scent of her arousal flooded his heightened senses, driving him wild on smell alone, to say nothing of her taste on his tongue, her sweat moans, or just her very presence there with him.

Finn slid one finger inside, and Eliza bucked against him, her walls clenching, so perfectly slick and tight. He stroked once, twice, aiming to find that special place inside her, and then she broke, shaking and grinding against him as her release took her.

His gaze snapped to her face. Her eyes closed in rapture and lips parted, still crying her pleasure into the night. The covers clenched in her hand and her hair splayed around her.

There had never been a more wondrous sight in all of Wonderland.

30

*E*liza came back to herself, panting, nails dug into the coverlets, and a sheen of sweat dewing her skin. It had nothing on the wetness between her legs or the tingling warmth still coursing through every inch of her.

All that glorious pleasure failed compared to the sight of the man between her legs. Finn's golden gaze fixed on her face as he gave another long, slow lap of his tongue against her core, spurring a new wave of shivers. His pale hair teased her thighs and his hands, firm yet gentle, held her open for him—not that he needed to. She wouldn't close herself off to him, never again.

She'd had lovers before, casual dalliances that her parents would have frowned on. They'd been satisfactory, easing her curiosity and need, but not one had come close to making her feel the way Finn did. He treated her like a precious treasure to be worshipped and embraced her body in all its glory and flaws. But more than that, he ignited something deep in her soul that she would have sworn a thing of myth.

It excited her. It scared her—but not enough to pull away. Rather, it encouraged her to reach further into the darkness, to find something worth hanging onto.

Finn rose on his knees, exposing his whole stunning self and the proud appendage between his legs—a masterpiece all its own. When she first met the strange man who stood too close and all but kidnapped her, she'd never considered this outcome. And yet, now that they were here, she couldn't imagine not being with him. It was right.

Cool air swept in at his absence, stark against the warm wetness between her legs. She couldn't help the shudder that crawled up her form, a mixture of her fading orgasm and the lingering desire swirling within her.

Finn never took his eyes off her as he licked the wetness from his lips. He wiped the rest from his face before smearing it across his cock. That act alone nearly undid her all over again. She couldn't even find words as he leaned down, his forearms on either side of her, their faces a breath apart.

"I want all of you, Eliza." His throat bobbed, and she'd swear his voice cracked over her name. "Will you have me?"

Eliza took his face between her palms, savoring his warmth, the glide of his hair against her skin where it fell over his ears, and the bit of stubble that tickled her tender flesh. Looking into his eyes, she had no doubts. "Of course." She'd never wanted anyone half so much.

The grin he rewarded her with was blinding, even in the room's dim light.

His lips found hers, soft and gentle. His cock nudged against her entrance. She rolled her hips. That was all it took for him to slide inside her. *And Mother above, he is perfect.* He inched his hard length into her slowly, giving her body time to adjust to his girth, to savor the feel of him inside her.

"Ancient kings," he groaned. He closed his eyes, sinking in until a tiny whimper slipped from her. "You're perfect, Eliza. So perfect."

"You too." He couldn't fit her better if the Mother made him especially for her. "I—"

Whatever she planned to say vanished as he moved, pulling back and then sinking into her depths once more. As he did, his weight settled on her, but it wasn't the crushing press it should have been given his size. It was comfort, connection. They could be pressed together head to heel, and it wouldn't be enough. Eliza gripped a muscular shoulder. Her other hand slid through his hair and held him close as they moved together.

In moments, the knot of desire within her tightened, clenching stronger than her thighs around him. The world faded completely. There was no Alice. No Wonderland. Nothing but the two of them mattered.

Finn slid deep, rubbing against that magical place within, and she tipped over the edge. Her vision blurred. Everything spun as a wave of warmth flowed through her.

Finn groaned. "Fuck, Eliza, I—" His body shuddered.

They were helpless to do anything but hold one another close as they rode the wave of ecstasy together.

Slowly, the spots dancing in front of Eliza's vision retreated. The room solidified. Finn panted above her, his eyes still closed in the last lingering throws of his release. When he opened them, she'd have sworn stars still danced in his irises. So many things passed between them in shared breaths, looks, and their connection—something that linked them body and soul.

Eventually, Finn trailed his fingers along her cheek and broke the silence. "Are you all right?"

A delirious giggle burst from her lips before she could stop it. "How could you think otherwise?"

He grinned and nuzzled her cheek. "I had to be sure." His weight slid off her, but he drew her with him, cradling her against the hard planes of his chest.

"And you, Finn?"

His lips pressed against hers. "I've never been better. No matter what happens, I will never regret a moment with you."

The easy grin slipped from her face, but Finn didn't notice as he released her before climbing off the bed. Someone would have seen Finn outside her door. The queen would be furious if he didn't come to her, but there was no way she'd ever let him go now, even if he didn't loathe being near the woman.

Finn dampened a cloth using the pitcher on the nearby nightstand and passed it to her. Eliza's thoughts were far from the moment as she cleaned the evidence of their lovemaking, her body still warm and tingling. After he'd done the same, Finn returned to the bed, sliding them both under the covers until she was tucked into the protection of his arms, their faces barely an inch apart.

There was nowhere she'd rather be, and yet, every moment he stayed risked his life. "Should you... Do you think you should go?"

He stiffened, various emotions flickering across his features. "I thought—"

"No." Eliza all but leaped on him. She pushed him into the sheets with her palm on his chest, half her body sliding over his as if she could hold him in place. "I'm sorry. That's not what I meant."

Some tension slipped from his form as he settled into the sheets.

"I just... The guards saw us come this way. If they speak..."

"Ah." His thumb rubbed little circles on her hip, stirring emotion like a stick swirling in a still pond. "Worried about me?"

She swatted at him. "Of course I am."

"I can come up with some kind of excuse."

"Oh? So we'll say you just happened to faint in my room or some such thing?"

He shrugged ineffectually.

"I'm serious." Her voice grew sharp. "What'll happen if—" *If she finds out.* The words stuck to her tongue, unwilling to tarnish the moment by letting the queen into their bed. The threat of her already lingered far too closely in the shadows.

"I'll think of something." Finn leaned up to kiss her, but Eliza pulled away.

He had no plan. Come dawn, the queen could demand his head, and Eliza had little conviction that even a direct order from Alice could stop her. It was too great a risk. She couldn't lose Finn—wouldn't lose him.

"Run away with me."

Finn's hand stilled at her side. He blinked up at her, lips slightly parted. "I thought you said you had to stay?"

"I have to become Alice if I can't break the curse." She wouldn't let the world fall to war and ruin. "But I don't have to stay here." She gestured around.

His features lost their easy mirth. "It would be dangerous for you out there. The White Court—"

"Can't be worse than this one," she snapped.

He flinched as if in pain.

"What?" she asked. There was something more that he hadn't told her.

"You know I'm from the White Court."

She nodded. He'd said as much and that he could never go back. "You were banished."

"Yes." His focus was suddenly somewhere far away. "My mother and I both. She ran away with me."

Eliza gasped. "Why?"

"She was banished for being unfaithful to my father—not that he deserved her loyalty. The current White King had us hunted down after the banishment. She tried to protect me, and they...they killed her."

"That's horrible!" She reared back, shaking her head. Here, everyone seemed to sleep with everyone else, and no one blinked an eye. It was less common in her world, and some took great offense at being jilted for another lover, but to demand death? "And so ridiculous. Death for an affair?"

Finn's arms tightened around her as he rolled them to the side. Eliza pressed herself closer, offering whatever comfort she could.

"The White Court is a court of law," he said. "The opposite of Red. Red has many faults, but it tries to be a court of pleasures, of parties, life, and vibrance. It's everything White is not."

The White Court hunted for Alice, possibly even right now. But how could they ever hope she would choose them? One thing she was sure of, though, however horrible they might be, they wanted Alice alive.

"They won't harm me. They need me."

He stared at her in the dim light, his face unreadable. "There are many ways to hurt someone, Eliza. Not all of them physical."

"But if they hurt me, how could they ever expect me to choose them?"

Finn glanced away again. "They have their ways."

Her lips drew in a line. "Still, we can't stay here. You said you could keep me safe, right?"

His palms slid up her back, leaving shivers in their wake. "With my life."

"But I want you to live, Finn. Live and be safe. Could we stick to the wilds? The anointment is only a week away."

The hint of a smile pulled at his lips. "You'd leave all of this behind for me? Trust me to care for you until you become Alice and can go home?"

"Yes." *A thousand times, yes.* She had no doubts about him. Maybe that was why her grandmother had sent him, because she knew he was honest and true, that he'd care for her in this strange world.

"Tomorrow. During the croquet match," he said. "It's in the gardens. We'll find a moment and slip away."

"Why not tonight?" she asked.

"The guards are too alert. We'd be lucky to get down this hall without someone stopping us, much less outside. But tomorrow we're already outside the castle—most of the way free. I'll gather everything we need and have it ready."

A rapid fluttering filled her chest, carrying away some of her worries. "You promise?"

He kissed her, soft and sweet. "Yes. Now rest, Eliza. We'll need all our strength for what's ahead."

The future had never been more uncertain, but as she nestled into his protective arm and closed her eyes, Eliza had never been more excited for the dawn.

31

Finn left when the first rays of dawn began to lift the blanket of darkness from the room. He kissed her before whispering a promise to gather everything they would need and meet her at the croquet match that afternoon.

Too bad it couldn't be held in the morning, but many people likely still slept off their drinks from the night before. After all, it wouldn't do for prominent members of the court to look like a hungover mess in front of the monarchs.

Eliza tried to rise for the day, but between Finn's promise, the lingering pleasure from the night before, and his scent all over her pillows, she couldn't quite find the urge to move.

The maids woke her sometime before midday, insisting on preparing her a bath and shoving food her way. At least they let her bathe and dress in peace. Even better, the queen hadn't ordered an audacious outfit for the occasion, so Eliza was free to pick a simple dress of blue that was easy to move in and sturdy shoes that would be advantageous in their travels. She had the maids braid her hair and tie it back with ribbons, something that would keep the wavy mess manageable and out of her way.

Would Finn find them a horse? Would they flee on foot? She had no idea, but she prepared as best she could for whatever awaited.

By early afternoon, the Tweeds escorted her through the halls of the royal manor and out into the sprawling maze of the gardens that led to the pitch. Usually, they were silent statues, going about their business, but today they spoke to her, offering thanks for letting them enjoy the party as if it was rare as diamonds. Eliza looked at her escorts more closely, a tangle of regret settling in her stomach. Would they be punished for her escape? She pulled her bottom lip between her teeth. She'd have to find a way to keep them out of trouble before she departed with Finn, especially since one of the twins had consumed too much sweet wine and still struggled to walk a straight line. It'd be far too easy to blame him for her choices.

Tiered, wooden stands stood to either side of the open, grassy pitch. Crimson draperies hung over their tops, granting the many people crammed into the stands some relief from the afternoon sun.

Most people were here to watch—to see and be seen like the gatherings she'd been forced to attend during much of her youth. The king and queen selected the players, a few dozen at most, who would take turns through various rounds of play.

No sooner had they arrived than the king spotted Eliza across the lawn and broke off from the conversation he held with a gaggle of others. Sunlight glinted off the strands of silver in his hair and the golden buttons on the crimson coat he wore.

Eliza tensed, forcing a pleasant smile to her face as he hurried to meet them. The Mother help her if he tried to continue things from last night.

"Alice," he greeted her with a blinding smile before turning to her guards. "Thank you for escorting Alice here. You are dismissed."

With a few words and a wave of his hand, the king removed one of her worries and replaced it with another. The more hungover of the twins let out an audible sigh before they both bowed and left.

"Dismissing my guards?" she asked, if only to avoid the inevitable.

"Do not worry," the king promised. "We have plenty to keep us safe."

Now that he mentioned it, there were many more guards than she expected. The crimson-clad warriors stood along the sides of the pitch, in front of the stands, and near the maze entrances. Dread settled hard in her gut. Dozens and dozens were stationed everywhere. Protection from White? But how would she and Finn be able to flee?

"Alice." The king took her hand in his, and she fought the urge to pull away. "About last night—"

She tensed, bracing for the worst.

"I must apologize."

This time she did flinch back. "What?" Of all the words she prepared for, that was the last of them.

"I believe I had too much to drink and may have come off inappropriately. I only wished to show you the favor of a dance and then perhaps give your feet a rest if you were weary."

She blinked at him, stunned into silence. A king apologizing?

"I-I am grateful, Your Majesty."

"Your grandmother and I used to enjoy easy company and conversation, usually over a glass of wine or two. I hoped to do the same with you."

Grandmama? Her brows pinched.

"We were simply friends," he hurried on, perhaps noting her look. "Nothing more."

That wasn't where her mind had gone at all, but she appreciated the information all the same. Though it was strange that, if they were friends, her grandmother wouldn't have mentioned it.

"I realize this is all new to you and must be overwhelming, but in time, perhaps we can share the same friendship."

If that was truly what he wanted, she could live with that. "I would like that," she said, hoping to end the conversation.

He raised her hand to his lips, placing a chaste kiss on its back before releasing her. "If there is anything I might do to improve your stay with us here in the Red Court, please let me know."

Perhaps it was all a lie—some pretty words to lure her into his web. But she'd had a lifetime of dissecting such things, and the honesty she discovered in his tone spooked her more than the apology itself.

"I certainly will." Would he intervene where his wife was concerned? Would he help her and Finn? In that moment, he'd opened a door, another possible path that had been closed off only moments ago.

"Actually," she continued. "Perhaps you could help me find someone. I wished to speak with—"

"Alice!"

The sudden, exuberant call had Eliza twisting toward its source. It took a moment to place the figure who approached in her billowing teal dress with her white hair piled atop her head. Some kind of shimmering red glitter was dusted on her hair, sparkling like tiny bits of flame in the sunlight.

"Duchess?"

The king gave a nod of his head and turned on his heel. "I shall find you later, Alice."

"Your Majesty—" She nearly reached for him, but he'd already stepped away. The Duchess filled her periphery, a man at her side. She turned, recognition settling in. Her smile twitched, nearly dropping. Harry had given her that horrible tea that turned her world upside down and inside out for an entire afternoon. She certainly wouldn't be taking any offerings from him today.

"It's lovely to see you doing so well." The Duchess cooled herself with a lace fan.

"Duchess." Eliza gave a respectful nod of her head. "You didn't bring Baby today?" The woman hadn't been without her pet for a moment when she'd stayed at her manor.

"Alas, I miss him so." The Duchess gave a breathy sigh. "But he would hate these crowds. Best he stay at home. And so lucky we made it in time for the games today, don't you agree, Maddoc?"

Her other companion from tea picked that moment to walk up and join them. "Oh yes." He slid his arm through the Duchess's. Though he was a foot shorter than her, his large top hat made up the difference, presenting them at equal height if one only saw the tops of their heads. "We're just in time."

"Perhaps you'd join us for the first round, Alice?" The Duchess offered her other arm. "It would be such an honor." A waft of the woman's perfume rolled over Eliza, smelling of bergamot and reminding her of the headmistress at her boarding school. The older woman had found endless fault in Eliza and her inability to be the perfect doll of a young lady she tried to force all her girls to become.

What she wouldn't give to turn and flee. Only practiced decency rooted her feet in place.

"Actually, I need to find someone." She tried to glance past the Duchess, searching desperately for Finn. She assumed he'd find her, rescue her as he always did from these awkward situations, but she'd yet to catch even a brief glimpse of him.

"Oh, well, we can help you look." The Duchess slid her arm through Eliza's without warning and pulled her along. The older woman beamed, positively delighted to have Alice at her side for all the court to see.

Eliza stumbled after her, nearly tripping over her own feet. "Really, I need to find—"

"Ah, Alice." The hiss in the queen's voice chilled her to the bone despite the afternoon sun.

The Duchess stopped dead in her tracks and turned toward the approaching monarch, her arm tightening ever so slightly on Eliza's. She glanced at the woman from the corner of her eyes, catching her thinned lips as she gave a polite bow. *An ally?*

"Your Majesty." The Duchess plastered a smile on her face, one Eliza would wager was even more forced than her own.

The queen didn't spare a glance for the Duchess, Maddoc, or Harry. Instead, her piercing gaze focused solely on Eliza, a slight sneer curling her lips.

She knows.

Whether she guessed or someone told her, Eliza couldn't say, but that look spoke volumes, and none of it good. It wouldn't be a surprise if the queen swung at her with the gilded mallet she carried for the game. Suddenly, Eliza was grateful for the Duchess and inched closer to her side.

"Come." The queen waved her over. "We must get you a mallet if you're to play the opening round."

"Alice had just offered to join our group," Duchess said, patting Eliza's arm.

The queen threw her head back and cackled. If one looked on from afar, they might think the Duchess made a joke, but this was no laughing matter.

"Alice," the queen drew her name out, "will be playing with me."

Eliza stood frozen. Finn wouldn't be able to risk getting near the queen, especially if she knew what they'd been up to. Confronting the queen would cause unnecessary problems that might make it harder, or impossible, to slip away.

Duchess looked between her men, some silent conversation passing between them before she patted Eliza's arm once more. "We shall catch-up later, dear."

"Of course." Eliza's throat was suddenly so tight the words barely slipped out.

The Duchess released her with a quick smile that was more apology than anything. Reluctantly, Eliza forced herself to abandon the odd trio and join the queen, drawing near until she was in easy striking distance of the mallet.

"You look positively gloomy this afternoon. Long night?" The queen's broad, knowing grin made her stomach turn over.

She definitely knew, and nothing good would come from it if they didn't get out of there soon.

One game became two, then three. Eliza fanned herself, blaming the afternoon sun for the perspiration on her skin and the bouts of nausea that had her swaying on her feet. It was a poor excuse given that footmen held parasols to guard the players from the bright rays.

Each time the queen struck her ball, the clack of the wood was like a stake driven further into Eliza's chest. She'd seen no sign of Finn—human or rabbit. The queen never took her eyes off Eliza for more than a moment, that knowing look making her squirm in her boots and pray to the Mother for some relief.

The only respite had been a few moments with the king after the last round, an unexpected source of comfort. But the queen had quickly sent him off to play with another group across the yard, plying him with the knowledge that their guests needed his royal attention. She hadn't even had the chance to ask him about Finn, and every time the queen looked at her, Eliza's hopes plummeted further.

The queen scored a winning strike, much to the joy of the crowd whom she waved to as she basked in their cheers and adulation. She practically skipped as she returned to the shade of her waiting parasol, held inconveniently by a footman next to the one holding Eliza's. No matter where she moved, he followed, no doubt ordered to do so. The queen swung her mallet, nearly wracking another player before the handle smacked against her open palm.

"Alice, Alice, Alice." She tapped the mallet against her palm with each iteration of Eliza's title. "Whyever do you look so ill? Not enjoying the game?"

The game. Eliza nearly snorted in disgust. There was a nefarious game at work indeed.

Eliza faked a yawn, covering her hand with the back of her mouth. "I'm quite worn out. I had a long night."

Victoria's hands tightened on the mallet, her knuckles going white. Her lips wrinkled in disdain, and Eliza could no longer hold back a self-satisfied grin.

The queen stomped across the stretch of lawn separating them until she kicked her foot at Eliza's hem. "You should watch where you tread."

"Or what?" Enough was enough. Eliza placed her hands on her hips, staring the other woman down.

The queen waved her hand, and the men holding the parasols retreated. Eliza and the queen were left as an island unto themselves, the handle of the mallet a thin barrier between them, especially as the queen leaned in closer, her face inches from Eliza's. "Finn will pay for his disrespect."

Eliza saw red, and not the crimson of the court, but a bright blood red that seared under her skin and begged her to rip the wooden game piece from the queen's hands and wield it for herself. "If you lay one hand on him, I swear..." Her nails cut little crescents into her palms.

The queen straightened. Her brows rose. "Is that a threat?"

"It's a promise." She was done being the queen's pawn, her plaything.

Nor would she let the queen play with anyone else. If Eliza had even a shred of power in this strange world, then damn it all, she was going to use every last drop of it. "Am I not Alice?" She drew out the words, cocking her head to the side as she assessed her prey. "Do I not decide who rules in Wonderland?"

The queen's eyes flew wide. "You wouldn't dare—"

"I would." *And so much more.* She leaned in, forcing the queen back on her heels. "Lay one hand on him, and Red shall never rule again."

The queen lunged back with a veritable growl, pulling back the mallet and readying for a swing. "Why, you little—"

Screams erupted from the far end of the yard. The queen froze mid-swing and twisted toward the sound.

The ground rumbled. A deep, bellowing roar joined the rising chorus of chaos. She knew that sound.

Bandersnatch.

Eliza swayed on her feet. At the distant side of the pitch, forms in white clashed with those in red. People scrambled over one another in the stands, some leaping from the sides altogether. The players gathered on the field screeched, some turning to run her way, others rushing toward the action.

The queen turned toward Eliza, her eyes wide as saucers. The mallet fell from her limp fingers to thud upon the ground. She uttered one word before she fainted. "White."

Color flickered through the air, sparkling rainbows there and then gone. A wall of crimson rose on the far side of the stands, spreading from a figure with his arms held wide. It took a moment to recognize him through the crowd—the king, protecting his people, unlike his helpless wife. He wielded tangible magic like Finn had the night they fled the Duchess's manor. The sparkles, the rainbow, came from him and a few others gathered at his sides. A shiver wracked her body. More magic shot through the air, this coming from intruders across the pitch.

Bodies fell on the other side of the wall and did not rise.

Sound retreated. Maybe people still screamed, but she couldn't hear it. People ran past, nearly knocking her over, but she couldn't move.

And then a woman was right in front of her, blocking her view and shaking her by the shoulders.

"Alice! Eliza!"

Eliza blinked rapidly, finally recognizing the Duchess, who screamed at her to run. Another familiar form, Pilla, crouched by the queen, helping others lift and carry her away.

"We must go!" The Duchess grabbed her hand and yanked her away from the pitch.

She stumbled a step, but then Harry was there on her other side, taking her arm and helping her along, Maddoc beside him.

Of all the familiar faces, there was still one she did not see, one she could not flee without.

"Finn!" She twisted back over her shoulder for one last glance at the chaos. "Where's Finn?"

32

The steady drip, drip, drip of water ticked on like the hands of a clock, drawing ever closer to his demise. Finn's head thumped back against the coarse stone wall of the cell. What a fool he'd been, trying to go back to his room to grab supplies. He'd still been light on his feet, nearly floating on air from his night with Eliza, head in the clouds, seeing only hope in the morning sunlight.

If he'd been more aware, more himself, he'd have thought to shift into his rabbit form and take more caution when traipsing through the halls. But all his thoughts still lay with the sleeping woman he'd left. *Stupid fool.*

Would she learn that the queen's personal guards arrested him before the sun had fully risen in the sky? Would Eliza think that he fled without her? Surely not, but who knew what lies the queen would spin?

Any minute now, a troop of guards could walk through the main door prepared to end him. He'd fight with all he had, and he was stronger than most, but it might not be enough. His actions the night before may have doomed him. Still, he couldn't regret a moment of his time with Eliza. Given the choice to live his old life or have one more moment with her, he'd pick her every time.

Someone a few cells down sang a nonsense song, their tone so sharp it could shatter glass. Too bad the cell doors were made of iron. Apparently, they'd been here long enough to go mad, but that wouldn't be his fate. The queen wouldn't let him linger here, not when the king could learn of it and demand his release, or Eliza, or perhaps some other member of the court who felt something for him other than indifference, though he couldn't say who that would be.

Finn sighed and ran his hands down his face, wincing at the bruises forming from guards who had been none too kind. His lips thinned. He'd even trained some of the bastards. So much for loyalty.

A little light glinted through a window high above his head, slanting in at an angle that showed it to be afternoon. His chest drew tight. Eliza would be looking for him, and he wouldn't be there as he'd promised.

The ground rumbled, a tremor so slight it could have been a trick of the mind, until it came again. *Earthquake?* No one had reported one of those since his youth, but in this time before Alice's anointment, anything was possible.

Finn pushed himself up with a groan, attempting to ignore the aches in his body. He stretched on his toes, squinting against the sunlight as he peeked out the thin, high window.

Screams echoed from the gardens, followed by a deep roar.

His blood went cold. *Fuck.*

Another roar followed, this one from a slightly different direction. Only one thing made a sound that horrid—Bandersnatch.

Finn gripped the bars on the windows, attempting to wrench them apart to no avail. He could pull himself up, transform, and then—

No. He slammed his fist against the wall. There was no landing on the other side, and a drop from so high would kill him. For the millionth time, he lamented his other form being a rabbit rather than a bird or something infinitely more useful.

Eliza was out there, in danger. He slammed the wall again, earning more bruises.

The screams continued, but that wasn't all. Sparks of magic floated over the hedges. He glimpsed a distant bit of white and silver.

Shit, there aren't just Bandersnatch on the loose. White was here.

And I'm stuck in a fucking cell.

Finn whirled toward the iron door in the far wall. He couldn't squeeze through the grates and escape, but maybe he could blast the damnable thing off its hinges. It'd been too great a risk before, with guards likely stationed outside the cellblock, but if they were under attack by White, a few wayward prisoners were the last of their problems.

Finn called upon the magic in his blood, channeling it toward his hands, a glimmering ball of power forming in the space between his open palms. He concentrated on that blinding light, willing it to grow and expand.

Distantly, he heard the scrape of metal. Something clanked then clicked. A moment before he flung his ball of power toward the door, it swung open.

"What the—" His fingertips dug into the ball of magic, holding it steady and refusing to let it fly.

Chesa stepped through the door, wearing billowing pink pants and a matching top that left much of her stomach exposed. Her expression was calm, serene, as if she planned a casual walk through the gardens but ended up in a much different place.

"Hello, Finneas." She grinned.

Finn pressed his palms together, urging the magic to return to him and letting it soak in with a shudder that rolled down his form. Only when the power had faded and settled back under his skin did he respond. "What the fuck are you doing here?"

"I thought you could use some help?" She held up a set of keys, letting it dangle in the air off one finger. "You might need your magic later."

"How did you even know I'm here?"

She shrugged. "I have my ways."

He stared at the open door, itching to run through it and out to the gardens, but a tingle of unease held him back. "Why are you helping me?" It had to be a trick of some sort. "Won't the queen be furious?"

"Her opinion doesn't matter."

Finn snorted. *Tell her that.*

"Well?" Chesa snapped and stopped her foot, suddenly impatient as opposed to the calm woman of seconds ago. "Are you going to go save Eliza or not?"

Eliza. In danger.

The queen's threats no longer mattered. Finn raced for the door, brushing by Chesa without stopping. The cellblock door stood open. He didn't stop to consider that or the guards lying unconscious on the ground. Despite his speed, Chesa caught up to him, matching pace at his side as he raced through the halls.

"White?" he bit out.

She gave one jerking nod. "And some beasties." Then she grinned. "Look how you run to her. Such a gallant knight. Perhaps Alice was right after all."

Finn ignored her comments, skidding across the stonework as he turned a corner and then hurtled down a flight of stairs.

"What are they after?"

The grin vanished from her face. "You already know that."

Eliza.

He willed himself faster, practically crashing through a door and down another hall. *Damn the cellblock being far from everything.*

"Can't you just vanish and get to her quicker?" He wasn't sure how the woman did what she did or if she could move faster in her unseen state, but if it could possibly help Eliza, he was for it.

She cocked her head to the side. "You're right." Chesa vanished from sight—winked out as if she'd never been beside him at all.

Strange woman. Finn didn't spare Chesa another thought as he raced into the gardens.

33

*E*liza turned in a circle, staring down multiple paths through the hedge maze, which all looked annoyingly the same. "This cannot be right."

They were no closer to the Red Court than they had been minutes ago. If anything, they seemed to be further away.

The Duchess, Maddoc, and Harry had run with her into a nearby entrance to the maze as more White knights swarmed in from the opposite direction. The fact that they got so close without anyone noticing made her head spin. Though perhaps not as much as when Harry and Maddoc had turned just inside the entrance to the maze and used some sort of magic to cause the bushes to grow closed behind them.

Such a thing shouldn't be possible. And though it wasn't her first glimpse of magic or oddities by any means, her mind still struggled with it. Logic and reason fought a war with magic, and neither side was willing to submit yet. But she had bigger things to worry about—the knights; the deep, rumbling roars from numerous beasts far too close for comfort; and wherever the bloody hell they'd gotten lost.

"If you can close a path, can't you open a new one?" Eliza asked.

Harry huffed, hands on his knees, clearly worn out. "It's not the same."

"It's moving plants."

Maddoc dabbed sweat from his brow with a colorful handkerchief. "Growing and destroying are very different."

Her teeth ground together. *Fine.* He had a point there.

"Just a bit further and we'll be out of danger." The Duchess lifted her skirts and headed in the opposite direction of the towering spires rising over the tops of the hedges in the distance.

"But that's the wrong way," Eliza protested.

"Nonsense. Come on, dear."

The screams and sounds of battle had faded. Whether it was over or they simply couldn't hear it from where they were, she wasn't sure. But the roars of the beasts and occasional rumble of the ground below their feet had only grown closer.

"We cannot risk the Bandersnatch," Eliza insisted. Better the White knights find them than something that would turn them into its dinner.

"They won't come this way," the Duchess insisted. "We'll be safe."

Finn told her there was a Bandersnatch who lived in the maze, a strange guard dog of sorts. Apparently, it had wandered in by accident years ago and decided never to leave, making an easy dinner of any who should venture into its territory by accident. Otherwise, the beast seemed to keep to itself. Finn knew this maze and had lived around it for years. More than that, she knew he wouldn't lie to her.

If there were more beasts now, it could only be because the White knights had brought them. The coincidence of the timing allowed no other reason, even if logic was sometimes flimsy in Wonderland.

"Are you sure?" Eliza prodded.

"Certainly." Her voice rang with surety. Either the woman was daft or…

Eliza panned her gaze around the gathered group. A deep, hollow ache opened up in the pit of her stomach. For the first time, she noticed the white roses on the men's lapels—decorations that hadn't been there during the croquet match. The sparkling red powder had fallen from the Duchess's hair, or she'd shaken it off, leaving it a stark column of white.

Symbols of loyalty, but not to this court.

The Duchess had been so careful with the pink decorations in her home, she wouldn't make such a flagrant mistake now.

A silent look passed between the men before they turned their attention to the Duchess. Her shoulders drooped, and she shook her head. "Oh, Eliza."

"Why?" she asked, her voice cracking.

The Duchess clasped her hands in front of her. "Your flight from my home left me little choice. White demanded satisfaction."

Her ribs pulled tight toward her spine. They knew about the attack on the croquet match. They'd planned to hand her over to White from the start.

"They won't harm you, Alice," Harry said.

A hysterical laugh burst from her lips. They'd just killed or harmed who knew how many innocents during their attack. She was done being a pawn. The queen, the Duchess. Red, White. Damn them all, she was done being nothing but a piece in a game much bigger than herself.

Eliza turned and raced into the hedges.

"Alice!" the Duchess screeched, loud enough that anyone nearby would hear.

Eliza didn't look back, didn't stop.

The trio called after her in pursuit, but she was younger and faster. She could outrun them. She must.

Eliza turned down one path and then another, keeping the crimson towers in view. *Get out of the maze. Find Finn. Don't die. Get out of the maze. Find Finn. Don't die.*

She hazarded a glance over one shoulder, searching for danger and finding only hedges. She nearly stumbled into the greenery, shoving against the prickly leaves and earning little cuts to her palms before lurching down another path. Everything looked the same, like an endless maze she could never escape.

Another turn, and she skidded to a stop. A cluster of White knights stood at the end of the corridor. "There!" one called, pointing toward her.

Bloody hell.

Eliza turned and ran the other way. The heavy tread of footsteps and clang of metal echoed through the hedges—more knights in pursuit. The tingling fear echoed through her bones, urging her faster, heedless of direction.

The hedges widened ahead. *An exit? Finally!*

But as Eliza burst through the opening, her heart climbed up her throat. This was not a normal part of the maze, nor an exit. The square space had paths leading into it from each side, but within, grasses high as her waist swayed in a light breeze where they weren't trampled down in haphazard paths. She took a step back, her boot crunching on something. Eliza glanced down and swayed on her feet.

Bones.

They littered the ground. Some were bleached white by the sun, others browned. She jumped, stumbling back into more remains. A human skull fell free and rolled near her foot.

Eliza screamed.

A mistake. A terrible, terrible mistake.

She clamped her hands over her mouth, but it was too late. Across the grassy space, a furry creature as big as a horse raised its head, its muzzle red from a fresh kill.

The roar it let out was far too familiar.

Bandersnatch.

Its bellow echoed through her body, leaving a tremor in its wake. The ground shook as its paws slammed down. Elongated fangs stuck down over its bottom lip as its wide eyes settled on Eliza. A long feline-like tail swished through the grasses.

Eliza turned and ran back the way she came. Heavy thumping followed—the beast in pursuit. Cold sweat broke out along her skin. Tears burned in the corners of her eyes.

A White knight stepped from the opening in the hedge just ahead of her. Eliza slid around him, never stopping, never looking back.

The man screamed. Metal scraped and rang. Other voices joined the fray.

She couldn't look—didn't dare.

The Bandersnatch would keep the knights busy a moment, but one side would win out eventually.

Eliza zipped around a corner, tripping over something and going down hard. Pain bloomed on her knee and shot up her thigh. She whimpered, fingernails digging into the dirt. Some of her hair had fallen free, and she pushed it from her face. Ahead, a flash of pink caught her attention before sliding behind a turn in the hedge.

"Chesa?"

With a groan, Eliza shoved to her feet and limped forward. She turned the corner just in time to glimpse a show of dark arm and pink hair before it was gone again around another quick bend.

"Chesa, wait!"

A moment before she reached the turn, a form stepped out from the hedges. But it wasn't Chesa. A White knight blocked the way forward, his sword raised.

Eliza scrambled back, tripping over something she'd swear was invisible and going down on her backside. Noise from behind caused her to twist around as half a dozen more knights filed into the pathway.

No. Oh no.

"Finn," she whispered in a desperate plea.

"Alice?" one knight said, a question in his voice. "You're to come with us."

Eliza pushed to her feet as the knights spread out, trying to ring her in. "I'm not going anywhere with you."

Finn. Chesa. Anyone.

But no one was there. No one was coming. Eliza's fists tightened at her sides as she backed into the hedge.

Use your power. The voice from the night before echoed through her mind.

"I am Alice." She raised her chin, staring down the knights in turn. "You shall do as I order and leave this place."

They stopped. A small bud of hope blossomed in her chest as they looked at one another in silent question.

Then the one who'd spoken before stepped forward, palm outstretched toward the ground at her feet. "Not yet, you aren't."

Colorful poppies burst from the dry dirt around her feet. Eliza gasped, leaning into the hedges, but there was nowhere to go. As the blossoms unfurled, quick as a blink, they released something into the air—a shimmering dust. Pollen? A sweet scent tickled her nose, causing her to sneeze. As she gasped for another breath, the world spun and darkened at the edges. Her body refused to work, and then she fell into endless darkness.

34

Finn sprinted to the croquet pitch, dodging courtiers as they raced back toward the castle in fits of hysterics. Each face he searched, some familiar, some loathed—like the unconscious queen, but none the one he sought. A few guards tried to calm the chaos with little success.

Smoke billowed out from one set of the wooden stands, a few lingering flames licking at the remains of the canopy as the guards brought it under control.

King Jasper stood in the center of the pitch, shouting commands. He turned as Finn drew near, revealing a splatter of blood across his sporting attire, but from the easy way he moved and spoke, it wasn't his.

"Finneas!" The king raced forward and clapped him on the shoulder. His gaze caught for a moment on his bruised face before the wrinkles between his brows smoothed out. "We have White on the run. You're unharmed?" His gaze slid back to the bruise. "Mostly?"

Those few seconds were all it took for Finn to know that he wasn't aware of the queen's orders. His teeth ground together. So, she did plan to do away with him without telling the king. *Fitting.* A complication he'd have to address, but right now there were more important matters.

"Alice?"

The king's brows drew together once more. "She should be with the queen. They should be back at the castle by now."

The king continued speaking, but Finn barely heard him. The guards had the queen, but not Eliza. Dread threatened to bring him to his knees. "I have to find her."

He pulled the pocket watch from his pocket, one that pointed the way to the new Alice. The guards hadn't thought to divest him of his personal affairs when they found no weapons on him—thank goodness. He'd kept the talisman on him since returning to the Red Court, a loose connection to Eliza and way to assure himself she was safe. As he both feared and suspected, the hands pointed toward a section of the maze, not the castle. Without a moment to lose, he shoved the watch into his pocket and took off at a sprint.

"Finn!" the king called after him, but Finn ignored him.

How could these idiots lose Eliza?

Even if she didn't hold the place in their hearts that she did in his, she was Alice, or would be soon enough—as long as nothing happened to her.

A few different entrances to the maze loomed in the direction the clock hands pointed. If Eliza ran, which one would she have chosen? His brows pinched as he neared. None of them felt right. In times like these, though, the feel of something wasn't near as important as the smell. Finn shifted mid-stride. The air fled from his lungs as his rabbit form hit the ground. He ignored the pain and scampered on, sniffing for Eliza's familiar scent.

A bolt of energy surged through him as he caught it, nearly hidden behind the mass of other smells filling the area. He followed it, nose twitching as he advanced up on a wall of the hedge. Had she climbed over? He skidded to a stop. No, the section was much less dense than the rest and still smelled of new life and bitter magic. Someone had done this. To protect Eliza or trap her?

There was no time to ponder the motive. Finn dove toward the hedges, using his lithe form to squeeze between branches and pop out the other side into the maze. Her scent was clearer here, less obscured though not alone. Hints of bergamot, pepper, and something piney danced with Eliza's scent.

Finn tried to place the familiar scent as he rushed through the maze, stopping only for brief moments to make sure he took the correct turns and didn't lose the trail. He'd fixed so much on Eliza's smell that he didn't hear the people arguing until he was nearly upon them. One glimpse and the familiar scents suddenly made sense. Finn shifted mid-lunge, human hands shoving off the ground as his hind quarters shifted back a half-second later.

The Duchess shrieked, throwing her arms in front of her face to ward off an attack. Harry twisted around so hard he nearly fell—would have if Maddoc hadn't steadied him.

"Where's Eliza?" Finn snapped.

The men looked at one another. "That way." They each pointed in opposite directions.

A deep roar bellowed from somewhere further in the maze, an echo of Finn's fury. "You *lost* her?"

"We didn't mean to," Harry said.

Maddoc stomped his foot. "*She* ran away."

Eliza ran from them? Finn's gaze panned to the Duchess, who stood silent and pale, her wide-eyed gaze fixed on him. "What. Happened?" he grated. "Duchess—" Finn stomped across the space between them.

She swallowed visibly but held her ground.

"We're telling the truth!" Maddoc said.

"Honest," the other man echoed.

Finn stopped a foot shy of the older woman and turned to her companions. It was then he noticed the roses pinned to their lapels—white ones.

His head snapped back toward the Duchess. "How dare you."

"We had no choice," she squeaked out in a whisper. "The White King... He..."

That title alone had him shuddering. He was all too familiar with the wrath that bastard could met out. Another beastly roar split the air, followed by screams. *The Bandersnatch.* Finn whipped out his pocket watch. One quick look at the hands confirmed his fears.

"She's all right. She'll be all right," the Duchess muttered. For him or for her, he didn't know and no longer cared.

Eliza was in danger, and he'd wasted too much time on these fools. Finn took off at a sprint, praying he chose the right path that would lead him closer to her, begging all the Ancient kings to let him get to her before the Bandersnatch or any of the White knights.

It had to be their screams he heard, masculine ones filled with agony. Red knights would know better than to venture into the Bandersnatch's domain, but Eliza? She knew nothing of the maze. It'd be far too easy to end up in the wrong place.

It took only minutes to reach the site of the screams, but that was still too long. A White knight jabbed his sword toward the Bandersnatch. Other armored forms lay unmoving on the ground.

"Retreat!" someone yelled out of view. The knight swung again, sending the Bandersnatch rearing back on its hind legs, black stains—its blood—marring a striped leg. The knight turned and ran out of view, but the Bandersnatch followed, bounding on all fours faster than any human could run and shaking the ground. A scream speared through the hedges before being cut short.

Please... Finn's hand shook as he dared another glimpse at the pocket watch.

His whole body sagged in relief. The watch pointed behind him, away from the carnage ahead. Without waiting another moment, he ran in that direction, his pocket watch out to guide him. Traces of Eliza's scent hung in the air, but once again, it wasn't alone.

A sickly-sweet scent nearly burned his nose as he raced past a carpet of poppies growing alongside a hedge. Finn skidded to a stop, twisting toward the oddity. Poppies didn't grow in the maze. He drew near until the lingering scent caused him to retreat a step. Not normal poppies. They'd released sleeping pollen. A number of the flowers were crushed, trampled by feet? Dread bloomed like an empty chasm within. Or someone falling onto them in sudden slumber?

He drew near, sniffing liberally of the air. Finn's vision blurred a bit before he retreated, the lingering pollen at work. He let out a bitter scream of his own, one to rival the roars of the Bandersnatch from before. Eliza's scent swirled with that of the sleeping pollen. She'd been here, right here, probably only moments ago. And now—

"She's gone."

Finn whirled at the voice, ready to tackle the offender to the ground. But the space behind him was empty. A flash of color above drew his attention, and he found Chesa perched impossibly atop the hedges.

"Gone where?" Finn asked. But he already knew. One of his worst fears had come to life.

Chesa hopped down from the hedge to land a few feet away. "They need her as much as Red."

Finn bared his teeth. "If I find out you had something to do with this—"

"What will you do?"

His fingernails dug into his palms, nearly drawing blood. "I'll...I'll—"

"Not to me." She waved a dismissive hand through the air. "I'm not sure you could harm me if you tried."

Want to try me? He shifted his weight to the balls of his feet, ready to test his luck.

She blinked at him, completely unruffled by his anger. "Will you go after Eliza?"

"Of course! There's no way I'll abandon her now." They were supposed to run away together, flee this mess. If he'd been more careful, he could have upheld that promise and gotten her far away before White caused a stir.

"You'd risk returning to the White Court for her, even after your exile?"

Another reason the woman set him on edge. Not only did she vanish and reappear at will, but she seemed to know everything and had no trouble picking at old wounds. He'd never planned to return. Never wanted to set foot in the damned place again. But for Eliza, he would.

"What choice do I have?" It was that or leave her to whatever fate awaited her there, and he couldn't allow that. They may not harm her since they needed her to choose White over Red, but that didn't mean it would be a pleasant stay. Plus, she had to know he hadn't abandoned her, that he would never abandon her. "I can't just leave her there. They kidnapped her! Shouldn't Eliza have a choice in this?"

"It's her choice that matters. But didn't you bring her to the Red Court against her will?" Chesa cocked a pink brow at him.

"I—" *Shit.* "That's different."

"Was it?"

His teeth ground together. There was no time for this nonsense. "I have to find her. I have to explain things to her. I promised I'd always protect her, and yet, when she needed me, I wasn't there."

Chesa's nose twitched. "You love her."

"I—" He hadn't said it out loud, especially not to someone else. "Yes. I love her."

She blinked once, twice. And when her gaze settled on him, he took a step back. A genuine smile spread across her face, leaving her looking almost normal, almost human, instead of the otherness that always radiated from her. Maybe she was human beyond whatever magic kept her locked in time, but if so, this was the first time he'd truly glimpsed it.

"Good." She said at length. "That's very good."

Finn's chest burned, and he rubbed at it, suddenly self-conscious over the way she looked at him, as if she saw so much more than his appearance or words.

"Alice may have been right," she said.

Had Eliza guessed his feelings? His cheeks flamed. "Weren't you supposed to protect her too?" He moved the conversation away from himself.

"I arrived just before you did. Eliza is safe."

He snorted. *Hardly.*

Chesa snapped her fingers. "Well, are we going to save Eliza or not?"

35

*D*im light bled into the darkness, burning away the remnants of a pleasant dream. Eliza had been a girl again, sitting in the gardens with her grandmother and listening to fanciful tales of magic and talking animals. Dappled sunlight had glinted off her grandmother's blonde hair, which bore smatterings of silver. She'd smiled as Eliza handed her a small purple flower before adding it to the collection of little blooms pinched between her fingers.

Sleep beckoned again, drawing her back into its embrace, the world slipping away. But Eliza didn't mind. She wanted to be in that garden. There was so much to say, and her dream-self hadn't asked about anything important yet. *Important? Was there something important?*

The bed jolted, and Eliza blinked fully awake. The remnants of the dream fell apart like a brushed spider's web, leaving behind a sudden ache in her chest.

"Where…" Eliza sat. The fine hairs on her arms stood on end as she took in the unfamiliar surroundings. Memories rushed back. Finn. The croquet match. The maze. Encountering the Bandersnatch. Then being chased by the White knights and the strange flowers with their pungent sweetness. "The flowers put me to sleep," she mumbled, her tongue like cotton.

The bed lurched again, but it wasn't a bed at all. Sunlight filtered in through small curtained windows, teasing at the scenery moving beyond. The other half of her room that wasn't a room was the bench of a carriage. Her side was much longer than a bench, a simple cushioned pallet meant for sleeping on long journeys in a carriage that must be humorously long.

As her initial panic receded, her body's needs made themselves known. Her bladder threatened to spill, her mouth was dry as sand, and her stomach gave a little rumble. *How long was I out?*

Eliza slid from the sleeping space and peeked through the curtains. White knights rode on horseback two deep, voids of color against the riot of vibrant trees behind them. Even the horses were solid black, white, or a mix of both. Not a hint of brown or tan on any of them that she could see. The pit in her stomach told her she'd find a similar view on the other side. There'd be no easy escape, not that she knew where she was or where to flee to.

"Hello!" she called. Whether escape was reasonable or not, she needed information. And to pee.

Knights spoke to one another, passing word down the line. From the little she heard, there were even more of them than she expected. *Damn.*

Eventually, one of the knights hopped down from their steed and opened the door. "Alice."

"How dare you abduct me!" She scowled at the handful of knights she could see in turn. Not one of them even bothered to look sorry.

"King's orders," said the man who opened the door.

"And where are you taking me?"

"The White Court."

She assumed as much but hearing it confirmed made everything so much worse. She'd once thought the Tweeds to be silent guardians, but they had nothing on these knights who stood nearly still as statues and spoke less than they moved.

Eliza huffed and crossed her arms. Even if not for the abduction and everything she'd heard of the White Court, the cold reception did little to earn her favor. "Well, I need to relieve myself. And I'm famished."

That at least got them moving. Within a few minutes, Eliza had seen to her needs and was guided, somewhat gently, back to the oddly long carriage. The food did little to help her mood. Every bite tasted like sand —not the food's fault, but the emotions churning through her. She still had no idea what had happened to Finn. Had he abandoned her? Spent one night with her and decided she wasn't worth more? He wouldn't have been the first. Tears tried to form, but she blinked them away.

She couldn't think like that. Eliza took a liberal sip of water. But worse, what if the queen had done something? Her stomach twisted in on itself, terribly possibilities taunting her. Helping him from behind enemy lines would be impossible, but she couldn't just leave him, especially if he was in trouble.

Worry, mostly for Finn rather than herself, kept her company in the never-ending ride. It would have been a mercy if they'd kept her asleep, lingering in dreams where the pain of reality couldn't reach her.

At some point, Eliza nodded off. She woke to morning light peeking through the shades and voices speaking outside. She dared a look through the window and gasped. Gone was the colorful forest from the day before. White buildings filled her view. The orderly structures sat in neat rows, though each block sported unique shapes. One row of buildings was oddly thin, no wider than the front steps. The next was short and wide. But one thing was the same: all the buildings on a block matched with eerie precision. A few bore signs or symbols painted in black above their doors, but most were nearly indistinguishable from the one next to them.

Streets cobbled in pale tan stones ran between the blocks of buildings, little streams of clear water running along their sides. The air lacked the foul tang that accompanied many city streets. Instead, the subtle pleasant scents of fresh bread and flowers wafted through her window.

The people who milled about were dressed in neutral-colored clothes that were both simple and elegant all at once. They spoke and went about their business, a few stopping to observe the procession of knights. Children played without a care, but even that was more restrained than she was used to back home. There were few bursts of laughter and no loud squeals. But the childrens' smiles were wide, their clothes clean, and their figures not lacking for nourishment, as far as she could see.

This was the heart of the White Court. As orderly and lawful as the Red Court was colorful and wild.

You may have been right, Grandmama, sending me to Red.

Eliza had always thought she loved order. It was a staple of her life, especially in her job at the library. Everything had a place, a purpose. It nearly drove her mad when visitors left piles of books just sitting about, or worse, misplaced them on the shelves. But the library teemed with life and history. Each book had its own personality. Their spines had various colors and sizes. The bound pages within held more wonders than anyone could ever count.

Yes, she loved order, and the White Court was beautiful, but it was a cold beauty like icicles that sometimes formed on the eves of the library in winter. In the distance, a massive waterfall fell from steep cliffs, perhaps feeding the water that ran through the narrows steams at the sides of many streets, but even that seemed somehow tame.

Her stomach tried to eat itself as the carriage rolled closer to the destination. Sweat broke out on the back of her neck. Eliza tapped her foot to keep from leaping for the door.

Light dimmed as they entered some structure, eventually rolling to a stop. Eliza had to flex her fingers to get feeling back into them after gripping the seat for so long.

The knights opened the carriage door without a word. Eliza stepped out into a covered drive, the roof blocking much of the structure that stretched out as far as she could see to either side. Like the city, white stonework dominated. Thankfully, there was a breath of life from the shrubs and grasses growing near the building and along either side of the perfectly formed cobbled drive. She'd wager not a single blade of grass had been left to grow unchecked, all of it evenly trimmed down and the bushes perfectly shaped into balls, squares, and other designs.

"Come, Alice, we must not delay," a knight said, ushering her toward a set of massive white doors that had been thrown open.

"Where are you taking me?" she asked. Not that she had much choice in the matter.

"To the White King."

No queen? Eliza was in no fit shape to meet a royal—her dress marred with dirt, a hint of sweat on her skin, and her hair a tangled mess. Not that she cared. If they were going to attack another court and drag her there, whatever the king thought of her appearance didn't matter. He was beneath her care.

The castle was as starkly devoid of color as the city. Black and white checked marble floors dominated every hall, stairway, and room that Eliza saw. The walls and ceilings were white as well. Black metal sconces held lanterns at regular intervals. Occasional tapestries were displayed, but those too begged for a splash of color. A single colorful section of stitching would do wonders. The few people they passed eyed them in quiet wonder, speaking to one another in hushed tones.

The stark whiteness of the walls became blinding when the sun landed on them through an open window. The bright light urged forth the starting bloom of a headache, a harbinger of worse to come, but she didn't have Finn's tea nor the time to hide away and hope it passed.

At last, they reached their destination. The throne room was as plain as any other room, with the same checkered floors and white walls the court seemed to favor. A wide, white carpet stretched across the sparse room to the raised dais at the end.

Her near-empty stomach pulled in on itself as she crossed the carpets in silence toward the person—presumably the king—sitting on a massive silver throne at the end of the room. White hair cascaded down his shoulders, nearly the same shade as the clothes he wore. If not for the golden tan of his skin, he'd look like a ghost upon an icy throne. She'd expected a fearsome brute on a throne of blood based on the stories she'd heard. But life had taught her that the worst of men—and women—often looked nothing like the monster lurking under their skin.

The king was not alone. Sitting on a smaller chair to one side was a slight figure, hair dark as night falling around her like a veil. Unlike the king, her skin was pale, as if the poor woman hadn't seen the sun in ages. She did not turn or shift her focus away from a spot on the floor to look at Eliza as she approached, unlike the king who rose to his feet.

"Ah, Alice. At last." His voice rang with strength. As she drew closer, his features revealed prime maturity in the sharp angles of his face and bright violet eyes that could maim with their ferocity. He was younger than the monarchs of the Red Court, probably not too far past thirty if people in Wonderland aged the same as they did back home. For a moment, his hair and stance resembled Finn so much that she did a double-take. But this was not her lover. His cheekbones were too sharp and angular, his chin too pointed, and the aura that radiated from him lacked all the playful warmth of the man she knew.

The king crossed the space between them as if he owned the place, which, she supposed, he did. He stopped a few feet in front of her, brows rising expectantly.

Ah. I should bow. But Eliza couldn't quite force her body to comply with logic.

His nose twitched. "Most interesting." A ring-decked finger tapped against his lips, bearing the same clear stones dangling from his ears. "You must be tired after such a journey. That dress." He tsked. "We'll get you a clean one. A bath, perhaps? What can I do to please Alice?"

"My name is Eliza."

His eyes widened before smoothing out in a half-grin. "Well, how silly of me to forget introductions. Eliza, I am King Alvar of the White Court." He gestured to the woman still sitting and staring at nothing. "And my wife, Queen Neva."

The woman did not so much as acknowledge their presence or that they spoke of her.

Eliza stiffened as the king leaned in close, smelling of something spicy that nearly made her sneeze. "My *dear* wife is a bit touched in the head. The result of a most unfortunate accident."

Her blood chilled as the king stepped back. His tone lacked the sentiment of the words, and the sinking feeling within told her it may not have been an accident at all. Eliza bit her lip, trying to hold her emotions at bay.

"Now then, what can we do to make Alice feel at home?" the king asked, ignoring the name she'd given him.

"I would like to return to the Red Court."

The king froze. A few guards in the room drew in audible breaths.

"But you just arrived. Surely Alice would give us a chance?"

She swallowed, gathering her strength and trying to ignore the dull headache building behind her forehead. "There is someone there who may be in trouble. I need to assure myself of their safety." Eliza had no great love for the Red Court. In truth, it would be fair to give White a chance, but she couldn't leave Finn to the queen's fury, no matter if he'd changed his mind about them or not. She wouldn't—couldn't—give up on him.

"We go through all the trouble to get you here, and you just want to go right back?" His tone turned sharp, his violet eyes narrowing.

The doors behind her creaked open, but she dared not look away from the king. This was her one chance, and there was no time to waste. Finn may not have until her ascension. It had to be now.

"Just to ensure my friend's safety. That is all," she insisted. "Once he's safe, I will stay here until I'm anointed as Alice." It was a fair offer, one she could live with if she knew Finn was free.

The king's lips twisted into a scowl. Eliza braced for rejection. Damn it all, she'd beg if she had to.

"That won't be necessary."

Eliza gasped, turning toward the unexpected voice.

Chesa sauntered across the room, white skirts billowing about her legs and a short white top showing a strip of her dark-skinned stomach. Her hair was fully pink, a bold splash of color that shone like a beacon.

"What…" Eliza's mouth hung open. She swayed on her feet.

"Alice's guardian, of course," the king drawled.

Chesa swept into a deep bow. "King Alvis."

Thoughts chased themselves through Eliza's head, none sticking. Chesa was here. Not just that, she walked in like she belonged here, like she was expected.

"Why?" Eliza shook her head, still at a loss.

"What kind of guardian would I be if I didn't watch after my charge?" Chesa winked, as if this were all some big game, while to Eliza, it was anything but.

Chesa turned to the king. "Your White knights captured someone else in their foray into the Red Court. I believe you'll want to meet them."

Someone else? Eliza's brows knit together.

"Oh?" The king took his time making his way back to the throne. "Well, you have my attention. I assume you're not going to make me wait? Bring them forth."

Chesa bowed again. "As you will." Her gaze panned across Eliza, some message written there that she failed to comprehend. Then Chesa called to the guards, "Bring him in!"

Two guards scurried from the room. Awkward silence lingered in the wake of their departure. Eliza's feet wiggled in her boots as she fought the urge to move, to do anything other than just stand there.

When she could take it no longer, Eliza spoke. "Your Majesty, about my request to return to the Red Court—"

"Are you sure you want that?" Chesa asked.

The king looked between the two of them. "Well?"

"Yes, I—"

The doors groaned open, and the king went rigid on his throne. His hands gripped the sides like he might fall from his sparkling chair. Even more disconcerting, the queen finally moved, her head snapping up to stare at whatever came through the doors.

Eliza's stomach bottomed out. Her knees shook. Chesa's hand latched onto her arm, squeezing tight, but the woman didn't look at her, not even a passing glance before she released her arm and turned to stare toward the doors.

Eliza braced for the worse and forced herself to turn. She wasn't prepared—nothing could have prepared her for that sight.

"Finn!" Eliza made to race for him, but Chesa grabbed her arm again, fingers digging in painfully.

Two knights braced him between them, holding his arms and giving him little room to move. A nasty bruise marred his cheek. His clothes were torn and dirty—the same ones he'd worn the night of the ball that he'd stripped off before her and then redonned the following dawn before slipping out.

Something had gone wrong after he left. Terribly, terribly wrong.

His gaze met hers and held. Finn almost seemed to sigh as he said, "Eliza."

Eliza's heart cracked at the sight of him hurt and captured. The hint of a smile that touched his lips nearly slew her on the spot. That one look said so much. He hadn't abandoned her. He hadn't broken his promise to meet her and run away with her. Whatever kept him from her that afternoon wasn't his fault. And the ridiculous fool had gotten himself captured by the court that exiled him, probably coming after her of all things. Her lip wobbled, and she bit it. She would never deserve him.

"Finneas." The king's rumbling voice sent a chill down her spine.

The look on Finn's face transformed into something feral, his teeth bared, as he glanced past her toward the dais.

Eliza spun, flinging her arm out to try and block Finn from the king's sight. "He's here because of me. Please, don't hurt him."

The king had risen from his throne but stopped halfway down the short stairs. "Alice and the outcast." A smirk twisted his features. "How interesting."

He descended the rest of the stairs, a little jump in his step. "Oh, Alice, is this who you wished to go back for?"

Chesa's grip on her arm tightened. *A warning?* Eliza didn't dare look away from the king, only notched her chin higher and forced herself to stare him down. The knights dragged Finn forward until he stood even with Eliza and Chesa, but too far away for her to reach him.

"I didn't plan to get caught," Finn said, saving her from answering. His head twisted toward them. "That part was her fault."

Mine? Eliza flinched back. No, he looked past her at—

Eliza tore her arm from Chesa's grip. "What did you do?"

Chesa's gaze was far away. She didn't so much as blink at Eliza's accusation.

"Risking your life for Alice?" The king tsked as he drew near. "Is it love, brother?"

Finn growled in rage, jerking his arms and trying to free himself from the knights who held him firm. The king smirked, his amused gaze sliding from Finn to stare at Eliza.

She blinked, her chest squeezing painfully tight as her mind tried to grab hold of knowledge that refused to stick. Until it did, branding itself on her with such force it caused her to gasp and grab at her chest. The dull headache throbbing behind her eyes slammed into full force.

Finn wasn't just some random citizen of the White Court. The king who committed atrocities wasn't just his former ruler. A brother. Half-brother? Bile burned the back of her throat as she took in the man anew.

The bastard knew. King Alvis's feral grin stretching along his features proved just how much he relished the horror of her realization. And Chesa... Eliza glanced out of the corner of her eye, but the woman stood still as a statue staring at nothing, just like the sorrowful queen on her little throne.

The Red Queen was horrible. The Bandersnatch a thing of nightmares. But this...this king was the true monster of Wonderland, and now they were trapped in his clutches.

36

*W*hat was worse? Facing down the person Finn loathed most in the world or seeing Eliza standing in front of him? Probably the latter. Both together? A thing of nightmares.

The knights on either side held him firm. If Alvis were to try anything, to harm Eliza, he wasn't sure he could stop him in time. Her title of Alice should afford her some safety, but this bastard had exiled his own mother and had her hunted down like a criminal, all because she cared for Finn's father—whoever that was. She'd never said, and sometimes he was grateful not to know, not to be disappointed by whatever family he might have left. The former White King had been cold enough to him, even thinking he was his own son. A father who might not want him and probably didn't know he existed? Finn could do without that.

It was a wonder to have someone to love, though, someone he could gladly step in front of a blade for. Now that he had Eliza, he wasn't about to lose her, especially not to someone as awful as the White King.

"What am I to do with you?" Alvis taunted. "Our new, or rather soon to be, Alice and her unfortunate lover." He laughed. "I certainly could not have predicted this. What a bounty my knights have brought me. Though they aren't the only ones responsible, are they?"

Chesa blinked, coming back to the moment as if summoned.

"How kind of Alice's guardian to bring her lover here. Now she can stay in the White Court without needing to run back to Red, isn't that right?"

Chesa reached for Eliza, but she stepped away. He couldn't blame her for that. Finn had never trusted Chesa much, and the past days made him remember why. She'd literally freed him from one cell just to lead him into another. They had still been a few hours from the White Court when Chesa alerted the convoy to his location and handed him over to be brought before the king. Another betrayal. Another arrest. And more bruises for his battered body.

"Let Finn go," Eliza demanded.

The king stopped his pacing mid-stride. "Oh? And why would I do that? He was exiled from the White Court. He knows the cost of his return."

Not like I had a choice. He'd hoped to somehow sneak in unseen and get Eliza to safety. This? This was a disaster. The worst possible outcome other than a knight running him through with a sword before he ever reached the woman he loved.

Eliza stomped her foot, her hands in fists at her side. "I am Alice, am I not?" At this, she looked to Chesa, who simply nodded, her features carefully blank. "If you harm him," she continued, turning back to the king, "I will make sure that White never reigns over Wonderland."

Finally, she'd stepped into her power, owned it, as was her right. Finn's heart swelled with pride even as he nearly shook for fear of his brother's rage.

The king stepped within a foot of her, staring down his imperious, pointed nose at the woman before him. Finn jerked against the men holding him, trying to twist away without success. Power hummed under his skin, begging him to unleash it. He could use it, or transform, but neither act would earn him any favors. Most likely, he'd get a quick death and punishment for Eliza.

"Is that a threat, Alice?" the king demanded.

Her throat bobbed before she answered. "Alice is charged with deciding who rules. I will make my choice as I will."

The king laughed, though the sound lacked all humor. "Oh, you are an interesting one. Such a spitfire." He turned on his heel and marched toward Finn.

For once, Finn gave into the guards, shifting his weight and letting their bulk provide a bit of a shield between the approaching king. He knew what lurked under the man's skin, an alternate form entirely different than his own.

Truthfully, Finn didn't remember much of his half-brother. More feelings than actual memories. He remembered cruel taunts and being hammered to the ground during their weapons and magic practice. That, and he remembered the monster—the powerful beast his brother could become at will, something he'd always envied. To be able to transform at all was seen as a blessing from the ancient kings. But his brother? He was beyond blessed, so unlike Finn, who could only become a pitiful rabbit —prey.

"Sword," the king snapped, hand outstretched.

"No!" Eliza screeched. "What are you doing?" She made to advance on the king, but Chesa grabbed her again, holding her back.

This time, Finn was grateful. His heart pounded in his chest. Magic raced under his veins, waiting and ready should he need to use it. He'd have only a moment—seconds at best.

A guard near the side of the room rushed up and handed the king his weapon. Alvis took it, angling the blade so it glinted in the light.

"You wish to threaten me, Alice? Two can play at this game." He lifted the sword until the tip of it hovered an inch from Finn's face.

He gritted his teeth, forcing himself to remain still as his brother threatened him and the woman he loved. But from the corner of his eye, he noticed movement on the dais. When he'd entered, he'd seen a woman's slight form, but she'd hardly moved. Not a concern given the much greater problem in the room.

But now she moved to the edge of her seat, her dark hair pushed back, and Finn recognized her. *Neva?* They'd been friends in childhood. The talented daughter of a prominent noble, she was often at court, probably with the hopes of gaining the position she seemed to hold now. But Neva hated Alvis, and she was never quiet.

"What do you want?" Eliza's pained cry drew his attention from the queen. A streak of tears glistened on her cheek. She jerked against Chesa's hold, to no avail.

The sight gutted him worse than any blade. "It's okay, Eliza. Don't worry about me."

The king shot him a sideways look. "You're in no position to give assurances."

Finn bared his teeth in a snarl, earning a smirk in return.

"What do you want? Tell me!" Eliza begged.

He hated it, hated seeing her like this, her strong shell breaking before this tyrant.

"You know what I want. Promise that you'll choose White, and he lives. Choose Red, and well..." The king shrugged.

Don't do it. He pleaded in silence, trying to gain her attention, but all of Eliza's focus was on the king. She could give him more power. It wouldn't just be his life on the line if White ruled.

"Fine." Eliza's shoulders sagged, and Chesa released her. "I'll do it."

"See, not so hard," the king said.

"But," Eliza paused, making the king wait as she wiped away the stray tear and raised her chin.

The king adjusted his grip on the sword, the tip sliding a hair's width from Finn's nose.

Eliza caught the moment and hurried on. "But you will not harm either of us while we are here, and you will let us be together." She crossed her arms and stared him down. "Surely a king can allow Alice some comforts while she is in the White Court."

Alvis lowered the sword, a hint of amusement brightening his features. "We may get along well, you and I."

Finn nearly snorted. He knew that look she wore. Eliza would gut the king if given a chance. Perhaps she'd get it.

"Guards!" The king called the command unnecessarily loud in the quiet room. "Have rooms prepared for our guests. Ones close together. East wing, I think." He held out the sword, waiting for a guard to come and claim it. The man nearly tripped over himself in his hurry to do so.

"But Alice," the king added. "One step out of line, one hint that you plan to go against our agreement, and Finneas and I might have to have a little fun together in my dungeons."

The king pulled a thin dagger from the sheath on his thigh. The crystalline blade sparkled in the light. Panic spiked through Finn. He twisted against the guards to no avail.

"You see, I quite like my blades."

Eliza bravely held her ground as the king used the sharp point to pick at invisible dirt under his nails.

"This one, in particular, is quite precise, a small slip, and oops—" A thin trail of blood lingered in the wake of the blade, running down the king's finger. Alvis stared at it, his amusement growing as he turned it toward Eliza. "This is the only shade of red I like, the only I permit in my court."

Eliza's throat bobbed, but she did not respond. Finn yearned to be at her side, or better yet, be a shield between her and his brother. The king slammed the blade back in its sheath, and a bit of the tension between Finn's shoulder blades smoothed out.

"The blade is sharp, but do you know what is sharper?" Alvis held his finger out, letting the blood drip to the white carpets between him and Eliza. Chesa's gaze dropped to that splatter of crimson, seeming to garner her attention where the threat did not.

"Well?" the king prompted when Eliza did not respond.

"No." Her response was so quiet he almost missed it.

A feral grin spread across the king's face. "The claws of my other form."

A monster Finn could never forget.

"I don't think you want your *little rabbit* at my mercy, do you?"

"No," Eliza replied, stronger this time.

"Good. Then you understand what happens if you disobey?"

Eliza paled and wobbled on her feet. The threat was against him, but all he could see was the impact it had on her, the way the king's words nearly struck her down.

Her gaze slid to Finn as she said. "I understand."

It should have been a relief. They were alive—for now. However, the damning agreement slammed around him like the bars of a new cell, and worse, Eliza was trapped in it with him.

37

The White knights led Eliza to a room within the castle. The similarity to her former chambers in the Red Court nearly made her laugh. Except where those rooms were gilded with gold, crimson, and other colorful furnishings, these were as neutral in tone as the rest of the castle. White wood. White fabric. White carpets over white marble floors. At least it was clean, immaculately so. Any bit of dust or dirt would stick out like a sore thumb. The sunlight glinting through sheer curtains and reflecting off everything increased her headache two-fold. Eliza pinched the bridge of her nose and shut her eyes, a poor attempt to ease the steady pulse trying to split her skull.

"The maids will be along shortly," one knight said before movement sounded behind her.

"Wait!" Eliza sprung at them, grabbing the closest man by the arm. The sudden move had her head pounding worse than ever, but she couldn't let them just tuck her away.

He gawked at her as if she'd sprouted wings.

"Take me to Finneas," she begged. "The king said we could be together."

"If the king said it, it will be done," another said.

A humorless laugh caught in her throat. Could they truly believe that horrible man? "Then we can go now," she insisted. "Please—"

The knight gently pried her hand from his arm. "Apologies, Alice. We have orders."

She stared at them wide-eyed, her heart racing. They couldn't lock her up in here, not another prison of a room.

"Please," she begged again.

One winced, the other looked away, but still, they left, the lock clicking behind them with damning finality. Unable to sit still lest she give in to her pain, Eliza scoured the room. Locked windows and empty drawers greeted her at every turn. There wasn't even a false wall or stash of useful knickknacks to be found.

A handful of maids arrived quickly, as promised, filling the tub in the adjoining room with steaming water and sweet-smelling oils that did nothing to help her head. Another group arrived bearing armfuls of fabric —dresses of all kinds, if one ignored the fact that they lacked any color and were all modestly cut. Not that she minded the latter, she'd always preferred more modest and functional clothing, a far cry from the flamboyant and flimsy outfits she'd been forced into at the Red Court.

Finally, a maid brought in a tray bearing a steaming kettle of tea. The scent teased her nose, offering much-needed respite. She didn't know how they'd gotten the blend right or who they'd learned it from, but she didn't care as she gulped the steaming liquid and prayed it would work quickly on her migraine.

Pleased that she accepted the tea, the women insisted on seeing to every possible need, combing the tangles from her hair, bringing her a wide assortment of tempting foods, and finishing preparations of the bath. They fawned over her like she was a princess of some sort, yet not one would answer her questions about Finn or let her out to see him. Instead, they gave her too sweet smiles and plied her with words about how she should rest and recover.

Each dodged question sent her nerves fraying further. The headache faded, leaving a different frustration in its wake. When the women pulled at her clothes, half-undressing her for the bath, she snapped. "Leave me alone!"

The maids jumped back in a hurry, and Eliza winced, almost regretting her words. "I will undress myself," she said, more calmly. "And bathe alone."

"Yes, Alice," the women answered in a chorus of tones.

If they wouldn't answer her questions or take her to Finn, the least they could do was leave her to suffer alone. She waited, arms crossed and scowl fixed in place until the last woman left before Eliza shed the rest of her soiled clothing and sank into the embrace of the steaming water. It nearly scalded her skin, but she welcomed the pain, a distraction from her racing thoughts.

She had just rinsed the flora soap from her hair when the door to her bathing chamber squeaked open again. She hunched further into the water and drew in a sharp breath. "I said I wished to bathe alone."

"No one truly wants to be alone."

The familiar voice swelled the fury burning in her chest hotter than the bath water. Eliza leaped to her feet, uncaring of her nudity, and whirled on Chesa.

"Out!" She thrust an accusing finger toward the door.

Chesa tilted her head to the side, nonplused by the order or Eliza's dripping form still standing in the tub. "Care for some more tea?" She held up a dainty cup on a saucer, a tendril of steam wafting into the air. "It's a special blend."

The exact special blend that eased her headaches. "You had the tea brought to me."

"Of course. Finn mentioned that this helps you. I wish I'd known sooner."

At the mention of his name, Eliza's lips drew thin. "You've clearly sided with the king. Do you know what he did to Finn? To his mother?"

When Chesa didn't so much as look surprised, Eliza's nails dug into her palms. "Of course you do. You seem to know everything, and yet you sold him out to the White knights, to people who would see him killed!"

Still, the other woman barely moved, her focus drifting and not quite settling on Eliza. "I'm only on the side of Alice."

The scream building in her lungs finally tore free. Eliza kicked at the water, sending a wave over the side of the tub before she climbed out. She grabbed the nearby robe, shoving her arms through and stomping across the wet floor toward Chesa before she had the ties fully secured at her waist.

"You." She jabbed a finger toward Chesa. "Are certainly not on my side. I saw you in the maze. I know I did. You could have helped me, but you did nothing." Eliza was mere inches from her now, every last thread of restraint she had left given to not shaking the damn woman and demanding some kind of a reaction.

Chesa blinked, her eyes clearing. Her gaze flicked up and down Eliza's fuming form as if seeing her for the first time. "You and Finneas are exactly where you need to be."

Eliza sucked in a sharp breath, stomped around Chesa, and out into the bedroom. One more moment that close to her and she'd do something stupid.

"Finneas was in the Red Court dungeon awaiting the queen's judgment."

The statement stopped Eliza in her tracks. She spun on the balls of her feet to stare at Chesa, who lingered in the doorway, still holding the teacup.

"Should I have left him there? Rather, I brought him to you. You wanted him, didn't you?"

Eliza ignored the question, still stuck on her previous words. "He was in the dungeon?" Some of the strength went out of her. She barely found the bed's edge before she plopped down on it.

So that's why he wasn't at the croquet match. She'd feared as much, but hearing it confirmed made everything worse. The queen had known, or assumed, they'd been together. Would she have even given Eliza the chance to save him before carrying out her punishment? Would anyone have known? Would she have gone on to become Alice and chosen the Red Court, never having known what happened to him?

"The White Court isn't any better," Eliza mumbled, desperate for words to break the crushing silence.

"The courts are as different as night and day," Chesa replied. She left the tea on the bedside table before retreating a few steps. "Neither all bad nor all good, simply...different. White is a court of laws—order, balance, and restraint. Red, as you saw, is the opposite. A court of freedom, openness, and frivolity. Alice should know. She should see."

"The White King exiled Finn for a crime that wasn't his own. Alvis, the heir to the throne at the time, had them tracked down as they fled. He killed his own mother!" Eliza wasn't sure of that, but she suspected. Chesa's answering nod made Eliza's teeth dig into her bottom lip.

"White holds marriage sacred. The queen broke her vows. She loved another and deceived not only her husband but the entire court by claiming her bastard son was true-born."

Finn... "But such a severe punishment is ridiculous." Eliza shook her head. Scandals happened in Gamor all the time, but rarely were they met with such vitriol. The royals were rumored to have affairs, but such things were always cloaked in so many layers of false-truths that no one ever knew the reality of the thing. Better to cover it up than bring it to light with punishment.

Chesa merely shrugged. "It is the way of White. Their laws keep order. A king would be punished just the same, and Finn was punished for defending his mother even knowing her crimes."

Which made it all that much worse. Of course he defended her. He loved her. Eliza hugged her arms about herself. "It's too cruel."

"Is Red better?" Chesa asked. "Finn was imprisoned for no other reason than loving you instead of the queen."

Loving me? Or making love to me? She shook her head. "How am I supposed to choose when neither choice is good?"

"That is Alice's burden."

A terrible one to bear. Eliza snorted air through her nose. "You could have just told me these things instead of surprising me in front of the king. And why bring Finn here? You freed him. Why not just let him be free?"

A grin spread across Chesa's face, rekindling the spark of fury that wanted to blaze through Eliza and burn down the world for its offenses.

"The fool would have gotten himself killed if I'd let him."

Eliza reared back. "What do you mean?"

"He never spared a thought for himself. When the knights attacked, he only wanted to save you." Chesa drew near and took up a perch on a footstool like a cat about to lick its paws. "His plan was terrible. He planned to try to sneak in and then sneak you out." She shook her head. "He would have been caught, probably killed, and ruined everything. I couldn't have that."

"Everything?"

Chesa's grin widened. "I brought you something."

Eliza leaned forward, pulling her robe tighter. "Wait, what do you mean by everything?"

The other woman ignored her and pulled out a small square of paper from her pocket. "Here."

Eliza sighed and took the offering.

"Open it." Chesa leaned forward, her eyes sparkling with anticipation.

Fine. Eliza began unfolding the page. "But what did you mean by—" Words died on her tongue as she spied the familiar looping handwriting. Tears stung the corners of her eyes.

"Grandmama."

"I believe you were missing a page from her letter to you."

Her mouth gaped. "You had it this whole time?"

Chesa's head bobbed in a gleeful nod. "I saved it for the right moment."

The right moment would have been days ago. But Eliza held back the retort.

"Read it," Chesa said.

And so, Eliza read:

...he can help you break the curse.

"Finn," Eliza whispered.

I came upon something only recently, a truth which both courts would see buried forever.

King Jasper and I often share wine and stories, but recently he shared one I had not heard before. In his earlier years, he loved to hunt in the wilds of Wonderland, sometimes venturing off by himself for days at a time. One such time, he met a woman of the White Court. She was smart and kind—the things he longed for but could not find in his arranged marriage to the queen.

That should have been the end of it, but he could not make himself forget her, even when he learned she was Queen of White.

Eliza gasped. Finn's mother? It had to be. A tingling raced under her skin, willing her to continue.

They met in secret various times for over a year until the queen ended things and vowed never to meet him in their special place again. She kept that vow for several years, until the day she died. Jasper heard of her exile and knew where she might go. The king was too late to save her from the fury of White, but he saved her son, vowing to offer him the sanctuary he could not give the woman he'd loved.

I could not ask the king about the boy he'd claimed and if he was his son, nor did he admit as much, but I can see it. They smile the same. The king's smiles are rare these days but so pleasing when they come.

Had she seen the king smile? Truly? Her brows scrunched. Maybe once, at the ball, but even that was fleeting and fueled by drink and lust.

A mixed-blood child in Wonderland is rare indeed. One of royal blood? Unheard of. If Finneas is as I believe, then such a man may be able to help you. He may be the key that the rest of us have lacked.

Either way, I trust that he will keep you safe. He has the honor and consistency of White, yet the free spirit and joy of Red. A balanced heart, if ever there was one.

You have that balance too. A love of knowledge and order but a heart that's not afraid to dream and wonder. Such a combination is powerful. A curse breaker if ever there were one. Be strong, my girl.

With all my love,
Grandma

A tickle in her nose had Eliza sniffing and pressing her eyes shut. "You know what it says?"

Chesa nodded.

"And you believe she's right?" Finn's father lived. More than that, he cared for him—in a way.

"I do."

A shiver wracked her form, and Eliza swallowed the lump in her throat. "Why keep this from me? Why share it now?"

Chesa sighed. "It would have been dangerous to leave it where anyone, say the queen, for instance, might read it. This truth would have been lost. As for now…" She looked across the room, her gaze going distant once more. "It is time."

"Time for what?"

"Time to see Finneas." A toothy grin spread across her face. "I can take you to him."

Eliza leaped from the bed. "Yes. Where is he? Is he safe?"

She giggled. "You love him too."

"I—" She stopped short. Yes, she did love him. And more than anything, she wanted to assure herself that the king had spoken truly—at least in this matter. She needed to know that Finn was safe and would be safe while they were here. If they were together, she was certain they could survive whatever was to come.

"It's okay. You don't have to tell me." Chesa winked. "He's in a room of his own. Hopefully cleaned up by now too."

Only then did Eliza remember she still wore nothing but a thin robe. "Let me change." She aimed for the wardrobe where the maids had stashed the dresses.

"Why? Finn will just undress you anyway."

Eliza skidded to a stop and snapped her head toward Chesa, who grinned like a cat. A blazing flush already crept up her neck and to her cheeks. Eliza opened her mouth, closed it, and turned back toward the wardrobe, ears burning as Chesa cackled.

38

Finn paced back and forth in his assigned room. It should have been familiar, he'd grown up here after all, but the room lacked anything that sparked sentimentality. The furnishings were beautiful—wood lovingly crafted in delicate designs, the softest cushions, and perfect angles. All of it cleaned and maintained to perfection as it always was. As a child, he'd gotten in trouble more times than he could count for tracking mud or other unsavory substances inside. The maids were always scowling at him, or at least, he thought they were. He couldn't remember any of their faces anymore. Even his mother's memory had blurred around the edges.

Alvis though, that was a face he could never forget, one that liked to pop up to haunt him in the worst of his nightmares.

The knights had shoved him into the room none-too-gently and locked the door. No matter how he pounded against the polished, pale wood or demanded to see Eliza, they did not respond. The knights were still there, though, just outside the door. The unfortunate part about having heightened senses was knowing exactly when you were being ignored.

The door opened once for a gaggle of women to deposit a heap of clothes and tray of food before retreating just as quickly as they came.

With nothing else to do, he cleaned as best he could with the pitcher of water and cloths that had been left on a table and changed into a fresh set of clothes in shades of white and tan.

They better not be the king's. Finn scowled at his reflection in the full-length mirror, even as he savored the fine cloth and stitching—something Red never could seem to match. He and his half-brother were of similar size, but he doubted Alvis would ever give him anything but a blade to the heart. Even that might be too generous. It'd be much more likely his half-brother would just lock him in the room to starve.

Finn lifted a biscuit from the tray of food, his stomach rumbling. "Better make you last."

He had just finished off a handful of berries and licked the juice from his fingers when the door groaned open.

Wide skirts appeared first, and his heart jolted. But the slight woman who entered wasn't the one he longed for, but someone else entirely, a ghost from his past.

"Neva," he whispered. Finn hastily wiped his hands on his borrowed breeches.

"Should we accompany you, my queen?" A woman asked outside the door.

She barely turned her head before speaking. "No, thank you. I wish for privacy." She stood still inside the room, her hands clasped demurely in front of her. The expression on her face was carefully blank, giving nothing away.

Friend or foe? She'd been a friend once, the closest thing he had to a sister. All these years later, he still remembered her laugh's melodic sound and the strength of her magic that could knock him off his feet without causing her to break a sweat.

But that was a lifetime ago, it seemed, back when Neva frowned or rolled her eyes in disgust at the mere mention of his brother, and now she held a position at his side.

The White Queen. A title his mother once held. Just the thought of her stuck him like a dagger to the heart. He had to force himself still and not to give anything away if Neva had changed as much as he feared. He'd heard the White King had taken a wife some years ago, but if he'd heard the woman's name, it never struck his memory the way seeing her before him did.

The lock clicked closed. Finn held his breath.

Neva lifted her gaze from the floor to him, her veil of indifference shattering and falling away like shards of glass. "Finneas."

Before he had a chance to process the sudden change, she raced across the room and launched herself at him. The air whooshed from his lungs as her slight form crashed against him, and she wrapped him in her embrace.

Her face burrowed into his chest, but he still heard her muffled, "I thought you were dead."

"Neva." Tentatively, he trailed his fingers along her dark, silken hair. "I'm quite alive. For the moment anyway."

Interesting that she thought him dead. His identity wasn't exactly a secret. Many throughout Wonderland, even those who lived outside the courts, knew him—the white rabbit, the king's ward, the queen's favorite. Though, it was true that no one called him White prince. In some ways, that boy was dead. The man he'd become had stepped out of his grave and never looked back.

Wetness leaked through his shirt a moment before Neva sniffled and released him. Reluctantly, he let her go as she pulled away to wipe away the last trace of tears from her face.

"My apologies," she said.

The tightness in his chest held firm, and he fought the urge to rub at it. "There's no need to apologize." He'd long wondered what became of his friend. "I'm glad you're all right."

"All right?" She huffed air through her nose and turned her attention to the teapot on the table, fiddling with the lid as if it were the most interesting thing in the world. "I guess you could call it that."

With her perfect posture and refined air, she was as graceful and proud as any queen. The Red Queen could certainly have taken a lesson from her. But she was nothing like the spunky young girl he remembered, one who'd always been a bit dirty from sparring or spending time outdoors and who could light up a room with her high laughter. This woman, this queen, was dim by comparison, a pretty figurine whose spark had been snuffed out.

"What happened to you?" he forced out. Part of him didn't want to know, but the rest of him demanded to, even if it was as terrible as he feared. "In the throne room... I didn't recognize you at first."

Her fingers stilled on the teapot. "Well, you know my parents always hoped I'd become queen." She shot him a sad smile. "They got their wish— eventually. The last queen died just a little over a year into her marriage, but I suppose you know that."

"No." Somehow, that had never reached the Red Court, or if it had, he'd missed it entirely. "I didn't know." Few ever spoke of the White Court within Red, other than to proclaim them monsters. They weren't wrong, at least where the king was concerned.

"Ah, well, I'm not surprised they covered it up." She left the teapot alone and turned toward him. "She fell down a flight of stairs and broke her pretty little neck. Or so they said."

A tingling chill spread beneath his ribs. "My brother."

It wasn't a question, but Neva nodded all the same. "My parents put me forward as a new bride." She dropped her gaze to stare at the carpets. "My magic has always been strong. They suggested perhaps I was made of stouter stuff and could enhance the royal bloodline with my abilities."

She had always been powerful—skilled both physically and with magic. "Why didn't you run? Fly away?" Like many powerful wielders of the White Court, she had an alternate form, a great hawk, fierce and proud as the woman herself.

Neva glanced up with a sad smile. "You know what happens to queens who run."

The reminder struck him like a punch to the gut. All these years later and the memory of his mother threatened to bring him to his knees.

She winced. "I'm sorry. I shouldn't have mentioned it." She reached for him but dropped her hand. "I miss her too. She was always kind to me."

Finn merely nodded, unable to find the right words.

"My parents were right about one thing, though. I'm strong. And I've found a way to protect myself. At least, it's worked so far. Alvis has never liked people who speak against him or stand up for themselves, so as you can imagine he wasn't thrilled with that aspect of me." She glanced toward the windows and the sun slanting through sheer curtains. "The first time he hit me, he knocked me unconscious."

"What?" He straightened. "How dare he—"

She held up a hand. "It's fine."

"It's not!" He took her raised hand in his and squeezed. "Neva... You deserve so much more."

"I know." She gave his hand a squeeze in return before pulling free.

"It's against the law to harm another." It was a vile act to hurt someone else outside of war and sparring. At least it had been when he'd lived in the White Court. Everyone learned the principal laws as children and the punishment for breaking them. The king and queen were the figureheads of their people, responsible for upholding the law and setting a good example. He understood now it was the reason his mother was banished and he with her, though the pursuit that followed wasn't. Such vengeance wasn't tolerated...before Alvis. Finn shut down the thought, his eyes squeezing tight as his fists at his sides.

A gentle touch on the back of his hand brought him back. "It is," Neva said. "But kings are often the worst offenders of the laws they're meant to uphold. Alvis thinks himself above the law. Beyond it. That's why things must change. It's why *I* must change them."

"How?"

"Ill behaviors have a way of making themselves known, even when the perpetrator would have it hidden on the threat of death."

Death. Finn hissed in a breath. It shouldn't surprise him that his brother would go so far, but somehow, it still did.

"Some things are hard to cover up, though." She touched her face as if remembering a long-ago wound. "The maids saw. They knew, as did the guards. Word spread—in shadows and whispers. The people remember your mother, Finn. And you. They hurt for the queen before me, who was gentle and lovely as a flower but too weak to stand against a monster. But beasts like Alvis trample the things in their way. Pretend you're nothing but a leaf on the breeze, easily drifting out of the way, however, and they dismiss you." She looked at him, meaning clear in her bright eyes.

"You pretend to be..." He searched for the right word.

"Damaged?" she offered. "A little soft in the head now?"

Just hearing her say it was painful. Someone like Neva should never have to hide their brilliance.

She shrugged. "It keeps the king's attention off me and gains a certain sympathy from the people—those who understand the ruse and those who do not. My maids know, as do my guards. No one has outed me to the king."

At that, Finn's brows drew skyward. "You have their support."

"The court is ripe for change. With the help of your Alice, we could save the White Court—make it what it should be."

My Alice. "Eliza." He looked toward the door, heart lurching in his chest. "I don't even know what they've done with her."

"She's safe," Neva promised. "I'll see to that, as long as you don't do anything stupid." She gave him a hard look and shook her head. "I'm glad to see you, Finn, but coming back here and riling up the king is dangerous."

He swallowed the knot in his throat. "I couldn't just let them take her." Magic shivered under his skin, responding to his anger. "I couldn't risk my brother hurting her."

"You do love her." A genuine smile twitched at her lips, so reminiscent of the girl he once knew. It broadened out into something wide and genuine. "I'm happy for you, Finn. If something good could come of all you've suffered... No one deserves happiness quite as much as you."

Did anyone really deserve happiness? If so, it surely wasn't him. He'd spent half his life idling away his time on drink and fruitless pursuits. "*You* deserve happiness," he said to her. But she wouldn't have it with his brother, ruse or not. Finn was many things, but not a fool. "Sooner or later, he's going to figure out you're pretending."

"I know. Which is why we must act soon." Her hands drifted down to cradle the slight swell of her belly. "I won't let the past repeat itself. Not anymore."

Finn stumbled back as the realization of what she meant took hold. "You're pregnant."

Neva rubbed her belly as she bobbed her head. "And now the king truly has no need to pay attention to me, at least for a while."

He stiffened. "It's his?"

"Yes." The look on her face hardened as she stared Finn down. "But I will not let my child become its father. You must believe that. This child will be the future of the White Court, and I will see it be a brighter one."

"Neva." He scrubbed a hand down his face. Her passion, her fervor, was strong as ever, honed into a blade of vengeance to give a better life to her unborn child. But such blades had a way of cutting those who wielded them. He knew that better than anyone and had witnessed it firsthand. "It's too risky for you and the child."

The utter hope shining from her begged him to believe, but so much had gone so wrong in his life lately. The queen took his hands in hers and beamed up at him. "Some things are worth risking it all for. Isn't that why you came after Alice?"

"Yes." For her, he would risk it at all and more.

"Then you understand." Her focus was suddenly far away as she whispered, "A well-placed blade can fell any monster."

Finn opened his mouth to ask more, but Neva simply shook her head and turned her focus back to him.

"I will do all I can to keep you safe," she said. "Be patient. Don't try anything foolish. And once Alice's ascension comes, ask her to believe in the White Court. Don't forget us. Don't leave us to ruin. We're not all monsters."

Tears rarely visited him, but the passion Neva laced into every word threatened to bring them forth. Finn tugged her to him, wrapping her in his arms and squeezing tight. "No, you're certainly not all monsters." If he could help his friend, if Alice could somehow give her and her child a better life, he would ask her to try.

inn had just released Neva when the door groaned open.

Eliza walked in, turned, and froze. Her lips parted as she blinked at them. Thankfully, she hadn't been a moment earlier. Their hug could have given the wrong impression.

"Eliza." Finn darted past Neva, running to the woman he longed for above all others. He barely skidded to a stop before pulling her into his arms and burying his face against the top of her head, breathing in her scent. She leaned into his embrace, some tension slipping from her form as her fists bunched sections of his shirt against his chest.

Someone cleared their throat. Finn looked up to find Chesa standing in the doorway, a too-bright grin on her face.

"You." He spun Eliza away from her, shielding her with his body. "How dare you—"

"It's okay." Eliza grabbed at his arm.

"What?" Finn glared over one shoulder. The tricky woman had literally handed him over to the White knights and ruined all his plans. Even if she had freed him from the Red Queen.

"I'll explain," Eliza said. "But…" She cut her gaze to the side of the room he'd just come from.

Neva. Damn. She has no idea. Eliza probably thought the queen just as terrible as her husband. Finn glared back at Chesa. "Get in. Close the door."

For once, she complied without a word.

Only once the door was closed did Finn step back from Eliza and gesture to the queen. She said many of the maids and knights were her allies, but one could never be too careful, so he lowered his voice to a whisper before speaking. "Eliza, this is the White Queen, Neva."

To his great surprise, Neva dropped into a low curtsy. "It's nice to finally meet you, Eliza."

His eyes widened. *Shit.* When the queen looked up again, he slid his gaze toward Chesa, but Neva only smiled and said, "She knows."

Finn looked between the three women, none of them appearing to bear a shred of his concern. Chesa had the gall to wink at him. "You handed me over to the White knights," he accused.

"I saved you from doing something stupid and getting yourself killed," Chesa replied. "I will always do what's best for Alice, and right now, that involves keeping you alive."

"Right now?" His eyes narrowed.

Chesa shrugged.

"It's okay, Finn." Eliza twined her fingers through his. "We're okay."

For the moment... "And you?" he asked the queen. How could Chesa possibly know the queen's secrets when she'd just arrived that morning?

The two women shared a look. "We're acquainted," Neva said.

"As I said," Chesa continued. "I will always help Alice, and the queen has vowed to be an ally to Alice as well."

"Why me?" Eliza asked. Her fingers flexed against Finn. "Just because I am Alice?"

The queen narrowed the distance between them, her skirts swishing across the marble. "That was the reason," she confided. "Alice can make real change in Wonderland, and we need that change. Not just the White Court, but all of us. I believe you can make things better than they are. But also," she glanced at Finn, and the sincerity and the hope in her face nearly gutted him, "because Finn loves you, and I know he would not love anyone unworthy."

He felt Eliza stiffen against him, then relax. "You know each other?" She tilted her head to the side and stared up at him.

"A long time ago," the queen replied before he could. "We were friends as children."

Eliza's brows furrowed. "But the king...what he did..." She glanced between them, a dozen questions lingering unspoken.

"I'll explain it all to you, I promise." He squeezed her hand.

One brief nod in return was all he needed. That and a shared look that said she trusted him, believed in him. That faith sent a wave of warmth through his chest.

"We should give you two some time to yourselves," the queen said, a knowing look glinting in her eyes. She held out her hand to Eliza, who took it. "We need you, Eliza. We need Alice. Do not forget about White." She dropped her hand and turned to Finn. "I will see that you two can remain together. Just don't do anything foolish." Her smile turned lopsided, a ghost of the friend he knew long ago, before she strode passed them toward the door.

"I will be near," Chesa promised. "And I am always on Alice's side. Do not forget that."

With a final farewell, the two women departed, leaving Finn alone with Eliza.

He gasped as her arms wrapped around him from behind. Eliza's head came to rest against his back. The simple touch broke down all his walls. She was safe. They both were, by some miracle. Whatever it took to keep them that way, he would do it. Finn barely had the chance to savor her embrace before Eliza pulled away and shoved him—hard.

"What—" He twisted toward her, halting at the deep scowl on her face.

"You idiot!" She stomped. "What were you thinking coming after me? There were dozens of knights. More."

Finn reared back. "You wanted me to *leave* you here? With that bastard on the throne?"

"You could have gotten killed!" She flung her arms to the sides. "Chesa told me your plan about sneaking in. You should thank her, you know. No way would they have just let you slip in and sneak me out."

When she puts it that way... He rubbed at the back of his neck, cheeks flaming.

"They could have *killed* you, Finn! You would be dead, and I would never know." She started to pace, arms gesturing in wild motions. "The whole time I was at that bloody croquet match, I thought maybe you had abandoned me."

"I would never—" he began, but she kept going as if he'd never spoken.

"You'd figured out I wasn't that special after all and moved on, decided I wasn't worth the risk, or that trying to escape was a horrible plan. I was so angry."

"Eliza—"

"But no," she whirled on him. "You were in a dungeon, waiting for the Mother only knows what kind of punishment from that selfish bitch queen, and yet, I was mad at you?" Tears glistened in her eyes. "And now you're stuck here, with a man who already tried to kill you, trapped under his roof under yet another threat of death."

The emotion pouring out of her was more blinding than the sun. Her pain drew him closer, every instinct begging him to pull her into his arms, hold her, and promise that everything would be okay.

That was a promise he couldn't make. Not yet. But hold her? How could he not?

"Eliza—"

"And it's because of me, Finn!" She railed, flinging her arms down at her sides. "You should never have come after me."

With a grunt of frustration, he closed the distance between them and pulled her against his chest. A sob cut off whatever words she tried to say next. Her head thumped against his breastbone. Eliza's arms wound around him, holding on as if she might collapse without his support.

"You truly wished I didn't come after you?" he asked, petting her hair.

Eliza twisted her head to look up at him, her cheek plastered against his shirt. "It's the one thing I wanted more than anything else and the thing I feared most in this world."

His fingers stilled in her hair, cupping the back of her head. "Why?"

Her nose twitched over a sniffle. "Because I love you."

A fluttering sensation erupted in his belly, leaving him lightheaded and swaying on his feet. "You love me?" He had to be hearing things.

"Yes, Finn." She stared up at him in wonder. "I love you."

"You love me?" A jolt of laughter escaped before he could stop it. In all his years, he thought the White Court held only death for him, and on this worst of all days, it managed to deliver something beautiful too.

Eliza smacked his arm, not too hard, but enough to get his attention. "Yes, how many times do I have to say it?"

A bright grin broke across his face in response to her scowl. He dipped his head close to hers. "At least a few more."

His grin widened at her eyeroll.

"You're ridiculous," she said.

Maybe so. He cupped her cheek, drawing her face a hand-width away from his own. "But then, you know why I had to come for you."

She blinked at him, her lips parted in an invitation he wouldn't be able to ignore much longer. "I do?"

"Yes, Eliza."

That tempting pink tongue slipped across her lips, and he followed the movement with his thumb, rubbing away the slight trace of wetness. "I love you. I could never leave you," he promised.

The space between them vanished. Eliza kissed him like her life depended on it, like the strength of her kiss alone might save them from whatever lay ahead. She wiggled her arms free and flung them around his neck. He'd never been so grateful that Wonderland had an Alice, and more than that, that she was his. Whatever choice this beautiful woman would make, it couldn't possibly be wrong. It didn't matter that he was in the place he loathed most, surrounded by people who likely thought him dead or wished it so. They were together. That was all that mattered, and whatever time he had left, he planned to share it with Eliza. Only her.

Her taste was pure intoxication, sweeter and more dizzying than any wine. *She loves me.* Desire burned low in his abdomen. *She loves me.* Eliza pressed against him, rolling her hips against his erection. *She loves me.* Finn groaned against her lips, giving her one more all-consuming kiss before pulling away.

Eliza whimpered at the lost contact and strained toward him. He didn't give her long, only a heartbeat before lifting her off her feet and carrying her toward the bed.

40

He loves me.

When Eliza had seen him hauled into the throne room and heard he'd come for her, she knew. It was there in his eyes when he looked at her, when he told her not to worry for him while facing down his brother's blade. He loved her. But how could she not worry or be angry with him for risking himself when she loved him too?

Somehow, hearing it from his lips, being close to him once again, made that anger vanish. She loved him. He loved her. They'd both done and promised foolish things, but what did that matter when love was involved?

He loves me.

It was all Eliza could think as he carried her to the bed, all the while staring at her like she was a precious treasure. He was the diamond, though, enduring so much for so long and yet emerging as the powerful, brave man before her. Still strange, still foolish, and with a lopsided grin that made her knees weak. He was both soft and hard—delicate and quick as a rabbit but sharp as a blade. Grandmama was right. He truly was balanced in the best of ways.

Even if they couldn't break the damnable curse, he was what her heart, her soul needed to survive this place. A true wonder in Wonderland.

Finn laid her on the bed, and before he could pull away, she grabbed onto his shirt and pulled him down with her. His knee slipped between her thighs, planting itself on the mattress and supporting his weight over her.

The feel of his body against hers, the scent of his swarming her, was a dream come true. But it wasn't enough.

"I need you," she said.

The grin he gifted her in return tugged at the invisible string pulling tight between her chest and her core. The look alone twisted her into knots in the most delicious way—something only he could accomplish.

"Then you shall have me," Finn promised, but again he tried to rise.

"Right now." Eliza tugged on his shirt.

She needed him right then, before anyone could interrupt, before anything else could happen to separate them again. Eliza trailed her hand down his chest, then lower, savoring the way his stomach muscles contracted under her touch before she tugged at the waistband of his pants.

A deep groan rumbled through his chest. He nipped at his bottom lip, a sly grin spreading across his features before he nuzzled her neck. Finn's hair tickled her, his breath raising shivers across her skin before he whispered, "Right now then."

Finally! Eliza nearly cried out in excitement. She'd never been a wanton, needy woman, but that was before she met Finn. Having almost lost him, she needed him now as much as the air in her lungs.

When he rose onto his knees, Eliza didn't stop him. She was too busy bunching up the skirts of her dress as Finn tugged at the ties of his pants with fervor. When he freed himself, Eliza still struggled with her blasted underthings. Her fingers slipped over the thin, silken fabric. It would be a lie to say it wasn't mostly because her hands shook.

"May I?" Finn's fingers easily slipped under the edge, a touch cool against her heated skin.

Already she was wet for him, ready. "Please, I—"

Finn jerked the cloth. Eliza gasped as it ripped off, bearing her to the man kneeling between her legs. Cool air rushed in, teasing her sensitive skin and the moisture already dewed there.

"Kings," he hissed, staring at the sight he'd just exposed. Eliza wiggled her hips, eager to have him back where she wanted him. An expectant sigh slipped from her as Finn leaned his weight atop her, their lips crashing together as his hips pressed her into the bed.

Fire ignited under her skin everywhere they touched, swelling in her center and spreading the moisture growing between her legs. Finn's tongue flicked against her own, teasing and taunting, distracting her as he reached between them. The slightest touch of his fingers against her folds had her bucking against his hand.

"Wet for me?" He nipped at her lip, the slight bit of pain heightening her pleasure.

"Yes," she sighed. He stoked up and down her slit, eliciting a whimper. "You. Only you. I want you. Please."

His hand vanished, only to be replaced by the firm press of his cock. "As my Eliza wishes."

That first slow thrust nearly shattered her right then and there. The fullness, the completeness of him inside her pulled a moan from deep in her throat.

Perfect. A missing piece. That's what he was. Body and soul, they fit.

He pulled back slowly and drove home again, letting her feel every inch of him and driving her mad with need. She rocked her hips against him, desperate for more—a hunger to match her own.

"More," she begged. "I need—"

The simple request had Finn's eyes widening like he spied an open door in a cell and now was free. He shifted the tempo in an instant, no longer slow and torturous but starving—ravenous.

"I know what you need, Eliza." Finn wound his fingers through hers, pulling one hand above her head. "My Eliza."

One hand remained unclaimed, and she tangled it in his long hair, sliding her fingers across his scalp, down his neck, and to his back, never able to get quite enough of him as they moved together in a quick, heady rhythm.

The knot of pleasure low in her core drew tight as her release neared. Eliza wrapped her legs around him, holding him as they rocked together, his cock grinding against that magical spot within her.

This was no slow seduction. It was a joining, a claiming, a promise to never let go.

A sheen of sweat broke out across her skin. Her fingertips dug into the firm muscle of his shoulder. Then she broke, carried away in a tide of ecstasy. Her thighs clamped around Finn, and she held on for dear life, even as he quickened his pace before letting out a groan of his own. Finn jerked back abruptly despite her legs around him, sliding free before a warm wetness splashed across her most sensitive skin.

"I love you." He panted, his fingers twined with hers, flexing but holding firm.

"Finn," she gasped his name, the last of her orgasm still coursing through her with a shiver. Eliza brushed back his hair back behind his ear before cupping his cheek. She held his gaze all the while, basking in the wonder of him. "I love you too."

A little laugh slipped from him. Relief? Could he truly not think she'd say it back?

"I love you, I love you, I love you," she promised.

The kiss he pressed against her lips was so tender it nearly brought a tear to her eye. "I believe you."

Finn closed his eyes, a smile upon his face as Eliza caressed him again. Some of his weight eased onto her, and his length softened against her thigh.

His brows pinched, and he opened his eyes. "I'm sorry if I was too rough."

A little chuckle rattled her chest before she planted a kiss on his nose. "You were perfect."

He grinned. "Perfect, huh?"

*a*fter cleaning up and righting some of their clothing, Finn and Eliza nestled together in the bed. Prison or not, Finn had no desire to leave. In fact, he'd be perfectly content to spend the remainder of his life wrapped up with Eliza—which might not be long if his brother had his way and Neva failed to come through on whatever she had in mind.

Eliza made lazy trails down his bare chest with her fingertips. Simple touches, yet each one distracted him more than the last. A few times, she'd asked her questions twice, but he wasn't about to tell her to stop—the conversation or the touches. Just having her beside him, safe and contented, was all he needed.

"So you didn't know your friend had become queen?" Her fingers stilled right over his heart. *Can she feel it racing?*

"No." He turned his head to look at her across the pillow. "That must seem strange to you."

She lifted a shoulder. "A bit odd being that the courts are somewhat close, well, closer than some kingdoms back home. But some of them are secretive—even though I work in the great library, the hall of records, we know little about them. The Red Court didn't have spies keeping an eye on White?"

She'd yet to resume her distracting caress, so Finn pursued one of his own, twisting that lock of hair near her face that always liked to spring out on its own. "Yes, though whatever they learned wasn't widely shared. If they knew, it never reached me." Not an altogether surprising revelation. King Jasper shared what was essential to the protection of the Red Court. Anything else he learned? Sometimes it slipped out over a drink, and other times, it didn't.

"And yet Chesa knows everything."

He laughed. *That she does*. He had taken their time together to fill her in on what Neva divulged, and Eliza had done the same, explaining Chesa's actions. Still, it didn't explain why the tricky woman couldn't have told him her plan. He wasn't *that* bad of an actor—he'd fooled the Red Queen for years. "If I could become invisible, then I might too."

"You can become a rabbit." She waggled her eyebrows at him.

Finn smirked. "Not quite the same." Pity that. The ability to disappear at will might have saved him a heap of trouble over the years.

The humor fled her face as she shifted closer on the bed. "Do you think it's possible for Alice, for me, to demand a different king? That's what the White Queen wants, isn't it?"

Truly, he wasn't sure exactly what she had in mind. If Neva was still the same as the girl he once knew, he'd wager she had a more violent solution in mind. She was always quick to act, to demand forgiveness rather than permission, even with him. Not that he minded much. She'd been a friend, perhaps his only true one.

"I don't know. Maybe?" He wanted to give her more than that, but lies would never do. "It would be worth trying."

"Perhaps I could command him to step down. He has violated the laws of White."

"Doubtful." The bastard never had a shred of kindness. They used to train together as boys. With the difference in age and size, Finn never had much of a chance, but it didn't stop him from trying. Too many times, Alvis hadn't let up even after Finn yielded, when his young body was bloody and bruised on the ground. The king then had been indifferent, insisting that his sons needed to be harder, stronger if they were to one day rule. There was no mercy or leniency shown to Finn, even though he was younger.

Only his mother ever showed him praise. She tended his wounds herself, spoke sweetly to him, and held him close. Maybe that was why his brother and the king both hated him—and her—because she'd loved Finn, the son who was nothing like her husband or her elder child.

"He isn't the first king to breach the law without recompense," he said. Though, he couldn't recall former monarchs being quite so flagrant about it as his stepbrother seemed to be. "I'm not sure if Alice has unseated one. Smaller requests, sure. Choosing which court rules, of course." Changing the royal line? Surely, he'd have heard about that if it were possible.

"Did your grandmother's letter say anything?" Eliza had told him that Chesa finally gave her the rest. The previous Alice had said to trust him. A kind gesture, but he wasn't sure how that would help Eliza break the curse.

Sorrow washed across her features, and she glanced away. Instantly, he regretted bringing it up again. Any talk of her grandmother always seemed to dim her spirits.

"No," she said at last, barely a whisper. "I wish she had. I wish…" Eliza closed her eyes. "I was a terrible granddaughter. I should have written more, visited more. If I'd been a better granddaughter to her, maybe I would have learned more about this world, about being Alice, and about the curse. Things could have gone so much differently."

Finn cupped her cheek, demanding her attention and drawing his face close to hers. "It's true that she missed you, but your grandmother always spoke of you with love and affection. Your letters were the light in her life. Talking about you always made her smile." She'd loved to talk about her granddaughter who raced through her gardens or lounged in the grass with her nose in a book. But all her stories painted her as a young girl, carefree and innocent. He'd never been more surprised than when he first glimpsed Eliza and found a grown woman in place of the girl he expected.

"I could have done so much better by her. I loved the times I spent with her as a girl, but my parents put a stop to that when they sent me off to boarding school." She sighed. "But after that, when I was no longer a schoolgirl and had my own life, I could have—should have—gone back more often. At first, I stayed away because of my parents. In the capital, I was out of their reach, but visiting Grandmama always drew their attention, and not in the best of ways..." Eliza pinched her eyes closed before opening them again. "I was a coward, I guess you could say. Then later, I was so consumed with my life and wishes that I all but ignored her. I should have visited her regardless of my parents or my obsession with my work. She deserved that."

Time could be tricky like that, teasing a person with all they could have done with it but didn't. He knew that better than most. So many years spent with little to show for it other than his head still attached to his neck.

Finn trailed the back of his hand across her skin. "She was proud of all you accomplished." A white lie. Proud, yes, but Alice gave little in the way of specifics. "If you ignored your own passions, you wouldn't have become the woman you are now." That, he was sure of. The former Alice was a lovely woman, but she didn't have the fire and determination of Eliza. That was something all her own.

"Maybe," she whispered before closing her eyes once more. She lingered like that so long that he almost wondered if she'd fallen asleep. Eventually, she cracked her eyes open again. "You never knew who your real father was?"

"No. I didn't know it wasn't the former king until the charges were brought against my mother." Finn had been dragged into the throne room along with her to bear witness to her crime, or so they had said. Looking back now, it was probably to force her obedience. She'd been strong—gifted with magic. But with her child in the hands of the White knights, she wouldn't be able to act against the king.

Finn hadn't fully understood her sins, yet he'd wrenched himself free of the knights to stand at her side, to defend her. Even when the king threatened him with exile as well, his half-brother smirking all the while, Finn hadn't budged. Somehow, he thought he could make a difference. What a fool he'd been. He never considered his exile or the attempt on his life. Even so, he'd have defended her again in a heartbeat.

"After that..." He swallowed hard. "We had precious little time after that."

The king, the man he'd once thought was his father before he learned of his mother's crime, hadn't sent the assassins. He was almost sure of that, especially since one of his half-brother's friends led the assault and chased them through the wilds. The former king was cold, stern, and followed every letter of the law. He might exile his wife, but if he'd wanted her dead, the sentence would have been carried out in the light of day, not the shadows of the wilds. Finn sometimes wondered if it was a broken heart that killed the king not long after his exile, though he'd wager Alvis had something to do with that too.

Eliza covered her hand with his. "I'm sorry."

"It's not your fault." He forced a smile for her benefit.

She returned it. "Even so. Finn…" Eliza bit her lip, fighting some kind of war he couldn't quite discern.

"Yes?"

"If…if there were a way to find out who your father is, or was," she added quickly. "If Alice could figure that out, would you want to know?"

Finn rolled onto his back and stared at the ceiling, void of all the colorful decorations he'd grown accustomed to while living at the Red Court. It was a question he'd asked himself a thousand times. *Do I want to know? Should I try to find out?* The thought picked at him more than he'd ever admitted, but he landed on the same conclusion each time.

"No." He turned back to Eliza. The White King, whom he'd believed to be his father for years, had been a cold, hard man, never showing him the slightest glimmer of affection. If his real father knew about him, he'd never sought him out—never tried to make a connection. True, he might have thought Finn dead, but it was easiest to believe his father simply never knew. It saved him from false hope. "I've lived this long without knowing."

Her nose wrinkled, lips pressed together. "But maybe you don't have to?"

The start of a laugh caught in his chest. Stubborn woman. "Maybe I don't. But the truth could hurt more than I care to risk."

Eliza opened her mouth as if she might speak again but closed it and shook her head. "I suppose it doesn't matter anyway since I'm not anointed as Alice yet, right? Neva wants us to just sit tight and wait until then?"

"For now." Much as he was loathed to admit it. One step outside this room, and the king would see it as a reason to punish him, if not kill him outright. The best way forward for them was to trust Neva and Chesa and wait for the right moment to act.

Eliza trailed her fingers along his jaw, down his neck, stirring up gooseflesh in their wake. "I'm not very good at waiting." Her eyes hooded, and she shot him a look that struck him like a bolt of lightning straight to his cock.

"Neither am I." Finn rolled on top of her, wrenching a gasping sigh from her lips as his hard length pressed against her. "But I can think of a few engaging things we can do to keep ourselves busy."

42

The handful of days before the anointment passed in a blur. Eliza spent much of them entangled with Finn, a blissful respite from the otherwise grim realities before them.

But the White King found ways to pollute even that. Each day he ordered Finn and Eliza to join him at dinner. They sat on opposite sides of a long table, the king at its center and no other guests except knights looming near the doors and footmen serving the meal. Much of the dinner was filled with painful silence. The rest? Punishing verbal reminders of what would happen if they stepped out of line or if Eliza should fail to choose White upon her anointment.

At least Eliza and Finn were allowed to stay together in one room. The queen had seen to that, true to her word. Neva visited a few times along with Chesa. Both shared what they'd heard about the world outside their walls. Beasties threatening settlements. Red promising war, and White's eagerness for it. With every passing day, the bloodlust grew, until Neva confided that she wasn't sure if even the power of Alice's choice would prevent all bloodshed.

An element of the curse, Chesa told them. It would continue to build, to blind the senses of man and beast alike until Alice made her choice.

Should she not choose? The people would suffer and die, forced to fight by whatever madness wrought this punishment on the land to begin with.

That impending fate consumed Eliza's thoughts on the long carriage ride to the shrine, the spot of Alice's anointment. Worry was her constant companion, the only one the White King would allow since neither Finn nor Chesa were permitted to ride with her.

"Alice shouldn't be forced to share," the king had said, his grin all too feral.

More like he wanted her alone with only his parting reminder about the importance of her choice.

They stopped twice, only briefly, to refresh both person and horse. Both times, Chesa lingered nearby, offering an encouraging look and word, but she never caught sight of Finn.

"He's safe," Chesa said.

Oddly, Eliza believed her, and not just because it was in the king's best interest not to harm him—yet.

When they stopped a third time, the sun was already low in the sky. The blinding rays streamed through the curtains, all cheery and bright. Maybe Alice's ascension was supposed to be that way too. It would be for whatever court was picked and for those who lived outside the courts and were harassed by the increased wildness of the land. To Eliza, though, a raging thunderstorm would have been more appropriate. Maybe then she could have screamed out some of the fury boiling within her.

The door to the carriage swung open. Eliza barely had time to gather her nerves before the one face she least wanted to see blocked out the sun.

"Alice," the king all but hissed, a mockery of the way Finn sometimes drew out her name. "You shall ride the rest of the way with me."

There'd be no arguing. Any dissension would cause problems for her and for Finn. Reluctantly, she emerged from the carriage and took the king's offered hand. He led her to his horse, a stunning white stallion. The great beast snorted as the king lifted her into the saddle himself before leaping up behind her.

"Now, this is more like it." His breath tickled her neck as he reached around her to grab the reins. "We shall ride to the shrine together. What better sign could there be of Alice's allegiance than riding in, clad in white, and sharing a mount with the king?"

Eliza fought the urge to shove him away or, better yet, smack him across the face. She'd had no choice in her clothing. It was wear what she was provided or go naked, and she wasn't sure she could handle the shame of the latter. The bastard would probably have found a way to spin that to his advantage as well.

"Even your hair..." He leaned in and nipped at her earlobe. The unwanted touch made her skin crawl. "Lucious and dark. The perfect complement to my own, don't you think?"

Perhaps the perfect complement to Finn. Never to you. It was a pity they looked so much alike, traits inherited from their mother, no doubt.

Chesa drew her horse near. "We should continue on. The ascension is almost upon us."

The king let out a drawn-out sigh but eased back. "So it is."

Chesa looked to Eliza. "We're almost there."

Eliza nodded in return. The woman was as present in the moment as she'd seen her—eyes clear, her hazy faraway look nowhere in sight. It was almost as if she slept-walked through life, only to awaken fully for this occasion.

The other woman kicked her horse into a gallop, leading the way. Knights collapsed around them as the king followed suit. Eliza turned her head this way and that, searching for Finn but never finding him. Nor did she spot the queen. However, multiple carriages loomed in the procession. They could be in any one, hidden from view.

Or left behind.

The thought left her stomach hollow, and not just from the lack of food. It had been offered, but who could eat on such a day?

Eliza searched the horizon for the shrine. Chesa described it as an old ruin near a lake, walls and pillars of grey marble half grown over with vegetation. The shrinewas big enough to house a whole troop of knights, she'd said, but only Alice and her guardian could step foot on the grounds. Even so, people from all over Wonderland would travel there as a sort of pilgrimage. And if Alice were to make a proclamation, such as naming her choice of court, or more significantly, switching it, such a choice would happen there on a night with a full moon. One choice per moon. One decision made and no more. Only there. Only where the ancient magic ran strongest.

Forest gave way to sweeping plains, sunset cutting harsh rays across the tall grasses. A smudge of red stood out among the golden strands, stretching far and wide like the crimson river she and Finn had crossed weeks ago. For a moment, she thought it might be the same one.

"Bastard," the king growled behind her. "Of course."

Her brows scrunched as she glanced back at the king, but he looked straight ahead. She turned back toward the advancing sight. Realization crept in like a slow morning fog.

"The Red Court." Hundreds of them. At least as many as accompanied them, if not more. The revelation made her head spin.

"Always putting on a show." The king snapped the reins harder, urging their mount onward down the sloping hill. "Though they shall be the ones leaving in disappointment, don't you agree?"

The speed of their pursuit pulled away his laughter, but not before it could turn her stomach. Her decision would not be made in shadows but in front of both courts.

As they drew near, a sight off to the side drew her attention: grey rock glimmering in the sunset. A wide flight of stairs led up to what must be a shadowy entranceway. Great pillars stood at the top of the stairs—at least three people high—supporting a roof of the same grey stones. Vines and foliage climbed from the field like fingers of green, grasping onto the sides and pillars and trying to drag them down into the ground. The whole structure appeared to slant backward as if the plant life had already partially succeeded in its task.

The king led his horse to the front of the procession, pulling alongside Chesa. They advanced the growing wall of Red head-on. Red knights sat aside their horses in rows so perfect they may as well have been statues. Foot soldiers stood behind. At their front lingered the king and queen, each resplendent in armor bearing their court's color.

The White King did not slow until they drew near the visible line running from the center of the shrine across the plain. No grass grew on the strip of barren dirt wide as a person. A result of the curse or some age-old marker created by man, she couldn't say. The Red Court stood several feet behind the line, and White took their position on the opposite side.

Eliza dared a glance at the monarchs she had once resided with. The Red Queen fumed, angry as ever, her cheeks a shade not too distant from her dress. The king, however, bore a look of disappointment, something far worse than fury. Guilt twisted her stomach into knots the longer she looked at him. Surely, he knew it wasn't her choice to be stuck with White or astride the king's horse? It wasn't her choice to be in Wonderland at all.

Chesa was the first one off her horse, walking around its head to hold out her arms to Eliza. Without waiting for permission from the king, she slipped down with Chesa's aid, her legs and backside quaking from the brutal ride. The king leaped down after her. Knights rushed forward to lead the horses away. Another drew up on horseback, the queen nestled side-saddle in front of him.

Eliza's heart leaped at the sight. She was here after all. An ally— hopefully—on this field of war. The king stood smirking at his opponents across the line. Eliza would even say he basked in their displeasure, letting it draw him up higher than his already towering height. The arrogant man didn't spare a glance for his wife as another set of knights rushed to her horse to help her down. Rather, more like lift her down for all the help she gave them. They set her on her feet like a doll or a child. Her white gown remained resplendent despite the ride. Even dirt didn't dare touch her. A silver crown ringed her head, much like her husband's, sharp points sticking up through the fall of her straight, black hair that nearly reached her backside.

The queen walked to her king's side, all the while maintaining a distant look about her that could rival Chesa's common façade. The queen's expression was a careful ruse, where Chesa's was more like a comfortable outfit she chose to wear on occasion but had shed for today. Even so, Eliza had hoped the queen would offer her something, some look or promise that the night wouldn't turn to bloodshed, but she gave her nothing, not even a twitch of her fingers where they clasped together in front of her.

The king turned to his knights. "Where is my dear brother?"

Finn. Eliza stretched on her toes, trying to find him amid the crowd of knights behind them. The last rays of sunset glinted off their white and silver armor, nearly blinding her, but she squinted against the light, refusing to look away.

A pair of knights led him forward, one holding him firm by either arm, not that he tried to run. Where would he go with both armies present? He found her unerringly and gave her a weak smile, the only glimmer of hope she'd received from anyone.

Though fear tightened its icy grip around her throat, she forced a fleeting smile in return. It was the best she could give.

The king drew his sword and marched toward Finn.

Cold sweat broke out along her neck. Eliza rushed after him, only to be hauled back by Chesa, her iron grip tight around her forearm.

"He won't harm him yet," Chesa said in a harsh whisper.

Eliza whirled on Chesa but was stopped by some unspoken warning on the woman's face.

Yet. He wouldn't harm Finn yet. But he would. The moment Eliza declared her choice of one court or the other, little would stop the king from harming the man she loved. It would be another moon cycle before she could choose again, and that was only if she could make it to the shrine. The bastard would more than likely lock her away to prevent just that.

Eliza turned back just in time to see the king grab Finn from the knights and jerk him across the field to where they stood.

"Finn!" The call came from across the line. The Red King's mount danced in agitation, its rider wide-eyed and suddenly very un-kingly as he took in his ward.

The tightness around Eliza's neck slid down to crush her ribs. Perhaps he knew or suspected. Maybe the king wasn't oblivious to the identity of the ward he'd taken in. Eliza's nails dug into her palms. However, that made the queen's actions and his blind eye to them all the worse.

Alvis held Finn, facing the other monarchs, and raised his sword to his throat. The White King cut his sharp gaze to Eliza, a hard smirk cutting across his features. "Do remember our agreement, Alice."

"Don't worry about me," Finn said.

The king jerked his arm, bringing the blade entirely too close for comfort.

Eliza looked only at Finn as she said, "I remember."

She needed a way out. Now. There was no more time left. The clock hands had ticked their last, and she had to do something other than follow the path fate laid before her.

Eliza stared hard at the White Queen where she lingered just beyond Finn and Alvis, but the woman still didn't so much as flinch.

"We must go now." Chesa slid her hand down her arm to grab her hand and gave it a gentle tug.

"But—"

Chesa gave a quick shake of her head. "Not here. You can do nothing here. But there..." She slid her gaze to the shrine. "It's the beginning," she said, her voice barely a whisper. "It can be the end. Now come."

The king laughed, the sound grating against her senses like sharp stones against one another. "Make a good choice, Alice!"

43

Finn stared helplessly as Chesa led Eliza toward the flight of stairs leading up to the shrine. She might as well have been on the way to slaughter for the panicked look in her eyes.

The stories he'd heard always talked about Alice's Ascension as a grand moment, something of beauty and wonder. He was too young to have any memories of the last ascension, however, he always pictured it as something beautiful. But this? *A nightmare.*

The last colors of sunset were quickly fading from the sky, leaving the bright moon overhead a pale eerie specter of the event. Red knights lit torches across the field, passing them through the ranks until their line looked like a living flame in the dark.

Horses behind them whinnied their agitation. The shift and clang of metal from uneasy knights were a dark symphony all its own.

Whatever Alice's proclamation, it wouldn't stop bloodshed. There was too much eagerness, too much anger, on both sides for that. King Jasper's horse still high-stepped around, as uneasy as its master. Finn refused to look at the Red Queen. Maybe, by some grace of the ascension, she'd take a tumble that would knock some sense of decency into her head.

Eliza twisted back to stare at him, stumbling and nearly falling in the process. The silent plea broke something in him. A tingling sensation started under his skin, burning away the fog jumbling his thoughts.

He couldn't leave her to this choice alone. He wouldn't be a liability or a tool to be wielded—never against her.

His half-brother made mocking calls to the Red Court across the divide, stirring up the knights who shifted in their perfect precision and alignment. Lizardo stood near his queen, hollering something foul back that sent the White King howling with mocking amusement.

Better than that, it distracted him, making his blade dip low, hostage near forgotten.

Finn was out of time. No better opportunity would present itself. And so, Finn released his magic, shifting in a blink and dropping into the tall, yellowed grasses. Knights gasped. The king's laughter choked off. Finn sprinted away.

"You bastard!" The White King roared. A heartbeat later, the air pulsed with magic. The ground rumbled as a beast's heavy paws landed with a vicious thump. A woman screamed—possibly the Red Queen based on the direction.

Finn sprinted into the clearing of the division line, just a brief enough exposure to confirm his fears. His brother had shifted into his alternative form, a vicious and powerful beast of legend—a Jabberwock.

Clawed, reptilian legs supported a long but stout body that slimmed into a long, pointed tail behind its hind legs. Silver scales covered him from tail to snout, fangs long as a Bandersnatch's visible in his open maw. A set of wings covered in a thin membrane protruded from the monster's back.

His little heart pounded against his ribs. Every footfall of the mighty beast rumbled the ground. Finn bolted down the dividing line in an attempt to draw the beast away. In that horrible form, Alvis was likely to swing at anyone, and even metal armor was little defense to his horrible claws.

A jaunt to either side would land Finn amid knights of one court of the other. Momentary protection, possibly—if horse or human didn't squash him—but death to innocents was certain.

The Jabberwock had a taste for blood, and little else could quench it.

"Finn!" Eliza's screech cut through the chaos. It tugged him like a rope, nearly sending him tumbling tail over foot. He glanced back but couldn't see anything from his low position.

He reached for his magic, and once again became a man, fingers digging into the dirt as he scrambled upright.

The sight near the shrine chilled his blood. Alvis, as the Jabberwock, paced back and forth across the dividing line at the base of the stairs. Eliza stood still and pale halfway up them, Chesa in front of her, arms outstretched to block the monster from her charge.

"Ruunnninnngg aawwwaayy?" The words rumbled from the beast like rocks down a hill.

A shiver raced over his skin. His brother could talk in his alternative form. A thing that shouldn't be possible.

The Jabberwocky's bottom fangs thrust up over his upper lip, glinting in the moon's light. He reached up with a massive, clawed hand and swiped toward the women on the stairs. Sparks of magic rained down over the monster where he scratched against the magical barrier preventing people from entering the holy shrine.

Chesa screeched like a cat. "You dare threaten Alice?"

His tail slammed into the barrier in response. The whole complex shook. A stone from the roof crashed to the ground, shattering on the stairs as Eliza screeched.

Finn lurched forward, teeth bared in a snarl. *He wouldn't fucking dare.*

A commotion rose on both sides. Knights inched forward. War was a heartbeat away.

"Fight me!" Finn yelled. "Stop cowering as a beast and fight me man to man!"

Something caught between a roar and laugh rumbled across the field, shaking him to his core. Finn was a great fighter, one of the best in the Red Court, but he'd lost hundreds of fights to his brother in youth. Not once had the duel gone in his favor, and he still had some scars to prove it. The odds couldn't be more out of favor, a rabbit versus a beast in truth, but he couldn't let the bastard bring the whole shrine down on the woman he loved.

"No!" Eliza screamed. "Run, Finn!"

He swallowed down the tightness in his throat. *Ancient kings do I want to.* He was good at running and evading. His specialty, really. After all, rabbits were quick and skittish creatures.

Finn shook his head, hoping she could see. "Go, Eliza! Make your choice!"

Pick Red. Any choice but this monster. He might not be able to beat his brother, especially unarmed, but he could hold him off long enough for Eliza to do what she must.

"Finneas." The familiar voice at his side stole his attention. King Jasper's horse kicked its legs as its rider drew him to a sharp halt. The moment they pounded into the tall grass, the king drew his blade. "If you're to fight, you need a weapon."

The king took the bare blade in his gloved hand and held the hilt toward Finn. A silent look of gratitude passed between them as Finn grabbed hold of it, testing the weight and the grip and finding it to his liking.

"Thank—" A bellow from the Jabberwocky cut off his reply.

"Step back!" Finn roared instead, adjusting his stance and reading for the beast that tore across the ground in his direction.

Alvis was on him in seconds, too quick to think. Finn lunged out of the way, barely dodging a killing swipe of the Jabberwock's claws as he fell into the tall grass, the ground stealing the breath from his lungs on impact. He'd barely gained his feet when it charged again. This time, he anticipated the swipe, swinging with his sword and nicking the beast's leg enough to cover the tip of the blade in blood.

The sweet sight barely had time to register before the Jabberwock caught him with his tail and smashed him against the ground once more. Finn's body roared in pain from the impact, his lungs like fire as he tried to suck in a pained breath and regain his footing. His ears rang. Screaming voices begged him to run.

A blade alone wouldn't bring him victory. *The asshole knows it, too.* The beast pawed at the ground and flicked his tail as he laughed. A cat playing with a mouse, that's all this was.

He gritted his teeth, set his feet, and prepared for the next assault. A new strategy took form in his mind. Finn raised the blade in front of him, a sign of readiness, beckoning the monster on. Alvis didn't disappoint. He charged across the space between them, and this time, Finn raced to meet him. But instead of wielding the king's blade, as his brother expected, he dropped it to the side and raised his open hand—one holding a tight ball of pure magic.

The Jabberwock leaped. Finn slid low across the ground. He held his breath and at just the right moment, let the magic fly.

It zipped from his palm like an arrow, striking the beast in the belly and sending it flying to land on its side with a booming thud that shook the ground.

Now that was satisfying.

The Jabberwock roared, pushing itself off the ground and shaking its body like a wet dog. Too bad it hadn't broken its beefy neck or those bat-like wings. It was too much to hope for, but landing the blow satisfied something deep within Finn, even more so once he saw the smear of dark blood on its pale leg. He already accomplished more than had had as a child.

"Too afraid to fight me as a man?" Finn goaded.

"Finn!" Eliza cried out behind him.

He couldn't see her, but the fear in her voice nearly brought him to his knees. What he wouldn't give to hold her, to look upon her again, but he couldn't divert his focus away from his brother, especially not as the beast shook himself again.

"Coward!" Finn yelled at the Jabberwock.

It snarled in response and finally, *finally*, transformed back into the loathsome White King. Only the small smear of blood and a little wildness in his hair gave away any tells of the battle. "You're right," the White King mocked. "It would be too easy to shred you apart as my beast. Far less...satisfying."

"Please," Eliza whimpered.

"We must go," Chesa warned.

"Go, Eliza! Listen to her." *Please.* "If I win, he's out of the way. If I lose..." He bared his teeth in a snarl, never looking away from Alvis, who drew his blade and stalked forward. "Make him pay."

The two brothers met in a clash of swords, the impact ringing up

Finn's arms. *Fuck.* The asshole was even stronger than he remembered. Their blades met again, forcing a satisfying grimace to the king's face.

Whatever went on around them, Finn couldn't say. His focus lay solely on his opponent and the way he moved in the moonlight, a true predator through and through. One wrong step, one blink, would be too much to give away.

Again and again, their blades clashed, trading minor wounds and advantages. A cut on Finn's arm. A slice of the king's leg. Bloody surface wounds, just enough to paint their white clothes with smears of color. Even members of the White Court bled red. Funny, that.

Sweat slid down Finn's back. He breathed hard, eyeing his opponent, looking for some weakness or tell that might finally tip the scales.

"Giving up, little Finneas?" Alvis smirked.

Little Finneas. How I hate that fucking nickname. He *had* been little once. Young and desperate for his father and brother's regard. No more.

Finn raised his weapon and charged, swinging with all his might. Alvis met the swing with one of his own, metal ringing as the blades collided. But in his anger, Finn and given too much to the swing and threw himself off balance. The horror of it struck him just as he lost the slightest hair of control. Alvis's grin widened. He shoved Finn back with the force of his blade and leaped, free arm shifting in a blur of magic, long claws flashing out.

Finn roared as the sharp claws scoured his side, leaving fiery pain in their wake. He stumbled back, spots dancing at the edge of his vision as he clutched the wound.

His brother shook his clawed hand, blood splattering onto his clothes and the ground before the partial transformation vanished. "I've learned a few things since you've been away."

"Dirty trick," he groaned.

His brother shrugged as if they discussed the weather, not the three deep cuts he'd left on his side. "A king plays all cards to his advantage." The sword shifted as he righted his grip, the tell of another incoming strike.

Damn it all. Finn was in no shape to defend. Every time he tried to lift his blade, his side roared in agony.

But two could play a game of tricks.

The White King swung. Finn dropped his sword and shifted into his other form. The blade whizzed through the air above him as he landed on the ground. The impact made his body scream out in pain, his rabbit form echoing it in a horrifying squeal.

Worse was Chesa's horrified yell behind him.

Eliza. What happened?

"Bastard!" Alvis stomped, his boot far too close to crushing Finn.

He sprinted in the direction of Chesa's scream, away from his brother and hopefully toward the woman he loved. His little heart threatened to burst as it pounded against his ribs. Blood leaked down his side. Every bound and twitch was agony, but he couldn't stop, couldn't give in until she was safe.

"Stop!" Chesa yelled, to whom he didn't know.

"I'll gut you!" The king's footfalls fell heavy in his wake.

Speed was his ally, but injury slowed Finn. Tall grass obscured his vision. Someone stepped in front of him, and he skidded to stop, screeching in pain as it pulled at his injuries.

Hands grabbed him, lifting him off the ground. He tried to squirm away, but they held fast, tight but tender all at once. "I've got you."

That sweet voice knocked the fight right out of him. *Eliza*. She ran, hurrying toward the shrine.

"Foolish bitch!"

The king's enraged curse made Finn twist to look behind them. His half-brother gave chase. Close. So close. He snarled and pulled back his arm in preparation to swing.

Eliza leaped, fell.

Finn shifted, growing to human form within her arms and twisting to take the brunt of the landing. His back cried out as they slammed onto the stairs of the shrine. Eliza yipped, pulling him tight.

The king's blade struck the barrier, magical sparks flying.

Then Chesa was there, appearing as if from nowhere and standing between them and his brother, a human barrier in addition to the magical one. "You dare swing a blade at Alice?"

An enraged roar split the air, but it had nothing on the whimpers of the woman whose arms were still bound around him.

"Are you hurt?" he managed.

She moved her arm, winced. "I'm fine." Her gaze grew wider as it flicked down him and back up again. "Finn, you're—"

"Make one more move against my charge, and I'll obliterate you," Chesa said, hands on her hips, blocking them almost entirely from the king beyond.

"The guardian is not to intervene!" he snarled.

"Except in the defense of Alice!"

Lightning flashed across a mostly clear sky. Eliza jolted, and he sucked in a breath as she brushed against his wounded body.

Chesa leaned in, her face inches from the barrier. "You have forgotten your place, White King." Her voice carried an other-worldly resonance and power that hushed the gathered armies.

Alvis snorted air through his nose but finally lowered his blade. "This isn't over."

"You're right," Chesa said, drawing out the words. "Alice still has to make her choice. You think it will be you?"

"I'll hunt you!" He stomped outside the barrier, shouting obscenities and foul promises.

Chesa turned her back on the king and grinned down at them. "Shall we?"

inn was alive, safe from the terrible king and his monstrous beast. Somehow, she'd been able to take him over the barrier. Eliza hadn't been sure it was possible. Actually, she had been pretty sure it was impossible. But when she saw him injured, she couldn't stay in the safety of the shrine and leave him to such a horrible fate. He stayed and fought for her. He suffered for her. No more.

Let the king dare raise his sword against her. It would be his end, but she would not let him be Finn's.

The brave, reckless man had even taken the brunt of the fall after she'd launched herself the last few feet to the stairs. His poor body. The sight of his wounds crushed her heart.

Chesa said something, but it was a meaningless buzz as Eliza took in the blood coating Finn's side and the other smears and splatters on him. He gritted his teeth, trying to push himself up, despite the obvious agony of the act.

"Let me help you." She reached for him, trying to find a place to hold and steady him that would not do further harm.

Outside the barrier, the king still raged, but that was no more than a distant annoyance to her ears. The first words to truly sink home were Finn's.

"H-how am I here?" He glanced down at the stairs.

"Alice brought you across the barrier," Chesa said matter-of-factly.

"That's possible?" Eliza asked. She bid Finn wrap an arm around her shoulder and lean his weight on her, which he did.

Chesa shrugged. "It would seem so. But come, more important things await."

"I won't leave Eliza," Finn said.

And she would not leave him. Barrier there may be, but he was hurt, and she wouldn't risk him worsening or someone else finding a way across.

"Good." Chesa flashed a grin at Finn before shifting her focus to Eliza. "Let's get him inside." She ducked beneath Finn's other arm, and they moved him as quickly as they dared.

The inside of the shrine was nothing like Eliza expected. The entryway opened to a single room bearing a staircase descending below ground. Torches flickered on the walls at even intervals, lighting the way, though who lit them, she couldn't say. The whole place reminded her of a tomb—cold, musty, and most of all, eerily silent. They'd yet to reach the bottom of the stairs before all she could hear was their footfalls, an occasional pained groan from Finn, and the steady drip, drip, drip of water somewhere below.

At last, when they must have been several feet below ground, the staircase spilled out into a large, square room. The sight of it chilled Eliza to her bones. Strange symbols were carved on the walls, the floor, the ceiling—none of them a language or style she'd ever seen. Swirls, dots, and the occasional square made up something caught between a language and art. Lit torches hung along the walls, burning just enough to make shadows dance among the shapes.

In the center of it all was a dark space, an opening in the floor, which served as the central focus of the designs. No other exits led from the room. If the White King lost his temper and battered the barrier enough to bring the ceiling down, they'd all be trapped—or squashed. A shudder raced through her body.

"Is this it?" Finn asked, his voice echoing back at them.

"Yes," Chesa replied, her gaze distant once more.

"Set me down here," he said, slipping toward the ground.

That simple movement caused him to cry out. Blood dripped onto the stones. Eliza's stomach bottomed out as she spied the trail of splatters leading back up the stairs.

"We need to get you help, a healer." Eliza jumped to her feet, refusing to look at the blood smeared all over her white gown.

"I'll keep," he groaned.

"Nonsense!" Tendrils of panic skittered down the back of her neck. "I won't let you bleed out down here. This was a mistake. We have to go back up." She twisted around, searching for Chesa, but the woman was nowhere to be found. "Bloody hell!"

"You have to listen first," Chesa demanded.

Eliza gasped. Finn jolted before groaning in pain. Where once there was nothing but air a moment ago, Chesa stood on the other side of the hole, staring into its depths.

"I most certainly do not. I'm not going to sit around while Finn suffers." Getting Finn back up the stairs would be difficult at best. She couldn't risk him pulling the wound open further and bleeding out. *Pressure.* She had to apply pressure and stop the bleeding. Eliza grabbed at her hem and ripped the fabric up to her knees.

"You heard him," Chesa said. "He'll keep."

Eliza tore at her dress, ripping off a large section from the bottom.

"Such a high opinion of me," Finn muttered.

Chesa cocked her head to the side. "You'd rather go back out to your brother?"

"I could get a healer." Eliza dropped her knees beside Finn. He seemed to understand her aim and raised his arm with a wince. "Bring them back across."

"No!" Chesa roared.

Eliza froze as the command rang throughout the room, reverberating through her mind. Stones ground against one another. Shock bled into horror as the pillars on either side of the door shifted to block it.

"Fuck," Finn snapped.

Eliza dropped the rest of the cloth and sprinted for the quickly closing opening.

"Eliza! Don't!" he yelled.

She ran fast as she could, heart hammering, but it was no use. The pillars stilled just before she reached them, leaving only a small opening no bigger than her hand. Even Finn in his rabbit form would have trouble slipping free, to say nothing of his injured side, which would make it nearly impossible.

"You. Must. Listen!" Chesa's voice came again, echoing more not only in the room, but also within her mind. Whatever consumed her now, this was not the woman Eliza knew. She was as strange as the first time they met. Human, but something more, something other. "Alice must hear before she makes her choice."

On wobbling feet, Eliza returned to Finn. "Then speak." She did not wait for Chesa to continue before she resumed binding the fabric around Finn's side. It might not do much, but it was better than nothing.

Chesa didn't continue until Eliza finished knotting the fabric and looked at her. "Now that I have your attention."

Eliza bristled, her lips curling, but then Finn grabbed her hand and gave it a little squeeze. His face still bore a bruise from the rough treatment he received when he was brought to the White Court. His body bore so many more. Between the two of them, they looked like slaughtered lambs, but his presence, his touch, gave her strength. It calmed and centered her. If he were still out there, still at the mercy of the White King or any others who wished him harm, she would not be able to sit and listen to Chesa. With him? Anything was possible.

Chesa swept her hand toward the hole in the floor. "The well."

"A well?" Eliza's brows pinched together.

"You brought us here to show us a well?" Finn echoed.

Chesa paced back and forth near its edge. One slip on the damp floor, and she might tumble in. The thing was plenty wide enough. Three people could stand side-by-side within and not be too squished.

"Not just any well. This well has been here for ages. Before Wonderland was Wonderland. Before humans lived upon this island."

Not just old; ancient.

"It lacked such interesting housing." Chesa gestured around. "But it still existed. In time, people found it. They discovered its wonders and the powers it could grant. A source of raw magic. It became a holy place, sacred, used for ceremonies and special celebrations. Not a place to be visited lightly."

In all her learnings, Eliza had never heard of such a thing. Magic, to be sure, and holy places, pixie doorways, mermaid reefs. But a well? Such an odd thing wouldn't escape her memory.

"Once upon a time, a young woman named Alice Carrol heard of such a place. Yes," Chesa said in response to Eliza's raised brows. "That Alice." She sat down, crossing her legs under her as if settling in for a long tale. "She had a knack for adventure and a wild heart that wasn't satisfied with the daily going-ons of her life. Her family thought her such an odd young woman, quizzical and different. But she didn't mind. It only encouraged her yearning to learn and discover."

"Sounds familiar." Finn shot her a sideways glance.

Quizzical and different. Just the descriptors her parents would have chosen. She could have smacked him for that if he weren't hurt.

"Alice heard the legend of the well and the island known as Wonderland for its unique flora and beasties. Eager as she was and longing for travel, she took her savings and booked passage on a ship. But it would be improper and unsafe for a well-to-do lady to travel alone, so she convinced her dearest friend to go with her."

Finn eased his head onto her shoulder, letting his weight rest on Eliza. Her arm encircled him, her fingers rubbing a gentle caress on his uninjured shoulder.

"The women quickly fell in love with the strange land, so different from their own," Chesa continued, her voice light as if she told a joyous tale. "If that were all, it should have been a successful journey. But Alice, being fair of looks and bright of spirit, fell in love with more than just the place itself. Wonderland was governed by two noble families, different as night and day but both reasonable rulers in their time. Alice and her friend grew to know them both, and love them both after a fashion. Again, not a problem if only it had stopped there." She tore her gaze from the well and gave Eliza a sad smile.

A creeping suspicion took root at the base of Eliza's spine.

"A son of each noble family fell in love with Alice and professed their feelings to her on the very same day. She came to her friend in distress, for she loved two men. How could she choose? Her friend encouraged honesty, to tell them both about the dilemma. So Alice did, but the men were unsatisfied. How could she also love their rival? Threats of violence grew between the two families. The place that had once been peaceful became unsettled. A decision was made to meet here, at the well, for surely that would give Alice the clarity she needed to make a choice." Chesa trailed her fingers across the opening as if it were a pool and she could tease the fish. "Alice's friend could see how upset she was. She warned against giving in to the demands of the men who now seemed more villains than lovers. The women should book passage on the next ship out, return home. After all, they'd had the grand adventure they'd hoped for, and their families must miss them dearly."

Chesa stood, brushing off her pants and gazing down into the well. "But Alice was stubborn. She didn't listen, of course, and went to meet her lovers on that fateful day. They came to the well. Right here."

A sudden chill slipped through the room, bringing out the gooseflesh across Eliza's skin. What had been a happy tale of romance and adventure turned dark, and she knew deep down it would only turn grimmer.

"But still, Alice could not choose. The men fought, drawing blood in this sacred place, for if Alice could not choose between them, then they would force a decision with their swords. After all, if one were dead, he would no longer be a choice. Alice tried to stop the fight. The men never could say exactly what happened or who was responsible, though the fact they fought at all put the guilt squarely on both of their shoulders. When Alice's friend arrived, it was already too late. The men still fought, each blaming each other, for Alice had fallen into the well and struck her head." Chesa stared down at her upturned palms. "There was so much blood."

Eliza's skin turned clammy. "You were her friend. Alice's. The first Alice."

When Chesa looked up, her eyes were glassy, tears leaking down her cheeks. "Yes."

"But that was generations ago." It had to be given the history of Alices. "How are you still here?"

"How is any of this possible?" She shook her head. "There is more. We retrieved Alice's body, but it was too late. Her spirit had left, and her blood tainted the well. The men fled, vowing vengeance upon one another, and I was left to cradle my dead friend's body in this place."

The horror of it stole her words and the warmth from Eliza's skin. Chesa had been alone and far from home, her friend dead in her arms, and those responsible had been so consumed by their anger that they'd ignored the woman they'd killed. No wonder Wonderland was cursed—damned. But Chesa? Alice?

"You think it seems unfair." Chesa wiped at her cheek.

"Of course. Why were you punished for their anger? Why should all of Wonderland suffer for the crimes of two men?"

"Who can say what is fair and what is not? I did not stop Alice from coming here. Alice did not choose to avoid a fight. The men demanded a choice Alice was unwilling to make. Everyone shared some fault."

Some more than others...

"They loved Alice, passionately, fervently. They were not bad men in their hearts, different as the courts that grew from their legacy, but neither was fully good nor bad, just different."

Just like the courts now, different, but neither good nor evil at their core, though evil lurked among them both. A sharp warmth burned in her chest, demanding vengeance. But there was still more to the story. "If Alice died, then how did the curse come to be? How did new Alices come here?"

"You ask the right questions." Chesa paced around the well as she spoke. "I'm not sure what I said in my grief that day, what may have caused the well to curse us all as it did. But hours later, when my body was cold and numb, a mirror appeared, just there." She pointed to a wall. "And through it, I saw Alice's sister. Her name was Eliza too."

The revelation had her sitting up a little straighter.

"Though not much like you," Chesa offered. "She fell in love and wed young. Raising her small children was the joy of her life. When I saw her in the mirror, I called out. I never expected her to hear me, to turn and answer. She saw her sister lying in my arms and rushed straight through the mirror to come to her. I didn't even have the chance to tell her it was too late, that Alice was gone. We wept, but when we tried to take Alice's body back through the mirror, to take her home, we could not go. It was solid as glass once more. So we went the only other way available to us. Up the stairs, out into the night with the full moon shining down upon us."

"The barrier had already begun to form over the land, a haze of green that crept over us like a distant fog. We watched it in a trance, unable to move or comprehend the horror unfurling. It wasn't until later we learned that Wonderland was sealed off from the world, the barrier stretching into the sea and leaving us a world apart. Then a voice spoke from nowhere, echoing up from the shrine and into the night. *Alice must choose.*"

Eliza's brows pinched together. "But Alice was dead."

"That she was. But her sister was not. We didn't understand that, not until two days later when the men returned, each bearing a contingent of soldiers. They fought as if compelled by madness, showing no mercy. All the while, the voice whispered to Eliza. It begged her to choose. Eventually, she yelled back. *Fine, I choose white!* So named for the color their leader wore."

"And the battle stopped." Eliza didn't need Chesa to fill in the blanks anymore. The rest seemed so obvious now. So horribly, painfully obvious.

She bobbed her head. "It did. The armies returned home. And Eliza was able to return through the mirror."

The same mirror her grandmother had shattered most likely, though for what reason, Eliza still didn't know. "And all that time, ever since then, you've been stuck here?"

Chesa held her hand in front of her as if seeing it for the first time. "Unageing. Unchanging. Though with certain gifts I never had before."

Like her ability to disappear. The well had both blessed and cursed her. "And that's why I must choose," Eliza said. "To stop the sides from fighting. To continue this cycle of nonsense?" She shook her head. "There has to be another way. Grandmama said all curses have a weakness. They can all be unwound. Surely, this one can too. What do you think, Finn?"

She turned to him, only then realizing his eyes were closed, his lips parted. The sight punched straight through her chest, leaving her hollow and reeling. "Finn!"

45

Finn's body was limp, a heavy dead weight as she shifted him carefully to the floor. Chesa was there, kneeling on his opposite side. She touched his wound, her hand coming back crimson.

"Finn!" Eliza called again. Her palm caressed his cheek, her fingers sliding through his hair. Gently she shook him, to no avail. Tears burned her eyes, blurring her vision and falling with unchecked ease.

"He still breathes." Chesa nodded toward her hand on his chest, the slow rise and fall that Eliza nearly missed.

"You said he would keep!" She shouted at Chesa, her grief fueling a fury that shook her. "If he dies, Wonderland can bloody fight itself to the death."

Chesa lurched back as if struck, but Eliza did not stop. "Do you hear me, Well?" She turned toward the hole. "You talked to the last Eliza. Can you hear me? If you can curse this land, you can bloody well heal it and Finn!"

"Eliza…" he whispered.

She gasped as Finn's fingers grazed hers.

"Finn! Speak to me." She cupped his cheek, tilting his face toward hers. "Don't leave me."

"Never...leave you." His hand tightened on hers ever so slightly. "Just...tired."

"No. No, no, no." Every muscle in her body clamped tight. She rocked on her knees, unable to sit still. "Please, don't leave me. Please." Grandmama had said he could help her break the curse, maybe. But that would never happen if he was dead. Another lost life, more blood sacrificed at this cursed place for no reason other than pain and suffering.

"Make a choice, Eliza." Chesa had risen, standing a few feet away. "You've heard the tale. The magic is satisfied. The stones will open once you do."

Eliza ignored her as she pulled Finn's head into her lap and caressed his forehead, praying to the holy Mother for a miracle. Maybe she couldn't hear her in this strange land held in thrall under a curse. If the world didn't know Wonderland existed anymore, perhaps the Mother didn't either.

"Please. I love him. Don't take him from me." She wasn't sure who she pleaded with anymore—anyone, everyone. "Alice couldn't choose because she loved them both." Her brows scrunched. Was that true? Had Chesa said it? It didn't matter. Somehow, she knew that was true.

Both men had her love. The courts that sprang from their legacies, their characteristics shared with those men. Law versus freedom. Restraint versus excess. White versus Red. Both good and bad in their way.

She caressed Finn's cheek. *He was both. Is both.* A blend of the courts, a balance of extremes, and Eliza loved all of him, every last bit. If he were simply one or the other, he would not be the man she'd fallen in love with. To truly love, she had to embrace it all.

Awareness slowed the racing of her heart. Warmth returned to her limbs, tingling with encouragement. The very air around her seemed to still, waiting with bated breath for her choice.

"Alice couldn't choose because she loved them both," she said again, staring at Chesa. The other woman gave a slow, hesitant nod as if afraid one drop in the pool of Eliza's thoughts might send her off course.

But it wouldn't. She knew. She finally understood the thread her grandmother wanted her to pull. It was Finn. He was the key to unraveling the curse, but not by his blood or death.

Eliza turned her focus to the well. "I am Alice." Something rumbled deep below the ground. Acknowledgment? She hoped so.

"I am Alice, and I love this man, a child of both courts, White and Red. I will not choose between his two halves, between the two courts that bore and shaped him, because I love all of him, every bit, just as the first Alice loved both her men. They tried to force her to choose. That was wrong. When you love so deeply, such a choice is impossible." She stopped —waiting, hoping. The silence lingered, but she refused to give up or back down from her choice. "I choose Finn. I choose both courts. I love both. Please, let that be enough. Let it end now."

The ground beneath them rumbled. Eliza gasped. A sound like tumbling stones echoed in the distance. A quick look showed the stone pillars still in place, blocking the exit. "Chesa?" Eliza's voice cracked.

"I don't know." The other woman rushed over on unsteady feet. "This is different."

Bloody hell. In trying to break the curse, she'd brought the whole place down on their heads. "Don't punish us for love!"

The ground felt like it rolled and bucked, but the stones did not appear to move. Then all at once, a green mist like that which hovered at the edge of the horizon burst in a plume from the well. Eliza screeched, clutching Finn tighter. Chesa dropped to her knees, throwing her arms around them both. The mist drifted toward them and seemed to coalesce, forming itself into the hazy image of a young woman.

"Alice?" Chesa gasped. Her eyes grew wide as saucers, her mouth hanging open.

Eliza waited for a ghostly chill to consume her, to shake her down to her soul. But as the form drifted near her, a comforting warmth spread over her instead, like being wrapped in a blanket near a pleasant fire. Everything in her screamed to hold perfectly still as the woman knelt at her side, opposite Chesa. This close, she could spy a hint of color amid the green; straight blonde hair, pale skin, a blue dress in an old Gamorean style that hadn't been in fashion in centuries.

The woman—Alice—smiled at her and placed a ghostly hand on Finn.

What are you doing? She tried to ask, but her mouth wouldn't move. The words wouldn't form.

After a brief moment, Alice lifted her palm from Finn's chest and placed it on Chesa's cheek. The two shared a smile, a look that spoke more words than could have ever been uttered. And then Alice rose to her feet and curtsied, the hem of her dress spread in a wide arc. The moment she dropped it, her form burst, the green mist speeding out in all directions with such force that it pushed Eliza back. Only a quick move of her arm kept her head from smacking the stone floor.

"What the bloody hell..." Eliza pushed herself up, searching the room for any sign of Alice. She was gone, and so were the pillars blocking the stairs, though Eliza couldn't recall hearing them move.

"Ugh," Finn groaned.

Warmth radiated throughout Eliza's body. The strange event moments before didn't matter, not as Finn opened his eyes and blinked up at her.

"Finn!" She touched his no longer clammy cheek with shaking hands. "You're awake. You're alive!"

His brows knitted together. "I am." He moved to sit up.

Eliza reached for him. "You should—" But the words died on her lips. Her hand dropped into her lap as she gaped at his side. Through the torn and bloodied clothes, she spied clean, smooth skin.

Finn seemed to realize the same thing as he undid the length of cloth Eliza had tied around him. When it fell away, only unblemished skin remained. He glanced at his arm and touched his face. The older bruises were gone, too, healed as if they had never been.

"You're all right?" She struggled to wrap her head around it, to make sense of the impossible.

"Yes." A slow smile spread across his face. "I think I am. Maybe even better than all right."

"I think the curse is gone." Chesa, who had been staring at her upturned palms, looked over at them, her eyes completely clear, the sense of otherness that hung about her gone as fully as Finn's injuries. "I...I feel like time has suddenly restarted. Like I can almost feel the ticking of clock hands that had been rusted over for ages."

Gone. The curse is gone. Eliza's sucked in one deep breath after the next. "Truly?"

Finn rose to his feet and held out his hand to help her up. No sooner was she steady than he pulled her into his strong embrace, his lips claiming hers in a passionate kiss that left her light-headed and reeling. "You did it," he whispered. "I knew you could."

"We can't be sure yet." Even so, Eliza couldn't stop smiling. Finn was alive and healed. Chesa was...normal? Even if that was all, it was a victory in itself. "Let's go and see."

46

Together, the three of them climbed the stairs and exited the shrine. Outside, both courts gazed skyward, speaking in a mix of excited and fearful tones. Finn looked up, finding the full moon glowing bright and bold overhead, a shade bluer than he remembered, not the green-tinted light he'd known all his life.

As he squinted at the sky, he spotted movement in the darkness. Sections of the sky fluttered like the torn end of fabric, little pieces dangling and slipping apart. One section moved off to the right, the opposite section moving left, as if the whole of Wonderland had been covered by a cloth that now split and fell away. Beyond, it revealed a carpet of blackness, white and yellowish lights sparkling in its midst.

"The barrier is coming down," Chesa said. "The curse is truly gone. Look." She pointed to people gathered in the field. "Alice did not choose a side, and yet, they do not war."

She was right, in fact, many had wandered toward the dividing line, standing not far from their opponents, yet their eyes were trained on the sky, not grabbing for weapons or taking up defense.

"You didn't choose?" Finn took Eliza's hand in his, giving it a squeeze.

She drew her attention from the sky and smiled at him. "Actually, I chose both courts. Or rather, I chose you."

"Me?" The last thing he remembered was Chesa speaking about Alice falling in love with two men, which must have been the origins of the courts.

"You," Eliza said. "A child of two courts."

His brows pinched together. "I was born in the White Court."

Eliza's smile faltered for the briefest moment. "Yes, but you lived much of your life in Red. It shaped you into the man you are now just as much as the place of your birth. My love for you, for all of you, Red and White, was the loose thread that unraveled the spell. I did not pick one nor refuse to choose. I simply chose both with all my heart and soul."

She stepped closer, caressing his cheek in a way that left him closing his eyes in ecstasy, only to force them open so as not to miss a moment with her. "You were the key, Finn."

The key? He hardly felt like it. All he had done was the most natural thing in the world, love the woman before him who was smart, fierce, and most of all, kind.

"She loves you with her whole heart," Chesa said, joining them. "As Alice loved her two men. She could not choose, but Eliza finally fulfilled her dying wish of not having to, of choosing both. But it wouldn't have been enough, I don't think, to simply make that choice and not believe it. She had to love you." She grinned. "And what a powerful force that love is."

Protective instinct rose in Finn as Eliza stepped closer to him, her face weary. He adjusted his stance ever so slightly, putting himself between Eliza and Chesa.

"You knew how to break it, and you never told me," Eliza said to the other woman.

Something tight gripped his chest, only inflaming the spark of fury kindled by that accusation. "Chesa," he warned, baring his teeth.

"It was your grandmother's idea."

Of all the things she could have said, that was the last he expected and perhaps the only one that could ease his anger so quickly. Alice was many things, but like her granddaughter, cruel was not one of them.

"What?" Eliza scoffed.

"She theorized that if Alice could love both courts, the way the original

Alice did, fully and with all her heart, it might break the curse. We weren't sure, but it was the best theory we had after generations of trying. But it had to be real love. True love." Chesa planted her hands on her hips. "If I simply told you two to fall in love, would you have?"

A huff of laughter escaped through his nose. No, he would have run away fast and hard. Loving Alice? A fool's wish.

"I—" Eliza started but stopped herself.

"No," Chesa answered for her. "You wouldn't have."

"So all this time, all of your sudden appearances and disappearances..." Eliza looked from Chesa to him.

"You played us." His teeth ground together. He could love the result and still hate the method of it.

A touch of color rose to her cheeks. In all his years, he'd never seen Chesa embarrassed, though she'd never been so open, so...human, before either. "I told you I was always on Alice's side. I have been from the very first Alice and now to the last. It is done."

"What is this?"

That hated voice made every muscle in his body go tense as he whirled toward the crowd where his half-brother stalked forward.

"Something is different, and now the sky is falling!" He gestured overhead. A rumble of concern rolled through the gathered crowd. "What was Alice's choice?"

Eliza tried to step forward, but he gently urged her back. The kind of fury radiating off his brother was not the kind that words could tame. Finn might not have seen him in years—the past week withstanding—but some things never changed.

"Alice chose both courts," Chesa replied, projecting her voice for the crowd. "The curse is over."

The words cut through the assembled like a snake through the grass.

"Finn," Eliza whispered, pushing his arm away. "Please. Trust me."

The full force of the love in her eyes nearly gutted him. When she looked at him like that, he could deny her nothing. Instead, he offered her his hand. "Together then."

She nodded and took it, stepping up near Chesa until she was in line between the two of them. "Chesa speaks truthfully," she said. "I was your

Alice, but I am no more. I am simply Eliza Carroll of—of the other land."

"Then who rules?" someone yelled from the crowd.

"Both and neither," Eliza spoke with the confidence of a born leader, her head raised and proud. "You have two courts already. Both will rule their territory. Each shall be equal, for they were both beloved by Alice."

"Ridiculous." The king laughed as he stalked forward. "Clearly, the girl has knocked her head."

Finn's teeth ground together, the urge to rush down the stairs and resume his dual nearly overwhelming. Only Eliza's hand in his kept him still.

"If there is no choice," Alvis continued. "We must war to decide." He stepped forward, one boot landing on the bottom step.

Finn's heart skipped a beat as all eyes glued to the king's act—his step upon the shrine that before had not been possible. His stomach sank as the king lifted his head, a smirk upon his face, and stared at Eliza. There was nothing to protect them from his wrath now or that of his Jabberwock. Nothing, but himself.

"Eliza..." Finn urged her back, but she shook him off and pressed forward instead.

"I am the last Alice, and I command peace in my name. No more war. The courts once lived in harmony, and they can do so again."

The sharp whinny of a horse drew the crowd's attention, even that of the White King, as King Jasper made a path through the crowd, only stopping at the foot of the stairs where he leaped from his mount and bowed toward Eliza.

"The Red Court shall keep Eliza's command."

The use of her true name wasn't lost on him, nor on Eliza, whose lips parted as she stared at the monarch promising her peace.

Finn searched the members of the Red Court, spotting the queen in their midst, still on her mount not too far from the king. Her expression was hard, but she said nothing. She would obey, at least in this.

"Afraid of a little fight?" The White King mocked. He placed his boot one step higher, leaning his weight onto that foot in an obvious taunt.

"Are you afraid of peace?" Eliza snapped before the other king could reply. "There doesn't need to be bloodshed. Your people have been subservient to Red for decades. No more. Is that not enough for you?"

Again, the crowd spoke among themselves. A wave of noise rose and fell as the assembled discussed and debated the unexpected outcome. The king panned his gaze across his subjects, his smirk growing, but he didn't see the one person Finn suddenly could not tear his focus from. Neva strode through the crowd, heading with purposeful intention toward her husband.

"White has bowed enough!" The king yelled. "It is our turn to rule! Our turn to enforce our will upon all of Wonderland!"

"Is it not against your laws to do others harm?" Eliza yelled, but noise from the crowd threatened to drown her out. "You would follow this king who mocks his own laws? Who harms his own wife and would be death to the land once more?"

The tide of conversation shifted. The White King snapped his gaze to Eliza, a snarl on his features. "I knew you were trouble. And if you're not Alice, you don't belong here." Alvis drew his sword and pointed it at Eliza.

Something in Finn snapped. He wrenched himself free of Eliza's grip, her bellowed "No" ringing in his ears. Unarmed he may be, but he wouldn't let that bastard touch one hair on the woman he loved.

Halfway down the stairs, feet from his brother and his vicious snarl, Finn saw Neva finally reach her king's side. Time seemed to slow, nearly grinding to a halt, as she raised the silver dagger clutched in her hand and slammed the blade through the king's throat.

She jerked it free, blood spurting all over her white gown. Nearby knights stumbled back. The king clutched at his neck before falling to the ground as life fled him in a torrent.

It was over in moments, the king's lifeless eyes staring up at the sky as his wife stood silently by, bloody dagger still clutched in her hand.

The death should have brought Finn some measure of relief if nothing else, but all he felt was uncertainty as he stood frozen on the stairs, his gaze fixed on the scene mere feet away.

Neva turned to the crowd and raised the blade high for all to see. "The king broke his own laws and turned his fury against me, his people, and against Alice! No more."

Neva's determined gaze roamed over the court—her people. At last, she turned her attention to Eliza. The moon itself seemed to shine brighter on the woman he loved, illuminating her apparent shock, with one hand still pressed to her lips.

"The White Court shall follow Eliza's command," Neva said, her voice loud and clear for all to hear. She swept into a low curtsy, the picture of grace in a dress that was anything but. As she raised, she turned to her court and placed her empty palm over her belly. "Would any care to dissent?"

The pause was full of risk. The White Queen claimed to have many of the court on her side. But did she? Would they follow her?

The knight closest to her dropped to one knee. Those near him followed, spreading out in a wave as the court acknowledged their queen.

"We welcome peace with the White Court." King Jasper had crossed to the boundary line at the bottom of the steps, the Red Queen now at his side. She would not look at Finn, and he was grateful for that. She wobbled a bit on her feet, her gaze locked on the dead king. For a woman known to be violent and bloodthirsty in her own right, she did not handle the sight of a bloody death well. But she managed a nod to Neva, showing agreement with her husband's proclamation.

The White Queen stepped over the body of the king and advanced on the other monarchs, stopping just at the edge of the boundary herself. "As we welcome peace with the Red Court."

Jasper turned to the gathered knights. "Let it be known that both courts pledged peace on this day, honoring the commands of Eliza, the last Alice."

47

*E*liza and Chesa told the monarchs the full story of Alice and what had happened deep within the shrine. As they did, members of the two courts began to mix and speak to one another. Just a few at first, sharing hesitant greetings and wary glances. But as they finished the tale, Eliza heard the first burst of laughter from a cluster of people that represented both courts.

There was a part of the tale, however, that they did not tell. They left out the Red King falling in love with a White Queen and her bearing his child. Unknowingly, they had begun something that freed their land. Perhaps one day that story would be told too, but Eliza was not about to reveal that secret to Finn, not now. Maybe one day, when he was ready.

As for the Red King... A peculiar fondness passed over his features as he stared at Finn. Perhaps he knew, or maybe he simply cared for him because he'd loved Finn's mother. Eliza didn't ask, but there was one favor she had to request. She pulled the king aside.

"I'm so glad he's all right," he said, glancing once more toward Finn, who spoke with the White Queen and some of her knights. "When I saw the White King strike him, I feared the worst."

"It's a miracle, to be sure." Something she could not fully explain but was grateful for, nonetheless. "Whatever the well truly is, it possessed a power unlike any I've ever heard of."

The king rubbed at his jaw. "An unhealthy temptation at best. We will have to come up with a solution. Perhaps find a new way to seal it off now that it seems anyone can access it."

"Please do." History loved to repeat itself and leaving it open to all only begged for another tragedy to occur and the horrible cycle to resume. "But that's not what I'd hoped to talk to you about."

"Oh?"

Goodness. She'd rehearsed the speech in her head, but now that it came time to say it, the words tried to run away. "It... Finn mentioned that he had relations with your wife, the queen." She all but spit the words out, her cheeks flaming.

"Ah. Yes, our marriage is mostly a formality." His lips pursed as he glanced away at nothing. "I believe Alice, your grandmother, said that's not as common in your land?"

More common than Grandmama would have liked, at least in the capital where Eliza had worked. "Yes, well," she said, fighting through the awkwardness. "The point is, Finn was not interested in such...affairs, but was told he had no choice."

The king's attention snapped back to Eliza.

"In fact, when the White Court attacked the croquet tournament, Finn was rotting in the dungeon for refusing the queen's request to attend her in her bed. Did you know that?" She probably didn't need to add that last part. The dawning horror on his face was easy enough to read.

"Victoria!" The king boomed, his voice lacking all its customary warmth.

The Red Queen halted her conversation with another and stared at them, brows raised in arrogant question. The king looked meaningfully at Finn, then back at his wife. The woman paled.

"I shall speak with her," the king said, finally tearing his scowl away from his wife. "This—How did I miss it?"

"Sometimes the things we don't want to see are the easiest to overlook," Eliza said.

It seemed he finally realized that and gave himself a shake. "It won't happen again," he promised.

"Or to any others," she added.

"I vow it." He took her hands, causing Eliza to gasp. "Thank you. For telling me. For trusting me. I've been...lazy in my duties, but you have renewed my spirit and given me new purpose. I will not fail again."

If it hadn't been for what her grandmother's letter revealed, she might not have. But her words, her belief that he was a good man, and his role as Finn's likely father gave her hope that he would listen. Thank the Mother he seemed to have, though only time would tell if he followed through.

The Red King took his leave, and Eliza forced a smile in farewell, but all the while, the same thought chimed through the back of her mind.

Time.

How could she have forgotten? It was said that time in Alice's world nearly stood still while she was in Wonderland, but with the curse gone and the barrier broken, would it return to normal? Wonderland should be part of her world again, accessible to outsiders. Time would have to fix itself, wouldn't it?

"Chesa!" Eliza found her sitting alone, simply looking around with the brightest smile on her face.

"Eliza." She grinned.

"You said you felt the hands of time ticking again. Does that mean my world's time and Wonderland's time flow at the same speed now?"

Her nose twitched. "Well, since they are part of the same world, yes. Wonderland was kept apart by the curse, but no more. I should think any time that passes here will pass in the place you left just the same."

Damn. That was what she feared. Which meant sooner rather than later, her absence would be noted if it hadn't been already. Her parents would worry, and even if they didn't see eye-to-eye on most things, she didn't want that. Her lips drew thin. If she were gone too long, she wouldn't put it past her father to find a way to claim her inheritance for himself.

Chesa jumped to her feet. "We should get you home," she said as if reading Eliza's thoughts.

"The rabbit hole Finn brought me through is days away." Assuming she judged their location right. Even if they were closer than she expected, it was still quite a ride.

"Hmm... We'll need some fresh clothes. And food. There should be a village not too far away." Chesa grabbed at her stomach. "Wow." She glanced down at herself. "I...I think I'm hungry?" Her quizzical expression nearly made Eliza laugh.

"I can help with some of that."

Just looking at Finn as he walked to join them made Eliza smile. Behind him trailed knights bearing food and drink. Chesa rinsed her hands with a splash of water and dug into a loaf of bread with gusto. As for Eliza, she could barely manage a sip of wine after washing the blood from her hands. And the dress... Well, she tried not to look at it. Seeing the blood stains on Finn and Chesa's clothing was already too stark a reminder of how close she came to losing him.

"So, home," Eliza said. "I guess there's no easier way than a bit of a journey?"

Finn flashed her a half-smile. "At least the Bandersnatches should have returned to the deep wilds. Well, we can hope, anyway."

More beasties. Just what she wanted.

Chesa gaped, nearly dropping her bread as she stared behind Eliza. Others gasped. Even Finn looked startled. Eliza twisted around and had to do a double-take. The entrance to the shrine had been an open passageway of stone, but now, standing at its front, was a massive mirror framed in gold.

"The looking glass," Chesa whispered in awe.

"Like the one that appeared before? The one my grandmother destroyed?"

Chesa shoved her loaf to an unsuspecting knight and advanced on the anomaly. "It looks just the same."

"A gift from the well?" Finn asked.

It had to be. What else could create such a thing from nowhere and place it over the entrance to the shrine?

The mirror shifted, the reflection dissipating into swirling grey as if a morning fog had settled over it, but there was none around them. The grey mist cleared slowly, slipping away in little tendrils to reveal a new scene, this one, Eliza knew. "Grandmother's garden."

Chesa had stopped halfway between Eliza and the mirror and now turned back toward them. "You wanted a way home. I think this is it."

An easier way. A faster way. Right back to where it all started. But... She glanced at Finn, who wore the saddest smile she'd ever seen.

"You should go," he said. "It's your home. You can finally go back."

Tears welled and blurred her vision. "Not without you. I won't leave you." *Not now. Not ever.*

His shoulders slumped. Something sparkled in his eyes, but Eliza didn't get the chance to examine it before he wrapped his arms around her and tugged her to his chest.

"I don't want to leave you either, Eliza. Never." He cupped her head. Her ear pressed against his chest so that she could hear his heart thumping wildly. "I love you. I'd stay with you all my days, but I'm not sure if the mirror will let me through."

Eliza twisted her head until she could look up at him. "I think, if I wanted it to, it would." Something settled within her, drying her tears, a knowledge she couldn't name and reason that was no better than nonsense. Still, her very soul believed her words as truth. The mirror was a gift to Alice. It would let her bring those others through.

"You'd take me with you?" He leaned down until their noses barely touched, and his breath ghosted across her skin.

She grinned. "I think you know the answer to that."

"Yes, but I like to hear it anyway."

"You'd want to come to my world? My home?"

He laughed. "You have to ask? I think *you* know the answer to that."

Warmth swelled through her chest. "I love you, Finn. There or here, I have no desire to leave your side."

"I love you too, Eliza." He closed the last of the distance between them and sealed his words with a kiss, neither chaste nor passionate, but simply a perfectly balanced expression of love that Eliza eagerly raised onto her tiptoes to meet.

"Ah-hem," Chesa cleared her throat.

Eliza pulled away, a deep flush heating her cheeks.

"The looking glass?" Chesa said, pointing to it.

"Right," Eliza said. "Shall we try it?"

Finn and Eliza said their farewells to the Red King and White Queen, who both vowed to keep the peace between courts and work toward a better future for all of Wonderland. The entirety of the commotion in the field came to a halt. People rose from their places near cookfires and tents that had been hastily erected. The monarchs stood on the wide landing atop the stairs.

"Farewell, Eliza," Neva kissed her cheek before giving her hands a squeeze and releasing her.

"Best of luck to you and your child."

She cradled her belly. "You've given them a bright future. I will not forget it."

Chesa waited near the looking glass, the last to say farewell. She defied all expectations, wrapping Eliza in a near bone-crushing hug. "We shall meet again, Eliza."

"I hope so." No sooner had Chesa released her than a thought struck Eliza like lightning. She grabbed the other woman's hand. "Come with us."

"What?"

"Through the looking glass. You're supposed to, I think." Somehow, she was sure of it. "You came from my world, my country originally, right? It's about time you go back. If you want to, that is." Perhaps after so long she preferred to stay in a place that was familiar.

Chesa grinned like a cat. "Yes, I think I shall."

Eliza stood in front of the looking glass, one hand clasped with Finn and the other with Chesa.

"Whenever you're ready." Finn gave her hand a squeeze.

"No time like the present." *Please let this work.*

Eliza stretched out one foot. It slid into the looking glass like stepping into a lake, cool and strange. She tightened her grip on her companions and completed the step. Whatever lay beyond, or within, pulled at her and begged her to come. She wasn't sure she could pull her foot back out if she tried, so she took the next step, holding her breath and closing her eyes as she passed beyond the veil.

Going through the looking glass was like swimming in honey—thick, a bit cold, and strange, but not entirely unpleasant. Even so, a bubble of panic rose in her throat as the feeling lengthened. What if they were trapped? Stuck forever? Only the hands holding hers kept the panic at bay. And then, as suddenly as it began, the feeling vanished, popping like a bubble and spitting them out.

48

The fall knocked the wind from her lungs and left Eliza with a sore arm and mouth full of grass. Finn groaned nearby—the most beautiful sound in the world. He'd made it through. Eliza opened her eyes and glanced around. A familiar sight stared back—her grandmother's garden.

"It even smells different," Chesa remarked as she pushed off the ground to sit.

Leave it to Chesa to comment on the smell of all things.

"You're home," Finn said.

"I am." Though she still couldn't quite believe it. Eliza found the rabbit hole that Finn had taken her through only a few feet away, but it was just that now, a hole, not the gaping chasm they'd disappeared into. The looking glass was nowhere to be seen. A one-way trip?

The sky overhead had begun to lighten, harkening the dawn of a new day—the day after her grandmother's remembrance gathering, with any luck. If not for her companions, she might be able to convince herself the past weeks were nothing more than a strange dream she'd suddenly awoken from.

"We should get to the house. People may be looking for me, and—Oh!"

She clasped a hand over her mouth. "I guess you'll have to meet my parents." She gave a toothy grimace.

"I've faced worse monsters recently," Finn said, completely unruffled. Leave it to him to handle such a revelation with ease.

"Not like that, you won't." Chesa stood with her hands on her hips before gesturing to their attire.

Ah, yes, the blood. That would be a problem. To say nothing of the different fashion, or that she wore a completely different outfit than she'd fled the party in.

"You have more clothes in your room?" Chesa asked.

"Yes, plenty." She glanced at Finn. "Some of my father's clothes might fit Finn, but how would you get in? They may be asleep, they—"

Chesa vanished.

Finn shook his head and gave a little laugh. "Some things never change."

Minutes later, Chesa returned baring clothes and a pitcher of water. "I picked this one out for myself." She held up an unfamiliar dress. "Found it in your mother's things. She won't mind, will she?" Chesa winked.

Eliza rolled her eyes. Either her mother would be in distress over the loss or would never notice. It was hard to say with her.

Once they'd changed, Eliza asked, "Will you be staying with us? You're welcome to." It was the least she could do.

"I appreciate that. I may visit from time to time, but I want to see what's become of the world since I left." She vanished, only to reappear a few feet away. "Plus, I'd like to see if there are others like me. Curse tainted? Is that what we'd call this?" She shrugged.

"A gift for all you've suffered?" Finn asked. "I certainly received one." He put an arm around Eliza's shoulders and drew her close.

"And that is why I'm leaving." She wagged a finger at them. "You two need some alone time. But yes, a gift, I like that."

"Until we meet again." Chesa gave a dramatic bow and vanished.

Eliza sighed. Somehow the world was a little dimmer without Chesa around.

"We'll see her again," Finn promised.

"Yes, I think we will." Eliza leaned into his side, savoring his warmth in contrast to the morning chill. "Shall I show you the house?"

Together, they walked through the gardens, arm-in-arm, to her grandmother's estate—*Eliza's* estate. Well, hers and Finn's. She certainly wasn't going to leave him out in the cold.

No sooner had they reached the front stoop than the main door swung wide, and Eliza's mother appeared, dark circles under her eyes. "Eliza!"

She winced. "Mother." *Damn.* Perhaps she had been gone longer than she thought.

"Where have you been?" She flicked her gaze to Finn for a brief moment before focusing back on her daughter. "You vanished from the gathering last night, and then the maids said you weren't in your room this morning."

Eliza let out an audible sigh. *Thank the Mother for time in Wonderland being nonsense.*

Her father all but shoved her mother out of the way to join them on the landing. "Eliza, dearest, you gave us a fright." His focus landed on Finn but did not move on. "And who is this?"

Finn glanced at her from the corner of his eye, a grin on his lips that seemed to say, "Should I explain?"

She gave the slightest shake of her head in answer. "Mother, Father, this is Finneas, my fiancé."

"Fiancé?" her parents echoed. Her mother swayed on her feet. Her father simply looked perplexed.

"But the Admiral's son?" her father asked.

"That's why I could not accept your gracious arrangement." She smiled up at Finn and laid her arm on his. "I am already promised."

"But he's next in line for his father's position. Such an offer may not come again."

And now for the fun part. "Finneas is a prince, father." He stiffened ever so slightly under her touch but kept his smile in place. "Son of the Queen of Wonderland." No need to mention that she was the former queen or that there were two, the title alone should satisfy.

"Oh, oh by the Mother, a prince!" Her mother placed the back of her hand on her forehead, all but swooning right there on the threshold.

"My, that does put a different light on things." Her father swept into a deep bow. "Apologies, Your Highness. I had no idea. I have not had the pleasure of visiting this…Wonderland."

Finn's chest shook with laughter, which nearly had Eliza doing the same. "Apology accepted," he replied flawlessly. "We have been isolated for quite some time, but I believe you may learn more about our fair country soon."

"Oh, of course, it is an honor you're here. If only you could have arrived in time for the remembrance ceremony. Eliza will have told you of it, yes? That's why you're here?"

"Finneas was unfortunately delayed," Eliza said. "We planned to announce our engagement once you'd met, but things didn't quite go according to plan."

"Indeed," Finn added, "I've just arrived, and I'm quite worn out. Perhaps Eliza could show me inside?"

"Oh, of course!" Her mother snapped to attention, leaning her head in the door and calling for the servants. To Eliza's surprise, she held the door open herself, beckoning them in.

"Thank you," Finn nodded his head to her. "I look forward to getting better acquainted once I'm rested."

"Shall we?" Eliza asked. Together they stepped over the threshold of Folly Hall. As they wandered down the long entryway, her parents' whispered voices carried to them.

"This is such a dream. A prince!" her mother said.

"Hush, Darling, we mustn't appear too eager."

Eliza giggled and shared a secret glance with Finn.

"When did you come up with that story?" he asked.

She nudged his side. "It's true, isn't it?"

He halted, his brows knitting before smoothing out. "I suppose it is." He lifted her hand to his lips and placed a kiss on its back. "Would my fianceé like to help me rest?" The look on his face implied many things, but none of them were resting.

"Perhaps a bath first?" She ran a finger down his arm.

His eyes hooded. "Yes, I think that would be quite nice."

They laughed, arm-in-arm, sure that whatever obstacles awaited in the future, they would face them together.

Thank you for reading! Did you enjoy? Please add your review because nothing helps an author more and encourages readers to take a chance on a book than a review.

And don't miss more Reimagined Fairy Tales coming soon, and find more from Megan Van Dyke at www.authormeganvandyke.com

Until then, discover THE BINDING STONE, by City Owl Author, Lizzy Gayle. Turn the page for a sneak peek!

You can also sign up for the City Owl Press newsletter to receive notice of all book releases!

SNEAK PEEK OF THE BINDING STONE
BY LIZZY GAYLE

The magic is palpable. It tingles as it radiates up and down my arms. My eyes snap open the moment I feel it.

I let the power drift over and through me, soaking it up like a human does sunlight. My fingertips crackle with it. Voices become clear now, and sounds assault my ears like daggers after the blissful silence of nothingness. I prefer to sleep. When I do, there is no need to think. Or remember.

Whoever dares disturb my century-long slumber will suffer my wrath. That's a promise.

"Really? Only ten?" The voice of a young man attracts my attention.

He is close, but my senses remain dulled from my sleep inside the gemstone, so I choose to be cautious, staying invisible to human eyes. His voice, warm like honey, soothes the edges of my anger. But some qualities can be deceiving. I know from experience.

"Jer, remind me not to bring you along when I buy a used car," comes the voice of another young man. "Your haggling skills need some serious work."

I stand in the center of a modern marketplace. It is small but cluttered, centered in front of a brick house with several people milling about the lawn and walkways. Whatever time I'm in, the women wear far less clothing than I remember. Near the outskirts of the unkempt grass, I spy a girl who is closest in appearance to me. A small child tugs at her arm, but the woman is distracted. A smile pulls at the corners of my mouth, and I quickly change from the draped fabrics of my last master's time, mirroring her outfit. I nod in approval. I'm going to enjoy this century.

Now to locate and destroy the source of the threat. It is not difficult. I follow the same girl's blushing gaze toward the honeyed voice I'd heard before.

"I'll take it."

He stands a mere table's width from me, and it is clear he is indeed the One. His aura glows like none of the others. A rainbow of iridescent colors pulsates and bleeds around him like a force field. This is too easy.

A gasp draws my attention. It's the young mother, frozen in a state of horror. I've seen that look before, so I follow her stare to find the toddler examining a flower growing in a crack in the concrete. A machine of some sort zooms toward her, so big it will surely crush the child in seconds. Time slows as I raise my fingers and invisible hands lift the young one out of harm's way, setting her securely back near her mother. No one has seen, save the woman who will likely never again be so negligent.

Focusing on the rainbow aura, I raise my hands. All it will take is one blast, directed at the handsome man busy handing a piece of green paper to an elderly woman. He will cease to exist. But I feel it as I let go, and even before it bounces harmlessly off his aura, I know. So I scream. It is not as though anyone can hear it. Not yet.

"Never figured you'd go for the whole bling thing," says the one with glasses and a dull, human aura. "Try it on."

I watch helplessly as Jer slips the ring on his middle finger. The large opal in the center gleams a little too brightly, and I tug at the choker around my neck, running my thumb along the matching stone. I hope the ten-paper is worth more than it appears. Why must I care so much for the innocent after all these years? If I'd let that machine crush the child...

No. I am not, nor will I ever be, one of the human Magicians. It is what sets me apart, and the only thing that may make up for some of my past sins. The ones that were within my control.

"Great. Can we go now please?" It seems by his rush that the friend does not like it here. I cannot blame him. My nose wrinkles up as I scan the rest of the market—a few scattered tables covered in odd objects, dusty boxes stacked and interspersed between them. Most things I don't recognize, but it all looks like junk to me. So how did I end up here? Just one more indignity to add to the list.

I trail behind as the two boys move away and down the wide street. The homes surrounding the market are similar to each other, yet closer together than in my last master's time. It saddens me to find far fewer trees and greenery to balance all the brick and mortar surrounding us as we walk.

The chilled wind carries the ozone-tinted scent and humid feel of a body of water nearby, which pleases me. It is refreshing after my sleep. I let my bare arms stretch out behind me, allowing goose bumps to prickle along my skin. A few buildings away, the men amble up the uneven brick walk, scattering fall's last crisp leaves from the single maple tree in front, before bursting inside the four-story rectangle. I've seen worse. Although I'm certain this "Jer" will be upgrading soon. I continue following them up creaking metal steps and into a small room, containing a sagging, cushioned seat big enough for two, a square table and chairs, a well-worn bed, dresser, and a desk.

"Do you think it's real?" Jer's friend inspects the ring.

"I don't know, Gabe. There was something about it. Like I couldn't put it down."

Of course not. You sensed the power. My power.

I suppose I should reveal myself. If I do not, the stone will force me, and at least this way I can have a little fun with the friend.

I loosen the invisibility and freeze Jer's friend before he can touch the ring. I will teach him not to touch things that do not belong to him. I grin and let my eyes glow green with power so there can be no doubt as to my nature.

My new master's reaction is immensely satisfying. About to sit in the chair near the desk, he spies me and misses, falling to the floor with a *thud*. His face is pale, his eyes huge as his gaze darts between me and his friend. I would not be surprised if he fainted. Instead, he licks his lips and clears his throat.

"Hel...hello?"

Well, that's different.

Don't stop now. Keep reading with your copy of <u>THE BINDING STONE</u>, by City Owl Author, Lizzy Gayle.

Don't miss more Reimagined Fairy Tales coming soon, and find more from Megan Van Dyke at www.authormeganvandyke.com

Until then, discover THE BINDING STONE, by City Owl Author, Lizzy Gayle!

A thousand years of servitude left Leela more than a little jaded. The betrayal of the man she loved was only the beginning of the nightmare.

After centuries of abuse by greedy masters, her hope for freedom for herself and her fellow Djinn from the magical stones that bind them has dimmed to a barely-there glimmer.

But it hasn't yet been extinguished.

When the young, handsome, and idealistic Jered inadvertently becomes her new master, Leela wonders if his tenderness and concern may be real. He doesn't even realize that he's a magician and wields magic of his own. Despite her years of suffering, her heart begins to open to him. And the chance of romance.

As she inches closer to trusting Jered, the original masters she assumed long dead resurface. They've found a way to survive, using young magicians' bodies to hold their essence. And when they discover her whereabouts, they come for her—and Jered. If the evil ones succeed, then she'll once again be in the service of the man who betrayed her, this time forever.

In the past, her choices led to unimaginable suffering. Now, when freedom or an eternity of torture both loom as real possibilities, can she dare risk everything for love?

Please sign up for the City Owl Press newsletter for chances to win special subscriber-only contests and giveaways as well as receiving information on upcoming releases and special excerpts.

All reviews are **welcome** and **appreciated**. Please consider leaving one on your favorite social media and book buying sites.

Escape Your World. Get Lost in Ours! City Owl Press at www.cityowlpress.com.

ACKNOWLEDGMENTS

Thank you so much to my incredible family for the love and support you show me every single day. I could not do this without you all. A huge thank you to my CPs, writer friends, and Street Team for your constant support and encouragement. You all pick me up when I get down and push me to keep going. Thank you to my editor Heather McCorkle for helping this baby shine and loving it as much as I do. Finally, to my readers, thank you for letting me live my dreams by sharing my stories with you. Each time one of you reaches out to tell me how much you loved a story, or you post about it on social media, or leave a review, it completely makes my day. I am so grateful and wouldn't be able to keep putting out stories without your support.

ABOUT THE AUTHOR

MEGAN VAN DYKE is a fantasy romance author with a love for all things magical and romantic, especially fairytales and anything with a happily ever after. Many of her stories include themes of family (whether born into or found) and a sense of home and belonging, which are important aspects of her life as well. When not writing, Megan loves to spend time with her family, cook, play video games, and explore the great outdoors. Megan currently lives with her family in  Florida. Be sure to sign up for her newsletter so you never miss a minute!

www.authormeganvandyke.com

instagram.com/authormeganvandyke
facebook.com/AuthorMeganVanDyke
twitter.com/AuthorMeganVD
tiktok.com/@authormeganvandyke
bookbub.com/authors/megan-van-dyke

ABOUT THE PUBLISHER

City Owl Press is a cutting edge indie publishing company, bringing the world of romance and speculative fiction to discerning readers.

Escape Your World. Get Lost in Ours!

www.cityowlpress.com

facebook.com/CityOwlPress
twitter.com/cityowlpress
instagram.com/cityowlbooks
pinterest.com/cityowlpress
tiktok.com/@cityowlpress